The River Warriors

Michael Arnold lives in Hampshire with his wife and four children. His interest in British history is lifelong, and childhood holidays were spent visiting castles and battlefields – a passion he now inflicts on his own kids. He is the author of the acclaimed Civil War Chronicles; one of which, *Devil's Charge*, was chosen as a *Sunday Times* Book of the Year.

Also by Michael Arnold

The Savage Isle series

The Savage Isle
The River Warriors

THE RIVER WARRIORS

Michael Arnold

CANELO

 Penguin Random House

First published in the United Kingdom in 2026 by

Canelo, an imprint of
Canelo Digital Publishing Limited,
20 Vauxhall Bridge Road,
London SW1V 2SA
United Kingdom

A Penguin Random House Company
The authorised representative in the EEA is Dorling Kindersley Verlag GmbH. Arnulfstr. 124, 80636 Munich, Germany

Copyright © Michael Arnold 2026

The moral right of Michael Arnold to be identified as the creator of this work has been asserted in accordance with the Copyright, Designs and Patents Act, 1988.
All rights reserved. No part of this publication may be reproduced or transmitted in any form or by any means, electronic or mechanical, including photocopy, recording, or any information storage and retrieval system, without permission in writing from the publisher.
No part of this book may be used or reproduced in any manner for the purpose of training artificial intelligence technologies or systems. In accordance with Article 4(3) of the DSM Directive 2019/790, Canelo expressly reserves this work from the text and data mining exception.

A CIP catalogue record for this book is available from the British Library.

ISBN 978 1 83598 427 7

This book is a work of fiction. Names, characters, businesses, organizations, places and events are either the product of the author's imagination or are used fictitiously. Any resemblance to actual persons, living or dead, events or locales is entirely coincidental.

Cover design by Becca Thorne

Printed and bound in Great Britain by Clays Ltd, Elcograf S.p.A.

Look for more great books at
www.canelo.co | www.dk.com

For my niece, Ellie.

PROLOGUE

Bledri knelt in the long grass. Absently, he found himself wondering if his trembling limbs were the result of fear or cold, sodden as he was.

A big shape loomed over him. Bledri looked up. A man studied him. He was tall and broad, wearing red *braca* and tunic over a mail corselet that was beaded with water. Golden hair, dark with moisture, sprouted in thick clumps from beneath the rim of a helmet that was crested by the figurine of a large, pouncing cat, forged in copper. He had come from the river, and he looked every inch a monster of the deep.

'We sniffed you out, little man,' the monster said, his words, though clear in the common tongue, heavily accented.

Not for the first time, Bledri cursed himself for a fool. He should not have hidden. Should not have gone to ground. For these were no mere hunters.

More men came, dismounting to gather around him. They seemed like halflings to his eyes; part-Roman, and yet something else. Gaulish, perhaps? They carried long body shields, each painted with the same pouncing cat that adorned the leader's helm. They carried throwing spears too, in the Roman style, though their saddles were hung with blanched skulls, in the manner of native tribes. Close up, he could see the water still dripping from them. The dampness of their beards, too, and the sodden tails and manes of their magnificently harnessed horses. Perhaps the river goddess had sent them herself, unhappy with Bledri, and keen to punish him, though he could not fathom her reason. Whatever the truth, his decision to hide in the ruins of an old byre had been a bad one. He had crouched and watched the river and prayed to every god that would come to mind, making promises of perpetual piety if the water-sprites would just throw his pursuers off the scent. And then he had heard himself whimper like a child, and felt the shameful heat as he soiled his own braca, as men and horses, in full tack and armour, clambered, inexplicably, onto the west bank of a waterway too deep to ford.

The leader of the water-lords stepped closer. He had blue eyes that were so pale, they seemed flecked with ice. One eye had a strange pupil, shaped like a tadpole, and there was an old, deep scar running from his forehead to his jaw, vanishing amongst the yellow growth of a beard that was long and plaited, terminating in a huge tooth or tusk.

'You have been a worthy quarry,' the man said in his lilting words.

'Not worthy enough,' Bledri said bitterly. He had encountered them in the thick woods not a mile west of the battle at Swamp River, and they had chased him, relentlessly, all the way to this smaller watercourse. He had swum across, certain they could not follow.

Ice-Eyes gave a grunt of amused acknowledgement. 'I am Grimoald. You have heard of me?'

'I have not.'

Grimoald shrugged to show that it was of no consequence. He lifted a huge palm, in which were clustered half a dozen tiny strawberries. With his free hand, he plucked one from the pile, popping it into his mouth, and Bledri glimpsed a ring of gold on the man's forefinger. Set into the thick band was the likeness, in black, of a large cat's head, its jaws gaping. 'They call me the leopard.'

'Leopard?' Bledri echoed the unusual word.

Grimoald twisted his shoulders slightly, so that his heavy-looking cape could be seen. It was clearly a pelt of some kind, in black and gold, not so dissimilar to that of a lynx, though it would take several lynxes to make this particular garment. 'Leopard.'

'What do you want with me?'

Grimoald ate another strawberry. 'Mine is a task of destruction,' he said as he chewed. 'I would know where to find your nearest warbands.' The cold gaze flickered to take in the surrounding woodland. 'Are there steadings hereabouts? A local chief, perhaps, or a strong sept? Even a notable Wise One would suffice.'

Bledri did not want to say. Did not want to undermine his people. But, more than that, he did not want to die. Besides, this strange man had not asked for sensitive information. Simply a nudge in the right direction. It seemed a small price to pay for his life. As the balance tipped in his mind, a face resolved before him. Lean and hard, milky-eyed and amber-toothed. An annoying face. One he would not lose sleep over betraying. He turned his head to look into the western sunset. The blood-red sun was sinking behind the hills. 'That way. Fifteen leagues.'

'And what will I find that way?'

'A fort. A big one.'

'Defences?'

'Many, but the garrison have gone north.'

'Then why should I go?'

'The Wise One remains,' Bledri said. 'He guards a great treasure.'

'Why does he not flee?' Grimoald asked suspiciously. 'Is this treasure too heavy to move?'

'He means to leave,' replied Bledri, 'but he cannot. Not yet.'

Grimoald tipped back his head and upended the remaining berries into his mouth, taking a moment to chew. 'You have been most helpful.'

'How could you?' Bledri glared up at him, his own shame burning his cheeks now that the deed was done. 'You are of our blood.'

Grimoald laughed through his swallow, teeth stained with juice. 'I am no more kinsman to you than I am to Emperor Claudius. I am Grimoald, Leopard of the Batacgwi. Warrior of the raging river, Renos, at the northern edge of the empire.'

There were rooks looking on, up high in the trees, their beady eyes shining with brutal judgement. Harbingers of the Otherworld, come to beckon him home. The sense of resignation gave Bledri a belated pang of defiance. He spat. 'A vassal of Rome.'

'Not so, little man,' Grimoald said, drawing his sword, which was long and double-edged. 'Rome honours the Batacgwi as the greatest of all war-givers. She respects our people. We fight for her glory, and, in return, she leaves us alone.'

'It will not always be thus,' Bledri said, thinking of the alliances his own tribe, the Cantiaci, had made, and how, in the blink of an eye, they had been torn up and cast into the winds of conquest. 'You will see.'

Grimoald shrugged, lifting his blade in a two-handed grip above his head. The fading light caught its edge, gold and red and dazzling. 'But you will not.'

CHAPTER ONE

Cullen of the Atrebates hunched behind his horse's neck, the beast's breath roiling past him in vaporous plumes. He braced as the snorting palomino vaulted a narrow stream, righting himself just in time to duck under a low bough and swerve a densely spiked holly. He twisted briefly, checking his companions had cleared the obstacles too, then tucked in his elbows as the track narrowed alarmingly, branches slapping and snagging at his bare arms, leaving scratches across the blue life-wheel etched into the skin by those who were conduits of the gods. He hissed apologies to the spirit world and pressed on.

The land eased into a gentle slope that seemed like a cliff-fall at the speed they travelled, and he clung on for all he was worth. He rounded the gnarled sprawl of an ancient oak, his heart in his mouth as the big horse whinnied and stumbled. He flinched, cursing, but the anticipated impact did not come, and thanked the gods as the sweat-streaked animal regained its footing, crashing into a thick stand of bracken that marked the end of the incline and the extent of the little wood.

The party burst from the gloom into a clear meadow of wildflowers and grass. They were a ragtag group, scarred and weathered. Many had lost the weapons or helmets they had once cherished, while their carefully daubed warpaint was besmirched by filth, blood and sweat. Once noble fighters, turned to frayed shadows of themselves.

Cullen kicked the snorting horse's flanks, urging ever more speed. Shouts came from behind, sharp above the hoof-thunder, heralding the pursuers' doggedness.

'Still with us!' a tall, slender man called from the flank as the group fanned out, gathering into a full gallop on the meadow's surer terrain.

Cullen lashed the reins, as if there might be more to eke from the tiring mount. Soft, warm drizzle welcomed them into the meadow, flecking his brows and the wisps of a nascent beard. It stung too. The big gash in his head already smarted, but the rain seemed to worm beneath the matted red hair and irritate the raw line of flesh, opened two days earlier by a Gaulish blade. He berated the pain through gritted teeth, clenched thighs tighter astride the four-horned saddle and scanned the horizon. It was summer, but uniform blue had given way to the metallic grey of pregnant clouds which obscured the high ridge that was his destination.

The taller man squinted at the dark blur that marked the ridge's position, long legs dangling incongruously at his stocky horse's flanks. 'That's it.'

'Should we see the dun, Andoc?' Cullen asked. 'From this distance?'

Andoc shook his head. 'Scarp runs east–west. We're looking at its rump end. Need to get up on the crest and follow it.'

'How far?'

Andoc's sallow face bunched as he considered. 'Eight leagues. Nine, maybe.'

'We're close.'

Another of his companions drew alongside. 'Not close enough.' She was entirely naked from the waist up, save a leather belt circling her chest, just wide enough to cover her nipples. Her lithe torso and sinew-knotted arms were smothered in a rich, blue paste that had since been scraped and smeared by the throes of battle. Her black hair was cropped severely close to her skull, spiked like so many raptor's talons, and her cheeks were streaked with dark patches of blood and charcoal. 'They'll run us down before we reach the dun.'

'What lies beyond this field?' Cullen called out.

'Woodland,' came a contribution from behind.

'Another stream,' offered someone else, 'then a quarry.'

Cullen stared hard at the indefinite mass that betrayed the ridge's place on the horizon. 'To the quarry, then,' he said, 'where we shall greet them properly.'

—

The ridge was a great wooded run of grey ragstone banded with sand, starkly elevated above the river valley. At its foot, the trees had been cleared to make way for a small hamlet, and the smoke trails from a dozen roundhouses meandered up to the crest, mingling with the rain clouds and invading the dense canopy with a heady fug that tore Cullen back in time, reversing his seventeen winters to stride amongst his oldest memories. His mother and aunts at the hearth. His grandparents at the quern and the loom. The lowing of cattle, the bleat of sheep, the laughter of his sisters. All gone, now.

He looked around, startled, blinking, aware that someone was speaking. The painted woman, standing over him. He said, 'Maeveen?'

She folded her arms impatiently. 'I said I hear them.' She tapped a foot on the twig-latticed track. 'Hooves. Are you ready?'

He eased out of his crouch, looking at the others. They had reached the eastern extent of the ridge, knowing that time and distance were no longer their allies, and had duly tied all but one of the mounts in an almost impenetrable thicket that would be shielded from the path. There was a man-made ravine close by, hidden amongst the deep, dark wood, steep sided and treacherous with loose lumps of rock made slick by the drizzle. A quarry, they reckoned, though it had long since fallen out of use, the sides clothed in thick green moss and clasped by exposed roots that seemed like the skeletal hands of extinct giants.

Cullen took hold of the bejewelled harness and walked his whickering mount to the pit's edge. He had known the horse just two days. Claimed it as plunder from a battle that had ended in stalemate on the banks of the Swamp River. Killed its owner as its owner had tried to kill him. Now they were twinned, he and the war-beast, with its striking golden coat and contrasting cream-coloured mane. Joined by horror and blood. Watched over by the spirit of the Gaul who had died in its saddle. He whispered soothing words into its pricked ears, begging trust, as he coaxed it to the edge and down the first few feet of slimy boulders, skirting logs that had been lashed together in huge piles, evidently the building materials of the villagers down in the valley. Once they had reached a shelf of firm rock, he left the horse and continued alone, crabbing and sliding his way to the very bottom, mindful of the ancient pick-marks that spoke of ancestors long gone to the next life. At the base of the crater, one of his comrades waited, curled on his side like a foetus, knees drawn tight to his stomach.

'Life with glory,' Cullen said.

The curled man's foot twitched as he murmured, 'Death with honour.'

It seemed mere moments before the chasing pack arrived. They were down to a dozen, a determined squad having broken away from a larger body of cavalry several leagues back. These, Cullen presumed, were the keenest riders on the freshest steeds, which was why it seemed a fool's errand to keep running.

He watched them skirt the edge of the quarry's bowl. He could see them because he was lying on his back, soft rain flecking his cheeks as he writhed and moaned. They studied him for a short while, discussing his fate in that strange language, so out of place on these shores. They wore ring-mail on their bodies and plumed helmets on their heads. Each man was armed with a short lance, an oval shield, and the long, slashing sword that was the mark of Roman cavalry.

He bucked, groaned, scraped his heels on the damp stone, let his eyelids flutter inconsistently, a brace of dying butterflies. Laughter reverberated above. Orders, unintelligible to his ear, streamed down with the rain, and then footsteps scrabbled. They were coming. Two at first. Not enough. Then several more, shuffling gingerly down the mossy descent until they filed into the echoing basin.

Cullen touched the wheel at his forearm as the dismounted enemy approached. He shut his eyes and prayed.

One of the Romans spoke with the harsh, choppy cadence of his native tongue.

A second man replied, though Cullen could disentangle none of it with the paltry Latin he had learned. A rumble, like distant thunder. Cullen opened one eye. Above him, a burly soldier loomed, his mail-coat beaded with rain, the horsehair plume the rich crimson of fresh blood. In his hands he gripped a spear, its point trained upon the prone man at his feet. But he was turning away, his victim all but forgotten.

Because the rumble was not thunder, but timber. A lot of timber, rolling, bouncing, flying down the uneven slope towards them. The felled trees, stacked so neatly by hands unknown, had been unleashed and shoved into the quarry by hands very much known, and now they gathered speed like a herd of startled bullocks, careening down the scarp, jarring from one jagged spur to the next so that their paths were as unpredictable as they were unstoppable.

Cullen rolled away, snatching up the sword he had secreted in brambles close by, and he was screaming for his comrade to rise. The second supine form was miraculously resurrected, limbs unfurling even as the first Roman was tossed into the next life by a speeding tree trunk that jumped at the last moment and smashed him at the midriff.

The others dodged and leapt the runaway spars, but one, careless of all but escape, ran straight onto Cullen's poised blade, the gap at his throat, just above the protective mail, proving soft and inviting. Another man came on, just as the first slumped, gargling. His spear was levelled and his shield girded before a big, brawny body, and Cullen knew this would be a fight he might not win. Except that there was more than simply drizzle coming down from on high. Stones, small and smooth and lethal, flung from leather thongs that whirred above the heads of a half-dozen slingers that descended the slope as they attacked.

The Romans fell, plucked from the waking realm in a welter of blood and a chorus of shocked yelps. Cullen, wincing as the smooth river pebbles rained down like the vengeance of Andraste herself, threw himself at his opponent as the bigger man diverted his shield in the face of the new onslaught. Out the corner of his eye he glimpsed Maeveen, her lithe frame melding with the trees, vanishing and reappearing like rippling shadows in a pool as she skirted the melee. He wasted no time, jammed the tip of his iron blade hard into the hamstring of the distracted Roman, who juddered backwards, collapsing under his own suddenly gargantuan weight.

Maeveen screeched as she erupted from her hiding place, whirling her own blade high above her spiked head. A huge man, with shaggy silver hair, plaited whiskers and a handless wrist that had been armoured with a mass of metal studs, lolloped in her wake, a long necklace of badger teeth rattling with his heavy strides. As the great timbers rolled harmlessly to the far side of the quarry, the pair charged into the centre, joining the slingers who had come down from the heights, and together they fell upon the remnants of the enemy, dispatching them without mercy.

They were good, the Romans. More than good, for they had conquered a continent. Built an empire on the foundations of smashed armies, annihilated kingdoms and subsumed cultures. But theirs was a power derived from the corporate. The legions were vast machines, achieving stellar success through discipline and joint enterprise. Here, in the base of a quarry at the foot of a ragstone ridge covered in trees, these soldiers fought as individuals against the blade-brothers of the Isle of the Mighty. They did not stand a chance.

When it was done, when the fight's snarls ebbed to the soft moans of the dying, and the sounds of circling, hungry crows echoed about them, Cullen stooped to wipe his sword on the cloak of a dead Roman. He lifted it to kiss the hilt, which was shaped into the form of a man, the exquisitely wrought legs and arms providing a guard. He closed his eyes as the cold metal grazed his lips, silently thanking the gods and the ancestors for their favour. When he opened his eyes, the reflection staring back made him start. A year, that's all it had been. One turn of the seasons since he had tended his goats on the chalk hills of his forebears, worrying only about the threat of wolves and the growl of his stomach. Now a man stared back at him from the depths of the iron. Muscle layered the sinew of his neck and shoulders. Hair grew on a face blighted by scars. The old, deep groove that split his right eyebrow tugged permanently at the lid. A big cut across his head, crown to temple, that had not even begun to heal. Bruising across the bridge of his nose, casting it in blue shadow. He was the same person, and yet utterly, shockingly different.

A deep, guttural groan drew him from his reverie. He turned, weary, to see the man he had hobbled, lying in a pool of his own blood. Sheathing the blade, he went to stand over the grimacing Roman. 'You fought with honour,' he said in the common tongue, knowing he would not be understood.

The wounded man hissed a reply in his native Latin, spitting to show his disdain.

Cullen glanced at Maeveen. 'What did he say?'

She wiped blood from her painted cheek with the back of her hand and grinned. 'That the Catuvellauni will all perish.'

'Then I need not lose a wink of sleep,' Cullen said. He looked down at their captive. 'I am Cullen of the Atrebates. Cullen Wolf Scourge. Slayer of Branna and beloved of the thunder god, Taranis. I do not fear you, nor your legions, nor your emperor, whose balls I will cut off if ever I meet him.'

Maeveen laughed at that. The Roman spewed a torrent of words that Cullen presumed were not complimentary.

'Shall I?' said the burly fellow with the badger necklace. In stark contrast to the others, he was not sinewy and lean, but a bear of a man, all bulky flesh and powerful muscle. He held up the stump of his left arm, which was bound in bull hide and spiked fit for nightmare.

Cullen smiled as the horrified Roman's eyes widened to orbs. But he shook his head. 'Leave him, Garn.'

The big man sucked his teeth, annoyed. 'Now is not the time to build your repute.'

But Cullen was already walking away. 'Let him tell his friends of the fate that awaits them,' he called over his shoulder. 'Let the legions come, and let them quake.'

CHAPTER TWO

A ribbon of soft pink hung above the far hills, heralding the new dawn, as Cullen stared into the embers of the dying fire. He blew gently on the layer of pristine white ash, disrupting the thin smoke trail that mingled with the scrawny fronds of the overhanging birch.

They had traversed the ragstone range the previous afternoon, halting only when the fading light had made the going treacherous. To spare the horses, they made camp on a step of flat terrain just below the crest at the ridge's western extremity, and had talked into the night, telling tales of old fights, glorious victories and narrow defeats. They had eaten well – a welcome replenishment after the strain of the ambush – and had thanked the gods for delivering enemies with abundant rations. Bread and cheese seemed to be the common theme, though a few Roman saddlebags were supplemented with strips of dried fish or beef. The welcome fare was shared amongst the nine, enhanced by yarrow leaves and whortleberries growing wild on the ridge. Now, the others snored as the sun climbed, and Cullen, snug in the thick beaver-skin cloak that had belonged to his mother, stared out at the valley below, watching a pair of crows dance on the breeze.

'Did you lose any?' a woman's voice broke his reverie.

Cullen looked to his left, where Maeveen was lying on her side, propped on an elbow beneath a cloak of fur. 'Any what?'

'Sleep,' Maeveen said. She had spared a little of her drinking water to dowse her face after the fight at the quarry, purging it of both blood and paint, so that her true face was revealed, sharp cheekbones and chin more prominent than before. Her eyes, too, which were blue and intense as they bore into him. 'You told that Roman you would not lose a wink.'

'Because I was not of the Catuvellauni,' Cullen explained. He felt no need to apologise, for he barely knew her, having first encountered the formidable warrioress on the banks of the Swamp River only two days before. But that encounter had seen her fling herself into the melee, tearing at oncoming mounted Roman auxiliaries with teeth and nails as well as iron. Those riders, battle-frenzied Gauls who had known no fear, had been stunned by her intervention, their briefest hesitation going more than a little way towards saving Cullen's life. Which was why, as a distant dog barked and the crows climbed to harry an approaching raptor, he decided against hog-headedness. 'I have offended you, Maeveen. It was not my intention.'

The blue eyes were unwavering. 'You fight for our tribe, but you would have us killed?'

Cullen reached across to where his shield lay. It had been painted on the eve of battle with the symbols that were way-markers of his life. The wheel of Taranis, the red serpents of King Togodubnos, the magpie who seemed to shadow his every move, and a three-tailed horse, which he tapped with a forefinger. 'The sign of my tribe.' He met her gaze levelly, which was not an easy task. 'I do not love the Catuvellauni, but I will fight for this island against our mutual enemy. On my honour.'

'Cullen,' a low growl of a voice joined theirs, 'was at Calleva when Caratacos made conquest of the dun.'

'I was there too,' Maeveen said.

The growling Garn, who they called Grey Boulder, pushed himself upright with a groan reminiscent of a wounded ox. 'He witnessed the passing of his people to the next life, sent there by Catuvellauni iron.'

'Calleva?' one of the others asked. He was fresh-cheeked, without the hint of whiskers, though he was about the same age as Cullen. Golden eyebrows, the same colour as his thick hair, knitted together as he frowned. 'Capital of the Atrebates?'

Garn nodded as he scratched the scarred mess of skin that was his forearm stump. 'Seat of old King Berikos.'

The baby-faced youth stared from the big man to the subject of their discussion. 'How did you survive?'

Garn laughed darkly. 'Stone me, Clesek, but you do not know?' He rummaged beneath his cloak, pulling out the studded leather thong that would be wrapped around his stump. 'He sent Branna back to the soil, lad.'

Clesek's jaw lolled as he ran a veiny hand through his tousled locks. 'Branna the Slayer? First shield of Caratacos?' He looked to Cullen for confirmation of what he clearly deemed the tallest of tales.

But Cullen was not listening, the questions tumbling over him like rainwater across thatch. For Maeveen's four words had been like daggers, driven into his ears, pinning his mind in place. He looked into her hard eyes. 'You were there too?'

She sat up, pulling the cloak around her almost bare torso. 'I go where I am sent,' she said, a defensive slant to her tone.

'And they sent you to kill my family.'

Maeveen shrugged. 'I could not say for certain. But I did not see Branna the Slayer that day.' She put her long-taloned hand to her heart. 'On my life.'

A man with a bushy iron-grey moustache leaned forward. 'I heard you fought Arthmael the Learned.' The earnestness of his words was starkly at odds with his stern eyes and hatchet face. 'Is it true?'

'Fought?' Cullen said. Flashes of remembered lightning streaked across his mind. The smell of roasting bull-flesh. The baying of the mob. The leering face of Arthmael the Learned, wisest of the Wise, counsellor to mighty Caratacos, the high king's brother. He suppressed a shudder. 'He tried to burn me alive. With the help of Lord Taranis, I managed to avoid the flames.'

The moustachioed man nodded reverently. 'Then he truly does favour you.'

Garn chuckled, reminiscent of stones shaken in a barrel. 'Why else would we suffer this whelp as our leader? Ulla Jagged Cliff trusted him.' He looked for another. 'Did he not, Rues?'

'That he did,' confirmed a short, wiry man whose bare chest and face were streaked with painted symbols. His scalp was limewashed pale yellow, the hair, like Maeveen's, styled into severe spikes. He gave a wry smile. 'Saw something the rest of us did not.'

'And Aoife the Dread,' Garn went on, 'gave him his name.'

'Mine too,' Maeveen said.

'Spurn Joy, they call her,' Garn said to Clesek with a wink. 'On account of her talent for the telling of jests.' He ignored her withering look, sweeping his stump before the assembled faces. 'Aoife gave him this nine. Ulla could judge a man's substance,' Garn continued, warming to his theme. 'Judged Cullen worthy. That was all Aoife needed, and all I need.'

Cullen smiled, unable to hide his appreciation for what amounted to high praise indeed. 'Long as you can fight, drink and swive, eh?'

The huge man chuckled, his badger-tooth necklace rattling along. 'What else is there?' He fixed the studded strap around the terminal of his severed arm and set about tightening the thick plait of his silver beard. 'I will fight for your nine, Cullen Wolf Scourge. By the gods, you might get me killed, but I'll fight.'

Cullen nodded his thanks, but found himself averting his eyes, casting them back to the pulsing embers as potent memories stirred. *His* nine? The term rankled a touch, for they were not really his. Everything about his appointment had been a matter of expedience above all else. Battle had been joined on the Swamp River's banks, reeds trampled, a bridge destroyed, waters dyed red with the blood of Cantiaci, Catuvellauni, Gaul and Rome. It had been little more than a tactic of disruption. Cullen had been tasked with delaying the advance of the legions, and he had succeeded, since they had stalled and were now forced to locate an alternative place to convey their men, equipment and supplies to the west bank. But the native warbands – those called Britons by the enemy – had retreated all the same, outnumbered and overwhelmed. The real fight was yet to come. Which was why, as the dead had been arranged on great pyres and the Wise spat curses at the invaders still lurking on the far bank, mounted nines had been dispatched into the west. Some would take a northerly route in order to report the action to High King Togodubnos, who waited with his main force at a ford on the River Vaga. Some would veer south to reach the tribes of the chalk hills and the windswept coast, there to rally them to the fight. Cullen, though, would head due west. To that end, Aoife, the great war-chief, known far and wide as the Dread, had stood atop her chariot on the bloody turf, Belinos's dazzling brilliance shining through her long, red tresses and dancing along the twists of bronze at her neck. She had rewarded men and women for their deeds, Cullen, to his surprise, amongst them. He had found himself at the head of a small warband, a blend of youth and experience, furnished with fresh mounts and a fresh task. He could hardly believe it still.

It had been a whirlwind. A night of battle, a morning of grief and a dusk of farewells. He had taken his new horse, one that had almost killed him only hours earlier, and then they were away, Aoife's orders ringing in his ears.

But the Romans, as bloodied and hesitant as they now were, had remained undaunted. Their auxiliaries had found a way over the river to make chaos of the natives' retreat. They rode in all directions, killing messengers, hunting warbands and burning villages, employing terror as an effective vanguard. And one such party had spotted Cullen and his nine within an hour of his departure.

He clambered to his feet now, blinking away the memory and stretching expansively as he yawned, feeling joints crack and ribs complain, bruised as they were by an enemy shield boss during the battle. 'We must be on the move.'

The others responded without demur, gathering their belongings and kicking the last of the fire so that its soft ash rose with the languorous smoke. Cullen brushed flecks of dirt from his yellow, bloodstained tunic and folded the cloak that would return to its place at his saddle. He picked his way to the edge of the flat step, looking out over the valley stretching below.

At his back, Maeveen Spurn Joy said, 'Where is the fort?'

Cullen vaguely indicated the far side of the valley. 'That way. Beyond the trees.' He turned back, climbing. 'Let's not tarry.' They had put paid to the Roman hunting party, but more would come. The enemy were a multitude. A host, as numerous as the stars in the night sky. And they were not to be denied. He imagined the rendezvous chosen by Togodubnos. The raging river, Vaga, placed in the earth at the dawn of time by Danu, the mother of all gods. It might be the only obstacle that could prove truly insurmountable, even for the Romans. He hoped it would be wide enough, deep enough, to protect the high king's forces. Disquiet gnawed at his guts as he strapped the shield to the waiting horse, checked its ornate harness and leapt up, nestling his rump between the four horns of the saddle.

'Ready?' asked Maeveen.

Cullen cast his gaze across the party, still feeling uneasy as their leader. He had earned his command, earned his name and his status, but he was still young, the knowledge a thorn to his confidence. Others here had more sword-prowess than he, had fought more fights and shed more blood. But he had learned his craft with the best. Ulla Jagged Cliff had been his chief, and the nine known as the hawks had been his war-brothers. It was a reality he would have to embrace if he was to succeed.

He whispered a plea for guidance. To his mother, who had fallen at Calleva, and to Ulla Jagged Cliff, who had shown him how to be a man when all had seemed so bleak.

'To the fort,' he said, and they kicked on.

—

The wain rocked alarmingly as it negotiated the run of exposed roots that had broken the road's surface like clawing hands. A wheel spun intermittently, made slick by the short-lived rain. The vehicle slewed to one side, its pair of oxen growing more plaintive as they wrestled to regain momentum, and it was only when a pair of burly warriors put shoulders to the tailboard that it came back into line, juddering violently over the last of the roots.

'Smoother now,' Cassia crooned into the wounded man's ear. 'Try to sleep.'

The man lay flat on his back, wedged against the side of the wain. Contradicting her words, he made a loud, if futile, effort to sit up. 'They're coming.' He possessed only one eye, for the other had been reduced to a grotesque mess of cleaved tissue and congealed blood by the stab of a *gladius*. That lone eye widened, rolled back into his skull, and then fixed Cassia with a look of sheer terror. 'They're coming. The javelins.' He grasped her shoulders, shaking her, as if trying to get through to a slow-witted child. 'Take cover, girl. By Belinos, take cover.'

'Hush,' she urged softly, shrugging herself out of his grip. 'You are out of danger now, I promise.' She found herself glancing furtively over her shoulder, wondering if that was not a sensible pledge to make. The rear-guard action, not a mile away to the east, was ongoing. A desperate attempt to delay the inevitable. 'Rest, brother. Regain your strength.'

'You saw the battle?' a silver-haired woman said. Like Cassia, she had clambered onto the cart to perform a healer's duty, and she dabbed a pink-stained cloth to a prone man's brow as she spoke.

Cassia glanced at her. 'Saw?' The word itself seemed to stick in her throat, its inadequacy offensive. Yes, she had seen. But she had smelled the battle too, the unmistakable tang of fresh blood on the air. She had heard the screams of dying men, women and horses. And she had felt it. The thrum of hooves in the earth, the pounding of her own heart against her ribs, the rushing of blood in her ears as terror overtook her. She had felt the body of an old king resist and then sag as she plunged sharp iron into his guts. She nodded. 'Yes.'

'What was it like?'

Cassia threw her eyes up to the lush canopy that cast the world in premature twilight. An apt description was not perching there like a bird. 'Bad.'

The older woman's crinkled eyes lingered on her for a moment. 'I cannot place your accent, child. Are you from the north? Parisi? Even further. The Caledonii, perhaps?'

'You didn't see?' Cassia deflected, suspecting a discussion of her heritage might lead her to require the ministrations she was currently administering. 'The battle, I mean.'

The silver plaits shook. 'I lived close by. Word reached my home. I went to see what could be done.' She offered a forlorn smile. 'Here I am.'

Cassia nodded, understanding. Because nothing, in truth, could be done for the defenders at the Swamp River. The battle had gone as well as could be expected. The Britons had been outnumbered, the bulk of their army – an uneasy confederation of tribes – had already fallen back on the wide and deep waters of the Vaga, further north and west. What had transpired, then, had only ever been a matter of disruption and delay. The first step of what would become a drawn-out, brutal action of sporadic fight and incremental flight, designed to frustrate the advance of the legions. But that advance was inexorable. If Cassia remembered anything of her countrymen, it was that once a decision to invade a territory had been made, there would be no stopping the machine of conquest until it had achieved its aims. Britannia would be subjugated, of that she had no doubt. But that did not mean the Britons should not resist. And she, in spite of the tug of home, would be with them every step of the way.

A water jug made its way, hand to hand, through the packed vehicle. When it reached Cassia, she held it to the one-eyed man's blue-tinged lips. 'Drink this. Do not complain.'

'You've a healer's touch,' the older woman said.

'Thank you, grandmother,' Cassia acknowledged. 'I studied with the Wise.' Which was almost true. Her first tutor had been her father, who had tended the legions at the great infirmary of Gesoriacum, but the less said of him, the better. Her teacher on this remote and warlike island had been an equally warlike woman named Critheanach, who had fallen short of acceptance by the Wise Ones, and cleaved to her resulting bitterness for the rest of her days. But she had known her potions and remedies well enough, and had shown Cassia the ways of the Britons, just as Cassia had reciprocated with her father's knowledge. They had worked well together, their friendship flourishing, until Critheanach had vanished at Swamp River. Taken or killed by Cassia's countrymen.

'Which was why you were at the battle,' the woman said, touching a finger to her temple to show that the pieces had fallen into place.

Cassia nodded. That was indeed the reason for being at the fight. The fact that she had crossed the water – foolishly – been captured – briefly – and ended her day with the murder of Berikos, seemed an unnecessary tale to tell. In slaying the toppled, exiled and returned king of the Atrebates, ostensibly so that she could escape, she had uncovered a list of tribes who had struck deals with Rome. Friendly natives in return for client thrones. She was Roman, and it had occurred to her that perhaps she should have stayed on the east bank. Found position with the legions. But Britannia – Isle of the Mighty, as the Britons knew it – had been her home these past few years. She had found comradeship here. And love. So she had made her stand amid the chaos of screams and death. Made her choice.

The wains had come and fetched the wounded in the hours after the Romans had aborted their river crossing, retiring into the forests of the east bank to lick their wounds, both literal and figurative. Then the massed retreat had begun. With some of the warriors lingering to guard the Swamp River's fords, most marched and rode into the west, corpse-pyres belching black as the sun had risen at their backs. A great tide of humanity, spilling out of the trackways and into the fields, all heading to the Vaga, where the over-king had raised his banner and issued his call.

But who would rally to the standard of the twin serpents? Who would come in the hour of need? King Berikos, hounded from his throne at Calleva the previous summer, had found his way across the Narrow Sea, and then on to Rome itself. There, it seemed, he had plotted with Adminios, youngest brother of Togodubnos, who had himself been exiled from the Isle of the Mighty. Together, they had set about charting a return, harnessing the strength of the mighty Roman eagles. They would become vassals of the emperor, but would be restored to their thrones. They had sold themselves for power, and seduced many more chieftains along the way. Cassia had requested that she be sent to Togodubnos with the news, for it was she who had uncovered the treachery. But the commander on the Swamp River, Aoife the Dread, had bade her stay, for the majority of the Wise Ones had mostly coalesced around the main army on the Vaga, leaving a dearth of healing hands with the smaller force that now made its painfully sluggish retreat. Cassia's skills were required. Others had been dispatched with the news, and she would tend, instead, to the wounded.

But all roads led to the Vaga.

'There's to be a great gathering of warriors,' the old woman said hopefully. 'On the big river's far bank.'

'Yes, grandmother, so it is said.' It would be, so King Togodubnos hoped, the largest massing of fighters since the days of Casivellaunus and his tussle with the original Caesar. 'But the enemy must not be underestimated.'

'The Romans'll struggle to cross the water. It is wide and fast.' A little bubble of laughter escaped her wrinkled throat. 'Not that I have ever seen it, but folk talk.'

'The Romans are clever,' Cassia warned.

The woman shrugged. 'If they get across, they shall be cut down like wheat before a scythe. We'll toss their corpses in the Vaga. Let them float out to sea.'

Cassia offered the wounded man another sip, so that she could avoid the old woman's gaze. 'I am sure you're right,' she said. Which was a lie.

CHAPTER THREE

A buzzard circled above the valley as the horses took them down. Cullen picked at what was left of the bandages at his hands. They had enwrapped most of his fingers, the digits having been cut to ribbons during the battle, though most of the dressings had come away in the hours since, so that it looked now as though he wore a pair of ragged, dirty gloves. All the same, the memory of their binding made him smile. Cassia had tended his wounds in the aftermath of the fight. Even as the pyres had belched black smoke and the warriors had patrolled the west bank, lest the enemy attempt another crossing, she had seen to his injuries, of which there were several, and told him of her travails with her captors. Told him what she had discovered, and whom she had killed. Berikos. King of the Atrebates. Cullen's king, before the Catuvellauni had sacked the great dun of Calleva and ground his tribe to dust.

'The Vaga is wide,' Garn Grey Boulder was saying, his great bulk swaying precariously in a saddle that was dwarfed by his rump. 'They'll have to swim it.'

Laughter greeted that. Clesek said, hopefully, 'Drown in all that armour.'

'May the river goddess swallow them whole,' Garn growled.

One of the front riders twisted to look back, an unshaven face, blighted by angry welts, betraying his youth. 'And if she doesn't?'

'We'll fight, young Kenal!' Garn declared, the enthusiasm of his delivery suggesting he rather hoped the Romans would cross the river safely. 'And you'll earn your warrior's name!'

Kenal visibly blanched, swallowing thickly as he nodded, and clearly not relishing the prospect. The third of the nine's raw young fighters, a lad named Erbin, reined in beside Cullen. 'How many will we have?'

'Many,' Cullen said bluntly. 'Togodubnos and Caratacos have sent delegates to every corner of this island. Help will come.' It was a surreal thing, to play mentor to these new warriors, who had drawn and shed blood on the Swamp River, and deserved their shields and their dignity, for Clesek, Kenal and Erbin had all shivered through a similar number of winters as Cullen himself. But, he supposed, when a boy reaches the age of choosing, it matters not which seasons he has seen, but rather what moments he has experienced. He was a lord of war now, whether he felt comfortable with the title or not. A battle-giver, and a leader of spears. That was what mattered.

Erbin – a squat, muscular barrel of a warrior – drew a vein-webbed forearm across his brow. 'What of the traitors?'

'It is a blow,' Cullen conceded, 'but not yet mortal.'

'The Regnenses on the south coast,' Andoc chimed in dolefully, 'and the Brigantes and Coritani in the north. Not to mention the Dobunni to the west.'

'Do not speak that name,' Cullen said, even as a bitter knot formed in the pit of his stomach. They had abandoned the spear-wall at Swamp River, the Dobunni tribe, and he could still picture their star-spangled shields being slung as they turned their backs, leaving the defenders at the mercy of the Roman advance.

Andoc shrugged his thin brows. 'Our confederation has crumbled.'

Cullen threw his friend a caustic glance. 'If you believe that, we are already defeated.'

Andoc turned his sunken eyes upon Cullen. 'Perhaps we are.'

'The names of the betrayers are many,' Cullen said, 'but it is not as grievous as it appears. King Togodubnos has sent riders in every direction. The Damnonii, Parisi, Ordovices, Cornovii have all been summoned to his banner.'

'He is high king because he commands the most spears,' Andoc said sullenly, 'not because the lesser kings owe him fealty. He can ask them for aid, but he cannot summon.'

Cullen made to respond, but the wind was knocked out of him as his horse stumbled on a patch of loose rocks and attempted a half-buck that had him clinging on for dear life. 'Gods,' he hissed, 'but the Gaul did not have this trouble.'

Andoc grunted. 'The Gaul is dead.'

Maeveen reined in beside Cullen, grinning as she grabbed the palomino's harness. 'I'll keep you safe, Wolf Scourge.'

Cullen felt heat burn his cheeks, and he steered the horse away, shedding her grip. 'No need.'

Garn Grey Boulder laughed, like a bucket of gravel poured onto rocks. 'He is green, Maeveen, but he learned his craft from the best there was.'

'Ulla Jagged Cliff,' Cullen reminded her testily.

That stopped her in her tracks. 'May the gods honour his name,' she said, suddenly sheepish.

'Besides,' Garn announced, 'if he soils his braca, I am here to wipe his arse.'

Cullen glanced pointedly at the iron nodules studding the stump that had once been Garn's left hand. 'Not with that, you won't.'

—

The high ridge loomed above them as they followed a well-worn track to the valley floor, emerging from the thick canopy to bear the brunt of the dazzling afternoon sun. At the foot of the slope, a river meandered through stands of ash and bracken, a glistening band of silver against lush greens, light and dark. The skies had mostly cleared, revealing a blanket of cornflower blue, save a smudgy pall that clung above a cleared hillock at the far end of the vale.

A small settlement, encircled by ditch and fence, occupied the low ground, making use of the meandering waterway. The cleared area before the gate was given over to outbuildings, grain pits and wickerwork livestock pens. On the valley's opposite slope, the dark forest had mostly been purged clean, grazing sheep showing as brilliant white dots against the green of the hill.

The nine forded the river at a narrow crossing place that was marked by a pair of withies, each hung with what looked to be a tiny straw doll. Those who had spears dipped them to the figurines as hooves frothed the shallows, acknowledging the authority of the water spirits. They traced the line of the bank a little way, stifling smiles as Garn practised his most intimidating growl upon a pair of lads fishing from a coracle below. Then they moved into the area containing the animal pens and grids of carefully tended soil that dazzled with the colours of herb, vegetable and petal. There were men toiling therein, and the gazes were suspicious, if not outwardly hostile. One of them – a stooping greybeard leaning heavily on his mattock – acknowledged Cullen's hail. 'Can I help you, lord?'

Cullen offered a short bow from the saddle, stifling the sense that the salutation had been uttered a little ironically. He tried to add a guttural undertone to his voice, hoping it would give the gravitas his youth clearly denied. 'I seek the fortress known as Smith's Ring.'

The greybeard pivoted slightly on the tool's long haft and extended a bony finger in the direction of a smoke cloud that smudged the hill's crest. 'Yonder, lord. Ask for Coel.'

—

'Andoc says you've made enemies of the Wise,' Maeveen Spurn Joy said to Cullen as they urged their mounts up into the steep pastures that comprised the valley's southern edge.

'Andoc has a big mouth,' Cullen said, glancing back to throw baleful eyes at his friend. The tall man, within earshot, made a theatrical show of inspecting the hillfort that had steadily emerged on the high ground, its defensive ring of ditch, bank and palisade becoming more defined with every passing yard.

'Does he lie, then?' Maeveen pressed.

Cullen shook his head. 'It is not the Wise, but one of their number.'

'Arthmael?'

'Arthmael,' he confirmed.

They passed through a wicker gate, which, like the withies, was protected by a pair of straw dolls, and moved into grasslands cropped low by grazing flocks. Above them, the smear of smoke seemed to have broken down into individual streaks, betraying the presence of dozens of hearths.

'You said he tried to burn you.'

'A sacrifice to Taranis,' Cullen explained. He lifted his right hand a touch, angling the forearm so that the light played across the vivid wheel that had been etched in bluish green into his skin. 'But the lord of thunder had other plans.'

'And he hates you for that?' Maeveen asked.

'That,' Cullen nodded, a smile cracking the corners of his mouth, 'and because I stabbed him in the leg.'

She laughed, a high cackle, and he realised it was the first time he had ever heard the sound. 'He limps,' she said. 'That was you? And Caratacos let you live?'

'I think he was in two minds. Either he could anger Arthmael, or he could anger Taranis. He made the sensible choice.' Now Cullen allowed himself a chuckle. 'Besides, I think he enjoyed needling his counsellor.'

'A great man, Caratacos.'

'Great,' Cullen repeated the word, weighing it, as he would a nugget of precious metal. Son of Cunobelin, the old high king, Caratacos had certainly been one of the most powerful princes in all the Isle of the Mighty. Brother to the new king, he was now a peerless and formidable warlord, with realms of his own. Those things made him great in one sense, Cullen could hardly deny.

'Forgive me,' Maeveen was saying, 'if I offended you before. I am unused to following one so young.'

He looked across at her. She was a hard thing. All angles and knots, like a sack full of pebbles. Her lithe arms were corded with sinew, and her spiked pate bore all the softness of Garn's studded fist. Yet, as she regarded him in turn, he saw, for the first time, a warmth in those glinting eyes. 'It is forgotten,' he said truthfully. 'I can hardly begrudge you your reservations. In truth, the path my life has taken has surprised none more than me.'

'I saw you at the battle,' she said. 'You fought savagely.'

He remembered the desperate shield-wall on the riverbank. Felt again the churning terror in his guts and saw again the oncoming charge of Gaulish horsemen who formed the vanguard of the Roman advance. He remembered how he had winced and braced and prepared to step into the next life. And he saw once more, scorched vividly on his mind's eye, the impossible, screaming woman who had leapt over bodies, alive and dead, to fling herself into the face of the snorting golden horse which had once been the steed of his enemy. That horse now walked, placid and obedient, beneath his own rump, its owner having taken the ghost-step that had been intended for Cullen. 'And you fought like a crazed shee, riding the wind,' he said, with feeling.

She gave a spurt of that high-pitched laugh. 'It was all I was good at, fighting. I could never weave, and I would always burn my aunt's bread.'

'I tended the goats, before fate intervened.'

She winced. 'What happened at Calleva... I fight where I am told to fight.'

'I know. I have no ill-feeling towards you, Spurn Joy.'

She nodded, brightening. 'And now fate brings you to the notice of great ones. Aoife the Dread. Ulla Jagged Cliff. These are the mightiest of all the Isle of the Mighty.' She lowered her voice conspiratorially. 'What of the high king? Garn says you have been in his presence.'

'He has honoured me,' Cullen said, though he tried not to expand on the subject. It was true that he had spoken with Togodubnos on several occasions, but he was acutely aware that that was due, in no small part, to the influence of the king's Wise One, Moranna of the Silver. And her interest could be attributed to Cullen's friendship with Becan, Moranna's adoptive son. Cullen had risen fast and high, it was true enough, but always there was the nagging truth that luck and happenstance had played a huge role. The knowledge that he was an imposter gnawed at him always, whispering in the quiet moments.

'What is he like?' Maeveen asked as they reached the crest, the high summit marked by a collection of mossy, weathered standing stones.

'Togodubnos? A good man, I think. Generous. Fierce when required.' He shrugged. 'A king.'

'Can he unite the tribes?'

The high palisade of sharpened stakes reared up a hundred paces before them. The gates, adorned with more dolls, were closed, and spearmen waited conspicuously above. 'If any man can, it is he,' Cullen said as he eyed the lank fox-tail banner that hung from a high pole. 'But many of his alliances have fractured.'

Maeveen spat. 'Cowards.'

'They do not fear war, but what will become of them should we lose. They'd rather make peace now and salvage their thrones than resist the empire and be ground to dust under the feet of the legions. Rome has been busy. She lured our chiefs before ever she launched her great ships.'

Maeveen spat again, allowing her mount to drop back with the others so that Cullen led the final approach, as was his right. The ditch, bank and timber wall stretched for hundreds of paces in both directions, curving away over the crest of the hill to encircle the settlement. As they drew closer, he could see carvings set into the timbers, depicting horses, wolves and raptors.

'A beauty,' Clesek's voice rang out from the following group. 'We have a few forts above the cliffs, but not like that.'

'That's a dun,' Rues Seeker replied. 'More than a fort. An entire town, defended against all comers.'

'*Oppida*, the Romans call them,' Cullen said, recalling the word Cassia had once used.

'The Romans,' Garn growled, 'can shove it up their arses.'

'Lower spears,' Cullen commanded above the ensuing gusts of laughter. 'Let them know we mean no harm. We must find this Coel.'

'Are the rumours true?' She was tall and willowy, her long cloak, trimmed with rabbit fur, doing little to hide the meatless nature of her frame. 'Have the eagles crossed the Narrow Sea?'

Cullen and his band had been permitted entry to the dun after a brief discussion with the guards, who had been swiftly and gratifyingly cowed by his credentials. They had traversed the middleway through the settlement, flanked by spearmen on foot. The way was lined by freshly painted roundhouses of varying grandeur, eventually opening out into a half-moon-shaped space at the centre of the hillfort. The space, presumably intended for large gatherings, was about a hundred paces across, adjacent to the grandest of all the buildings they had seen, and at its centre, like a chariot wheel's axle, was an ornately carved pole, taller than the greatest thatch. It was there, in the pole's shadow, that they dismounted, as Coel – who looked to have suffered around fifty winters – appeared from beneath the big roundhouse's sturdy oaken lintel.

Now, having watched her pad barefoot across the gathering space, Cullen bowed deeply. 'They have, lady.'

She nodded, apparently unsurprised. 'We have seen fighters. Moving in ones and twos, nines and great packs. Horsemen and chariots.' She twitched her chin – the sharpest jag in a harshly angular face – vaguely indicating the north. 'That way.'

'There was a battle, lady. Our warbands came together, thanks be to the gods, under the banner of Togodubnos.'

'To whom do I speak?'

'Cullen is my name, lady.'

'And have gods and men proffered a different name?'

'Wolf Scourge, lady.'

'Just so,' she said, evidently satisfied that he was worthy of her engagement. 'Was the enemy defeated?' Her voice was steady, but her thin fingers went up to adjust a pin in her grey hair, the rest of which was fixed in a single, thick plait, extending all the way to her buttocks.

'We bloodied them, but still they come.' Cullen observed the closest houses. Pale faces lurked in the doorways, watching and listening. Most, he noted, were women and children. 'I suggest you leave this place.'

'And where do you *suggest* we go?' asked Coel, waspishly, the strain of the news making each word stab like a challenge.

'The over-king has convened a grand horde, encompassing all the Isle of the Mighty.'

Her hand moved to fiddle with the boar-shaped brooch fastening her cloak. 'On the far side of the River Vaga. Our chief has gone to him. Taken a number of our fighters.'

Cullen glanced about, pointedly. 'A large number.'

Coel pressed her thin lips together, as if pinning the truth firmly in place. He did not begrudge her reticence, for revealing the diminishment of the dun's strength would have been reckless. 'A number,' she reiterated.

'Then you would be prudent to join him, lady.'

Her eyes narrowed. They were muddy-green and weasel-shrewd. 'Abandon Smith's Ring?'

'You intend to hold the fort with children and grandmothers?'

'With blood and fire, if that is what the gods demand.'

'Save your people, lady, I beg of you.'

She folded thin arms across her chest, a barrier to his words. 'Are you bound for the Vaga, Cullen?'

'We are, lady.'

'Then what brings you to our hill? If it is refreshment you seek, the valley below would have sufficed, I think.'

'I am commanded to locate one of the Wise,' Cullen said. 'Serwil is his name.'

Grey brows twitched upwards above the dark green eyes. 'Commanded?'

'By Aoife the Dread.'

The name had the required effect, as he guessed it would, for Coel's arms slid to her sides, the barrier descending. 'He will return at sundown. Until then, you will be my guests.'

—

'A magnificent site,' Cullen said, as Coel led the way across the gathering space. He glanced back up at the carved pole, writhing with all kinds of beasts, expertly stylised to swirl and morph, one into another. He was struck by how clearly those animals were etched, without any sign of rot or weathering. The houses, too, seemed bright, their painted murals vivid. 'Newly erected?'

'Commissioned by Lord Adminios,' she said, 'not four summers back.'

'Expecting trouble?'

Coel stopped, looking cooly at him. 'Trouble came.'

Cullen nodded, embarrassed, for trouble most certainly had come to the Cantiaci and their vassal clans. Adminios, the third and youngest son of the great king, Cunobelin, had been given the overlordship of the Cantiaci. His rule, though short, had brought undeniable prosperity to the territory, for its proximity to Gaul and the lands of the Belgae had secured trade links with the ever-expanding empire across the Narrow Sea. But that prosperity had been Adminios's undoing. When his father had died, his elder brothers had come to dominate the Catuvellauni hegemony, and they had set about dismantling the relationship with Rome. Their little brother had been deposed, exiled, and had fallen on the mercy of Emperor Claudius, there to foster plans for revenge.

What Adminios had left behind was a kingdom without a king. The Cantiaci went their own way, clan by clan, sept by sept, village by village, so that loyalties were hard to predict, from one hill or valley to the next. Generally, Cullen had come to understand that the peoples nearest the coast, who had been most prosperous in the days of great trade, would naturally hark back to the tenure of Adminios, while those inland, closer to the great rivers and neighbouring tribes, might be less fervent in their nostalgia. But nothing at all was certain. And for that reason, he held up his hands, placatingly. 'I meant nothing by it, lady. No offence was intended.'

'Do not be concerned. You are welcome here.'

'Even so,' Cullen muttered, feeling the colour rise in his cheeks and wishing, for the thousandth time in his short life, that he had not been cursed with his mother's red locks and pale complexion.

She smiled. 'Did I not say we had pledged our spears to Togodubnos?'

'Just so, lady,' he said. Still, he inwardly reproved himself for a childish fool. Ulla would not have blurted so mutton-witted a remark. Nor even, for that matter, would Andoc. A truth that smarted more than he would have liked. He looked over his shoulder at the warband, who waited beneath the engraved pole, taking refreshment brought by the youth of the dun.

'Many Cantiaci are reticent to bend the knee to the Catuvellauni,' Coel went on, 'given what transpired between the sons of Cunobelin.' She extended a thin arm, sweeping it expansively to indicate the entire settlement. 'But we, the Bibroci, make our own alliances.'

'Bibroci?' His eyes went to the brooch at her collarbone. He had thought it a rendering of a boar, but, now that he was closer, finer detail revealed its true likeness. 'The beaver people?'

'The Cantiaci are our overlords, just as your Catuvellauni rule over many smaller nations. Indeed, over the once mighty Trinovantes and Atrebates.'

'I am of the Atrebates.'

'Then you know of what I speak.' Now it was Coel's turn to stare at the group of warriors who had come together at the centre of the gathering space. They stretched and yawned, squatted as they drank. Some lay on their backs, gazing up at the white clouds, and one groomed his horse. 'Yet you bear the mark of the entwined snakes.'

Cullen realised that her gaze lingered upon the shields that had been stacked upright against the base of the pole, overlapping one another like huge scales. His own was outermost, facing them, quartered by the four devices that Moranna of the Silver had identified as his life's hinges, on the night when she had bestowed upon him his hero's name. Along with the red serpents of Togodubnos, there was the life-wheel of Taranis, and Cullen's personal device, a magpie in profile. 'You will see the mark of the many-tailed horse, lady,' he said, for the fourth sigil was that of the Atrebates tribe. 'My own blood.'

'You carry both marks,' Coel said, almost wistfully, as if considering the implication.

'The Romans are the greatest enemy. I fight for the Isle of the Mighty.'

She inclined her head. 'An example to us all.' She beckoned for him to walk, and they soon reached the gloom of the largest roundhouse. 'Have the Sun Hound's offspring truly brought the tribes together?'

'They have,' Cullen said as he followed her through the rippling door skin, though he knew the assertion was a stretch. Great Cunobelin – the Sun Dog – had built a hegemony out of the military prowess of his Catuvellauni, combined with treaties that ensured Rome would remain in the background, looming like a big brother, so that other tribes remained submissive. But when the old high king had died, and his three sons had inherited the confederacy, its complex bindings had immediately begun to fray. First Adminios, the youngest, had attempted to harness his groundswell of support in the Cantiaci-controlled southeast, in an effort to dominate his father's territory. Then, no sooner than matters had cooled, the remaining brothers had launched their own campaign of conquest, attempting to expand Catuvellauni borders by destroying the Atrebates. Their ambition had proved as successful as Adminios's had been catastrophic, but it had thrown the Atrebates king, Berikos, on the mercy of Rome. The twin voices of Berikos and Adminios proved too much for the new emperor, Claudius, to resist. Cullen could imagine the narrative spun in the gilded halls of Rome. Upstart brothers, building their own power base, while smashing long-standing treaties. Rightful kings deposed. Deference to Caesar thrown to the wind, replaced by laughter and contempt. A land rich in tin, lead, copper, silver and gold, all taken out of Rome's reach by bloodthirsty usurpers. It must have been irresistible.

Yet Rome's thrust had had an effect not seen in these fractious islands for generations. The tribes – bitter adversaries for so long – had begun to consider a reality where togetherness was the only way of securing a future free from the yoke of empire. At least, Cullen's inner voice nagged, some of the tribes.

'It is a fine desire, if a little hopeful,' Coel said, her voice contemplative, as if weighing his words.

'You see my thoughts, lady. The high king understands there are many factions preferring friendship with Rome above that with the Catuvellauni.'

'There are many factions, Wolf Scourge,' she said archly, stern like his aunts back in Calleva, 'who do not consider Togodubnos king at all, let alone one set higher than all the rest.'

He diverted his gaze, awkwardness drawing heat up his neck, looking instead at the cauldron that hung from a high beam on a stout chain. Children, jostling and whispering, squatted at its edges, stoking new-kindled flames beneath. The room smelled of woodsmoke and herbs, heady and inviting. 'As you say, lady. That is why I have come.'

Coel's grey brows shot up. 'Serwil?' Her voice was ripe with scepticism. 'You believe our Wise One can bring together the tribes?'

'Not him,' Cullen replied. 'But what he possesses.'

CHAPTER FOUR

Cassia knelt up, gripping the side of the wagon to steady herself against its ceaseless roll. She yawned deeply, for her dozing had been fitful and short, curtailed abruptly by a shaken elbow and a garble of excited words. She blinked, blearily, and stared down at the great, shimmering band of the River Vaga as it spread across the horizon. The day was ebbing, the sun low in the west, lighting the broad waterway like a vast serpent of liquid silver. She was immediately glad her companions had roused her, for this was a sight she would not readily have missed.

The convoy had finally cleared the interminable miles of dense, dark woodland, and had climbed a rise of open pasture that, at its crest, looked out over a wide, marshy vale. And in the centre of that low valley ran the Vaga in all its rushing pomp, splitting in places to spread glittering channels across the plain, like splayed fingers, each one forming little islands that were dotted white with gulls and terns. Cassia squinted against the sun, dazzling away to the left, shielding her eyes with a palm as she inspected the estuary far below. It was a vast mosaic of muddied earth, tangled vegetation, and shimmering, reed-edged waterways. On the far bank stood what appeared to be dense stands of low trees and tangled bushes, shadowy smudges at this distance. It was a vista of otherworldly beauty. A haven of the gods. She felt her mood lighten, knowing that safety, however temporary, was at her fingertips.

The rocking wain gathered a little speed as it crested the hillock and embarked on the long, gentle descent to the plain below, one vehicle amongst scores, a surging tide of humanity fleeing before the Roman advance. The retreating column had swelled by the hour since departing the smoggy pyres of Swamp River, so that now it stretched for mile upon mile, as far as the eye could see. She looked back, a matter of instinct, half expecting to see a galloping cavalryman, clad in mail and plumed helm, crouched behind a big, red shield, the long *spatha* sword poised to strike. There was nothing, of course, except the endlessly trailing ranks of warriors, chariots, beleaguered families and their plaintive livestock. Still, the image of the Roman made her guts twist, evaporating the wisps of hope as quickly as they had come. Before she knew it, she had reached into her shoe, pulling free the little pin concealed therein, and gently, persistently, began to scrape its sharp point against the inside of her wrist, revelling in the sudden shock of pain, letting it smother all else.

It took more than an hour for the wain to inch its way off the firm ground of the slope and onto the flat marshland, for the sheer weight of traffic made the column bunch and falter, and the terrain of the valley floor was soft and unstable, transformed to precarious sludge by the hooves, wheels and feet that went before. When eventually Cassia's wagon chuntered and jangled onto the new track, it creaked madly as it sank and slewed, stirring up a cloud of damp, earthy scent. Mud clung to the axles and sucked at the wheels. The air was muggier here, for the reed beds fended off the breeze. She felt sweat bead at her temples. The bellowing of oxen and horses, exhausted from their labours in fetlock-deep mud, seemed to echo around her skull. Drivers snapped in frustration, warlords barked orders for spearmen to help push the mired vehicles, and a chorus of croaking frogs and shrill marsh birds overlaid all.

Occasionally the wain veered, causing it to tilt and sway precariously. Cassia ignored the accompanying curses, content instead to let the pin do its work, stifling her fears with raw, pure pain. She stared out at the stagnant pools and the trickling brooks. At the labyrinth of twisting pathways, spurring off to places unseen, obscured by tall grasses and bent trees. A smattering of low clouds cast an ethereal glow over the landscape, lending the valley a peculiar, haunting beauty. It would be, she hoped, enough to put fear into Roman hearts. It might, she thought, even slow their advance. Might.

The stands of reeds thinned as they progressed westwards, and the great river came once again into view. They were low enough now so that the sun's glare no longer lit up the Vaga, and the terrain on the far side was suddenly easier to discern. The breath caught in her throat. In sudden, jarring understanding, she saw that the shadows smearing the west bank were not stands of vegetation at all, but people. A lot of people. And chariots, horses, sharpened stakes, supply carts and caches of weaponry. An army, no less, mustering for battle.

The sheer number of bodies, clustered in tight groups on the far bank, was something she could never have imagined. She had seen legions in her time, armoured and pristine in their massed ranks as they awaited ship at the great port of Gersoriacum, her former home, but this was another matter entirely. Ten thousand? Twenty? Impossible to tell. Too many to count. This was what the Britons required without doubt. They were not strong as individuals, nines or septs, despite what their outlandish traditions and incorrigible pride told them. These skilled, mad, courageous warriors found strength in numbers. In unity. That was what they needed. The only way they could possibly turn back the legions. The horde that spread across the horizon was, then, precisely the remedy she would have prescribed to cure the Roman blight. But, she knew, if things went awry, then an entire generation of Catuvellauni, Atrebates, Trinovantes and their allies, would die here, in these marshes. The vista was exhilarating and horrifying, all at once.

Her mind ran to Togodubnos and his brother, Caratacos, the Catuvellauni princes whose ambition had arguably caused this catastrophe, but whose determination to fight had seen them achieve the impossible and unite at least some of Britannia's disparate factions. Were they down there, she wondered? Conspicuous amongst the gathered nations in splendid finery, or racing atop gilded chariots, rallying spearmen and beseeching gods? She thought, too, of the message that would certainly have reached them by the now. That of Berikos and his treachery. The king Cassia herself had slain, and in whose possession she had discovered a list of native chiefs he had apparently wooed to the Roman side. Had riders gone to those tribes already? Emissaries of the new high king, carrying honeyed promises and iron threats. And that, inevitably, brought her mind to Cullen. The boy she had known, who had made her laugh, and stared at her as though hers was the only soul in all the world, and who she had lain with under a torchlit wych elm on a magical Nos Callan Haf. And who she might never see again, for the boy had become a man – a warrior, with a nine of his own – and he had ridden into the west on a quest handed down by none other than Aoife the Dread. She shuddered. All was changing. The world was about to burn. She dug the pin hard into her flesh, letting the pain smother her anxiety.

'He will return,' Aoife's voice filled her head. 'Taranis will protect him.' The sound seemed so close it could almost be real, even as far as the accent, which was the softly lilting brogue of the Isle of Destiny – Hibernia, to her countrymen – that sister island away to the west, beyond the white-crested swells of the Clear Sea.

'How can you know?' Cassia muttered bitterly, staring out at the huge expanse of marshland that spread into the distance.

'Because it was a simple enough task, girl,' Aoife said bluntly, 'it's not as if I asked for the emperor's balls in a velvet purse.'

Cassia's head snapped round as every inch of her skin turned to gooseflesh. 'Lady, I… forgive me.'

Aoife gave a snort of laughter. Even that was fearsome. She stared down at Cassia from the back of a chariot that was drawn by a brace of muscular bay geldings, clinging to the wicker rail as the driver negotiated the track's ever deepening ruts. Cassia half-suspected her eyes of playing tricks, for the visage looming over the rocking wain was more goddess than woman.

Aoife, battle chief to Togodubnos, dismissed her apologies with a peremptory wave. 'No matter.' She was tall and lean, with flame-red hair that fell like a molten waterfall over her fur-swathed shoulders. Her face had been beautiful once, but time and battle had given it a sardonic, cynical aspect, only deepened by the ghost-marks of long-healed scars. There was a huge sword at her waist, thick bracelets on her wrists, and snakes, stained in woad, coiled around her bare, knotted forearms. She gazed down at Cassia with eyes as green as sour apples, and ten times as sharp. 'A wagon for the injured. You are hurt?'

Cassia shook her head, forcing herself to stare at a fixed point somewhere beyond the warrioress's shoulder, for it was hard not to stare at the deep scar vertically bisecting Aoife's chin; a battle-standard rendered in flesh. 'Not hurt, lady.' She swallowed thickly. Few women were honoured with battle names, but, by all the gods, those that earned them were a sight to behold. 'It is my honour to tend the wounded.'

Aoife nodded. 'I recall. With—?'

An uplift on the final word prompted Cassia to complete the thought. 'Critheanach, lady.'

'Just so.' The hard gaze swept over the vehicle. 'And she is?'

Cassia groped for the right word, finding nothing satisfactory. 'Lost.'

'Dead?'

'I know not. She was at the battle. The Romans crossed nearby. When the fight was over, she had vanished.'

Aoife knuckled her own chest. 'On to the next.'

'Lady,' Cassia muttered. An offering of respect in lieu of the words she could not bring herself to repeat. Not yet. Not until she was certain Critheanach had truly left the waking realm.

To her relief, Aoife chose not to press the matter, instead perusing the cart once more. 'There is a place for the sick on the far bank. Will you go? Assist the healers?'

Cassia dipped her head. 'As you wish, lady.'

'Ask for Gwidion. Mention my name.' She tapped a hand on the elaborately painted wickerwork of the chariot's side panel, and the driver issued an order to the horses with a rapid succession of tongue clicks. But no sooner had the vehicle begun to veer away, than the great woman barked another command and it slewed back alongside, the sunlight winking upon the golden circlet on the driver's head, marking him out for respect. 'I am not ignorant,' said Aoife the Dread, 'to the service you rendered at Swamp River. It must have been... difficult.'

'I am loyal to the king, lady.' Which was almost true. She was Roman, and the ties to that old life endured, in spite of everything. Her loyalty, she thought inwardly, lay with Critheanach, if she still lived, and with a russet-haired former goatherd from Calleva.

'Even so. You did well. I will ask after this Crith...?'

'Critheanach, lady.'

'Critheanach.' Aoife issued a percussive command, and the chariot drew clear once more. 'I promise nothing, mark you,' she called after the jangling cart, 'but I will do what I can!'

'Your servant, lady!' Cassia called back, trying not to let the kernel of hope sprout shoots unmerited.

-

They crossed the swirling, brown River Vaga by way of a wide wooden bridge that clattered angrily under so many feet and hooves. A silver-stubbled warrior with a pronounced limp and an ancient but highly polished breastplate greeted them on the north bank with small, gritty loaves and baskets of dried peas and filberts. They juddered to a halt, allowing the ponies time to rest while they awaited further instruction, and the passengers – healers and wounded alike – took the opportunity to fill their growling stomachs.

Cassia gawked as she chewed. The entire west side of the river teemed with life. Supply wagons, livestock corrals, weapon caches, pens for workhorses and warhorses, and, of course, scores of fighters and their kin. Whole tribes had come, it seemed. From the tiniest hamlets to family septs and entire clans, the peoples of the lands south and east of the Vaga had fled before the might of Rome, while those of the north and west had answered Togodubnos's call, sending emissaries and fighters. Here they would gather. Here the sons of Cunobelin would make their stand.

Cassia watched as outriders came and went like bees at a hive, the bridge rattling as they crossed. They brought messages, food and skins of fresh water from distant springs. One such horseman paused briefly to exchange pleasantries with the bridge guard, who took a drink and told a ribald joke. When the rider had gone, the guard sidled over to pass the skin about the group.

When Cassia took the water, she asked him, 'How many have come?'

The old warrior chuckled. 'How many stars did you count last night?'

She caught sight of herself in the mirror-sheen of the breastplate. The image staring back was somehow out of kilter with expectation. Long hair, of course; crow-feather black and tightly curled, flowing thick and unkempt across her shoulders. Eyes dark, shaped like almonds, mouth a little too wide for the angular chin. But the light was somehow dull behind the eyes. The full lips were pressed tighter than she expected. Worry for Cullen? Grief for Critheanach? Fear over what her countrymen were about to inflict on the place she now considered home?

Guilt.

No, keener than that; shame.

She was Roman after all. The daughter of an army physician, lost to the same foaming depths that had cast her onto Britannia's ragged shore. She had betrayed her people, her blood, her father. Exchanged all she had known for this new life amongst those she had once considered savages. The knowledge gnawed at her soul.

The woman in the reflection had aged years these past months. A weight had descended, and she wondered if it would crush her to death. She reached for her pin.

–

'The reds came in a great tide. A fleet of ships, large and small, blanketing the Narrow Sea so that not a wave could be seen for oars.' Rues Seeker spat into the dancing fire, the hiss of his evaporating spittle seeming eerily loud in the echoing chamber. 'Foreign men and their foreign gods.'

Night had long since descended. There were few clouds above the fortified hill, and a myriad of stars, and the bright moon dyed the sky a rich purple. Inside the great roundhouse, light had replaced the earlier gloom as the hearth had been fuelled with seasoned logs to a dazzling, pulsing crescendo. Above those lambent flames, the gaping cauldron bubbled and steamed, the rich aroma of its thickening pottage rising about the room, entwining with the woodsmoke.

Rues was the only person to stand, and he paced as he intoned, the orange light animating the blue markings that swirled upon his wiry, bare torso. He dropped suddenly to a squat before a huddled row of children, making them gasp. 'Traitors,' he hissed, 'pouring honey and poison into the ears of their generals. Encouraging their greed. Informing their every step.'

He straightened, eyes roaming, picking out the half-lit ghost faces, rapt by his words. 'They swarmed inland like ants.'

'Rats,' Clesek's voice rose out of the gloom.

Rues nodded, grinning. 'Like rats.' He lingered a beat, playing to the audience, put gusto into his next words. 'And the Cantiaci fought like bears.' Cheers – murmured at first, but rising rapidly – echoed about the structure's high places. 'They lashed the reds as the interlopers swept towards the Swamp River.'

Cullen, seated upon a bench in the place of honour beside Coel, stifled a rueful smile. The Cantiaci were as soft as the pelts cushioning his rump, as far as he was concerned. There were exceptions, naturally. The insular marsh-dwellers like young Clesek, and fisher-folk of the cliff-fanged coast. But, in the main, the tribe's proximity to the sea, and therefore to the trade brought by the avaricious and ever-expanding empire, meant that they were uncertain as to where their loyalties should lie. Some of the Cantiaci, like Coel's Bibroci, had readily flocked to High King Togodubnos's banner, but a great many had not. A fact best left unvoiced in this company. As if reading his thoughts, Rues embarked on a stirring rant that made plain the courage of the great maritime tribe.

Cullen gave him a nod of approval and let his eyes travel the cavernous room. He and Coel were at the front, before the fire. Too close, if anything, for his cheeks and neck were slick with sweat. Further back, ranged in carefully set concentric rings, dignitaries of the ruling families were nestled on benches and stools and piled skins. A gathering conspicuous for its lack of men. There was a handful of elders at the rear, chewing dried leaves, their faces grizzled and their demeanour susurrant, but they were the grandfathers of the dun. The young bucks – those not patrolling the walls – had all gone north.

'And the brave Cantiaci,' Rues was enthusiastically intoning, 'were joined in their endeavour by the great conquerors, the Catuvellauni, and their vassals, the Atrebates and Trinovantes, and together, beneath the banner of Togodubnos, they held back the red tide.'

Which was not entirely true, thought Cullen, but then one did not gather at a moon-watched hearth to hear tales of frightened men facing disaster, and the near-collapse of an entire way-of-life. So he looked at the flames instead, letting the memories of that day wash over him.

'But the river was too slim,' Rues said, truthfully now, lowering his tone to a regretful husk, 'too shallow to waylay the evildoers for long. The heroes of the Isle of the Mighty, who had fought like Camulos himself, were forced to fall back.'

To the River Vaga, thought Cullen. Fierce and wide and deep. The great hope. The last hope.

'The Vaga!' Garn's gravel-hewn voice erupted.

'The Vaga,' dozens of others echoed.

'It will be the site,' Rues announced, 'of Rome's final defeat. It is where our brave men and women, our war-givers, wait even now. Preparing for the arrival of the greed-crazed reds and their golden false-gods. We will drown them in the Vaga, and melt their eagle-standards to precious liquid, and forge coins from their defeat to enrich our own people!'

'You are young to lead spears,' Coel whispered to Cullen while the assembly bellowed.

He was glad of the shadows that must be dancing across his face, for it would disguise his self-consciousness. 'The gods have favoured me.'

She watched Rues bow low as the applause faded, going to take up his seat on the far side of the great cauldron. Then she leaned a touch closer. 'As has Aoife the Dread.'

He nodded, following her gaze to regard his warriors, talking softly amongst themselves, their iron glinting. From the back of the large room, an itinerant poet, a lesser member of the Wise, began a wistful song of ancient heroes and of the times when gods fought for supremacy over the earth. A whistler played a soft tune, and folk chattered as they awaited the meal, two-score voices filling the high chamber like sparrow-song before dawn. Cullen's party, honoured guests, took the seats nearest the food, and amongst their number, those bearing warrior's names were given the most comfortable seats.

'After the fight at Swamp River,' Cullen went on, 'she honoured me with my task, and gave these spears to see it done.' He indicated his companions, beginning with those whose rumps were privileged by the best furs. 'Maeveen Spurn Joy.'

Coel gave a nod as she met Maeveen's gaze through the hazy firelight. Cullen was gratified to see the notoriously hard-nosed woman return the gesture amiably enough. She had donned the simple tunic offered by Coel's people, so that now, swathed in her fur cloak, she seemed much smaller and softer than he had thought possible. He had to suppress a smirk. The unassuming woman could dispatch every soul in the room if the mood took her. 'The tall one is Andoc the Staunch.'

'Well met,' Coel said.

The fire popped, sending a shower of sparks into the compacted dirt at their feet. A lean, sour-faced warrior thrust out a foot to snuff one of the embers. Cullen pointed at him. 'Baglan Day Break.'

Coel smiled. 'We are honoured to have those bearing hero's names at our feasting hearth.' She picked out the massive shape of Garn, his studded stump glimmering like a jewel trove in the tremulous glow. 'And you are the one they call Grey Boulder?'

'The same,' Garn growled ominously, a sound belied by the grin that formed on his wide mouth. 'I am honoured that songs of my renown have reached Smith's Ring.'

'Rues Seeker,' Cullen said of the man who had regaled them with the invasion tale. With a sweeping hand he indicated those of his nine who had yet to earn their names. 'And we have Clesek, a son of these lands.'

Her brows lifted with interest. 'Bibroci?'

'Cantiaci, lady,' Clesek said, 'from down on the salt marshes.'

'Erbin and Kenal,' Cullen continued, 'of the Catuvellauni. Noble fighters, both, who shed blood at Swamp River.'

'And all welcome,' Coel said. There was a screech outside, a barn owl or vixen. Folk started and gasped, though the hounds, dozing at the back, were reassuringly unmoved. 'If the Romans come this night, we shall feel safe.'

'They will come, lady. Not this night, but soon.'

'To be stopped at the great river,' she said hopefully.

'May Belinos let it be so.' Instinctively he glanced skyward. Wisps of smoke lingered in the conical apex, creeping gently through the thatch. The smell, mingling with the viscous pottage, made a heady brew that took him back to Calleva. How long had it been since he had supped at his family's hearth, his sisters and aunts huddled for warmth, their own Wise One spinning stories to the homely crackle of flames? It felt as though a lifetime had elapsed, and yet the seasons had taken only one full turn. He had seen his kin slaughtered at the hands of the Catuvellauni, only to join those same warriors in defiance of an even greater foe. He had learned the ways of the warrior, had earned a sword and a name of renown. Had stood at Swamp River and faced a strange and terrifying enemy, and tasted the unlikeliest of victories for the shortest of moments. Then he had experienced a betrayal that still stabbed like a knife in his guts, sharp and raw and bitter. The poet sang on, his tone querulous and lilting, as otherworldly as the tales he told, but Cullen's own mind had been transported to a time and place that was all too real, all too visceral. As he watched the embers rise, they became the spangled stars of painted shields. And those holding them, Dobunni warriors, sneered as they abandoned Cullen's hastily gathered shield-wall, even as the Romans advanced.

He shuddered, despite the cloying warmth of the roundhouse. 'King Boduoc sends his regards,' the scornful Dobunni commander had said, as he had led his men away. They had left the Catuvellauni to perish on the riverbank. It was a betrayal that would be repaid, Cullen silently vowed, even if it took a whole lifetime.

The story reached a crescendo, snapping Cullen from his brooding reverie. He was old and shaggy, the poet, like an aged wolf of the wild woods, and he tilted back his head as he addressed the smoke-haunted rafters, capering in his rough woollen robe, and shaking his shock of long, white hair. He regaled the assembly with the story of the ocean god, Manannán, who ruled the wind-harried rock that dominated the seas between the Isle of the Mighty and the Isle of Destiny. Folk gasped and laughed, cheered and jeered.

'Take your people,' Cullen said quietly to Coel. 'There is a ford across the Vaga, to the northwest of here.'

'I know it,' she said.

'The Romans do not.' He glanced at his nine, their faces aglow as they enjoyed the poet's performance. 'Collect your things. Bring your kin, young and old. You cannot hold this place against the legions.'

'We move slowly. If we are caught in the open, we stand no chance at all.'

'I intend to leave soon,' he warned.

'When you have found Serwil.'

'Indeed.'

She looked across at the door skin, which was rippling, animating the smoke and causing the hearth's flames to gutter manically. 'Then your quest is almost complete.'

—

Serwil, Wise One of the Cantiaci and their vassal-nation, the Bibroci, strode imperiously into the roundhouse, silence greeting him as resoundingly as any herald. The crowd parted, letting him approach the room's centre, and he made his way to the fire, a lean shape in the wisping smoke, jamming a long staff into the ground as his features resolved in Cullen's gaze.

Beads of opaque yellow glass hung from a chain at his throat, and a bird-skull headpiece perched upon close-cropped, brown hair. Despite the obvious accoutrements of the Wise, he seemed an incongruous creature to Cullen, for his neat beard and unweathered complexion marked him as a little young for a denizen of Mona. That mystical isle, the world's greatest seat of learning, took each tribe's best and brightest when they were barely free of the teat. Keeping those young tributes for anywhere between a decade and two, the Wise Ones would impart the sacred knowledge of stargazing, engineering, healing, law-making, history, verse and everything in between. What they produced was a caste of cultured and learned philosophers, counsellors and sorcerers, but very few who retained the fresh-faced youthfulness with which they had begun their journey.

'Summoned, am I, Coel?' Serwil asked in a high, effete voice that jarred with the itinerant poet's abruptly curtailed tale-telling.

The dun's temporary leader stood, acknowledging him with a bow shallow enough to convey respect without deference. 'Serwil, we are pleased you have come.'

'We?'

Coel opened a palm, angling it towards her guest. 'I present Cullen of the Atrebates.'

Cullen looked down as he rose to his feet, hoping he had managed to smother the proud smile that threatened to spread across his face. 'An honour, oh Serwil of the Wise.' He straightened, meeting the newcomer's eyes, one of which was sharp, restless and intelligent, the other milky and unseeing. Both were rimmed red, as if irritated by the smoke. 'I have been tasked with conveying you to the king.'

'*The* king?' Serwil said pointedly. His eyebrows were delicately arched, giving him an air of permanent scepticism, but they furrowed now in outright surprise. 'Has not your king fled these shores?'

'As has the king of the Cantiaci,' Cullen said, trying to keep his tone free of a growing waspishness. 'Togodubnos, then, is lord of all who oppose the invader.'

The Wise One's lips pressed into a thin line. 'You're too young to lead spears.'

'A great many battle-chiefs died at Swamp River.'

'Then you are the beneficiary of a dearth,' Serwil observed dryly, one corner of his mouth curling. 'The heir to slaughter.'

Cullen shrugged. 'I do as Aoife tells me.'

'The Dread?' The Wise One's knuckles whitened about the head of his staff, which, Cullen now saw, was more like a battle-mace, capped by a rectangular stone block, its edges rounded smooth. Below the hand, trailing along the stick's upper portion, was a carved lizard, its zigzag tail coiled about the shaft. 'She commands you?'

'After Ulla Jagged Cliff crossed to the otherworld.'

Serwil's sharp jaw faintly quivered. The tip of his tongue flickered out to wet his lips as his crimson-edged eyes roved, as if searching for escape. He seemed to sigh. 'What is it Togodubnos requires of me?'

'The Whetstone of Gobannos,' Cullen said.

'Then the gods do not favour you. The stone is no longer at Smith's Ring.'

CHAPTER FIVE

The first of the wounded arrived as dawn light slithered across the dun's palisade and over its smoking thatches. They came in twos and threes, some slumped over horseback, but most leaning heavily into makeshift crutches, decrying what horrors had befallen them at Swamp River. Their arrival honed the cutting edge of Cullen's warning, bringing stark experience to what had, hitherto, been nebulous anxiety.

He watched Coel as she hurried to organise a welcome. Provisions needed gathering, remedies and poultices had to be mixed, and youngsters were tasked with fashioning hurdles with which they would convey the exhausted newcomers up the hill's steep slopes. All the while, the interrogation came thick and fast. Folk wanted to know what had transpired. What was still to come.

This was all to the good, as far as Cullen was concerned. Perhaps now Coel would heed his advice. Gather up the vulnerable human flotsam she had found herself warding and lead them north, across the river. If she had thought this hillock, with its timber walls and enchanted straw dolls, would offer safety, perhaps now, at last, she might see her folly.

Cullen and his nine passed the morning beneath the carved pole at the centre of the sun-drenched gathering space, putting stitches to clothes and bite to blades. It was all in readiness for the time to move. But when would that be? As Clesek sang a mournful ballad of sea goddesses and drowned adventurers, Cullen stared across the clearing at the fort's big gates, hoping to glimpse Serwil on his return. He had vanished after their encounter at the hearth. Slipped through the smoke and into the night, gone wherever the Wise go in the darkest hours.

'Oily bastard,' Garn Grey Boulder muttered in the wake of a hawked wad of spittle.

'Hazardous to speak ill of the Wise,' Rues Seeker chided, though the lines at his eyes deepened as he spoke.

The pair moved to sit with Cullen and Clesek, who, perched on upturned bushels, were sharing a salad of mushroom and dandelion as the surrounding buildings crackled, their shimmering skeins of dew burning away.

'The Wise were ever showmen,' Cullen said. He had known members of that order who were kind, and others who were cruel, but all shared an irritating penchant for the dramatic.

Garn grunted, taking a seat and some crumbly cheese from the sharing bowl. 'We've no time for tricks. Send Rues to sniff him out.'

'And Garn,' Clesek said wryly, 'to knock him senseless.'

Cullen laughed as he rolled a leaf into a tight ball and crammed it into the side of his mouth. 'It is tempting.' He bent to pick up the sword at his feet. Lightning-Strike, anointed at his choosing ceremony by the Wise One, Moranna of the Silver, had received the care it deserved, stone and oil working to recover its lethal edge. He eased it from the scabbard, the cold iron slipping silently free. He curled his fingers around the hilt, which was shaped like a man, splayed legs and arms forming a guard, the pommel becoming the head. 'Alas, we cannot simply abduct him. We need the stone too.'

'And he says he no longer possesses it?' Garn scoffed. 'He is lying.'

'I cannot prove it.'

Garn's pale brows climbed meaningfully into that leathery forehead. 'Again...'

Cullen shook his head. 'We cannot harm a member of the Order of Mona, as well you know. His kind are lower only than the greatest chiefs.' He glanced down at the pommel again. At the face of a warrior, expertly etched into the gleaming metal, complete with eyes, hair, and a turned-down moustache. 'They would flay the skin from our bones.'

Garn sucked his teeth, unconvinced. 'What does Aoife want with him, anyhow?'

'I do not know. I was told to fetch him to the Vaga.'

'Then we must find him,' Garn said.

Rues nodded. 'And his pebble.'

—

They noticed Coel as she engaged in a meandering tour of a half-dozen large roundhouses that had been allocated to the sudden influx of wounded fighters. She shifted between the circular structures and their many outbuildings like a ghost, pale hair falling long behind her paler cloak, muttering words of encouragement into dark doorways.

Cullen threw the dun's de facto chieftess a hearty wave, and, having waited for her to complete a visit to the final building, he watched as she glided serenely over the grass, acknowledging him with a sedate nod.

'You would know when Serwil returns,' she said without perambulation, and not seeking a reply. 'He travels where he may. Stays in the wilderness for days – weeks – at a time. If he does not wish to be found—'

Cullen stood abruptly, cutting her off. He moved away from the group so that they would not be overheard. 'I do not trust him, lady.'

She smiled, as a mother to a naïve son. 'I do not suppose he will lose sleep at the news.'

'I explained the nature of my task,' Cullen persisted, hearing the irritation rise in his own voice, powerless to quell it, 'and still he vanished into the dark.'

Coel touched him lightly at the elbow, coaxing him into a slow stroll. 'As I say, the Wise are a law unto themselves.'

'Has he no respect for your position?'

She swept out a bony hand in a half-circle. 'I do not rule this settlement. I am merely all that is left of the noble caste. Besides,' she offered a wan smile, 'Serwil was sent to us from Mona. We must revere him, as duty dictates.'

It was all Cullen could do not to spit on the lush turf. 'He made clear his disdain for Lord Togodubnos.'

Her thin brows rose. 'So says a son of the Atrebates.'

Cullen opened his mouth at her shrewd thrust, instinctively ready to offer riposte, but the words died on his lips. It was not so long ago that he would have slid a knife between the king's ribs without a second thought.

Again, the indulgent smile. 'The folk of these lands have ever mistrusted the Catuvellauni. Togodubnos may be the strongest king, and perhaps we would be sensible to offer him our fealty, but the blood of the Sun Hound flows in his veins. Perhaps Serwil merely shares the cynicism common to many hereabouts.'

All he could do was nod. Cunobelin, the old king of the Catuvellauni, had been the most powerful warlord in the Isle of the Mighty. The Sun Hound, as he was known, had instilled fear in his enemies, but little loyalty. Now that he was dead, many hitherto subjugated tribes chose to break from his hegemony, rather than cleave to it.

'Now you come here,' Coel went on as they reached the huts where folk treated the wounded, 'demanding our Wise One, offering little explanation. Moreover, you ask us to leave the protection of our dun and fall on this new king's mercy. You can surely understand our reticence. Serwil's,' she looked steadily at him, 'and my own.'

A small girl emerged from one of the huts, her arms laden with blankets, which she carefully set upon a bench. A pair of men, too old to wield spears, helped a warrior as he limped out into the open. His right ear was thickly encrusted with black blood, and his opposite shin bore heavy splints. He winced with every faltering movement, hissing oaths under his breath as the attendants propped him on the bench.

Cullen turned away, letting his gaze roll over the expanse of the fortress. The timber palisade climbed high beyond the buildings, the pits and the pens, splitting green hill from blue sky. It might have provided stout defence in the old days, when local rivals or brazen cattle thieves were the greatest of the chief's tribulations. 'This dun is no protection, Lady Coel. The reds will sweep it away.'

'Better to meet the enemy behind walls,' she said, with terse finality, 'than on the road. And what is Serwil's role in all this?'

'I have been tasked with bringing him, and the whetstone of Gobannos, to the gathering place.' He spread his palms. 'That is all I know. All I was told.'

'I saw you.'

Cullen turned. It was a man's voice, soft but assured, cutting into their conversation like a swinging axe. He looked down at the warrior, who might have seen thirty winters. The man returned his gaze with dark eyes above raw, pustular skin that showed through a patchy, ragged beard.

'Saw?' Cullen prompted.

The warrior's eyes did not move. 'On the bridge. A child.' He smiled, revealing a gap where his two front teeth should have been. 'I could have laughed.'

Cullen supposed the man referred to the engagement at Swamp River, and he felt himself immediately bridle. 'Child?'

'The Gauls, they came,' the warrior grunted, an apparent surge of pain washing over him as he clumsily shifted his jutting leg. 'You stood in defiance. Like the battle god Caswallawn himself.'

The warrior's eyes glistened. Cullen felt himself swallow thickly, hackles settling as quickly as they had risen. 'Not alone.'

'But apart. A crag. Waves crashing on all sides. They came, you stood firm.' He placed a black-nailed hand over his heart. 'You bled. They died.'

'You were on the bridge?'

The warrior nodded. 'What is your name, lord?'

'Cullen, of the Atrebates people.'

That gaping smile again. The gums were torn and sore. Recently emptied. 'Your battle name, for one such as you must surely possess that privilege.'

'Wolf Scourge.'

'An honour, lord.' He patted his heart gently. 'I am Carax, of the Catuvellauni.'

Coel's eyes danced between the two men, as the little girl, still organising her blankets, tugged at the woman's sleeve.

Coel looked down at her. 'What is it?'

'I heard,' the girl said tentatively, the colour rising in her cheeks. 'You seek the Wise One?'

'I do.'

'I saw him, lady. He was in the woods, catching a martin. He chided me for spying.'

'A pine martin?'

She nodded, warming to her theme now, clearly pleased to impart something useful to so grand a lady. 'He means to read it at sundown, that's what he said. At the garden.'

—

The last vestiges of watery sunlight were leaking from the forest, so that the canopy, heavy with green boughs and buzzing with life, seemed to take on a portentous gloom. Cullen's spine prickled as he descended the narrow fox-track that slipped through the trees. He had come in full battle-wear, all the better to impress the denizen of Mona who lurked somewhere close, but, as he let his fingers curl about the hilt of his sword, he felt glad of the decision, for he could hear the spirits of the next life beckoning on the still air.

He understood Serwil to be in the region of a thousand paces to the south, at the foot of this bramble-choked slope. The garden to which the girl had referred was, in truth, a nemeton – a sacred grove – and it was there, in that place of mystery and magic, that he expected to find the elusive Wise One. The forest closed in as he picked his way deeper between the phalanxes of soaring ash trees, the ground becoming steeper. The air thickened, heavy with the earthy scents of moss, soil and sap. He glanced back, alive to movement, but saw nothing more than branch-thrown shadows. Asking Taranis for protection, he pressed on, ever deeper, the slope taking him further away from the fortress and into the realm that straddled this world and the next. He skirted a fallen branch, beneath which a score of tiny toadstools clustered, and slowed a touch so that he could listen for sounds above the soft pad of his feet, cushioned as they were by a blanket of leaves. Somewhere, a bird made its final call, heralding the deepening dusk. He caught the soft rustle of creatures unseen. And? Yes – the distant gurgle of the hidden stream that was his way marker.

The shadows deepened as he ventured further, the air strangely charged, imbued with the mystical energy that marked out the special, secret places of the world. Doorways to other dominions. The nemeton was close. He could almost taste it.

He heard the voice. A man's, pitched high and querulous, speaking words that were too muffled to understand, but unmistakably repetitive and rhythmic. A chant, meant for ears that were not made of flesh.

He stepped off the track, plunging into the tangled web of vegetation that existed beneath the ancient trees. His senses heightened as he moved towards the noise. A low, waxy pulse of light shone like a beacon just above the ground, thirty strides distant, diffused by the foliage. He stepped carefully, searching the ground for hazards, and approached the area that he rapidly understood was a clearing in the heart of the stands of ash, their great boughs intertwining to form a natural temple. Some of those trunks, he noticed, were placed more regularly, and, as he moved amongst them, he began to understand that they were not living trees, but great timbers, each the height of five men, standing at intervals to form a processional avenue. He followed them, staring up at the markers, and realising with a jolt that each one was capped by a human skull that was underlit by the warm glow of an oil lamp, placed at the foot of each thick pole.

At the end of the avenue, the space opened out. There was a stone wall, the height of Cullen's knee, running around the outer edge. It was clothed in thick ivy and crested with the skulls of tiny animals. Flowers bloomed at the wall's outer edge, a blaze of colour even in the failing light. He drew up, unwilling to cross the final boundary. The air seemed to hum with otherworldly energy now. The ground beneath his feet felt different, as if the power of the ancestors coursed up through the turf. He swallowed thickly, feeling cold sweat at his neck. He wondered if his mother was there, watching.

In the heart of the grove, a cloaked figure knelt before a weathered stone altar. The man did not turn, resuming, instead, the chant that Cullen had heard from the deep woods. The figure's hands worked busily. Cullen caught the flash of a blade, saw darkness spread across the altar's smooth surface. The pine martin, he realised, freshly disembowelled. Serwil was auguring the future from the way the glistening innards spilled. Cullen waited in silence, feeling uncomfortable just to watch, but the Wise One did not deign to challenge him, the ceremony demanding unadulterated attention.

When it was done, and the entrail strands had been pushed and pulled into their macabre patterns, Serwil unfurled himself slowly, stretching like a cat to reach his full height. 'You trespass, Cullen of the Atrebates.'

Cullen stared at the Wise One's back. 'You disappeared.'

Serwil turned, taking up the staff that leaned against the adjacent wall. The mace-head, Cullen noticed, was marked by thin stripes, the colour of ochre. Serwil put his weight into the long stick and peered from within the deep hood, his milky eye a jewel in the gloom. 'I have walked since last you saw me. Walked and contemplated.'

'You do not sleep?'

'Sleep is the cousin of death,' Serwil said sharply, as though affronted by the suggestion. 'This is the Waking Realm. I remain awake, in silent contemplation, hearing the spirits speak.'

No wonder his eyelids looked so sore, Cullen thought. 'And what do they say?'

'They ask about you.' The single good eye roved down to Cullen's feet and back up, as though he were sizing up a ram for the pot. Or a martin for the slab.

Suddenly self-aware, Cullen could not help but peer down at himself in the shifting lamplight. At the faded bloodstains, insignia of an ominous existence, that besmirched the green and yellow chequers of his braca, and at the frays and tears upon his patched tunic. Acute embarrassment rose in his cheeks, and he was grateful of the dark, for it would hide the blushes that ever afflicted one with a complexion such as his. He was thankful, too, for the foresight to bring his shield, and he brought it across his body, even as he inwardly berated himself for bashfulness unbecoming a warrior. 'Me?'

Serwil smiled, a gesture conveying more triumph than warmth. His teeth were mottled red, coated with the juice of whatever berry or leaf he had recently chewed. 'About how a stripling commands such famous names.' He was studying the shield face now. The painted symbols, which stood as a testament to his loyalty and status. 'Tell me, from which clan do you hail?'

'Near Calleva.'

'A great dun indeed. From a noble sept?'

Cullen shook his head. 'Though my mother was leader of our village, cousin to the chief of our sept.'

'And your king was Berikos.'

'A man I revered until—' Cullen bit his tongue, chiding himself for the unguardedness.

'Until he was no more.' Serwil's eye drifted down to the shield again, taking in the painted images. The life-wheel of the thunder god, Taranis, the three-tailed horse of the Atrebates, and Cullen's personal symbol, the magpie. The fourth quarter expressed a pair of entwined serpents, daubed in rich red. 'Now your loyalty,' Serwil said wryly, observing the sigil of Togodubnos with evident curiosity, 'rests with the sons of Cunobelin.'

With one of them, Cullen thought, keeping private his enmity for the king's brother. 'The Catuvellauni have welcomed me,' he said stiffly. 'Made me a warrior. Given me a name.'

'Not every Catuvellaunus.'

The single eye bore into Cullen, though it was the strange, unfathomable gaze of its milky sibling that sent a chill along the nape of his neck. The air seemed to hang heavy between them, a concoction of tension and derision, and Cullen knew precisely to what the Wise One alluded. 'You know of Arthmael the Learned?'

'Know of the wisest of the Wise?' Serwil scoffed. 'Show me a man or woman who does not, and I will show you a fool. I studied under him for a time.'

'At Camulodunon?'

'At Mona.'

Mona. Cullen felt ice creep around his guts. The sacred isle, whose mysterious groves and secretive halls were the seat of all the world's learning, whence the Wise went out into society. As a child, it had been as nebulous as the Dreaming Realm. An abstract notion. Somewhere Cullen neither wished to go, nor ever hoped to. Yet now it held something more in his mind. Something sinister. For it was the power behind his very real, very dangerous enemy.

'Arthmael tried to kill me,' he said quietly.

Serwil smiled sorrowfully, as if sympathising with a child that feared the sky would crash about his shoulders. 'To sacrifice your body and your soul to the gods. That is not murder, but freedom. To stride into the next world at the hand of so revered a man. That is a matter of opportunity, of honour. Instead, you sank your own blade into Arthmael's venerated body.'

'It was bone.'

'What?'

'I stabbed that old polecat with a shard of bone, not a blade.' In that instant, he was back at Camulodunon, beneath the black branches of tarred trees, with the drums hammering to the night, calling to the gods, beseeching them to attend and take the soul of a frightened boy. The Wise had capered behind their gruesome masks, and the people had cheered, and lightning had lit up the sky, and Arthmael had loomed over Cullen, his dagger poised, a rictus grin making him more hideous than ever. Fate had intervened. And Cullen had stabbed him. 'He screamed like a scalded baby.'

Serwil's pale face quivered as though he had been gently slapped. 'You speak wicked words.'

'I speak the truth,' Cullen said, and now all reverence was gone. The Wise One had antagonised him, and he was no longer in any mood to smooth away the man's concerns. This was an acolyte of Arthmael. It explained his pomposity, certainly, but also, he now realised, his antipathy. 'He screamed and he bled. Lord Caratacos himself bore witness, and knew I was favoured by Taranis. Knew that I must command spears, despite my apparent youth.' He paused, partly to relish Serwil's horrified expression, and partly because he was mindful that the cup was at imminent risk of over-chasing. 'Now I impart another truth. I have been sent here to bring you and your stone to the meeting place on the River Vaga. You will fetch that stone and you will come.'

Serwil drew himself up, his mouth thin and twisting. 'It is crucial that I remain. That the Stone of Gobannos remains at Smith's Ring.'

Cullen laughed bitterly. 'Then it *is* here.'

Serwil ignored him. 'Heuldro'r Haf is almost upon us. Midsummer. The time of light, when the country is fragrant, vibrant. The spiral of the year expands to its widest point, where the darkness is most fleeting. It is a time of magic. Magic that must be harnessed.' He pushed the cowl away from his head as he took a step towards Cullen. 'Why did I lie? Because Coel and her folk are simple.' He laughed derisively. 'They worship the beaver. What battles have beavers won? Gobannos, the smith god, is a wielder of power. He sharpens weapons for the other gods, in their perpetual wars against the forces of the netherworld.'

'Where is the stone?'

'If a brave man sharpens his sword on it,' Serwil went on as though Cullen had not spoken, 'his enemies will be vanquished. The opposite can be said for a coward, who will wither and die. The stone has great power, Cullen of the Atrebates.'

'Then bring it to the king,' Cullen insisted, realising now why Togodubnos would want the artifact at such a time.

'*Your* king can wield it not.'

'He is no coward, and he is king of all who resist the emperor.'

'The stone was made for Gobannos at the beginning of time. A gift from Belinos.' Serwil's voice was low, rich with contempt. 'It is useless in the dark seasons, until the sun god has touched it.'

And now Cullen understood. 'Heuldro'r Haf.'

The Wise One's forefinger extended skyward, pale flesh made bone-white as it passed across an errant moonbeam. 'The solstice.' He turned away, making to resume his vigil. 'The stone, and I, will remain until then. There is no alternative.'

The red kite was serene, dipping and wheeling before wisps of cloud, dancing on the vagary of warm breeze, entirely oblivious to the thirty riders emerging from a belt of trees far below. The bird circled, forked tail twitching, and issued its cry. A long, mournful call, followed by three short blasts, distinct and shrill, that had the leader of the riders staring up into the blue.

Grimoald, Leopard of the Batacgwi, drew his snorting black stallion to a halt as he cleared a low-slung branch that was laden heavy with summer bounty. He squinted, tracking the kite, trying to discern an omen in its lazy progress. Deciding there was none, he scanned the land that opened out before them. A slope of tall, haze-topped grass and wildflowers ran away from the trees. It was cut in half by a narrow, babbling stream, and terminated, some fifty paces away, at the shallow ditch that ringed a hamlet of small roundhouses, their conical thatches sprouting like giant mushrooms above a low palisade of hammered stakes and woven hazel.

'Gone,' he said to no one in particular. It had not needed saying, for the absence of life was palpable, even from this distance. No bleat of livestock, no shouts of children, no hearth-trails.

Grimoald muttered a word to the stallion, letting it amble down to drink from the stream while he kept his eyes fixed on the settlement. One could not be too careful in a hostile land. Soon, though, he was satisfied that the inhabitants had long since abandoned their homes. Which was sensible, he thought, for the Batacgwi had come. To stay and fight was a sentence of death. The notion made him smile, and he glanced down at the pale skulls that dangled from his saddle. Each one a banner heralding doom.

They crossed the stream in a broad line. The water was no more than fetlock deep, and half the force went ahead, thundering across the bridge of planks spanning the defensive ditch. They swarmed into the village, and Grimoald heard them call out that the place was indeed deserted. He looked for the red kite once more; its lingering presence might have suggested fresh carrion further off, but it had not been joined by other scavengers, and he was content that neither disease nor battle had put its blight upon the valley. The erstwhile inhabitants had simply run away.

'Empty, lord,' confirmed a heavy-set man on a mad-eyed gelding, returning from the village at a clip. 'We checked every building. They must have received word of the invasion.'

'Who can blame them?' Grimoald said. 'The emperor comes, Felix, with conquest in his heart. They're all headed north.'

'The Vaga?'

Grimoald nodded, shifting his pale gaze in that direction. Not that he could yet see the great river of which he had heard so much. The line of a great ridge would challenge his men first, and he eyed that dark line suspiciously as he spoke. 'The Britons gather upon its far bank. That is where they will make their stand.'

'Can they win, lord?' Felix asked.

'No.'

'But they will fight?'

'They are brave.' He chuckled, thinking of the ranks of spears that would be massing even now. They had no idea what awaited them. 'And the river is fast, deep and wide.'

A grin in response. 'They believe it cannot be crossed?'

'Don't they always? There will inevitably be fordable places, and the Britons will guard them in their ignorance.'

Grimoald let his eyes slide away from the ridgeline and down the slope, beyond the village, to another stand of trees. Before them, hemmed by a half-dozen earthen mounds that were the telltale sign of ancient burials, he noticed a circle of pale grey standing stones, and his fingertips rose unbidden to touch the leopard's tooth woven into the tip of his golden beard. 'There's power in this landscape.'

'Lord?'

'Come with me.'

Having halved his force, the rest sent into the village to forage what there was and burn what was left, Grimoald took a smaller party to the great stones, where they duly dismounted and removed their helmets. Bowing before they entered the circle, Grimoald touched each stone in turn, walking the perimeter with a pace that was reverentially slow. 'Placed by the ancient ones,' he said to the others, 'long before the Belgae crossed the Narrow Sea.'

Felix spoke. 'Who were they, lord?'

'From the south,' Grimoald said. He flicked a thick-fingered hand through his own golden hair. 'Dark as the Silures are dark. Great mariners, who challenged Britannia's murderous coast and tamed it. The Belgae,' he said with a sneer, 'came much later. Catuvellauni, Atrebates, Regnenses, Cantiaci. Pushed the older nations into the mountains. But these,' he paused by one of the biggest stones, placing a palm on its cold, rough surface, 'hold power, still.' He looked at each man in turn. 'We will rest here for a time. Harness what magic we may.'

'And then, lord?' Felix said.

'My duty is to harry this land. The legions advance, and they will eventually close with Togodubnos and the horde he doubtless gathers. But before that, the auxiliaries have been sent into this savage place. The Isle of the Mighty.' He hawked up a wad of phlegm and spat it, careful to clear the sacred stones so that no disrespect could be misconstrued by the unseen watchers of the Otherworld. 'There are eight parties of Batacgwi abroad. We are to wreak havoc. Ravage the people.' He glanced back to the village, from which, he saw with satisfaction, great columns of black smoke had begun to rise. 'Kill as many fighting men as we can. It is a matter of fear. We must sow the seeds. Let the Belgae know it is futile to resist Rome and her allies. But for us,' he deliberately sought every gaze, instilling meaning into each locked stare, 'for those loyal to *me*, there are opportunities too. You recall what that wretch told us? The treasure?'

'Yes, lord,' Felix said, and his words were bolstered by more grunts of agreement. 'Will we seek it?'

Grimoald nodded. 'We will find this druid. Take the flesh from his bones.'

Felix indicated one of the lower, wider stones. 'Here, perhaps?'

'That would be fitting,' Grimoald grinned. 'Stretch his skin over one of these. And we shall hang his head from my saddle. The treasure, we shall take for ourselves, with the gods' help.'

The others rattled their scabbards in approval as Grimoald moved to the centre of the sacred formation.

'You hate them, lord?' Felix said at his flank. 'The Belgae?'

'I knew a Briton back in Gaul. A slave. Full of self-importance. Arrogance. Tried to escape.'

'Tried?'

'Tried,' Grimoald said flatly as he pulled free his sword from a belt of interlinked bronze rings that were inlaid with winking flakes of jet. He slumped to his knees. 'I do not like them. We have been tasked with ridding the world of Britons, and their Wise Ones, the druids. It will be a pleasure to execute such an order.'

He closed his eyes, lifting the sword, revelling in its finely balanced weight. Loudly, he intoned, 'May the gods of the raging River Renos preserve us, the men of the Batacgwi. The *Batavorum equitata quingenaria*. May our enemies quake.' Gently, he kissed the cold hilt. 'Soon,' he whispered. 'Soon you will taste their blood.'

CHAPTER SIX

The sun rose and fell over Smith's Ring, bringing forth a crisp, clear night that afforded Cullen scant sleep. When he dreamed, it was an unsettled patchwork of sensations. Fragmented sights and half-recalled sounds and scents. He saw the home he had left behind, awash with the blood of his kin. He held Cassia, smelled her raven-black hair, felt the warmth of her skin against his, only to have her ripped from him, screaming as Roman *gladii* glittered, stabbing. He saw again the bridge over Swamp River, where he had made his stand and earned his name, but this time the timbers did not collapse and the enemy did not falter and they swarmed across like angered bees, grinning to the slaughter.

Morning brought relief at first. Buoyant birdsong heralded the flutter of his eyelids. A sound to cleanse even the most tarnished of nights. But almost immediately his mind went to the solstice, the ceremony of Heuldro'r Haf, dragged there by the reed-thin beams of sunlight filtering through the thatch above. The observance was only a few days away, but the thought of waiting made Cullen's teeth itch. Not least because acquiescing to the haughty Serwil's demands stuck in his craw. Of more immediate concern, however, was Aoife's command; bring the Stone of Gobannos, and its guardian, to the Vaga rendezvous without delay. He had been thrown from his course by the very man he had been sent to save, a fact that was as discomforting as it was unexpected.

It was glumly, then, that he clambered free of the layered pelts, padding across the chalk floor, groping for his shoes in the murky half-light, the snores of his nine fading as he pushed out through the entrance skin. He would walk, he decided, to rid himself of the lingering malaise that had settled since his encounter at the garden. An encounter that had both irritated and disquieted him. Serwil had been both stubborn and scornful, and Cullen had found himself quick to dislike the man. And yet, he wondered, had he been too quick to judge the Wise One?

Too ready to dismiss his assertions? If Serwil's claim was true, then the Stone of Gobannos was worthless without its power, and that power came on the longest day, when the sun god, Belinos, baked the earth. Did not Aoife – and, by turns, Togodubnos – seek the stone precisely for that power? Did it not, then, stand to reason that waiting for the solstice was the only logical course, however insufferable Cullen found the object's protector?

Either way, he chastised himself for antagonising Serwil. It was unnecessary and unseemly. As he pushed through a field of tall grass, just beyond the perimeter of the fort, he saw the disappointed face of Moranna of the Silver in his mind's eye. The Wise One was counsellor to the king himself, and her good opinion was something Cullen valued highly. He knew, deep down, that she would not have tolerated such a slight against a member of her sacred order.

With a bubbling sense of chagrin, he walked the hill's crest, the thinly patrolled palisade at his back. Two hundred paces away was a thick stand of trees, the beginning boughs of what quickly thickened into a vast forest, stretching away to the east. To the south was the low plain whence he and his party had come, divided into parcels of arable and pastural land, delineated by tree or hedgerow, piled stones or painted stakes with their dangling dolls. In the far distance, the rising hump of the ragstone ridge, one end dominated by a dormant beacon, a black bubo against the blue fastness. The air was alive with joyous sparrow-song. Swifts sped over the long grass, rising and dipping as they skimmed the seedheads in the perpetual search for insects. Roe deer lurked at the edge of the treeline, snatching a final graze before Belinos's brilliant disc had fully risen.

He looked out over the fields. Crows flew beneath him, cackling above the green expanse, and the skinny lines of glittering streams threaded the terrain like silver twine. An idyll, to be certain. Something deserving of protection. Coel's natural inclination to dig in her heels in the face of an advancing invader suddenly did not seem so foolish. He breathed deeply of the warming air, boosted by an unexpected uptick in his mood.

Which was why, when the man in his path suddenly straightened from out of the grass, his heart sank like a rock in a pool.

'Marjoram,' Serwil said, brandishing a fistful of leaves. In his other hand he clutched a sickle, which he tucked into the folds of his cloak.

'Abundant hereabouts.' Slung across his shoulder was a large leather pouch, into which he carefully placed the marjoram. He stooped, the yellow beads clinking gently at his neck, and drew his staff out of the grass like a dark snake. The stick, with its heavy head and carved lizard, demanded Cullen's gaze, not least because it would prove formidable if it came suddenly at his skull. He decided, then, to try a gentler tack.

'I understand you do not trust me.'

Serwil's snort was all scorn. 'Trust my lord Arthmael's assailant?'

'But I have been charged with this task by Aoife herself. I cannot simply ignore her word. If calamity were to befall you—'

Up came the mace-head to cut him off. 'I place my faith in the gods,' Serwil rejoined, 'and in the power of the stone. I will be safe, as will Gobannos's treasure, until such time as it might be wielded against the invader.'

'Will you come,' Cullen relented, looking south over the low fields to hide his dejection, 'as soon as solstice is complete?'

Serwil opened his mouth to reply, but found himself speaking into Cullen's raised palm. For the latter had noticed movement on the horizon. A blot at first, dark on the crest of the far-off rise. It became a smear, like spilled woad, as it grew against the clear sky. Cullen's legs moved unbidden, taking him towards the lip of the slope, as he shielded his eyes with a palm and squinted into the hazy distance.

'Smoke,' he said, sensing Serwil at his shoulder. 'The beacon has been lit.'

–

'Reds?' Rues suggested as he stared out at the rising smoke funnel.

'Too soon for the legions,' Garn growled.

'Cavalry,' Maeveen said sourly. 'The Gauls we faced on the bridge.'

Cullen had fetched the warriors, as eager for their solidarity at this moment as for their opinions. He nodded, recalling the fight on the river and the malevolent horde of Gallic horsemen they had been obliged to stop. The Gauls still visited his dreams. They had been creatures of the old world and the new. Men who stood astride the cultures of north and south. They had fought for Rome, in the manner of Rome. Donned Roman mail and hurled the fearsome Roman *pila* at Cullen and his comrades. Yet they had screamed the battle cries of the ancient tribes. Had painted their shields with images of the old gods, and, in the end, had been frightened into defeat by a trick of Cullen's own making; one that had invoked the spirits of the Otherworld. They had been, those formidable riders, neither Roman nor Gaul, but something in between. And that was precisely what he now imagined racing across the plains below Smith's Ring. 'Perhaps it is nothing,' he said eventually. 'A false alarm.'

'And perhaps it is something,' Maeveen said bluntly. 'Did you convince the sorcerer?'

Cullen met her cold, blue gaze. 'No.'

She ran a hand over her spiked scalp. 'The time for talking is over, Wolf Scourge.'

'Yes.' Cullen turned away from the ridge. 'It is.'

—

'We leave this place.'

Cullen had tracked Serwil to the dun's big gates, the Wise One having quietly slipped away with his stick and his marjoram when the warriors had gathered on the hill crest.

He turned now, sighing testily, as though the exchange were as arduous as it was unwelcome. 'Then may the gods guide you safe.'

'We leave now.'

'Again, I wish you the speed of the spirits.'

'Us,' Cullen said as he slowed his pace, some dozen strides from the Wise One. He pointed at Serwil and then himself. 'You wish *us* the speed of the spirits.'

Serwil's features tightened, almost imperceptibly. 'I am Serwil of the Wise.' The words were uttered stiffly, care given to their annunciation, as though in warning of extreme censure.

Cullen dipped his head, acknowledging the man's status. 'And I am Cullen of the Atrebates.'

Serwil's single seeing eye glittered with irritation. 'None may command me but the highest of lords. You are merely—'

Cullen pulled Lightning-Strike free of its scabbard. 'I am merely the one holding the sword.'

The Wise One's furious gaze was tempted elsewhere for a moment as hoofbeats shook the ground at Cullen's back. He spat as Cullen's warband hove into view. 'The Stone of Gobannos will never be yours!' Up came the mace, the staff clutched tight in both hands, as though Serwil was about to scythe corn.

Cullen stepped in, anticipating the blow, taking hold of the staff with one hand, wrenching it free. He pushed the hilt of his sword roughly into Serwil's face, stood on his foot, so that the shrieking Wise One tipped backwards, crumpling like a sack of turnips in a patch of mud worn bald by footfall. Serwil mewed, a hand clamped to his bloodied nose, fury blazing in his lonely eye as it bore into the younger man.

Cullen sheathed the sword and inspected the staff. He slid his hands to the heavy stone affixed to its end by way of straps and a deeply sunk hole. He held it up for the others to see. 'Behold, the stone of the smith god, Gobannos.'

A murmur of astonishment. Garn laughed, guttural as a lowing ox. 'By the mystical gills of Llyr.'

Cullen could not stifle his grin of triumph. 'It is a whetstone. One used by the gods themselves, but a whetstone nonetheless.' He touched a finger to the reddish stripes. 'Iron marks, formed by the strokes of a thousand blades.'

'Speaking of blades,' Maeveen said, and, as his eyes went to her, she tossed him a small knife.

Cullen caught it and cut the leather bands, freeing stone from stick, tossing the latter away.

'You have wounded,' Serwil seethed, still clutching his face, 'a member of the Order of Mona.'

'You are not the first,' Cullen replied, as Kenal brought up his mount. 'Perhaps you and Arthmael can exchange tales of my wickedness.'

The Wise One clambered to his feet. 'You will regret this.'

'I'd rather live to regret it than die never knowing.' Cullen kissed the whetstone, for which he had come to this high settlement, and dropped it into his saddlebag. 'Get on the horse, Serwil of the Wise, or be thrown across its arse.'

The furious Wise One did as he was told, all the while spitting curses of pure venom at those he considered abductors. Cullen clambered up in front, and, as he kicked at the horse's heaving flanks, wondered if he was the biggest fool in all the Isle of the Mighty.

They headed north and east, coming down off the ridge and entering thick woodland through which the horses were allowed to walk, the undergrowth too treacherous for anything more.

They came upon a river, which Clesek claimed was the Vaga, and began to track its course through terrain that was mostly low-lying, the great waterway deep and wide, rush-fringed and flashing with kingfishers. Their destination was to be the horde's rallying point, not far inland from the coast. Togodubnos had chosen the place for its proximity to both a ford and a bridge. The latter would doubtless be dismantled in due course, but little could be done about the ford, which was what made it the logical objective of the advancing legions.

'The river is a shield-wall,' Garn, at the rear of the line, explained to Kenal as they rested beneath a heavily laden rowan, the creamy-white blossom alive with birds and insects. 'The ford is a gap. The king will plug that gap with men and spears, and trust the water to protect his flanks. It is too wide and too deep to swim.'

'And if they build a bridge?' Kenal asked.

'Did you not hear, lad? It would take too long. We'd kill them as they drove in their piles.'

'A bridge of boats then?'

'A floating bridge will be too precarious,' Rues said. He paused to gulp at a water skin. 'We'd kill them as they wobble across, and they couldn't bring cavalry.'

Garn laughed darkly. 'Besides, we'd burn the boats as they tried to tether them.' He glanced up at the canopy. 'With the blessings of Belinos, the reds will stop at the river and realise they can go no further. In the end, they'll return to their ships.'

'Blessings?' Serwil repeated the word with a tone of astonishment. He was on the ground now, having slid from the saddle to attend a call of nature. 'Do not rely on the gods. You fools have enraged them.'

'You think much of yourself,' Garn said, before giving a great guffaw. 'Our many nations will be conquered, all because young Cullen drew a little blood from your nose?'

Serwil spat derisively. 'I am a member of the Order of Mona. One of the sacred Wise. You have committed a heinous crime, against myself, my creed and our gods.'

'A crime?' Cullen retorted. 'I have kept you alive.'

'You saw smoke on a hilltop and scurried away like the mouse you are.' Serwil let his baleful gaze slide from one warrior to the next. 'This is what comes of allowing a whelp to lead.' The lone eye found its way inexorably back to Cullen. 'You,' Serwil said in almost a hiss, jabbing a finger furiously up at Cullen, 'have negated the power of the Stone of Gobannos. Rendered it worthless with your impetuosity. Your cowardice.'

Cullen had to fight to smother his own feelings of guilt. Had he been rash? Had he, indeed, been craven? 'The beacon is only lit when danger is imminent. What can the threat have been, if not the enemy's approach?'

'Who can say whether a distant banner belongs to friend or foe?' Serwil retorted with a smirking sneer. 'You did not wait to discover what the watchmen had sighted. Too spineless to bide your time.'

'If we had waited to ask,' Cullen said, 'we might all now be dead.' He levelled an accusatory finger at Serwil's hollow chest. 'Our delay, do not forget, was caused by you and your stubbornness. If you had given up the stone—'

'Arthmael warns us,' Serwil hissed in stinging retort. 'Warns his people that evil has infiltrated the Isle of the Mighty.' The crimson-rimmed eye bore into him. 'Warns us that you are an enemy of the gods.'

'I am honoured he speaks my name in the company of his minions,' Cullen said, genuinely surprised – and more than a touch discomforted – that he featured at all in the thoughts of the wisest of the Wise. 'Did he not also tell you that I am favoured by Taranis?'

'Preposterous.'

Garn chuckled at that, though his face was grim as he, too, dismounted, taking a scrap of cloth to wipe the dust from the studs that shone dimly at the end of his truncated forearm. 'Taranis protect the folk left behind.'

'Coel had the chance to leave,' Maeveen said flatly. She stretched, arching her back in the saddle, putting Cullen in mind of a cat, lithe and strong. 'Our duty is to the stone, only.'

'Dragon's blood will suffice.'

Cassia ascended the portable steps and clambered over the cluttered wares that packed the rear of the wagon. She moved amongst crates and sacks, in which rested mortars, pestles, and sheafs of dried leaves, pushing through the invisible but heavy fug of exotic oils, pungent herbs and rich spices. Loose formations of bottles, bowls and earthenware flasks played a discordant tune as she picked a route awkwardly through them. She knelt in a cramped space amongst bags of anonymous powders, selecting a crimson vial from a dozen similar, holding it up to let the sun give it a glaucous glow. 'This one?'

The old man, crouching beside a narrow stream, glanced back at her. 'That's the one, *puella*. Mixed with vervain and honeycomb.'

'For the treatment of ulcers, *avus*.'

He grinned as he dabbed a cloth at his newly washed cheeks, pale eyes growing an impish crinkle at the corners. 'You call me grandfather. I am not so old.'

Cassia climbed down, the dragon's blood resin in hand. 'And I am not so young,' she replied in the common tongue.

His name was Gwidion, and Cassia had liked him the instant they met, despite his playful insistence on referring to her by the Roman name for *young girl*. She had sought him out, as Aoife had commanded, and finding him had seemed so unlikely amongst the vast ocean of humanity that had washed up on the north bank of the Vaga. But folk had heard of Gwidion, the Wise One who claimed to possess the cure for any affliction, from pustule boils to sore throats, from maladies of the brain to lovesickness. And, more importantly, folk had fallen over themselves to assist her search, once the name of the Dread had been invoked. A more effective weapon, she later reflected, than any axe or sword.

Gwidion unfurled himself, the movement greeted by a dozen cracks from ancient joints. He tossed the rag into the wagon, though his white beard still glistened with moisture, and held out a vein-mapped hand, skin papery and translucent. 'We will soak a strip of linen,' he said as he took the vial from her, 'and bind the afflicted area. The resin will do its work, *puella*, rest assured. Bring him to the nemeton, would you?'

Cassia said that she would, glancing at the circle of stakes Gwidion had hammered into the soggy turf for the task. It was not a nemeton in the strictest sense. It had been designated and laid out by the Wise One, for there were no existing shrines on this part of the Vaga. Not that she was any authority on the subject, but she had learned enough from Critheanach to know what she was looking at. Still, Gwidion did not seem to care. There was a wizened ash tree close by, which Gwidion claimed was brim full of magic, and that, he said, would suffice.

'Our patients believe this patch of land is sacred,' he said in his perpetually amused tone, as if reading her thoughts. 'Thus, it will work as if it were the very front gate of the Otherworld.'

She smiled, acknowledging the truth of it. Gwidion was a pale and ethereal presence. He was withy-thin, slightly stooped and wrinkled as an empty wineskin. His hair was long and plaited, as was his beard, which was the same snowy shade as his hair, and his robes were plainly coloured and generally grubby. The only concession to his status was a silver band, in the form of an intricately wrought snake, that coiled all the way up his puffy ankle. A wraith, then, to look at. A dried husk of a man. And yet he carried himself with a grace and certainty that was indicative of his order. There was a confidence in his own words that spoke of one educated on the sacred isle of Mona. One who knew himself to be the superior of those he addressed.

Cassia set to the request. The patient in question was a farmer of the Trinovantes, another one of the thousands who had abandoned their old life temporarily in order to preserve it. He had come to them with a pronounced limp and a voice that rasped through teeth gritted against the pain. On closer inspection, his lower right thigh was red, swollen and hot to the touch, leaking pus that stank like a midden in high summer. Gwidion had dispatched him to wait with the other patients a little further up the brook, one of the many tributaries of the Vaga. Cassia hailed him and he sidled, cursing softly, back to the wagon.

Gwidion wrinkled his nose as he applied the dragon's blood poultice. 'Putrid,' he muttered, as though it were the farmer's fault. 'I'll give you a little of the tincture and some new bandages. Reapply it after seven nights.'

'I will, lord,' the man hissed, trying not to flinch.

'Tish, none of that,' the old man waved him away. He winked at Cassia. 'Gwidion the Majestic will suffice. Ash sap,' he added before the confused man could respond. 'Rub a little into the skin beyond the bindings.'

Cassia frowned. 'I was told ash sap was for newborns.'

'A spoonful will imbue a fresh babe with unseen fortitude,' Gwidion agreed. 'Your Critheanach taught you well.' He pointed a bony finger at the afflicted leg, now thoroughly strapped and smelling more fragrant. 'But it will also provide that same fortitude to healthy tissue, guarding against creeping rot.' He stood, moving back to allow the Trinovantes to stand, offer profuse thanks, and sidle awkwardly away. 'Do you think her alive?'

'Critheanach? Yes.'

'I think you're right, *puella*.' Gwidion's eyes creased, warmly. 'Hold the notion. Nurture it. The gods will know and, perhaps, they will favour us.'

'Us?'

Gwidion made an about-turn, indicating the stream, the trees and the Vaga with the sweep of a hand. Many thousands of men, women and children had assembled at this hitherto anonymous riverbank, gathered in their clans and septs as far as the eye could see. 'Us.' He looked at Cassia again, expression growing suddenly grave. 'You want to search for her, no?'

'More than anything.'

'Then we need to win. The reds are coming. The whole Isle of the Mighty gathers here to meet them.'

She nodded dutifully, though inwardly her doubts rang like bells. For it was not the whole island. Not even close. There were enough fighting men and women in these wild islands to resist any invader. But they seemed incapable of setting aside their petty hatreds in the face of a common enemy. She could not help but fear it would be their undoing.

Even as she gazed in wonder at the sheer scale of this gathering, she felt a knot of foreboding tighten like a fist in her stomach. So many spears, so much armour. Scores of chariots, supply wagons, salt merchants, brewers and fishermen, fresh from the Vaga with groaning nets. There were purveyors of huge cheese wheels, carts laden with bread, artists with their dyes, offering to paint the symbols of the gods on any fighter seeking protection. There were capering Wise Ones, performing rites and singing the songs of the ancients. There were horse-traders, tack makers and armourers, buzzing from warband to warband, like so many insects. And banners. A myriad of styles and colours. Poles held high and proud, capped with pelt, bone, wood and fabric. The sigils of a multitude of petty chiefs. Despite the pomp and circumstance, she thought ruefully, this great gathering may yet prove inadequate to the task. The king's tribe, the Catuvellauni, were here in strength, the bulk of the force. The Trinovantes, long in the thrall of Togodubnos's tribe, had brought their spears, as had a good remnant of Cullen's people, the Atrebates, bolstered by large contingents from the Ordovices, the Durotriges and the Cantiaci, whose land this was. But where were the rest? She had seen the list of traitors. Taken it personally from the dead hand of Berikos, deposed king of the Atrebates. The Dobunni had been seduced by promises of Roman gold, along with the Regnenses, the Coritani and, perhaps most concerning, the Brigantes, the powerful rulers of the forbidding northern mountains. The Eceni had been named too, which had been a significant shock, but rumour suggested their ailing King Antedios might not be as treacherous as first feared. Especially since the rescue, by Catuvellauni warriors, of the Eceni princess, Betha, from the warlike Silures tribe. Time, she supposed, would tell.

All in all, it would not be enough, whether the Eceni contributed their spears or not. The peoples of Britannia's Belgae numbered in the tens of thousands, but the legions were no ordinary foe. Togodubnos had sent tributes further afield, of course. To the fearsome tribes of the southwest and the savage warriors of the extreme north. On the far side of Sabrina's Sea lurked the Silures, formidable in the field, but they were unlikely to help, since the rescue of Betha.

And all the while, the eagles of Rome were in flight.

'What if the gods have abandoned us?' she muttered.

Gwidion snorted. 'Perhaps they have, perhaps not. If you wish to find your Critheanach, you must hope the latter proves true.' He sidled to the wagon. 'Aoife the Dread offered to help?'

Hardly, Cassia thought. She shrugged. 'Said she would ask after her.'

'Wait a day or two. Then seek her out. Aoife, I mean.' He winked. 'Give her a gentle nudge.'

'That seems a little risky. She does not seem the type to welcome *a gentle nudge*.'

'Then do nothing,' Gwidion said. He fished a hunk of bread from amongst the wagon's clutter. 'Now, then. Who's next?'

Cassia glanced along the brook, to where the gaggle of patients waited. 'Broken leg.'

'How?'

'Kicked by a horse. It has turned bad.'

Gwidion pulled an ominous grimace. 'How long?'

'Several days, I'm told.'

'Have him brought up.' He returned to the wagon, delving once more, and pulling free a slim earthenware bottle. 'It may be a sleeping draught is all that is required.' He gave it a little shake. 'Henbane leaves and crushed mandrake root, all boiled slowly in oil to produce a potent tincture.'

Cassia went to collect it. 'My father preferred the juice of the poppy. The sleep was more peaceful.'

'That was because your father concerned himself with the lopping of limbs.'

She drew breath, poised to protest as a matter of instinct, but held her peace. Her father had been a military surgeon, after all. She gave a grudging smile as she closed her fingers about the cold bottle. 'Not always.'

'The poppy will induce a deep sleep,' Gwidion conceded, 'and henbane will be fitful, disturbed.'

'Then why?'

'Because in his torment, the Otherworld may be revealed to him. He may converse with his ancestors, or even glimpse the gods themselves. If the leg is as bad as I fear, the Waking Realm can offer him nothing.' Gwidion drew a deep breath as she walked away. 'And *puella?*'

'*Avus?*'

The old Wise One grimaced. 'Keep the tincture. Keep it close. When battle is joined, you will need it.'

—

'Dog piss!' The tall man grimaced as he swallowed, drawing a hairy forearm across the thick black whiskers that made him such an incongruous sight in the legion's marching camp. He collapsed testily into a nest of pillows, hastily plumped and positioned by servants who clucked about the three men like hens.

'*Posca*, my dear Adminios,' the shortest replied, so smoothly it was almost a purr. 'The wine is heavily watered.' He lifted his own cup in mock salute, tanned fingers crammed with jewels. 'Sour but refreshing.'

'Piss can be refreshing if served cold enough.' Adminios, erstwhile lord of the Cantiaci, junior member of the heirs of Cunobelin, and ally of Rome, took another reluctant swig. He belched, deliberately vulgar to irk the supercilious servants, and glanced up at the sky beyond the broad awning, beneath which they took their ease. 'Still, it is too warm to demur.'

The smaller man, disported languorously on a pile of his own cushions, plucked at the hem of his toga, the edges glimmering with silver thread. 'You should make better sartorial choices.'

Adminios stifled a sneer, settling for a grunt that would not betray his disgust at the suggestion. He tapped his own cup against the mail vest that settled snugly over his standard-issue legionary's tunic. 'A warrior's clothes befit a warrior.'

'Ignore him,' the third man, standing broad and imposing, boomed as he took a drink from a grovelling slave who followed him like a whipped hound. He wore a golden breastplate that was contoured to give the appearance of a muscular torso. A red cloak, trimmed with sumptuous white fur, was fastened at his oak-trunk neck. His face was broad and ruddy beneath restless eyes and brown, tousled hair. 'A bureaucrat seeks power, but not at the expense of his comfort. Your fame as a warrior goes before you, Lord Adminios.'

'I thank you, General Plautius,' Adminios said.

Aulus Plautius, commander of the Roman invasion force, clicked his tongue, a motion that made the white scar twitch where it bisected his upper lip. A platter of food materialised as if from the swamp itself. He did not acknowledge the bearer, taking some cheese as he spoke. 'By summer's end, you will be a king.'

Which was why, Adminios thought, his sartorial choices were important. Donning the outfit of a Roman was one thing, but the toga said something far more profound. The difference, he suspected, between liberator and oppressor. He might be harnessing the power of the legions, but he would not be seen as one of the oleaginous prigs that represented the emperor. He forced himself to look away from the dark, perpetually amused gaze of Narcissus, examining instead the deep, insect-infested swamp through which they made painstaking but inexorable progress. 'My brother is no fool. He may hit us at any time.' His eyes settled on a phalanx of legionaries that laboured along a raised timber walkway some two hundred strides from the patch of dry ground

Plautius had earmarked for his itinerant command hub. 'We may fight for our lives at a moment's notice.'

Tiberius Claudius Narcissus, the famed freedman who had risen all the way to the summit of Emperor Claudius's court, gave a leonine yawn that finished in a dazzling smile. 'You worry too much, dear Adminios. We have more than forty thousand men.'

'Stretched in a thin column,' Adminios said doubtfully, 'all the way back to the bridgehead.' He observed the cohorts of legionaries crisscrossing the area in their highly disciplined lines, throwing spears in one hand, long, curved body shields in the other. Those shields, the *scuta*, were dazzling with their bronze decoration and rich, intricate designs. The effect was an ocean of reds, golds and greens, gilt edged and formidable. It was all for show, he thought. Everything they did, these Romans, was to impress. To intimidate. He did not begrudge them that. Rather, it gave him ideas of his own. The Adminios Legion. Red shields, bearing snakes and stags and stallions. A great cohort of Cantiaci in legionaries' mail, marching on Camulodunon and Verlamion, each unified step a thunderclap of intention. How his brothers would quell. How they would beg his forgiveness. Yet out here, in the wild, murky depths, even the legions were vulnerable. He met Narcissus's restless gaze. 'We are outnumbered and exposed. Togodubnos will likely send nines, moving fast, into the forests to pick us off.'

'Nines?' Narcissus echoed dubiously.

'The tribes' best fighters are arranged in groups of nine, who come together in larger warbands.'

'Warbands?' Plautius muttered, as he absently watched work parties wading through the black shallows, seeking dry ground for the pitching of tents. The land hereabouts was a patchwork of stooping trees and stinking bogs, the stench of decay lingering always, catching bitterly at the back of the throat. 'Or wolf packs?'

'Call them what you will. If my brother has a shred of sense, he will attack the legions on the road, while they are strung out.'

Narcissus simply smiled again. 'The scouts report that the Britons have gathered on the far bank of a tidal river. There they await our arrival.'

Adminios looked up at Plautius, who nodded firmly. 'It is true,' the general said.

'The fool,' Adminios said, swilling his posca, staring into its dark contents. 'Always was fond of grand gestures.'

Plautius snorted. 'This gesture will get him killed.' He swatted at something with a meaty hand. 'Soon we will engage your swine-headed siblings, and you will see why Rome has conquered the world.'

Out in the swamp, an officer was furiously excoriating a subordinate for some misdemeanour, his voice drifting to them in broken chunks, like random pieces of a puzzle. Narcissus sipped delicately from his cup and regarded the inhospitable expanse of surrounding marshland. 'The longest day approaches. To think I shall spend it here.' He laughed grimly. 'How is it celebrated hereabouts?'

'Every tribe will honour Belinos.'

'We honour the goddess Fortuna. And before that, it is the time of Vestalia,' Narcissus said. 'An unborn calf is cut from its mother's womb and sacrificed in tribute to Vesta, goddess of hearth and home. Then we feast.' He swatted irritably at a mosquito dancing at his left ear. 'This year it is us who are feasted upon!'

'We feast also,' Adminios said, and it sounded as though someone else had spoken, for his mind had drifted elsewhere. To the past. To better times. He saw again the festivals of his youth. The laughter and the women. When the gods had favoured him. It made his chest tighten and his heart become leaden. 'We give thanks for the land's bounty. We set great fires on every hilltop to honour the sun god, and we dance and sing to honour Maponos, he of youth and wonder.'

'By Mars himself,' Plautius declared, 'when I receive my estates, the first thing I shall do is drain all the swamps.' One of his eyes flickered as an insect flittered at his lashes. 'I'll have none of these little bastards in my air.'

'You'll receive land, general?' Adminios asked, trying to keep the displeasure from his voice. This was to be his kingdom, after all, once his older siblings were dead and gone.

'Of course,' Plautius said. 'Why else are we here? You'll get your crown, Adminios, do not fret. But the lands will be shared by those who have shed blood for Rome. Worry not, man. Our legions bring violence. The weeping of fresh-made widows is the music to which we march.' He quaffed his posca. 'But after the fighting is done, when your painted wild-men have been hunted and broken and slain, peace will follow. We will build. We will make good.'

'We will civilise the savages,' Narcissus said slickly. He raised the cup with bright-eyed amusement. 'Whether they like it or not.'

CHAPTER SEVEN

Grimoald, Leopard of the Batacgwi, pulled his sword free of the old man's belly. The flesh sucked at it stubbornly, so that he was forced to twist the iron to set it free. Entrails, steaming hot, slithered out from the widened wound, as if a nest of enraged snakes pursued the weapon. The old man clawed at them, trying to catch his guts, scoop them up and return them to his belly, but they escaped through his fingers, and he was on his knees before he understood he was falling. The light quickly dimmed from his eyes.

People screamed. Grimoald stepped back in disgust, spitting on the bloodied grass as if that would expunge the stink quickly rising from the dying man's innards. He handed the sword to an aide for cleaning and planted his big paws on his hips, surveying the meagre population of Smith's Ring with less enthusiasm than if he had been asked to choose the prize hunting dog from a gaggle of mangy mongrels.

'Have you no shame?' a woman, shrill and furious, squawked like a maddened jackdaw from the front of the motley gathering. She was tall and grey, her clothes corresponding with the raincloud hue of her long hair. 'No decency?'

'You are chieftess?' Grimoald asked her, speaking slowly as he brought his passable grasp of the Britons' language to the fore. All the tribes would have their own dialects, of course, and some would bear closer relation to his stunted rendition than others, but they would all understand the common tongue to a navigable degree. 'You command?'

The grey woman shook her head. 'I care for those left behind, that is all.'

He beckoned her forward. She edged out from the crowd, though her eyes lingered on the felled grandfather, who now lay utterly still, an ashen island in a lake of his own guts. 'Fear not,' he began.

'Fear not?' she spluttered. 'Do—'

He shut her up with a raised palm, his golden leopard ring glittering in the sun. 'Fear not,' he said again. 'I have no interest in these raggedy creatures. Only in your druid.'

'Druid?'

'You call them Wise Ones, do you not?'

That threw her, and she frowned. 'He has gone.'

Grimoald smiled. 'But I know this cannot be.' What was it that wretch had told him? He dredged the words up from his memory. 'The druid must stay, with a great treasure, until the gods command him leave.' He took back the big sword, proffered – spotless and gleaming – by the bowing aide. The timing, he had to admit, was exemplary, and he made a show of inspecting the sleek iron. 'We know this to be true.'

The woman set her jaw with a look of defiance. Unsurprising, he supposed, for the fine beaver brooch at her collar marked her out as a member of the nobility. A more self-aggrandising caste of people he could not imagine. 'He is no longer here. He was taken.'

'Abducted?'

She nodded. 'By warriors. I know neither their motive nor destination.'

'The destination is Togodubnos himself, certainly. Their king will want this treasure for himself.'

Felix had sidled over, fresh from corralling another party of frightened-looking waifs, ancients and striplings. They had marched them past the small remnant of spearmen that had so ineffectually patrolled the walls. All now deceased and stripped to waxy nakedness, piled haphazardly for the inevitable crow-feast. The resultant terror emanating from the captives was as palpable as Grimoald had hoped. 'At the risk of offending the gods, lord?' Felix ventured.

Grimoald shrugged. 'Kings.' Who could read the minds of such men? He turned back to the woman. 'If you're lying to me, every skull here will adorn my saddle.'

'I tell the truth,' she said firmly, and he found that he believed her, so he looked again at Felix.

'Take what we require. Burn the rest.'

'Lord,' Felix replied, already turning.

To the woman, Grimoald asked, 'Which way did they ride?'

Her sharp chin jutted up insolently. 'I will not say, may the gods be my witness.'

Grimoald shouldered her out of the way and took hold of a small child, wrenching the snivelling runt clean off the ground with one hand, the sword still poised in the other. 'The gods be *my* witness; yes, you will.'

—

The forest petered into a dense jumble of brush, fern and bramble, interspersed with the occasional stand of birch, whose branches filtered the beating sun. Always, the dark line of undulating downland smeared the distant sky like an ominous thundercloud. It was beyond that ridge that Togodubnos's meeting place – a rare ford in an otherwise impassable watercourse – would be found, and Cullen kept his eyes fixed on the horizon, knowing that it represented success.

'I shall call him Valour's Fortune,' he said of the sturdy horse as they negotiated a narrow track that bisected a barricade of twisting thorns. He studiously ignored Serwil's scornful sniff. 'Fortune for short.'

'Not right,' Garn's growl came from the rear, competing with the rhythmic thrum of hooves and the persistent chatter of starlings and marsh tits.

'He is courageous,' Cullen called back.

'And your fortune,' Garn conceded.

'Then?' Cullen twisted in the saddle. 'A horse needs a name.'

'Better no name than the wrong one. I can tell if it is right, and your choice is feeble.'

The wind whispered as the others laughed. Serwil muttered something about soon-to-be former warriors requiring no mounts. The sun, at its zenith, cast intricate patterns of light and shadow through the barbed stems at their flanks, creating a mesmerising dance upon the ground.

'Enchanted,' Rues muttered to no one in particular as he stared into the impenetrable fronds. A murmur of agreement came in response. Even Andoc, so dour and reserved, whispered quiet acknowledgement to the spirits dwelling within.

A break in the thicket brought them to a flower-dotted clearing that was cut by a gentle stream, its waters liquid crystal. Cullen felt the palomino strain under him, the beast eager to drink. He nudged gently with his heels. The horse responded with a loud, guttural snort as its pace quickened.

'Hog,' Andoc said dryly.

'Hog?'

'That noise it makes is not natural. The creature's more sow than stallion.'

'If Fortune fits ill,' Cullen retorted, letting Rues go ahead, as was his role and his habit, 'then Hog is absurd!'

The Seeker's chin tilted up as he sniffed the air. He scrutinised the brush, and the trees beyond, questing for threat, waving them on when none was apparent, though a quizzical expression lingered on his weathered features.

The horse pushed past Rues's mount and thrust its muzzle greedily into the cool water. The slurping noise, tussling for pre-eminence with its usual snorting, was acute and embarrassing in Cullen's ears, now that it had been drawn to his attention.

And the others laughed, long and loud, as their mounts followed, hooves splashing as they lapped.

'Hog,' Garn said, with a finality that was far from encouraging. 'Good and proper.'

They splashed across the stream and rode on, emerging from the bramble kingdom and into less suffocating air beneath stoic alder and quaking aspen. Cullen let his mind wander with the rustle of leaves. Half-worn memories wisped into view, overlaid and obscured by the maelstrom of change that had engulfed these past few seasons.

His mind took him home, recollections assailing him like a hail of sling stones. At once he was the green youth, the callow goat-wrangler, barely thinking beyond his next meal or the next opportunity to see what was under the smocks of the local girls. He smiled to himself at the memories. Of stolen trysts on lonely hillsides. He half expected to hear the bleat of his lost charges, snagged on a bramble or stuck in a waterlogged ditch. He could smell his mother's cooking. Caught the laughter of his sisters.

That laughter faded. No, it did not fade, but was cut short. Brutally, savagely severed when the Catuvellauni had come with hot greed and cold iron. Catuvellauni, whose banner he now fought beneath. Killed for, and was willing to die for. Togodubnos's image swirled into his head now. He who Cullen revered as a true king, whose brother, Caratacos, he loathed for ordering the carnage that befell his village on that day of horror. He had sworn allegiance to one brother, and vengeance upon another. He was caught between, a fox in a snare. Tears stung his eyes and the weight of the sword became heavy at his side. His fingers slid, unbidden, to touch the rim of his shield, slung behind him from one of the saddle's four pommels. Upon that shield were painted two red snakes. The symbol of fealty to his greatest foes. The guilt physically ached.

'They will not condemn you for your choices,' Andoc's morose tones dissolved his reverie. 'Your kin would be proud.'

Cullen gave a half-hearted grunt that entirely failed to convey the unaffected façade he was hoping for. 'How did you know?'

'You get a look, Atrebates, when you wallow in the past.' Andoc brought his mount alongside. 'You have honoured their memory a hundred times over. You have fame. A name that will be echoing in the halls of the Otherworld even now.'

'I would give up my name, the fame, all of it.'

'To have them back? That is a trade even the gods cannot make. Do not mire yourself in regret. A life must be lived, Atrebates. That is something I have learned.'

Cullen thought, then, of Andoc's own story. The slaughter, not unlike his own, that had befallen his kin, at the hands of an Atrebates warband. Andoc had despised Cullen on sight, and he had learned to overcome that enmity. Of the two comrades, he was, Cullen knew, the better man. 'I will try to learn the same lesson.'

Andoc gave a wry smile that shouted his scepticism.

The day slowly waned, the sky becoming stained with hues of orange and pink. By turns, they traversed thick forest and open meadow, the trackway easing steadily away from the watercourse, leaving little to guide them but Rues Seeker's seasoned nose. The man himself had set off ahead, sensing something that sat uneasy. They followed a track between two fields of high, humming grass. The way was narrow, clogged by trees, and the route gradually descended into complete shadow, becoming a holloway beneath jumbled roots, carved into the landscape by turning seasons and trampling feet. The sudden darkness was almost suffocating, every sound seeming louder than before.

Cullen stared ahead with straining eyes. Over his shoulder. Up at the dense, interwoven canopy. No one spoke over the clomp of hooves and call of sparrows.

A unique birdcall. Pitched perfect, slightly tremulous, beautiful. Too perfect. Icy fingers played at Cullen's neck. He looked round. Garn met his gaze meaningfully. Andoc too.

'Rues,' Cullen said, and he was already freeing Lightning-Strike from its scabbard, comforted by the accustomed grip, reassured by the exquisite balance. They could not form a circle in so narrow a path, so they manoeuvred, awkward and cursing, into two banks of four, back to back, spears poised like the spines of some many-hoofed monstrosity. Cullen alone dismounted, for he could not fight with Serwil in the way, and he could hardly toss the Wise One to the ground, to be cut down as soon as iron began to sing.

He unhooked the big shield from the saddle, and paced out in front of Hog, bracing himself behind the painted and scarred barrier, ignoring the tremble in his hands.

Strangers, on horseback, trundled down into the holloway some thirty paces in front of him, cutting through a break in the trees that screened the high bank. Cullen counted heads. Eighteen, all carrying spears and wearing mail shirts above chequered bracae. They had an assortment of helmets, some with nose bars, a couple with cheek pieces, and one, presumably the leader, made tall by a prancing deer crest in copper or bronze. Roman outriders? They clearly were not reds, but he had fought Gauls at Swamp River, looking, for all the world, like his own people.

He waited, held himself in check. The trees swished and rustled above, unconcerned by what came to pass below. Behind him, Cullen's companions bristled, muttered, making ready. Maeveen, Clesek, Andoc and Kenal, facing away, would be holding their position, watching for an attack from the rear, though he sensed them craning their necks to see what transpired.

Then, pushing to the front of the approaching line of horsemen, came a man he recognised. Craggy eyes, cleanly shaven jaw, hair dyed yellow with piss and limewash, spiked to stiff points with a chalky paste of which he was incredibly proud.

'Cantiaci,' Rues Seeker called, lifting his spear to the sky, showing no threat. 'Found them up in the pasture.'

Cullen nodded, trying not to betray the cascading relief. Sheathing his blade, he took a step back to gather Hog's reins. He addressed the man in the deer-helm. 'Well met. I am Cullen.'

'I am Hilax.' The leader of the newcomers was perhaps forty, though age was hard to read under all that bronze. He had narrow eyes, grey as his mail-links, and a dark blond moustache that curled down to his chin like inverted bullhorns. 'Who commands here, boy?'

'This boy,' Garn boomed, his mount skittering nervously at the sudden squall, 'led the defence at Swamp River.'

Baglan, the one they called Day Break, let his own horse take a step. 'He was appointed to lead spears.'

Hilax eyed Cullen with suspicion. 'Appointed?'

'By Ulla Jagged Cliff himself,' Garn said. 'On to the next.'

'On to the next,' Hilax echoed, as was the custom. He seemed to take a moment, weighing the revelation, and glanced sideways at his flanking riders. Then he dipped his head, just a fraction. 'Forgive me, I—'

'I am engaged upon the high king's work,' Cullen said, feeling rising irritation. At what? Hilax's preconception, or the very necessity of Garn's defence? He could not decide, so he cut it dead. 'What news?'

Hilax took a quick glance back whence he came, as if unseen enemies might burst from the trees as he had. 'The Romans are marching.'

'Did you not hear?' Cullen bit back tersely. 'I have come from Swamp River. I know what we face more than most.'

'They have crossed that river. They march west in great columns. Their outriders lay waste to our villages. Kill the slowest. Take plunder and slaves. Their eagles will reach the Vaga in days. Our people retreat in great droves. The steadings empty, the livestock abandoned. Pastures left to ruin.' Hilax shook his head, reliving what he had seen, an expression of glassy-eyed disbelief passing across his face. 'It is chaos.'

'You travel to the meeting place?' Cullen asked. 'To the great horde?'

Hilax shook his head. 'We come from there. The reds have horsemen abroad, scouring the land, harrying the people. So, then, do we.'

'You bring honour to the Cantiaci,' Cullen said, but even as the words left his mouth, he saw Hilax's gaze shift away, taking in the curious creature perched upon Hog.

'Take me with you!' Serwil squawked as he caught Hilax's attention. 'These scurrilous villains have abducted a member of the Wise! A son of Mona! Do your duty, and—'

Garn had moved his horse closer, crowding Hog, jolting the man in the saddle, and lifting his studded forearm threateningly before the Wise One's face. The air hissed out of Serwil, wasted and wordless.

Hilax's grey eyes slid from Rues to Garn, finally alighting on Cullen. 'Abducted?' Behind him, spears moved. They did not fall level. Did not offer threat. But, subtle as the leaf-shiver above their heads, they twitched faintly. A latent readiness that put both parties immediately on edge.

'We take him to the gathering place,' Cullen said.

Hilax cocked his head like a dog gauging a distant sound. 'But he would not go?'

Cullen shook his head. 'He would not.'

'Then you see?' Serwil bleated, hope renewing his cries. 'It is abduction, no less.'

'I do not contest that,' Cullen said. 'He goes to the Vaga against his will.'

'Then whose will would see it done?' Hilax asked.

'Togodubnos himself.'

A moment's contemplation. Hilax looked around at his men, saddle creaking under his rump. 'I would add my spears to yours, but I must engage the enemy. Hamper their progress.'

Cullen breathed a silent sigh of relief. 'May the gods bring you joy of battle.'

'And may they see you safe to the gathering place.'

'I will tell the king of your valour,' Cullen said, slinging his shield and swinging up into the saddle behind an incandescent Serwil. He raised a balled fist. 'Life with glory!'

Hilax lifted his spear, even as his mount wheeled about, the other riders coalescing around him. 'And death with honour!'

'How fares Hog?' Garn enquired across a crackling fire, herbal scents of burning greenery flavouring the heady fug of smoke and roasting meat. He was standing, rolling his massive shoulders and bending into a stretch, limbering up his legs.

Cullen, opposite, hefted a pair of sticks, one in each hand, gauging the weight and length. Before he could muster a reply, the creature, tethered nearby to a low-slung bough, offered a guttural snort that belonged firmly in a pigsty.

'The beast does as I ask,' Cullen said, hearing the defensiveness in his own voice and regretting it immediately. He shook his head in exasperation, unable to stifle the rueful smile that forced its way onto his face.

The others, having organised a night-watch and, probably, taken a piss out in the woods, emerged from the trees to sit round the fire.

'A victory for a man barely able to canter,' Andoc called from where he crouched, poking the guttering flames with a black-ended log.

It was near dark. The party had made camp amid a stand of close-knit oak, the thick foliage and massive limbs screening them completely from the trackway. Maeveen worked a small knife, whittling a chunk of kindling into a delicate figurine. Erbin, kneeling close by the flames, sang a soft tune of home that was utterly at odds with his brawny frame and knuckle-flattened face. Serwil sat away from the group, eyes closed, mouth working wordlessly as he no doubt called retribution down from the realm of the gods.

'I do not deny it,' Cullen conceded, as he tossed one of the sticks to Garn. Taking such a horse had been a boon indeed. The Gaul from whom Hog had been captured had trained him well. The animal was a consummate professional, stoic and unflappable, requiring little instruction. Cullen looked up as the hectoring chatter of squirrels came from branches bathed in tremulous flamelight. 'We would ride at home. Finding the sheep or tracking roebuck. But I was happiest with my feet on the ground.'

'I would not have guessed,' Andoc said drolly.

'At dawn, Hog,' Cullen called fondly to the horse, 'you must root out this ford for us!' The others muttered agreement as he handed the second stick to Clesek, who had stripped down to just his tunic and braca. The younger man made a show of cracking both elbows and flexing his fingers. It did nothing to wipe the terror from his expression.

Garn sidled over, rocking his wide head from side to side. The thick neck crackled and popped. He grinned. A vast, hungry wolf. 'Come, turdling,' he commanded, beckoning Clesek to join him on a patch of turf away from the fire and clear of obstruction. He swished a cross in the air with his makeshift weapon. 'This is my shield arm, so you are already at an advantage.'

Clesek imitated the move. 'I am ready,' he said, which was the most hollow statement Cullen had ever heard.

Baglan and Kenal had flasks of strong mead, which were duly shared about, swigged, handed on. Cullen went to sit with them. The group, save Rues, who had taken first watch, shifted to get a better view of the entertainment. The song died on Erbin's lips. Even Maeveen stopped carving and looked up with interest.

Garn Grey Boulder launched himself at Clesek. The move could hardly be described as graceful, for one as large as he, but nor was it lumbering. The big man knew his business, had taken on foes of every shape and size, since before Clesek was a glint in his father's eye, and immediately the young Cantiaci was on the back foot, parrying as though his life depended on it. Cullen sincerely hoped that that was not truly the case, but in the heat of the fight, he suddenly felt less sure. Garn – huge and snarling – looked as though he meant to offer a blood sacrifice to the gods of the night sky.

Feet shuffled madly, sticks clattered, the fire popped and spat, the warriors helped the duel along with muted cheers and gasps. Clesek did well enough, all told. Managing, by the skin of his teeth, to keep the monstrous war-giver at bay. Garn brayed and laughed and snarled. When Clesek had retreated far enough, running out of room, the bigger man moved back, beckoning him to return to the clearing.

Cullen called out, 'Now, Clesek, strike!'

The Cantiaci duly obliged, using the superior agility that youth offered, and closed the distance with admirable speed. He swung the stick in a wild arc. Garn stepped nimbly aside like a Calan Haf dancer, spun on the balls of his feet, and unleashed a swiping backhand. To his credit, Clesek managed to turn in time, dropping reflexively, maintaining his stance but bending at the knees. Garn's stick crossed above his head, missing by a hand's breadth, and he grinned broadly, readied himself again.

Clesek pushed up from his slight crouch, darting in, and smacked Garn's stick aside.

'Stop!' Garn bellowed.

The fight ended. Clesek lowered the weapon, breathing hard, his face and torso sweat-drenched and gleaming in the flame-flicker.

Garn's barrel chest heaved. 'We do not attack the blade,' he instructed in a low rumble. 'We attack the body. Unless?'

'Unless,' Clesek panted, 'I am clearing a line.' He flicked up and out with his stick, mimicking the move he had just made. 'But I was—'

'Do not waste your breath,' Garn cut him off impatiently. 'Your eyes were on my staff.' His hand moved, the stick swiping between them as he made his own rendition of the aborted attack. 'You may strike at the blade in order to displace it, making the way clear for your own attack. But you do not attack the blade itself. Not without the next two, three, four steps in mind.'

Clesek nodded sheepishly. Garn beamed. 'Thank Belinos! He can be taught!'

'Continue,' Andoc urged.

'You're doing well,' Cullen said. 'Keep on the outside, move him around.'

'He's blowing out of his arse!' Maeveen called.

The fighters stepped back, took the stance, renewed the duel. Clesek, encouraged, did as he was told, more thoughtful in his movements, more measured in his ripostes. Garn gave a grimace that betrayed a flicker of annoyance. It was becoming harder than he had expected or wanted.

Cullen watched them. Cheered and applauded both men as they cut and thrust, blocked and faded. He recalled his early training at the school of Master Farrad in Verlamion. If he was honest, Clesek was better than he had been. Cullen had been thrown into the heat of battle before he was ready. It had forced him to learn quickly, death the only alternative.

A nudge at his elbow. Maeveen, handing him one of the mead-skins. 'What does it represent?'

Cullen saw that she was referring to the hawthorn carving that hung from his neck. He looked down at the red-brown disc, polished smooth, that bore the intricate design of a three-tailed horse at its centre. 'My people.'

'The Atrebates, I know,' she said impatiently, 'but what provenance? It is heartwood, is it not? The spine of the tree. The most sacred. I can tell by the colour. It means more to you than what it depicts.' She smiled in the gloom, a gesture that seemed like a demonic grimace, all white teeth, pinched features and spiked hair. 'A girl?'

'Cassia.'

Maeveen's eyes widened. An expression he had not seen before. Shock, perhaps. 'Roman?'

He nodded. 'Shipwrecked, many years back. Raised by the Catuvellauni.'

Maeveen grunted amusement. 'One cannot predict desire.' She touched a hand to her breast, then pointed at the sky. 'May Taranis reunite you when the time is right.'

Cullen felt his chest tighten, and chewed the inside of his mouth hard, tasting blood and regaining composure. He could not help but look through the flames to where, beyond the flickering haze, Serwil remained, sullen and cross-legged, near enough to catch some warmth, but markedly apart from the group.

Maeveen, watching him, said softly, 'You are no coward.'

'I did not say that I was,' Cullen said, taken aback.

She turned her glittering, baleful gaze towards the Wise One. 'I heard what that fool said.' She glanced down at her lap, where the figurine she had fashioned lay. 'And when a member of the Wise brands you thus, it is difficult to ignore.'

'I was afraid, it is true. But not of the beacon.'

'Oh?'

The distant cry of a wolf hung in the darkness. 'Aoife the Dread demanded this task done. I would not fail her.'

'Being afraid of the Dread is not cowardice, it is merely common sense.'

Cullen peered down at the figurine. It was the size of a thumb, bearing the likeness of a person, round-faced and wide-eyed. Deft little nicks defined a neat beard. 'Who is it?'

She followed his gaze. Put a forefinger to the carving, the touch unexpectedly tender. 'My father. Died when I was just a babe.'

'Mine too. I wish—'

Maeveen looked up at him. 'You fret over your lack of years.'

'Wouldn't you?' He lifted the mead, took a tentative sip, the honeyed liquid immediately warming his lips and tongue.

She nodded enthusiastically. 'You cannot even grow a beard!'

He laughed, took a deeper swig, stifled a cough as the mead burned down to his core.

Maeveen thumbed over her shoulder, at the men who played at duelling, and those who growled encouragement. 'The likes of these, their judgements are made on deeds alone. You have proven your courage. Proven you are unlikely to get them killed.'

'Unlikely?'

'I hope so. You're clever. The Stone of Gobannos tells us so.'

He frowned. 'You speak to it?'

She laughed. 'You identified it, Wolf Scourge. Saw the Wise One's staff for what it was. As I say, you are clever.'

Cullen stared through the flames to where the scowling Serwil sat. He could not hold back a slight shudder. 'Wise One.'

'We must revere the Wise,' Maeveen said. 'Honour them. But not at the cost of our lives. You did the right thing.' She took back the mead, quaffing a good few gulps with practised ease. She belched, wiped glistening lips on her slender, scarred forearm, and gave it back. 'At sunrise, we'll take the stone to the king, and your task will be complete.'

Cullen breathed deeply, trying to settle the nerves that came whenever he considered his near-overwhelming duty. He looked up, through a gap in the trees that jagged a sky full of stars. The line of the ridge had faded into the rest of the encroaching night, but he knew it was there, looming, a final barrier to success, a symbol of safety. He raised the flask. 'I'll drink to that.'

CHAPTER EIGHT

'I don't like her.'

Arthmael the Learned, wisest of the Wise, opened one eye. 'The ale-wench?'

'At the sign of the plough.' Above him, blotting out the hoary half-light that filtered through cracks around the window skin, the girl screwed up her face as though tasting something rancid. 'She's a bitch.'

Arthmael formed a plan of the dun in his mind. Camulodunon's busy streets, shops and nemeta unravelled before him, until he remembered the drinking-den in question. He sighed. 'What concern is that of mine?'

She was straddling his belly, naked apart from a pair of fox-trimmed boots, the stars and moons etched permanently on his skin stretching and contorting under the clammy heat of her thighs. 'You have the power of kings, lord.'

'The power of the sacred isle,' he corrected. And that power, if not quite imbued with the majesty of throne-blood, was potent indeed. Mona, the mystical island far to the north and west, hemmed by mountain and sea, peopled by sorcerers and gods. It was there that he had learned the ways of the seasons and of the skies. The formations of the clouds and what they told of Great Taranis's mood, the growth of moss on deep-wood stones, and how that described Cernunnos's plans for winter. It was on Mona that young Arthmael had discovered how the run of a stream spoke of a thing, the caw of a raven another. Learned to tell the future from the spill of a lamb's blood, or the way the guts toppled from a disembowelled badger. He had learned so much there. Gained so much influence. Yet, he thought with sudden chagrin, he required more. Certain scores needed settling.

She was pouting down at him, her loose, auburn hair sweeping his cheeks and chest, turning his skin to gooseflesh. She unbent slowly, stretched like a cat, arching at the small of her back, and reached behind to curl strong, work-roughened fingers around him, flashing a mottle-toothed grin as he bucked in response.

'I will see what can be done,' he rasped, throat rapidly thickening.

She worked harder at his reinvigorated erection. 'What can be done is whatever you see fit, lord, surely?'

He closed his eyes. 'I will see. I promise no more.'

Not breaking stroke, she reached with her free hand to take one of his, drawing it up to her pendulous breast, milky white in the ethereal gloom. Outside, a trio of dogs gave furious retort to a distant owl call. Arthmael, sagest of the denizens of Mona, let himself groan, the animals' din masking his lust.

'Do it for Myrna,' she breathed.

'Hold your tongue, girl,' he managed to reply, kneading her like fresh dough.

'Why don't *you* hold it, lord?' It peeped, moist and pink, from between wet lips as she let go of his prick and sank in. He gaped for it, radiant and lambent, as her nipples scraped his, lapped hungrily at her, forcing his own, forked tongue deep into her mouth. He wondered vaguely if she noticed – or minded – the shape. It had been cut on his tenth birthday, healed completely in the decades since. A snake's tongue for the spirit-leader of the serpent tribe. What would this girl, no more than sixteen, make of this old man's mutilated mouth? Fortunately, he did not care either way.

Myrna eased back, a thin tendril of salvia dangling between them, then she smiled again, slid stickily down until she found him, still hard as granite and pulsing gently against the flesh of her rump. She wriggled a little, taunting him.

'You are wicked,' Arthmael protested feebly.

Myrna stopped moving. Met his gaze. Hers was suddenly level. Callous, even. 'The ale-bitch?'

Arthmael lifted his hips, probing for her. 'She will be gone by the longest day,' he said, hearing the hoarse desperation in his own voice.

A smile of pure triumph. Arthmael groaned and shut his eyes, saturated with bliss.

–

The sun began to rise over Camulodunon, stirring to life the Isle of the Mighty's largest settlement. Within Myrna's hut, silvery moonlight had given way to dawn gold that flooded the interior, though she had been careful to keep the skin drawn across the building's single opening.

'Where does the day take you, lord?' she crooned, her breath hot in his ear. 'I imagine there is need for your wisdom at the horde-gathering.'

They were sprawled, naked, on the bed of pelts he had bought her. He tilted his head to look at her, their noses almost touching. 'I await Caratacos, and he is away to the north, summoning the tribes to the serpent banner. The king oversees matters at the Vaga.'

She pouted. 'Does not the wisest of the Wise advise the king?'

'Careful, girl,' he warned. He often chided himself for tolerating her impertinence. Often threatened to have her whipped for her loose tongue. Then that same tongue would perform a trick that made him row back on every promise he had made.

Even now, she pressed closer to him, entwining their legs, letting him feel her heat. 'Forgive me, lord,' she said coquettishly, 'I just do not like the notion that the king defers to others.'

He shunted himself up onto an elbow, looking down at her. 'I'm sure you don't.' Outside, a cockerel gave voice to the dawn, loud and long. 'The king keeps his own counsel. I can do little to remedy the matter.'

Myrna pulled a theatrical glower, like a child denied a treat. She ran a finger gently over his stomach, tracing the shape of one of the faded etchings that had been needled there a near-lifetime ago. The touch put a shiver to Arthmael's skin, sent ice along his back, though it failed to kindle the fire she had intended. He put a hand to her heavy breast, cupped it, kneading it hard, as if the motion would stave off his brooding.

She was clearly disappointed with his response, for she frowned, genuinely this time. 'What ails you, lord?' As she spoke, her hand was slithering down to his groin. 'I can ease your burdens.'

Arthmael pushed her away. 'I have but one burden.'

'The reds.'

He held his peace, allowing her to think herself right. In truth, the grievance that gnawed away at his mind was the same one that made his thigh ache when it rained. The score to settle. The itch to scratch.

It plagued him in his quiet moments, kept him awake at night, cried out for resolution.

'I ask my grandfather, gods preserve his soul,' Myrna prattled, happily now, though he barely registered her words. 'Ask him to speak to the war-spirits. Intercede for us that walk the Waking Realm.'

'As you must,' said Arthmael absently.

'I beg for the reds to be smashed upon our brave fighters' shields. To be drowned in the great river.'

'The king and his brother will defend these lands, girl, do not fret.'

'Do they have children?' she asked. 'Togodubnos and Caratacos, I mean.'

'They do.'

She smiled, visibly comforted by the news. 'Then they will see us safe. They'll fight to the death. I have a daughter,' she went on, the ghost of real fury clouding her expression, 'and I would flay the skin from every man, woman and child in Camulodunon if it guaranteed her safety. If the reds reach us here, I'll kill them all myself. With my bare hands.'

He stared down at her. At the tightness that had come into her mouth and jaw. At the vehemence that blazed behind her eyes. The inferno of a mother's wrath. 'Yes, I believe you would.'

And now he took her by the wrist, drew those delicate fingers down to where his member was beginning, finally, to wake. Because he was suddenly encouraged. She had given him an idea, and, if he trod carefully, it would see a great wrong become a stunning right. The itch, gloriously, scratched.

—

'A child,' said Serwil of the Wise. 'Nothing but a child.'

Cullen looked at him through the grey smoke as it filtered over the small camp, feet stirring up white ash, kicking the last embers dead. He lowered the dagger, in whose polished reflection he had been inspecting himself. 'Good morning to you also.'

The sun was climbing over the treetops and the ridge beyond, highlighting the land in pale gold. The horses cropped what little grass they could find beneath the boughs, whickering in a language all their own, sensing the day's prospects like everyone else.

Serwil, gaze red-rimmed as ever, spat at the cooling ash pile. 'A snivelling whelp with leveret fluff for whiskers. I do not know what is more pathetic, your presumption of leadership,' he cast his single, malevolent eye around the party as they broke camp, 'or these cheese-witted fools who follow.'

'You do not wish to abandon the Wise and join my nine, then?' Cullen asked. 'I could find you a spear.'

Andoc, saddling his mount, grunted nearby. 'And I was beginning to think we had charmed him.'

Serwil spat again. 'Jest, please. It is I who will laugh in the fullness of time.'

Cullen sheathed the blade. 'Because I will have fulfilled Aoife's orders?' he said, exasperated. 'Succeeded in my task?'

'Because you will be exposed as a coward and a fraud. Because you saw far-off smoke and presumed it an enemy, though you could see none. Because you stole the Stone of Gobannos from its true keeper. Because you delivered a treasure to your king having rendered it utterly worthless. Because you, yet again, insulted the sacred Order of Mona.'

'Now that you mention it, Atrebates,' Andoc said, 'that doesn't sound ideal.'

'You mock,' the Wise One said, curling his lip, 'but you'll share in his disgrace.'

They performed a quick inventory: shields, spears, swords, flasks, provisions. Arched their backs and cracked their jaws. Emptied bladders and bowels in the deeper scrub. Rues went further up the track, checking the way was safe and clear.

Serwil glowered, hawk-like, from the periphery. 'Arthmael shall hear of this,' he spat, as Cullen summoned him to the waiting Hog.

'Of how we rescued you,' Cullen responded wearily, 'from Smith's Ring?'

'Of how you robbed and abducted me.'

'Aoife—'

'Spare me!' the Wise One almost shouted. 'Aoife the Dread is a fighter, and nothing more. A wild beast from the wild lands of Inisfail. A weapon to be used. Moranna of the Silver holds your true allegiance. That dark sorceress, who keeps Togodubnos in thrall.'

Cullen shrugged. 'Get on the horse.'

The red-rimmed eyes narrowed to slits as Serwil stepped back. 'I know you are a mere vassal,' he retorted, spittle frothing at the corners of his thin lips. 'A lamb to the shepherdess. Moranna of the Silver wields the power that matters, and Arthmael will hear.'

'I believe he knows her already.'

'Again with your mockery. He will hear of Moranna's sedition. How she undermines my work.'

Cullen made to argue, but thought better than to waste his breath. Besides, perhaps the order had come from Moranna. What business was it of his? 'The king would not have the whetstone in the enemy's hands.'

Serwil gave a bitter little laugh. 'And what good will it do in the king's hands, when Belinos has been denied? If he demanded of you a spear, you would not first make it blunt. This *theft* will only serve to incur the gods' wrath.' He laughed again, this time almost manically, as if in disbelief. 'And yours is the very hand that stabbed Arthmael! This can only anger Gobannos, not curry his favour. Indeed, the invasion itself may be reprisal for your sacrilege.'

'Give it a rest, Lord Serwil,' Garn said, readjusting the necklace of badger teeth below his white beard and hauling himself up behind his groaning horse. He jerked his chin at Cullen. 'By Belinos's hairy arse, but must we tolerate this all the way to the gathering-place? Folk fall from the saddle all the time.'

Serwil's mouth fell slack. 'How dare—'

The massed cries of gulls and crows rent the air away to the south. Every head turned, the exchange forgotten. Birds erupted in great, black and white swathes from the high canopy about a league away, startled to sudden panic and flight.

'Too many,' Garn said. 'Unnatural.'

'It is an omen,' Serwil insisted.

'Boar?' Andoc asked, as if the Wise One had not spoken.

'Could be,' Baglan said, though his tone was far from sure.

'Let us not wait to find out,' Cullen said.

The nine mounted without demur. Even Serwil clambered silently into Hog's saddle, aware that the atmosphere had tightened somehow, a frisson of anxiety permeating the air.

The dark line of the downland range hove into view as they moved out of the forest, travelling at almost a full gallop. Cullen, gripping Serwil in front, stared up at the livestock dotting the high pastures, driven there by herders at the birth of spring along the network of ancient trackways criss-crossing the land. There were fewer animals than he expected on those slopes. A good thing, he supposed, for it proved word of the invasion had spread, and was, for the most part, heeded.

They found the Vaga again, reed-fringed, fast flowing, far too wide and deep to cross, and followed it northwards, anxiously scanning the horizon for the telltale smoke trails of the settlement they knew stood guard over an ancient ford. They watched the south too, with equal anxiety, though the thick woodland gave away little except the birds who still seemed to be vacating the high canopy in unnerving numbers. Something was in there, amongst the great oaks, moving at speed.

It was Rues's raised hand that finally slowed them. He was up front, leading the group, but his head continually swivelled like a watchful owl, for his eyesight was by far the keenest, and he made a swirling motion with two fingers that they all recognised as the sign to turn. They wheeled the horses about, dust and grass flinging pell-mell.

Rues indicated a section of treeline as Cullen drew up on his left side. Every pair of eyes peered as if it were dimming twilight rather than blazing midday, squinting to focus, scrutinising each flowering shrub and zagging treetop.

'I see nothing,' Cullen said hopefully, though his experience of the faultlessly reliable Rues Seeker informed a sinking feeling in his guts.

'Wait,' Rues said.

They waited, to maybe the count of twenty. It was a thrumming at first, faint, muffled, almost imperceptible, like a wasp trapped in a barrel. Then a drone, more definite. The wasp becoming a hornet, angry and persistent.

Another ten-count, and there they were. Silhouetted riders, bursting from the dark. They fanned out, forming a broad line as soon as the terrain opened, and thundered after their quarry, clods of earth leaping in the wake of a score of warhorses carrying large men in heavy pelts.

Cullen's palms hurt where he gripped the reins so hard. He glanced down, knuckles white, as though all flesh had been stripped from them. He forced himself to look again at the strange riders, ignoring the race of his pulse. Their approach was uncomfortably familiar. Similar, somehow, to his own group, yet subtly different. The shields, perhaps? The spears, which seemed shorter than their own? They were not even close to Roman cavalry. And yet the image threw him instantly back to Swamp River, and the battle for the bridge. The blood shivered inside his veins.

'Auxiliaries,' Andoc said, perhaps replaying the same memories.

'Yes,' was all Cullen could say. He did not know what to do. It was a hammer blow to his heart. The expiry of his ambition. There was no time. They could not outrun the pursuers. If they stood and fought, they would be outnumbered. It was all for nothing. He could sense the others' stares, looking to him for leadership.

Garn laughed, sudden and unexpected. The sound, like a gathering storm, so incongruous it snapped Cullen from his melancholy.

'I was recalling,' the big man growled as he brought his mare beside Hog, 'something the Jagged Cliff once said.'

'Something funny?' Cullen asked, incredulous.

'Ulla *was* funny.'

'I never once saw him smile.'

'You were a spot-faced turdling,' the Grey Boulder replied, voice low enough for only Cullen and, regrettably, his surly passenger to hear. 'Ulla Jagged Cliff was funny, but in the company of lesser men, he wore the mask of command. You understand?'

Cullen swallowed. It felt like he ate thorns. But he nodded all the same.

'You are young,' Garn said. 'You are inexperienced. Folk will doubt you. You will doubt yourself. But you, too, possess the mask. I have seen it. I would not follow you if that were not the case.' He smiled as Cullen managed only a mute nod. 'Put it on now, Wolf Scourge. Become the leader Ulla knew you to be. The leader Taranis sees from way up in his brooding clouds.'

Serwil opened his mouth to speak, but a look from Garn made the jaw clamp firmly shut. Cullen felt gratitude sting his eyes and thicken his throat. He nodded again, for words would not come.

Garn winked. 'Put it on.'

Cullen breathed, steadying himself. He reached for Lightning-Strike, the smooth pommel cold and reassuring. He hauled breath into his chest. 'Skin your iron, my friends, and make ready for blood!'

In front of him, Serwil tensed. His head swivelled, seeking escape. He shrank back, squirmed.

Cullen pushed him from the saddle, so that he landed in a heap in the dust. 'Hide,' he said simply. Then he looked around at the others, catching as many eyes as he could. 'Life with glory!'

'Death with honour!' was the bellowed reply.

And the horn blasts began.

The valley had been flooded; not with water, but people.

The broad, marshy basin either side of the Vaga had been a world of reed and rill, glistening pool, weeping willow, sprouting sedge and cruel gorse, all interspersed with islands of raised, grassy ground. Then came the Cantiaci, fleeing the advancing legions. Then came the Catuvellauni, their spearmen taking up positions on the patches of dry ground. Then came all the others. Delegations of Eceni, Parisi, Ordovices and the rest, with their own banners, their own provisions and horses and chariots. All the vegetation that had clothed the slopes quickly vanished. Cleared for camps or to give line of sight to the riverbank. The trees were cut down for weapons and firewood, leaving only the wetland species that thrived out in the shallows. The gulls loitered, of course, harassing for scraps, but the warblers and heron, the egrets and the grebe had long since taken flight. Cernunnos, the great god of all nature, had awarded sovereignty of this kingdom to mankind, if only temporarily.

Some folk had gone away too. The children and elderly, most of the women; all those who would not take part in the coming bloodletting, sent deeper into the interior, there to pray to every god and ancestor in the Otherworld while they anxiously awaited news. Those who stayed made makeshift camps around little firepits. Most would sleep in the open, but a few made ramshackle shelters from branches chopped in the forest up on the overlooking hillslopes.

Cassia felt bewildered as she crossed into the shade of an improvised awning, having had the unenviable task of picking her way through the burgeoning settlement. 'I am here to see the Wise One,' she said, relieved to finally locate this place. The awning, like so many others, stretched like a great sail between three bare trunks on one of the raised islets near the valley base. *Wise One*. The moniker, uttered in her awkward rendition of the common tongue, still seemed incongruous to her ear. If her father had been here now, he would brand her for a true barbarian. *Druida, child! Druida.* She smiled inwardly for him. How she missed his voice, his love.

The space, one of many in this quarter of the vast encampment, was cluttered with benches holding jars and potions, not far removed from the fare contained in Gwidion's cart, though vastly better organised. There was a central cauldron, and a row of pelts for patients to lie upon, though only one was currently occupied. *That will soon change*, she thought grimly.

'We have several here,' sniffed a tall, jug-eared man, peering down at her over a long, hooked nose. Despite grime-clogged nails, he made a show of smoothing imagined wrinkles from the front of his voluminous robe. 'All trained at Mona, as the law prescribes.'

'Forgive me,' she said. 'I seek Moranna.'

The thin lips made a disapproving downturn. 'Of the Silver?'

'I do not know of any other Wise of that name,' Cassia said patiently.

The druid gave a fleeting half-smile that reached nowhere near his eyes. 'Wait here,' he said primly, clicking his fingers to summon an orderly. After a spew of hushed commands, he gave Cassia another artificial smile, announcing, she supposed, the completion of the great favour, and swept importantly across the shaded space, appearing almost to glide, his feet covered by the hem of the flowing robe.

She watched as he reached one of his benches, upon which was a variety of herbs, roots and flowers, in various stages of sorting, drying and slicing, each selected for their potent healing properties. The man muttered some kind of incantation as he assembled what he needed, whispering a private oath as he inadvertently gathered up the detritus with cavernous sleeves that were woven with intricate knots and circles.

She was working hard to stifle a laugh when a woman padded, barefoot, into the dappled sunlight that filtered through the awning's tiny holes. She was in her fifties, Cassia reckoned, her frail frame draped with a cloak of many colours, denoting an exulted rank. Her neck was laden with a heavy lace of wooden dowls, and her ears were woven all the way up the sides with delicate thread that glistened like the surrounding pools.

'Daughter of Rome,' said Moranna of the Silver.

Cassia bowed low. 'Lady.'

'You are well?'

Cassia glanced at the male Wise One, who had taken his collection of ingredients to the copper cauldron that was suspended over a pile of twigs and flammable hoof fungus. 'I am an irritant, it seems.'

Moranna's pale eyes narrowed as she smiled, her snub nose wrinkling. 'He would like you to know how busy he is. And how your intrusion curtails the great work of the Wise.'

'He made that quite clear.'

Moranna watched her colleague as he crouched before the vessel. 'Do not take it to heart,' she said, in her curiously off-kilter cadence, slow and lilting, as if the words themselves were coming down through the canopy, riding the sunbeams. 'He means well. Come.' She had slipped an arm around Cassia's shoulders, ushering her to a quiet corner of her new domain.

Cassia went willingly. She caught the scent of honey and lavender coming from the druidess's silver hair, the long tresses woven with charms and feathers. 'Have you received word?'

They stopped, out of earshot, though they watched Moranna's subordinate as he worked to kindle the fire. The druidess shook her head. 'Cullen will return to us. Taranis protects him. And we will need him soon. The reds come in earnest.'

'How does the king know they will cross here?'

'They will not wish to traverse the great forests, for danger lurks within. Thus, they must take the road over the high pastures, which leads them to this place.' She was close now, so that Cassia could see the pits of long-faded pockmarks on her cheeks. Some had been marked out with permanent dye, as if she wanted to acknowledge the blight for all time. 'And here is where the river is shallowest.'

'The bridge will be destroyed, no?'

'It will. But there are places where a man might wade.' The older woman smiled kindly. 'But you fret for more than just the coming storm.' She glanced sideways at Cassia. 'Or is it the storm itself? You dwell on your bloodline. On betrayal, perhaps?'

The shrewd question was keener than Cassia would admit, though she shook her head. 'Critheanach. Lady Aoife offered to ask after her.'

The priggish druid, squatting attentively before the dented cauldron, had expertly kindled a small, crackling flame that danced gradually to life, casting a warm, golden glow over the pots and pestles awaiting his ministrations. With an air of reverence, he began sprinkling the ingredients into the gaping pot, his hands moving in deliberate, rhythmic swirls. He murmured softly as he worked, strange phrases that Cassia struggled to follow, though it was evident that he extolled the energies of the river and the marsh, infusing the brewing mixture with whatever power he brought forth. The cauldron emitted a gentle eddy of steam. The man was incanting again, his gaze firmly fixed on the vessel, reading the subtle shifts and transformations of the fragrant vapours as they rose and mingled.

'I am afraid Aoife is away,' Moranna said gently, 'upriver. She will lead the charioteers, when the time comes. But do not be too disheartened. I have other news.'

Cassia followed the older woman across a bridge of boards, black filth oozing between each slat, and onto an adjacent hump of dry ground. From here she had a good vantage over the nearest streams and the little islands they created. She quickly realised that Moranna had staked a claim to significantly more territory than she had first assumed. If the covered space was the epicentre of the Wise One's operation, then the rises crammed with piles of blankets, cartloads of vials and jars, leagues of balled thread, stacked pelts, and containers of every potion, balm and unguent Cassia could think of, were testament to the degree of Moranna's preparation. It was a small town within Togodubnos's melting pot of tribes.

Moranna was observing a nearby islet that was crammed with simple beds. 'Most are empty for now, gods keep them that way.' She glanced skyward, regarding the wisps of cloud. 'Taranis keep his temper too. We had no time to construct anything permanent, and we do not employ canvas as expertly as your people.'

That last went without saying, Cassia thought, as she recalled the vast, neat rows of tents that were the hallmark of a legion's marching encampment. 'You have news?' she prompted, impatience briefly outdoing respect.

Moranna beamed. 'Ah, yes.' Her gaze slid to a place beyond Cassia's shoulder.

'By the hairy balls of Lugos!' the man behind her exclaimed.

–

The horns blared.

It was Hilax and his riders. The instruments were fashioned from antlers, and his men blew hard, heralding their arrival, giving gusto to the attack. Perhaps they had caught wind of the auxiliary troop's presence, or perhaps they had returned to question Cullen, suspicion outgrowing deference in the time since the holloway. It hardly mattered now, Cullen thought, as he watched them intercept the approaching force. Watched them die.

Hilax was good. He led his men well, from the front, conspicuous in his bronze helm, the ornate running deer appearing to prance with the movement of the horse. His party came from the meadow to Cullen's right, hitting the long auxiliary line's extreme left flank, and Hilax met the first of the enemy riders himself, going low, skewering his opponent's mount with his long spear so that the rider crashed to earth in a melee of iron and hoof. The spear was lost, so he drew his broad sword and swirled it above his head in a great rallying cry to the rest.

The auxiliary troop appeared to shudder, a great ripple of shock running all the way along their line, and it seemed for a moment that they would cut and run. But they were disciplined, these strangers, and their own battle cries boomed across the din of whinny and metal, and instead of fracturing, their strung-out line began to tighten, the chinks of daylight between them vanishing in a series of tiny eclipses. Then they began to wheel. Subtly at first, as if by accident, but they reformed their line very deliberately on a single rider, who looked for all the world like an underworld beast, swathed as he was in a strangely patterned pelt. With that man at one end, they performed a perfect pivot, swinging about like a shutting gate, to envelop Hilax's disorderly mob.

Cullen knew immediately what was happening. Could read it in the bunching of Hilax's force, who were steadily realising that they were encountering a formidable foe. Hilax himself was prominent in the melee, hacking and chopping on all sides, his courage admirable, but any fool could see that his force had been overwhelmed and outmanoeuvred.

'He's taken a big bite,' Garn rumbled. 'It'll choke him.'

Cullen sheathed his blade and looked for Serwil. 'Get back up.'

'You cannot mean to run,' Serwil blurted.

'Up!' Cullen snarled, and the tone seemed to light a fire under the Wise One's rump, for he scrambled into the saddle without further argument. 'They are doomed,' Cullen said as he wrenched on the reins. 'If we go to their aid, we will all die. They have bought us time. We mock their deaths if we do not use it.'

—

The meandering funnels of smoking hearths climbed out of dense reed beds as they rounded a sharp bend in the river.

The fight was far behind, now. Only the song of death played out above the gull-shrieks, a distant nightmare, fading fast. What refused to fade was the guilt. It gnawed at Cullen as he dug his heels into Hog's heaving flanks. Pulsed like a fresh burn. His decision felt thick, cloying. A swamp in his mind that dragged on his wits so that his thoughts became cumbersome. He reached down for his saddlebag, putting fingers to the hard block of the whetstone, its solidity reassuring. He had done the right thing, he told himself. Even his inner voice seemed hesitant.

The village, strategically situated on a slightly elevated area beside the Vaga, was a mushroom-cluster of thatched rooftops, the buildings themselves partially obscured by a continuous fence of sharpened stakes and woven hazel, faced by a deep ditch, and broken only by a single gate. That entranceway, manned by spear-toting sentries, barred an earthen bridge that spanned the trench, but it was narrow and sheer-sided, a devil to attack and a dream to defend.

Andoc had taken the lead, and his cries were heeded by the heads that popped up from behind the palisade. The gate was manhandled open, and the riders clattered over the bridge and into the compound, the rearmost of them calling for the way to be barred with all haste, which was prescient indeed. Shouts of alarm rose up almost at the same moment, as lookouts sighted the auxiliary troop's approach.

'Catuvellauni,' Cullen said breathlessly when challenged by one of the sentries, 'bound for the king's meeting place.'

'Which king?'

'Togodubnos.'

The spearman threw his gaze over the perimeter. 'And them?'

'Reds.'

The sentry's drooping moustache fell even lower as he frowned. 'Don't look Roman.'

'Open the gate and see what happens.'

The sentry sucked his teeth, weighing his choices. Then he barked towards the men at the entrance. 'Keep them away, Yorn! Get the slingers up!'

—

Cullen learned later that the man called Yorn was a fisherman by day, a fact that mattered little as the horsemen bore down on the village gates. Yorn himself was a tall, sinewy man with a gentle stoop and arms that were slightly too long for his body. He also possessed an uncanny ability to sling a stone. As the sentry had demanded, Yorn gathered a dozen men at the palisade, each armed with a long, leather thong and a pouch of smooth river pebbles, and in moments their arms were whirling, a droning blur, their song like a disturbed wasp nest.

It was magnificent in its way.

Four deaths was all it took. Two horses and their riders. Necks turned to jelly, skulls dashed to shards. Most of the approaching cavalry wore helmets, and would be harder targets to unseat or injure, but the sudden, vicious hail of stones, so fast they whistled through the auxiliary line almost unseen, gave the attackers pause for thought. They pulled up, aborted the charge, peeled expertly away, regrouping in the outlying band of pasture, waist-height and fallow, that separated river valley from dark forest.

Cullen, having wheeled Hog about in the open centre of the village, was back up at the gate, spear and shield poised, girding himself for the onslaught. He could see the auxiliaries more clearly now. Mail shirts, throwing spears, big shields painted with some kind of large, pouncing cat. At their head was the leader he had identified earlier. A broad man, wearing red braca and tunic. He had long, golden hair beneath an ornate helm, atop which was the copper motif of a cat, similar to the image on the shields. The strange cloak was made of exotic animal skin. Gold, with black spots. Like the lynx that lurked in these very forests, but the pattern subtly different, and it was clearly all one piece. The creature from which it came had, in life, been much, much bigger.

Then the stones zinged their cruel paths amongst the riders, and their progress stalled, their smooth formation fracturing into ragged retreat, and Cullen was screaming with all the rest. Bellowing and cursing. Giving voice to defiance and challenge and relief, all at once. They were not warriors in any meaningful sense, these village folk, but, by all the gods, they could sling a stone so hard that it could shatter a man's bones like dry twigs. Even Romans knew when to retire with their brains intact.

Cullen turned Hog about, scanning the triumphal faces until he found the moustachioed sentry. 'The ford, where is it?'

CHAPTER NINE

'We came up with all the rest, though gods know we are next to useless.'

He was a curious sight, making heavy work of the gentle rise on a pair of blackthorn crutches, an ancient, cadaverous man walking gingerly in his wake.

'Becan!' Cassia rushed down the slope, almost knocking both over in her haste as she embraced them in turn. 'Drest! It is so good to see you!'

The old man, Drest, clinging to her for stability, offered a gummy grin. 'Apparently we are a hindrance!' He was a head taller than Cassia, and his rumpled brow gave him a quizzical countenance, though that was belied by the grisly chasms where his eye sockets had once been. 'It is disgraceful!'

Moranna tutted. 'You'd be safer inland.'

Drest's head turned sightlessly towards her voice. 'I was a great warrior in my day, lady.'

'Until the Eceni stole your sight,' the druidess chided.

Drest's withered, blue-veined hand reached up to the decades-healed sockets. 'Belinos bar those villains' journey to the next life.'

'I'd have to steer you at the reds myself,' Becan said.

'And you'd probably drop your sticks in the process,' Drest replied. 'You'd fall on your face and I'd trip over you.'

Becan snorted amusement. 'Useless as each other, did I not say?' He thrust his hips forward a little to accentuate the point, making himself swing between the crutches. Below his crotch there was nothing, the braca folded up and stitched. Born without legs, he had been captured by the Catuvellauni after an abortive raid by his native Silures. Still a child, taken in by Moranna, he was kept close by Cunobelin, part curio, part lucky charm, and raised at the high king's court. The fates transforming unfortunate birth to privileged adulthood.

He spoke to Cassia. 'I'd wager you've made yourself useful.'

'I assist Gwidion,' she said.

'A good man,' Becan said.

'Sage and honourable,' Drest added.

Cassia agreed, but could not disguise her own bemusement. 'But why are you here?' She glanced back at Moranna. 'You assist your mother?'

'Gods, no,' Becan retorted hotly, as if offence was very much taken. 'All that blood and vomit.'

'Then?'

He smiled warmly, round face beaming like sunlight through parting clouds, nut-brown eyes as bright as she remembered. 'We are visiting Dan.'

—

'I warn you, Cassia. He survived the fight, but—'

'But he did not survive,' Drest finished his friend's sentence, 'in the way the others survived.'

Dan was no longer a patient, for Moranna had told him he was free to go. That was why Becan and Drest had come. They would wave him off as he left the healing district of this vast, haphazard encampment. In theory, he could leave the river. Turn his back on the great horde and walk home, wherever that was. He had played his part. Togodubnos would not compel him to risk his life again. But they all knew that he would choose another path.

Cassia forced a smile when she saw him. Offered a shaky wave. He looked like something from her nightmares. The scar was still livid. His stitches, stretching in a wide, hideous smile across both cheeks, were dark criss-crosses on raised, puckered skin, remaining as a horrific reminder of the violence that had almost killed him. It had been only a few weeks since a Silures axe had cleaved straight through his mouth, mangling lips and teeth, leaving the lower half of his face a ghastly ruin and nearly severing his jaw completely. When last Cassia had seen him, his entire face had been wrapped tight in bandages that had turned brown with blood that seemed impossible to staunch. She had been certain he would not come through it.

Now, Dan bowed. He could not return her smile, but the corners of his eyes creased right enough. He held out a hand for her to take. Squeezed her fingers, letting her know he was not the monster she so clearly took him to be. She felt utterly wretched at how transparent she must have been.

'He is doing well,' Becan said as they watched his surrogate mother bustle away to advise one of her acolytes who was frowning with consternation at a brass disc, upon whose surface was engraved the eightfold season wheel. Dan made a chest thumping gesture in response. Becan grinned. 'He means to fight when the reds come.'

'Can you shoot a bow?' she asked.

Dan nodded emphatically, wiggling his fingers to show that he retained all necessary faculties.

'They've honoured him with a name,' said Becan. 'Can you believe it? A war-name!'

She said that she could certainly believe it. Dan had been on the mission to rescue Betha, an Eceni princess, from the great fortress of the Silures king, Lestinos. His skill with a bow made him a valued member of Ulla Jagged Cliff's nine – his hawks – a famed warband, which had succeeded in its quest, but been dismantled in the process. Ulla had died, Dan had been maimed. After the fight at Swamp River, Aoife the Dread had disbanded the group, feeling their experience better suited to different parts of her burgeoning army. Some had gone south with Cullen, others north to the main defensive line at the bridge. Dan had remained here, tended by Moranna and her people.

'And what estimable title now follows your birth name?'

Dan glanced at Becan. Becan said, 'Tongue-Torn.'

She spluttered, choking on her own laughter, impossible to hold it back. 'Why am I not surprised?' It was a serious business, the naming of warriors, not taken lightly. A man or woman could carry a shield for years, fight like a demon in countless battles, and yet not achieve a name. To fight was expected. Every child learned to ride to hounds, skewer a boar and accurately sling a stone. But to have a war-name bestowed, one's deeds required the earning of renown. The name and the fame were woven together, like the strands of a wattle fence or the fibres of a cloak. An unbreakable mesh. And yet, for all the heroism involved in its attaining, a name, she had learned, needed to be right. Needed to ring true. It spoke of the bearer's essence, as perceived by others, and, depending on one's friends, there would be no guarantee of reverence. She offered a deep bow. 'Dan Tongue-Torn,' she said. 'A hero of the Isle of the Mighty.'

He returned the bow, solemnly and with no hint of mirth. It meant everything to him, and she felt a surge of affection for her friend. It made her think of Cullen. Her eyes became hot suddenly, and she rubbed them clear with the heels of her hands, too quick and rough to be subtle.

Dan looked at Becan, who frowned. 'He'll return to us.'

'I ask Taranis daily,' she said.

'Good,' said Drest.

'In the meantime,' Becan said, 'Dan intends to go north, to the king's main force at the bridge. We'll go too. All of us.'

'All of us?'

He nodded. 'We four. We'll find Aoife.'

Drest's head bobbed. 'And then we shall find Critheanach.'

—

'Then we're cornered,' Andoc said morosely as he stared over the perimeter fence. The horsemen had regrouped, and now sat, waiting, watching, like a wolf pack at the den of a wounded animal.

The ford was not close. It was, so the villagers informed them, a reliable crossing point, established since the time before the Belgae peoples had crossed the Narrow Sea. A relatively shallow section of the Vaga had been identified, spanned by two parallel rows of large stones that formed a causeway that was hidden just below the water's surface. The snag, it transpired, was that it was located the better part of a league away from the village, east along the riverbank. A snip in peacetime. A toddler could find their way there. But pursued by vengeful Roman cavalry, it might as well have been back at Calleva.

'Boats,' Cullen suggested. He was talking to Nills, he of the drooping moustache. The village, much like many of the others they had encountered, was a shadow of its former self, the majority of folk having fled when news of the Roman advance reached them. Nills had been left in charge. Him and a score of fellow fishermen, able-bodied and ready to protect their homes. Cullen resisted the urge to tell him the gesture would be utterly futile if the full might of the enemy arrived.

They were as woodlice to a legionary's hobnailed shoe. 'You must have boats.'

'We shall not leave our home to ruin,' Nills warned. 'The river gives us everything. Our drink, our food, our transport. It gives life to our crops. It is the dwelling place of our gods.'

'It may yet prove the death of you,' Baglan muttered.

Cullen indicated Serwil, who was still mounted, glaring down at proceedings. 'Then give the boats to me. I must see that man safely to the king.'

Nills seemed unmoved by the reference to the Catuvellauni chief. He instead indicated the far side of the settlement, where there was no palisade or ditch, necessity negated by the swirling River Vaga. 'There,' he said as if it were obvious. 'Both sides.'

'Watch them,' Cullen addressed Nills's comrades, who milled confusedly at the fence, still unsure whether these new guests would prove more dangerous than the horsemen outside.

Nills, at least, gave a curt nod as he clambered up the smashed-chalk platform that nestled snugly against the inner face of the timber wall, there to poke his head gingerly above the wickedly sharp stakes. 'Still there.'

Cullen clambered back into the saddle and urged Hog into a dust-kicking hurry that had Serwil clinging on for dear life and hissing obscenities in his ear. The village was circular in layout, with round-houses positioned in clusters around the edge, surrounding a central path and a wide communal area that was conspicuous by its stone shrine and blackened firepit. Cullen thundered across the open space and onto the middleway, oblivious to the footfalls of many more running and riding in his wake. Homes whirred by. Hand carts and animal pens too, all a blur. Granary buildings, elevated beyond the reach of pests by stout stone stilts, and a number of workshops, presumably the haunts of blacksmiths, potters and weavers. There was a midden, wide and open, flyblown in the sun, and a larger hall that was doubtless intended for the elders, Wise Ones and their many feasts and ceremonies.

He came to the far side of the village, passing the last few buildings and beholding the aperture that, anywhere else, would have been filled by another section of substantial wall, supplemented by inner walkway and outer ditch. Here, though, the river took on the defensive role, keeping animals in and enemies out. He drew Hog to a halt. The sound of lapping water came to him before he saw it. The distant call of marsh and sea birds too. Then his eyes settled on the broad band of the glistening Vaga. The rush of its perpetual flow sounding like endless applause. He drew up short, just watching the weeds and branches race by. It truly was as folk had said. Wider and wilder than any river he had ever seen. Mightier than the Swamp River, on whose banks they had made their first, failed, stand. And suddenly he was overcome by a sense of defiance. The Romans had crossed before, despite the collapse of the main bridge. This time, they surely could not find a way. They would be forced to march all the way around, striving ever inland for forgiving shallows, continuously ambushed, and picked off in the swamps and forests.

'There.' Andoc, arriving alongside, was pointing down at the riverbank.

Cullen followed his outstretched finger. Sure enough, there were posts jutting from the marshy ground like rotten teeth, darkly mossed ropes extending from them into the dense bullrushes. Beyond those tall stalks, in the river proper, a couple of small, circular coracles swayed gently, pulling taut at their tethers. They would not be enough to bring everyone across, but, on the far side of the water, Cullen was gratified to observe another group of coracles, interspersed with more substantial, plank-built fishing boats. 'They'll do,' he said. He looked around, facing the rest of his warband. 'We'll get across on those boats, bring the rest back.'

Kenal looked at him hesitantly. 'Can we not make a run for the ford?'

'They'll give chase,' Maeveen said.

Kenal shrugged. 'We'll outrun them.'

'And then what?' Cullen asked. 'If they catch us, we're dead, and the stone is lost. If we make it clear, they'll discover the ford, and they'll return, squealing, to their masters. The reds can be stopped at the Vaga, but only if they are forced to cross at a place of our choosing.'

'Or forced to swim it,' Maeveen added.

Andoc peered downriver, grimacing. 'I fear the latter won't prove as difficult as we hope.'

In the end, the presence of the boats proved little more than a cruel taunt.

There were at least a dozen, tethered in a neat row, harried by the stiff current and tugging taut their moorings. On the far side, beyond the little vessels and dense reed beds, the immediate landscape was low lying, given over to crops of barley and wheat, rising to hills in the distance. The sun beat down, bathing the scene in gorgeous gold, and, on a different day, Cullen knew that he would have been content merely to lay his eyes on such a vista. Except that there were men in the river. Somehow, astonishingly – incomprehensibly – six members of the enemy warband had entered the swirling, lethal waters, wearing full kit, and were making steady progress to the far bank, drifting behind their swimming mounts, reins linking them like the mooring ropes of the coracles.

Cullen knew he should say something. Knew he should bark some kind of instruction. Show leadership in this moment of horror. Nothing came to his mind, no words formed on his lips. He stared, silent, jaw lolling, along with everyone else, as the swimmers reached the west bank and clambered out of the rush-clogged shallows, stumbling and cursing but never faltering. Two men mounted their steeds and coaxed them through the marshy foreshore, scouting for danger, while two more took the reins of the rest of the horses and watched the final pair of sodden warriors wade to the line of boats.

What ensued was not obvious, for Cullen's view was limited by vegetation and distance, but the men were crouched over, elbows working, and he could guess what they were about.

'They're gone,' one of the villagers said at his back. Yorn or Nills, it hardly mattered. 'By all the gods, old and new. The boats are gone. We are trapped.'

And so they were. Rats in a barrel. Cullen turned to stare at them. Many more had joined, running the length of the settlement in the wake of his thundering nine. Desolation settled like lead weights, in his mind, on his heart, deep down in his stomach. This had been a vibrant, resilient community once. Fed, watered and made prosperous by the great river. And, though many of the very eldest had left, along with many of the fighting men, a substantial number had stayed, the small fleet of boats their lifeline in the event of a legion's arrival. Now they watched as that lifeline drifted, bobbing and turning, downriver, ropes brutally severed by the blades of strangers.

'Now what?' Maeveen spoke into the heavy silence.

'Now we shall be starved to death or slaughtered like cattle,' Serwil said. He coughed up a wad of phlegm, spitting with exaggerated vigour, as if the disgust were not clear on his every syllable. He nudged Cullen in the back. 'Thanks to this spineless, brainless whelp.'

'They can swim, Wolf Scourge,' Garn grunted, pausing to kiss one of the badger teeth that hung about his huge neck. 'In full kit. I've never seen the like.'

'They can swim,' Cullen said slowly, eking out each word as it came, for his mind was frantically working, 'but not the reds.' He looked across at Garn. At all the others in turn. 'A legionary cannot cross the Vaga. Not without a vessel, a bridge or a ford.'

Andoc's sour gaze moved to the man sitting, ungraciously as ever, behind Cullen. 'What about him?'

'He is alive whilst here.'

'Maybe they'll grow bored,' Baglan suggested, 'scurry back to their masters.'

Garn fingered the badger teeth again. 'Maybe it is *him* they want.' He grinned suddenly, a wolfish, esurient gesture that almost made Cullen shudder. 'Perhaps we should toss him over the ditch.'

'You would not—' Serwil began a shrill protest.

Cullen concluded the burgeoning spat by wrenching Hog about hard. 'We need to defend this place first!' The horse whinnied in protest, but launched into a gallop, Serwil howling like shee on a winter gale. Cullen ignored him, raking his heels along Hog's flanks. Because frantic shouts were coming from the other side of the village.

—

Another attack. The strangers had split their force, unwilling to commit their full numbers to the effort, but a good score had come.

They knew better, now, than to bunch together. Whereas before they had offered a ripe, unmissable target for the slingers, this time they left gaps of thirty or more paces between each horse. The strangers, crouching behind the painted cats that pounced across their raised shields, had come at a swift lick, reaching the wattle fence before the alarm could be fully raised. Now their steeds, some of which were adorned with pale skulls, skittered along the outer edge of the narrow ditch. The foreigners thrust down with their long spears, stabbing the vicious points at any sentry bold enough to show himself. They were testing the defenders, Cullen thought. Probing the perimeter and, more crucially, the resolve of the folk within.

Cullen and most of his band had returned to the main gate, though he left Kenal at the river-breach to oversee a gang of villagers tasked with its protection.

'They'll try to jump it,' he said to no one in particular, thinking aloud as he gauged the gravest threat.

'They'll not cross,' Serwil muttered as he slid down from the saddle, getting himself out of the way so that Cullen might wield a weapon. 'It is too far.'

'The ditch is not wide enough,' Cullen said. 'It was meant to discourage. Keep out wolves and thieves. These are no mere brigands.'

Even as he spoke the words, one of the auxiliaries, finding little success from beyond the fence, hurled his spear to no effect and wheeled rapidly about, retreating briefly, gathering his mount for a charge. He screamed something in his own, strange tongue.

Cullen urged Hog towards the inner face of the palisade. He inhaled briskly, bracing behind his shield, letting the reins drop to control the horse with his knees. For a heartbeat, there was nothing, the timber and wattle screening his enemy entirely. A vanishing act, like some market-entertainer's sleight of hand.

A bay horse's wild-eyed face erupted above the sharpened spikes, ears pricked, muzzle slavering, teeth bared. The beast sailed over the fence, a flying dragon of old, and upon it was a rider in mail shirt, with flaxen hair and moustaches, his own lips pared back in a macabre grin. The animal landed just before Cullen, their mounts coming together, the human heads dangling from the other horse rattling chaotically, and both recoiled from the collision, snorting and whinnying. The auxiliary screamed again, drew a long blade and levelled the point at Cullen's neck.

Cullen threw his spear. It slammed into the bay's chest with a wet smack, dangling there, snagged by muscle and sinew, the shaft jutting awkwardly. The creature screamed, reared, righted itself as its rider snarled for obedience. Lightning-Strike came free with a chime, Hog skittered in, closing the distance, Cullen spitting oaths of his own. The auxiliary twisted back and forth in his saddle, adjusting his stance amid the horse's erratic movements. He had his shield up, fighting desperately to keep it between him and his red-haired opponent, all the while lining up his sword for when the attack came.

Cullen snatched up the reins with his shield hand, compelling Hog to step left, then wrenched him savagely to the right, dropping the leather strap as he did so. The auxiliary swung wildly at him. He took the blow on the shield, punched the heavy boss into the foreigner's face, and hued with his own sword in a vicious upward slash that took most of the man's face off.

The limbs went immediately slack. The body toppled, as if emptied of bones. Cullen guided Hog with his thighs, his eyes raking the fence, seeking the next. He heard himself howl as a crash of battle-lust filled his veins, shoving fear roughly, mercilessly aside.

'Atrebates!' he screamed. 'Atrebates!' Though, as the only member of that tribe present, he knew it was hardly an inspirational rallying cry. Still, it came, the name of his subdued nation, again and again, and it gave him an inner will, the same life-force he had felt at Swamp River, at the Silures fortress, and at Avalloc's Shelter before that.

At the gate, a half-dozen dismounted auxiliaries were fighting on foot, holding shields over their heads against the sling stones and careening over the earthen bridge. Yorn and Nills were directing their reluctant fishermen-warriors to that scrap, beating back at the bobbing heads with their spears. Garn was there too, standing on the chalk platform, thumping at the raised shields with his metal-embossed fist, smashing the boards to kindling.

The others were at different points along the perimeter, in the saddle or on the ground, engaging knots of attackers alongside parties of spear-wielding locals who looked to the seasoned warriors for guidance. Everywhere was pandemonium, violence.

A second rider leapt the barrier, landing in a welter of hooves and snorts on the inner side of the earthwork. Maeveen steered her horse to Cullen's side and they engaged the enemy together. They parted, she went wide, trying to flank the rider, while Cullen sent Hog straight at him, belting the horse in the face with his shield. The beast shied away, but its rider was unmoved, his battle-cry a scorn-laden laugh, and he echoed Cullen's move, battering Hog with his own shield, and then the horses were alongside, their riders knee-to-knee. There was a clang as the blades deflected one another. The enemy was stronger than Cullen, and the force of the blow sent a shock wave down the length of his arm, Lightning-Strike falling from deadened fingers, and the big shield came round, smeared with Hog's blood, to break every bone in his face. Cullen managed to sway back, mostly out of range, though the shield's edge bounced off his temple, opening up the tight scab that ran from the top of his head down to his ear. He felt the freshly healing skin tear. Blood sprung, warm and slick, to cascade down the side of his face. He was part blind now, with only the shield blocking his route to the next life, but then Maeveen arrived on the rider's off side, and she stuck him low with her spear, twisting as she went, grinding the razor-sharp point into his guts. He brayed like a gelded ox, dropping his weapons to grope at his abdomen. Cullen had taken the dagger from his belt and now he jammed it hard into the man's thigh, right through the padded braca and the sucking flesh, until it scraped on bone. He yanked it free immediately, leaning precariously across the other man's saddle so that he could smell his fetid breath, and he punched the slim blade directly upwards, taking the stricken man under the chin. The light left his enemy's eyes as he fell back.

Cullen turned a tight circle, scanning the boundary. Near the gate, where attempts had been made to clamber the defences, only to be immediately thwarted, one auxiliary had died, as had two of the villagers, but the assault had, finally, ebbed. Cullen straightened in the saddle, craning to see out to the clearing beyond the narrow bridge. There he was, some fifty paces short of the ditch, the man with the flaxen hair and the strange gold and black cloak, simply sitting and watching, calm and impassive. The man was thickset and powerful, though he had poise in the saddle as though very much at ease. His eyes met Cullen's and he cocked his head slightly, as if gauging his foe, then he touched a finger to his brow, acknowledging the blood spilt on their mutual behalf.

Cullen threw himself to earth, collected his sword and sent it rasping back into its scabbard. He thanked Maeveen, checked his shield for damage and then stroked Hog's bloodied muzzle. To his relief, the beast nickered contentedly at his touch, his injuries apparently minor.

'You're bleeding,' Maeveen said. 'The old wound has reopened.' She was still holding her sword, and she used it to indicate the dead horseman whose jaw Cullen had mangled. 'Take his lid.'

He did as she suggested, pulling free his victim's helmet, which was of a simple pot design, its cheek pieces engraved with swirls. He buffed it briefly on his braca, cleaning away the gelatinous gore shreds, and propped it on one of Hog's saddle horns.

A gentle breeze frittered in from the valley. It seemed to carry away the sounds of violence that had echoed from building to building just moments before. An eerie quiet settled, like a layer of fresh snow. Cullen stood by his horse and regarded the settlement, splashed now with bloodstains, hoof-marks and debris. A broken spear here, a scattering of sling pebbles there. A blanched skull, cut from its saddle string, staring sightlessly from beneath the palisade. One of the villagers mewed softly near the gate, curling miserably over freshly spilled guts.

The guilty disbelief whispered to him then. A voice, not his own, and yet very much of him. The imposter he knew himself to be. *You did that, Cullen Goatherd. He'll die because of you.* He may not have been directly responsible, but the guilt was so sharp, so painful, that he might as well have stuck the blade home himself.

'We must set a watch,' Maeveen said. Her voice, up high from the saddle, seemed disembodied, as though it were another of his inner tormentors, and he blanked it out, blinking, his eyes shuttering the world. 'Wolf Scourge,' she pressed, more urgently this time. 'They'll come again.'

'Yes,' he said, not quite understanding, but then, as his senses began to sharpen, 'Yes, we must. Summon the village leaders.'

—

Until news of the Roman advance had reached the village, it had been governed by a minor chief and council of elders. As was the way in such places, a hierarchy of families owned the largest homes and majority of land and livestock, while access to the river and its teeming life was shared by all, overseen by that same council. Now, as with the near-empty dun at Smith's Ring, only a shadow of the former community remained. Mostly men, and a handful of women and boys of fighting age. Nills and Yorn, senior amongst the remnant, stationed spears at the palisade's break, guarding against a river-borne incursion, while more armed men patrolled the rest of the perimeter from the vantage of the chalk glacis on the fence's inner face.

'They have enough to try again,' Cullen said, as they gathered in the largest roundhouse, flames bright at its heart. He took a long swig of weak but passable ale from an earthenware pot, wiping his mouth on his sleeve, before passing it on. 'More than enough.'

'We killed a brace,' Garn said as he stuffed his mouth with smoked eel. It was a matter of great fortune that the locals had possessed enough foresight to keep their stores well stocked. 'They'll likely lose their nerve. Why keep coming? Why risk more death?'

Murmurs of agreement rose into the smoky thatch. Two dozen bodies made the gloomy interior fuggy and acrid, but they had gathered here, Cullen's party and the local elders, to decide what must happen next. Most were eating as they debated, and some were treating their battle-dented weapons with flax oil brought up with the provisions. The mood was grim, for they knew the brief, savage bloodletting might not prove exceptional. But still there was hope.

'We are humble river folk,' Nills said. 'We have nothing they might want.'

'Aye,' nodded another. 'If their masters are advancing on the bridge downriver, they'll be going there, like as not.'

'Who are they?' Yorn asked Cullen. '*What* are they, if not Roman?'

'Tribes from across the Narrow Sea.'

'Do they not rail against the legions as we do?'

An image came into Cullen's mind then. Cassia, reunited with him at Swamp River, having come from the presence of Berikos himself. The old king of the Atrebates – Cullen's own chief – had made a deal with General Plautius. Before Cassia had killed him, she had discovered the tribes Berikos had coaxed, threatened and seduced into alliances with the empire. 'Not all of our people would resist.'

Yorn frowned in the smoke-murk. 'But surely—'

Cullen picked up a small whetstone, setting it to his slender skinning knife's cutting edge. It put his mind to the larger stone in Hog's saddlebag, which, in turn, made him grateful that Serwil was busy in another hut, tending to the gutted villager, who, even now, would be wailing and thrashing in his death throes. 'Chieftains want power. Rome offers them that in abundance.'

'If,' Garn grumbled, 'they bend the knee.'

'If they bend the knee,' Cullen agreed. 'In faraway lands, those alliances are many. Some, generations old.'

'We faced Gauls at Swamp River,' Rues said.

'They seemed more like our own people,' said Andoc, staring glassily into the flames, reliving those horrors in his mind's eye, 'than the legionaries whose banners they carried.'

Cullen waved his knife at the open doorway. 'These riders serve Rome, that is all that matters. They are our enemies.'

'Perhaps we might reason with them,' Nills said hopefully. 'They may share the same gods.'

As if in reply, a low horn sounded outside. A shout from the palisade, of summons rather than alarm. They stood as one, gathering weapons, whispering prayers.

Cullen put away the skinning knife. 'Let us find out.'

—

The cavalrymen had drawn up some fifty paces short of the village. A long line, shoulder to shoulder, adjusted to a curving crescent. Curious creatures, all. They looked, for all the world, like Eceni or Trinovantes, with their long hair and moustaches, their pelts and their votive skulls, yet much of their weaponry, their armour and their mounts' tack was very clearly of the Roman style. Too much of it, in fact, to leave any doubt as to the identity of their masters.

Within the defences, spears and slings were readied, the riverside watched and the gates bolstered by spare logs and the remains of a dismantled handcart.

Cullen, near the newly reinforced gateway, totted up their preparations, and knew that it was not much to speak of. He clambered up on Hog, improving his view over the spiked fence, and drew a deep breath. 'Who are you?'

A man in an expensive-looking mail corselet, red braca and tunic, and long animal pelt let his black horse sidle out of the line, shield and javelin slung from the saddle so that his hands were free. He was a big man, a decent target for the slingers, though it seemed not to bother him a jot as he lifted a palm in greeting. Gold winked from his fingers in the sunlight. 'Where is your father, boy?'

'Long dead.'

The big man canted his head, intrigued. 'You command here?'

'I do. I ask again, who are you?'

'I am Grimoald,' the man called out, speaking the common tongue, but heavily accented, 'the leopard of the Batacgwi.'

Cullen let Hog edge closer to the gate. 'And what is the Batacgwi?'

Grimoald laughed, as if in disbelief. 'Why, the mightiest people you will find on either side of the Narrow Sea.'

'Mightiest?' Cullen echoed, making clear his own incredulity. 'You are a conquered people, are you not?'

'We are a proud people,' Grimoald bit back, his tone tighter now, words clipped, as if he resisted a burgeoning annoyance. 'And I am here to accept your surrender or hasten your death. The choice is yours.'

'I choose neither!'

A slash of white split the man's dark-yellow beard as he grinned. 'You put up a good fight, lad. For that, I commend you.' He spread his arms, stretching languorously, and Cullen was put in mind of a great predator, like the huge cat that was his personal banner, to judge by the shields of his followers, and the sculpted figure on the helmet that he now removed. His hair fell, loose and shaggy, framing a broad, hard face that was marked by a deep scar from forehead to jaw. 'They say the Catuvellauni have the blood of warriors!'

'I am not of the Catuvellauni. I am Cullen, of the Atrebates.'

Grimoald offered a sardonic smirk. 'Then I commend the Atrebates for siring such as you. It pains me to end your life's path,' he leaned to the side, shunting his rump down a few inches so that his shoe could tap one of the dangling skulls, 'but I will keep your spirit with me, do not fear.'

'What do you want, slave?'

'I am no slave,' Grimoald said, voice becoming clipped again, and audibly dangerous. 'Careful, or your death will be slower than the others.'

'But I speak the truth. You claim to be of the Batacgwi, but your weapons and your banners are Roman. You are nothing more than armoured slaves.'

The black horse took a few steps closer to the fenced ditch, reacting to its master's evident irritation. 'We are not subservient, but allied.'

'Even grown men tell themselves tales when the truth is too painful,' Cullen called.

Grimoald forced a laugh. 'We pay no taxes, Briton! We have no Roman governor, but a magistrate, elected by our own people.'

'Elected by your nobles, who enjoy imperial favours in return for a bowed head and a bent knee.'

'You know nothing! The Batacgwi, a proud people, fight for Rome and receive power and wealth in return!' Grimoald reached for his belt, pulling free a long, broad knife. He came closer still, holding it up, to show that it was embossed with the badge of the wolf and twins. Rome's ultimate symbol. 'Such as this dagger, with which I will pare the skin from your flesh!'

From somewhere close, Garn muttered, 'Well you've poked the bear, that's for certain.'

'Ready the slings,' Cullen spoke, keeping his voice soft but urgent. He looked back over the fence. 'I ask again, Leopard of the Batacgwi! What do you want?'

'The treasure you hide within your thin walls,' Grimoald shouted back, returning the dagger to its sheath.

'I know of no treasure.'

'It is in the possession of one of your priests.' The Batacgwi shook his reins and the horse shifted a few paces closer. He affected a sneering rendition of a native accent. 'Your *Wise Ones*.'

'I know nothing of this Wise One,' Cullen replied, 'nor any treasure.'

'Witless maggot!' Grimoald snarled, his horse snorting as it turned a tight circle, reacting to his ire. 'Your lies will bring only death! I will come for you, Cullen of the Atrebates. Your warriors' heads will adorn my saddle!'

'And what of mine?'

Grimoald kicked the black steed forward. 'Yours will—'

'Loose!' Cullen yelled.

The slingers went to work, all along the chalk step their arms whirred in powerful circles, building momentum until they themselves were a blur against the wall of timber uprights, and then, one by one, they let the leather straps snap free. The pebbles, smoothed by the river and chosen for their optimal size and shape, sung as they crossed the ditch and the grassy terrain beyond, and Grimoald found himself cowering behind his stallion's neck, clinging to the mane, scrabbling with one desperate hand to unloop his shield, even as the stones careened on all sides.

Someone shrieked behind him. Cullen craned from atop his own horse to inspect the damage. One of Grimoald's men, further back, had been struck on the shoulder, plucked from the saddle to crash to earth in a welter of clanging iron and spraying blood.

Then it was over. The stones, in the main, had missed. Grimoald had taken a hit to the side of his grand helmet, the bronze or copper dented above his left ear, his beringed fingers probing to check for damage. But he had survived the lure, and he was already letting his impressively nonplussed mount take him back to the relative safety of the line.

Cullen swore viciously under his breath.

Grimoald slowed, made a half turn, bellowing, 'I will keep you alive, Cullen of the Atrebates! I will take your treasure and kill your druid! But you will live, without your balls! You will follow my horse at the end of a rope, staring every day into the empty eyes of your comrades' crow-picked skulls. You will watch as your people are conquered, crushed and enslaved! Until the legions have planted their eagles in every village this side of the Narrow Sea. Until my own men have satiated themselves on all the young, fresh girls Britannia can provide. We have been promised land. Good land. When your tribes are a distant memory, we will plough these fields and build new homes. And then – when you have seen our hearths lit and our crops sown – then will I allow you to step into the next life!' He yanked the helmet free, glancing down at the dent, then lifted it in mock salute. 'Yours will be the triple death, beloved of the gods! Drowned, strangled, dismembered. Your blood will fertilise my steading, and your body will be interred amongst my orchards, to ensure a bountiful harvest. That is your destiny, boy. Never doubt it!'

CHAPTER TEN

The night came and went. Cullen and his party assisted the locals in guarding the ditch and barricade. As the fledgling sun climbed over the eastern horizon, making molten gold of the Vaga, a proud cockerel heralded the new day. They buried the dead by the river, for the ground thereabouts was softer and easier to dig, and then they gathered around the central fire pit, Serwil leading them in solemn entreaties to the gods, begging for an unlikely intervention. All the while, back at the safety of the treeline, the Batacgwi brooded.

Cullen, wrapped against a chilly dawn breeze in the beaver-skin cloak that had once been his mother's, observed those waiting horsemen as they moved like wraiths in the branch-shadows. He could not ride out, for they would hunt him down, and he could not travel the river without boats. Would they come again? Leap the ditch and scale the fence, or simply starve him into submission?

'You've seen him, lord?'

Cullen looked down to see a youngster proffering a steaming bowl. He took it gratefully, breathing in the porridge of barley and rye. 'Seen?'

'The king of the Catuvellauni, lord. Togodubnos.'

'I've seen him. But he's king of all the tribes now, lad.'

'My grandmother said the Sun Hound was greedy as a winter wolf, and his sons are no better.'

'That's as may be,' Cullen said, 'but it's his arse on the throne of the Isle of the Mighty, or Emperor Claudius's. Which would you rather?'

'What's he like?'

'Togodubnos?' Cullen lifted the bowl and slurped down the hot porridge. 'Honourable.' He wiped his lips with a grubby sleeve. 'Fearsome when needed.'

A sudden movement behind the boy drew Cullen's eye. He felt himself start, realising with chagrin how frayed his nerves had become.

He forced a smile as he saw a bundle of iron-grey fur gamble into the space between them, one ear pricked sharp, the other as lolling as its tongue. The pup had disproportionately long legs and vastly oversized paws that foreshadowed the coming of a formidable dog.

'My war-hound,' the boy said proudly, scooping up the puppy and laughing as it licked his face enthusiastically. A black stripe split the uniform grey, clipping the side of the upright ear and extending all the way down its muzzle. 'I mean to train him.'

'He'll make a fine beast,' Cullen said, inspecting the puppy more closely, its fur already shaggy, the nascent growth of what would one day become a thick, coarse pelt. The hound stared back at him, almost challenging him to find fault, its polished-pebble eyes gleaming, tiny and black. 'Fine indeed. You wish to become a war-giver?'

The boy nodded eagerly. 'Like you, lord.'

A pang of guilt, settling in his stomach, tightening it. The voices, whispered but firm, taunting him. *Fraud, phony, deceiver.* He remembered Garn's words. The mask, put it on.

'What's your name?'

'Ludris, lord.'

'Well, Ludris. If you wish to become a warrior, you must first learn the ways of the spear and shield.'

Ludris seemed disappointed by that. 'When the riders come again, I'll kill one. I'll show Nills how useful I can be.'

'Do not be foolish, lad. Practise with blunted weapons, learn what must be learned. Do not fight men with sharp iron until you are ready.'

'That'll take too long, lord.'

'A quick fight will only bring you a quick death. Learn the war-giver's ways, Ludris. And memorise the three prongs of the noble triad, for they are the foundations on which a warrior's life is built.'

'To do no evil,' Ludris chirped with childlike self-importance, counting the prongs on his fingers, 'to honour the gods, and to practise bravery.'

Cullen ruffled his hair. 'You are well on the way. How many winters have you seen?'

The pup squirmed in Ludris's arms, and the lad put him down. 'Eleven, lord,' he answered, but he now appeared to be addressing Cullen's shield, which lay nearby.

Cullen grinned as he went to gather it up. 'Look, by all means.' He inspected its face, noting the scars left by the fight at Swamp River, overlaid now by those from Grimoald's attack. It had served him well in the main. The edging was becoming frayed, and some of the paint had flaked off in patches, but it would suffice for the time being. He indicated one of the quarters. 'The wheel of Taranis.'

'The thunder god,' Ludris said. 'I'd like to worship him, but we prefer Cernunnos here.'

Cullen ran through the remaining symbols. 'The king's snakes, the spirit horse of my tribe, and—'

'A magpie? Grandmother says they're evil.'

'Aye, it is often said. The white and the black together. It is seen by some as a way-marker for wickedness.'

'But not you?'

'The magpie has helped me.'

'How, lord?'

'You would not understand,' he said, though he knew it was a feeble response. 'The bird appeared at crucial moments in my life,' he began again, trying to offer something meaningful, and suspecting that he had failed.

'Have you seen one recently?'

'Yes,' Cullen lied.

'That's good. A good portent.' The puppy was sniffing at Ludris's ankles, keening softly. He fished a scrap of smoked eel from somewhere about his person and offered it to the impatient ball of fur. 'I'll have a shield like yours when I'm grown.'

'Practise, lad,' Cullen said.

'I will, lord. I want to fight the reds.'

'And a fearful enemy you will be. They'll run all the way back to Rome.'

'They won't run, lord, when my war-hound's finished with them!'

Cullen laughed. 'I believe the pair of you will be the fiercest foes the legions have ever faced.'

Ludris and the dog left, wrestling over a tattered scrap of rope as they slipped between two roundhouses.

Cullen felt his eyelids grow heavy, even as he watched them go. He wandered over to a vacant animal pen, its walls made of earthen sods, grass worming through soil, binding it like tree roots. Unclipping his belt so that he would be unencumbered by the scabbard, he leaned back against the wall, letting himself slide down until his rump hit dry turf. He had taken the whetstone from Hog's saddlebag, lest Serwil think to relieve him of it, and now he drew it from its place within the folds of his cloak, turning it in his fingers, considering the trouble it had created. A nondescript item, all told. Dull grey, with faint orange stripes, in any other scenario he might have walked over this stone a thousand times and never noticed it. He had been charged with its safekeeping, and he had succeeded, insofar as he was still alive and the stone was not lost, but they were trapped, the keeper of the sacred object detested him, and the power of its shrine at Smith's Ring a distant memory. In his hubris, he had hoped the Whetstone of Gobannos would be the making of him, the quest that put a hero's grandeur on his freshly earned battle-name. In reality, he knew, it would likely be the death of him, and, if Serwil had his way, the dissolution of any fame he had hitherto won. He slumped back, letting the stone sit heavy in his lap, shutting his eyes and pushing a hand wearily through his hair.

'What suffering may be wrought by unfettered ambition,' Serwil's plaintive voice scythed into his head. 'We are trapped like crabs in a net.'

Cullen opened his eyes wearily, looking up at the skinny silhouette. 'I was tasked with locating the grindstone and its protector.'

'Stealing one, and kidnapping the other.'

'Bringing both safely to the king. If you had stayed at Smith's Ring—'

'If I had stayed at Smith's Ring,' Serwil retorted, 'I would be preparing for Heuldro'r Haf, imbuing the stone with unimaginable power. What good is it to Togodubnos now? It is merely a hunk of rock.'

'These Batacgwi were almost certainly the riders seen at Smith's Ring.'

'That would be most convenient, would it not?'

'They are here because they want you and the stone.' Cullen clambered jadedly to his feet. 'They have tracked us. Where else can they have learned of our location?'

'Tell yourself whatever salves your conscience. We are all dead.'

'Here, take it.' He tossed Serwil the stone. 'Heuldro'r Haf comes quickly upon us.'

The Wise One laughed scornfully. 'You suppose I can work the ancient magic from this scanty place? Smith's Ring was the home of the stone, where the altar of Gobannos, the smith god, rises from the sacred garden, a conduit to the Sleeping Realm. I cannot simply find another such monument because it suits you.'

'It would suit us all,' Cullen said, 'if the people of this village could witness the rites performed by a venerable member of the Order of Mona. Can you not see the benefit of such a thing? I will ask Nills what features this valley may possess.'

'You suggest pretence?' Serwil spat, scandalised. 'You propose a fraudulent ceremony?'

'I propose you behave like the Wise, Lord Serwil. Give these people something to cleave to. Ask the gods to intercede, and, if we are still alive by the longest day, ask Gobannos to make an exception. Plead with him to put power in that stone.'

Serwil pulled a sour look, as if challenged to an impossible dare by a moon-touched fool. 'Why bother?'

'You said it yourself, Serwil of the Wise. We are all dead anyway. Perhaps Gobannos will reward our tenacity.'

—

Arthmael the Learned drew his cloak tighter. It was not a particularly cold morning, though it had begun with a bite on the breeze. Indeed, he reflected as sweat beaded on the end of his long nose, it was rapidly building into what would be another balmy summer's day. But his was not a cloak of warmth. Rather, one of obfuscation.

Of course, it was unthinkable that he should walk the vast encampment unrecognised. He had spent a lifetime modifying, adorning and etching his body with the symbols and teachings of the gods, in large part due to the pursuit of lasting recognition. It would be foolhardy in the extreme to hope now that a simple cowl would render him invisible. But a muddying of the waters would suffice. The fewer who saw him approach the apple glade, the better.

Naturally, there were warriors wherever he looked. It was, after all, the gathering of a multitude. But he squinted up at the banners as he strode. Deer and fish and wolf and bear and wyvern. Sun and stars, oak, ash and beech, fox, martin and wildcat. Enough to conceal any man for a short time. Especially one assumed to still be at Camulodunon.

He walked hurriedly on. Perhaps a hundred paces away, beyond groups of spearmen and slingers, he spied a run of gnarled-looking trees, and he thanked all the ancients for their guidance.

More banners. More fighters. Some eating, some dancing, some practising the ways of the sword, thrusting and parrying to the clanging song of iron.

There it was. A pole, jammed into the ground, just as he had been informed. Atop that blackened shaft, nailed in place, was a half-moon shape, cut from timber, and painted bright red.

'Blood Swill,' Arthmael muttered triumphantly. 'I have found you.'

'It was our chief's tomb.'

'On to the next,' Cullen said as he clambered up the inner chalk step, gripping the stakes of the palisade as he peered over the ditch. They were on a section of the earthwork close to where it terminated, flush against the river. The fence here overlooked a monument of some kind. An earthen mound that rose from the reedy bank some forty paces to the south. The feature was topped with a chamber made of standing stones with capstones forming the roof. A circle of timber posts surrounded it, each one carved with complex knot symbols, cleverly integrated with faces, half hidden from view. The posts, unlike the stones, looked fresh, the engravings sharp, the paint bright. 'When did he die?'

Nills's bushy moustache turned up at the corners. 'Oh, he is hale and hearty. It was to be his resting place, when the time came. He was overseeing the final touches when word reached us of the invasion. He led our families west, across the river.'

Leaving you to die, like as not, Cullen thought. But, he reflected, these folk had no concept of what was to come. Like Coel at Smith's Ring, they believed the gods would make things right. Believed they needed to stay to watch over their homes, as if brigands and thieves were the biggest threat. He supposed he could hardly blame them. If he had not witnessed Swamp River with his own eyes, he would not have comprehended the impending tribulation either. At least, he supposed, the most vulnerable had gone into the hinterland.

What was left rendered the atmosphere strange in the extreme, for the age-old sounds of children playing, pigs rooting and cattle lowing were conspicuous by their absence. Still, there were hints of the familiar, despite the lack of people and, of course, the menacing presence of the Batacgwi in the far-off treeline. The valley breeze carried with it the tantalising aroma of freshly caught fish, baking bread and the faint hint of wood smoke. And those that were left behind maintained their routines as best they could. Folk laughed and sang, they mended garments and daubed walls. They paid homage to the gods, leaving tokens of esteem at the small shrine near the ceremonial firepit, where rituals would later be performed to honour the forest deities and water spirits.

'The mound is very ancient,' Nills was saying. 'There is an entrance by the capstones. We maintain access to curate the bones of our ancestors. Our chief will be interred upon his death, and the ring of posts burned to ash. If he returns.'

'Your people will return when we have driven the reds back into the sea,' Cullen offered, trying his best to sound encouraging.

'I beg Cernunnos daily for such a victory,' Nills said. 'The river needs fishing, the crops and forests tending. Life must persist or nature will take back the land.'

Cullen gazed across the water, at the hills and woods. 'It is a beautiful place,' he said truthfully. It had been idyllic, to be certain. The proximity to the river made food abundant, while the surrounding forests and meadows provided game for hunting, timber for building and all manner of flora and fauna for the Wise Ones and their work. The Vaga was a trade route too, bringing the wares of other tribes to this backwater village. Pottery, tools and textiles would all have passed through, making the local chiefs wealthy and the village prosperous.

'She provided everything,' Nills muttered, his tone wistful. His calloused hands gripped the palisade, and his eyes were suddenly glassy in his weathered face. 'Now, she has us ensnared.'

'I regret bringing these men to your homes,' Cullen said. 'You must understand, we were followed.'

'Will you give the cat-lord your whetstone?'

'It is not mine to give.' He regarded the monument again, the archaic repurposed by the new, and wondered if that was what the Romans would do to their hamlets and duns. Or would they simply burn them all to cinders and build afresh? 'Besides, Grimoald will not be satisfied with only the stone. He wants Serwil in order to work the magic. Would you hand him a member of the Wise?'

Nills twisted his whiskers between thumb and forefinger. 'Forsaken by the gods, we'd be.' He rubbed his rough hand over his eyes. 'I have spoken on this with Yorn. He intends to parley with the Batacgwi. Send an envoy.'

'His envoy will not return.'

'Perhaps it is our only recourse,' Nills said desolately.

—

Cassia and Dan helped their companions from the cart as the sunset flew a banner of blazing flame.

'She'll be down by the bridge,' Becan said as he braced himself on his crutches and let Drest take his elbow.

Cassia followed Becan's gaze. They were at the top of a gentle slope that had, until recently, been thick with vegetation. Now it was barren, like much of the valley, spear shafts the only forest. At the bottom of the incline was the main encampment of the great horde, set amongst the criss-crossing brooks, and, beyond that, the brown torrent of the river. She let her eyes wander a little way upstream to locate the bridge spanning the Vaga, the huge timber edifice over which she had trundled when first reaching the gathering place. A shoal of humanity congregated on both sides of the water. A vast, seemingly infinite sea of heads and weapons. Some folk sat on their cloaks, eating and chatting. Others practised their weapon-craft, while more still slept or danced or mended garments and kit. On a large, flat section, set away from the riverbank and clear of the treacherous streams, upwards of sixty horses grazed on the meagre stubble, while, in an adjacent plot, their associated chariots were being checked and painted for battle. 'How will we find her?'

Becan thrust out his sticks, setting off. 'Easy. She'll be at the centre.'

—

'Name?'

Cassia smiled sweetly at the spearman who had stepped into their path. In his left hand he carried a shield marked by the twin snakes of the Catuvellauni. These, she noted, were daubed in white, the personal sigil of Caratacos. It gave her cause to tread carefully. 'Cassia the healer. I must see Lady Aoife.'

Becan had been right. It had become apparent, as they descended the slope into the midst of the vast encampment, that the human shoal was shifting and eddying about a knot of figures near the river's edge. By the pace, they discerned banners amongst the throng, telltale signs that powerful nobility, if not the king himself, had congregated beside the bridge. Sure enough, on approaching a suitably grim gaggle of warriors, they had been duly accosted.

The guard was chewing like cattle at the cud as he eyed them suspiciously, apparently unsure whether his gaze was better employed on Cassia's chest or Dan's grotesque stitches. He spat a long stream of green spittle out the side of his mouth, the strong scent of mint carried on his words. 'Business?'

'Please let the lady know I am here,' Cassia pressed. She dropped her voice a touch. 'Moranna of the Silver sent me.' It was a risk, for the enmity between Moranna and Caratacos's inner circle was well known. The guard, however, seemed not to care, and she let out a long breath as he turned to plunge back into the crowd.

The four companions bided their time at the edge of the throng, attention drawn to a diminutive Wise One as she performed a protection ceremony over a group of Cantiaci warriors. She wore a squirrel-tail headdress and a cloak of stitched scraps of fur, and in her miniature hands she clutched a thin branch, which she stabbed repeatedly with a slender knife. She chanted and sang, the tones lilting and rhythmic, taking Cassia's mind far away.

A shock, then, when the deeper voice of another woman cut abruptly across her reverie. 'The elder tree releases its sap,' Aoife the Dread said, 'which is the blood of the land, of the ancients. Magic distilled.'

Cassia spun on her heels, the squirrel-tailed druid forgotten, and lurched into a scrappy bow. Becan, to her left, almost fell off his crutches as Drest babbled incoherent surprise.

'But you know that, of course,' Aoife went on, smiling. Behind her, shield-bearers moved into a crescent, an ever-present barricade of leather and iron. 'You had a teacher. Now you wish to know what I have learned of her fate.'

Cassia straightened. Her eyes raked up the boots, past the long sword at the war-giver's waist, the rich metals at her wrists and the woad snakes that twisted over sinew-knotted forearms. 'I would, lady.'

'Rumours only. The healing place at Swamp River was overrun by legionaries, as you rightly feared. Some scattered, made it back to our lines. Others were taken. Others still slain. I have no word as to which of these three fates befell Critheanach, but her body was not recovered.' Aoife glanced over her fur-trimmed shoulder. 'And, as you can see, preparations have been paramount of late. I have not had leave to press the search.'

'I understand, lady,' Cassia said.

'But?' Aoife said, as a gang of honey collectors trundled by, offering jars full of amber liquid to eager warriors.

'But where there is doubt there is hope.'

'Indeed.' Aoife pursed her lips, regarding Cassia keenly. 'Which is why I have a task for you, should you be willing.'

'Oh?'

'Scouts tell us the legions are on the move.' The tall battle-chieftess indicated the bridge, around whose thick oaken stanchions great ropes had been wound many times over. 'The king has commanded the crossing be destroyed. We'll fall back, hold our position on the far side of the river, and let the water do the rest.' She dropped her voice to a lynx-purr, soft but somehow laced with danger. 'I want you to remain.'

'Remain, lady?'

Shouts rang out. Aoife turned. At first Cassia looked into the east, half-expecting to see the banners of Rome emerge on the horizon, but her hammering heart settled as she understood that the ripple of news was uncontaminated by fear.

One of Aoife's guards muttered rapidly in her ear. She replied in the affirmative, then, to Cassia, said, 'I need eyes and ears in the enemy camp. *You* harbour hope that your friend somehow survives. Does she speak their foul language?'

'She manages,' Cassia said, and, despite it all, felt the twinge of amusement play at her mouth, as memory of Critheanach's hackneyed attempts to grasp certain Latin phrases tumbled into her mind.

The moment passed Aoife by, for she was regarding the arriving banners, eyes assessing, calculating, but she nodded. 'Then they'll have put her to work. You want to find her and make a hero of yourself into the bargain, or would you rather mix poultices for the rest of your days?'

'Lady, I—' Cassia began, bewilderment making it hard to pin down the words.

But the great woman was already moving away, harried by a small flock of chirping aides. She called back to Cassia, 'You'll excuse me. I'll send word by sundown.' And then she was striding back into the mass of bodies, most of whom were looking up at the western slope, on the crest of which, where sprawling forest began, a company of cavalry had emerged.

Cassia and her companions stayed put and stared. The horsemen numbered around a hundred, their standard-bearer hefting a tall pole that was capped with the bronze effigy of twin snakes, entwined.

'The king,' Becan breathed at Cassia's side.

The party came slowly down off the rise, walking double-file, solemnly receiving the respect paid by thousands of dropped gazes and lowered spear tips, all falling in unison like a sudden, silvery murmuration. The over-king's guards wore gleaming helms, winged and plumed, and long cloaks that trailed over their powerful mounts' rumps. It was an ostentatious and formidable display. Brightly painted shields, glittering chapes, hilts and belts and brooches. They drew up before the vast assembly. At their head, beside the banner of his tribe, Togodubnos surveyed the scene from atop a gorgeous, dappled-grey stallion.

The great horde began to move and pulse, then, like a flock of sparrows split by a falcon's dive, it parted as one. A heavily muscled and intricately woad-etched man, on foot, strode out to greet the king.

'Caratacos,' Becan murmured. Cassia almost told him his commentary was unneeded, but she realised, embarrassed, that he was relaying the events to the sightless Drest.

The war-giver, black hair falling like crow-feathers over shoulders clad in battle-iron, dipped at the waist in submission. The crowd seemed to hold a collective breath.

Togodubnos's broad, ruddy face split in a grin as he plucked free his eagle-winged helm, tossing it to an aide, and slid down to gather Caratacos in a bear-hug embrace. The king himself was a specimen indeed. Not as tall as his younger sibling, but certainly as powerfully set. His reddish, sweat-darkened hair was woven into many small plaits that spread like tentacles from the sides of his head, and his neck and wrists were heavy with gold. Togodubnos, the most powerful warlord of the Isle of the Mighty, and, therefore, king over all other kings, slapped the bigger man's back as though he were beating dust from a blanket. Caratacos rocked on his heels, wrapping his impressive wingspan about his older brother and lifting him clean off the ground. Togodubnos barely seemed to notice the obliterated conventions, for his laugh was loud as a red deer's roar, and it, in turn, was drowned to nothing by the cheers of the throng.

Cassia cheered too, for that was what was expected, and the rousing din was joined by the wails of carnyxes. The sound was jarring, out of kilter. A droning yowl overlaying the shouts of men and women, but somehow inconsistent with what she saw. Her eyes went to the companies of carnyx players she had identified amongst the massed nations, seeking a reason for the incongruity she felt. None of them were playing. They clutched those bronze tubes, elongated and serpent-like, the flared mouths shaped into mythic beasts, mid-roar. Held them close, cheered along with the rest, but brought not a one to their lips.

Even as understanding dawned, forming like a lump of ice in her guts, she was turning to stare up at the rising terrain to the east, pulling at Becan, at Dan, urging them to comprehend. Because it was not the wail of the Britons' carnyxes she could hear, but the call of Roman *cornu*.

CHAPTER ELEVEN

Serwil pleaded with the gods as the light slowly dimmed.

Nills, Yorn, Ludris and the rest — perhaps thirty in all — gathered at the communal pit, joined by those of Cullen's group that could be spared from the walls. There they formed a circle about the small shrine and cold hearth. The shrine itself was constructed of pale boulders, each carved with labyrinthine patterns representing the tree of life. Perched atop that low wall was a huge set of antlers, appended to the empty-eyed visage of a stag's skull. In previous times, they would have congregated here, young and old, to share stories, poetry and laughter. To celebrate a successful hunt or bountiful harvest, a joyful handfasting, a winter survived or a child born. Now it was a gathering of fear. A coming together that was tense with desperation.

For his part, Cullen was encouraged by the Wise One's intercession. He had not expected anything to come from their conversation, but, sure enough, Serwil had bustled grudgingly off to an old healer's hut, and located some herbs and various plants. There he had concocted a pungent infusion, which he ladled into small bowls to pass through the crowd. It was far too hot to drink, but he instructed them to breathe deeply of the steam, for its properties would aid tired eyes and weary minds, sharpening senses for what lay ahead. Then he incanted words known only to himself. Words of Mona. Of the Otherworld, the Dreaming Realm, all the while clamping his good eye shut, raking the group with the milky eye that saw beyond what could be seen.

When he returned to the plane of men, and to the common tongue, he had the gathering transfixed, and he glared at each person in turn as he implored the spirits of the land to give the people strength, and begged the river goddesses to imbue their lives with good fortune.

'We ask of the sprites in the reeds and the piskies in the woods,' the Wise One droned, his red-rimmed gaze wide and intense, 'that they play havoc with the invader. Disturb their sleep and poison their food. Make their mounts lame and their piss burn.' He pointed at the huge antlers, almost accusing in his vehemence. 'Cernunnos, the great one, who rules over all the elements of the wilderness. We are your sacred people. Bring us victory, by your unlimited power. Instil in us your—'

A cry of alarm. Solitary and pitched high, fading quickly. A barn owl? Serwil's entreaties died on his lips.

Folk looked up, cocked heads to listen. More cries, from different directions. Screams of pain. Murmured disquiet rippled through the congregation. Cullen, amongst them, turned without a second thought, already freeing his sword and running for the gate, for he knew what came with the encroaching dusk.

—

They were spectral against the background of shifting shadow and watery light. On foot this time, their mounts left to graze on the fallow pasture before the woods, they scrambled over the ditch and hauled themselves up the barrier of timber and wattle, attempting to manhandle their way over, swords jabbing at anything emerging on the other side.

Within the perimeter, the whirr of the slings was starting up, but how to pinpoint wraiths in the treacherous wolf-light? Cullen had his shield up, and he dodged one of those circling leather straps, and he could immediately see the dull shine of a helmet bob on the far side. He moved to that place, keeping low, pushing his shoulder against the latticed hazel branches, bracing for the man's arrival.

A face appeared above him, teeth bared, eyes wide and white. Cullen stabbed up hard, taking the man beneath the chin, the blade crunching deep, skin, tissue, teeth. Time slowed as the Batacgwi floundered and thrashed, a trout skewered at the end of a fishing spear, and Cullen had to jerk hard to wrench the iron free. Hot liquid gushed down the fence's inner face, drenching him from above. The man fell back, perhaps not dead but no longer a danger, and Cullen scanned the perimeter. Duels played out, as they had before. Somewhere a female voice screamed filthy curses. Maeveen, or one of the villagers? Close up, Garn's guttural growl reverberated in his ears. They were holding their own, which pleased him. And yet a warning chimed in his head, hazy but nagging. Something was amiss. It was all too easy.

More screams, distinct from the rest. Not a woman this time, but pitched high and querulous. A child? But there was no one left here younger than Ludris. He stood, improving his view, for there were no more attackers at his section of the wall. They had all been rebuffed.

Too easy.

The inconsistent scream again. One borne of fear and desperation rather than the battle yowl of a fight.

'The water!' someone else was shouting. 'Water!'

Events crystalised in Cullen's mind. The real attack had come from the riverbank.

—

'How can it be?' Clesek was bleating as they ran. 'It is dark now, dangerous, the current is too fast!'

Cullen rounded the final corner to see the two auxiliary riders, without horses this time, pacing backwards towards the black river. 'And yet here they are.'

The Batacgwi had come with weapons and armour. They glistened in the failing light, dripping from their swim, and they seemed to Cullen like denizens of the Otherworld. The ocean-borne Fomorii of ancient times, sent to do battle with the gods of air and land. There were two still standing. One had already been felled by Andoc, who had been watching over this section of the defences. He had taken a blow by the looks of the blood leaking down between the knuckles of his sword hand, but he was ready to re-enter the fray.

The curious screams again, and Cullen saw that Serwil had been taken. He shrieked like a shee on a hurricane, engulfed by terror. One of the Batacgwi, a head taller than the Wise One and half as wide again, had him clamped at the scruff of his neck, the big fist shaking him like a child's doll, lifting him bodily so that only the very tips of his toes scraped the ground. Serwil, to his credit, was trying to resist, thrashing with his spindly arms and throwing back his head, but all it did was give the impression of a seizure, as if crazed convulsions took hold. The Batacgwi grinned at his back, the waterlogged beard, shot through with metallic charms, glimmered as if sprinkled with silver-dust. He shook

Serwil a little harder, just to let him know the futility of that moment, and in his free hand appeared a long, curved dagger, that slid up to his victim's pale throat.

Cullen and the others moved in, realising that the Batacgwi meant to return the way they had come, dragging with them their shuddering prize. The second Batacgwi moved to block their path. He was shorter and more wiry than his comrade, but the long, blond hair was the same, and the beard was plaited with identical charms. Unlike his companion, he had somehow managed to bring a shield on his unlikely swim, and he brandished it now, braying a stream of what must have been curses in his own language. All the while they backed away. All the while Serwil pleaded with them, with the villagers, with the gods and with Cullen.

Andoc was furthest advanced. He went forth without demur, feinting one way, lunging the other, hueing in with his long sword and receiving a smart parry for his efforts. The Batacgwi's shield came round in a sweeping arc, the boss clattering the side of his head, and sending him reeling. Cullen tried to edge round him to get to Serwil, but the shield glided about to intercept.

From the sides, Kenal and Maeveen came on, engaging the shield-bearer. Maeveen spewed her own oaths, her spiked hair and wild eyes a thing of horrific beauty to Cullen. She was small and lithe, but her sweat-sheened muscles shifted along her back and shoulders as she twirled her blade and the Batacgwi would be a fool indeed if he considered her an easy victim. Evidently he possessed sense, for he shifted his stance, beckoning Kenal first, and the young warrior did not hesitate. He went low and fast, on the shield side, driving his shoulder into the gleaming boss, deliberately taking the hit to ram it aside. With his other arm he thrust forth with his sword, straight and hard like a lance, hoping to push it through the wiry Batacgwi's narrow chest, but his foe was quick, and his own sword took the strike, knocked it away, and his heavy pommel smashed Kenal in the nose, crumpling him forward. The Batacgwi bellowed his triumph, stamped Kenal flat, and stabbed him in the back of the neck. Kenal juddered, his splayed arms quivering like branches in a storm.

Maeveen hissed like a scalded cat, rotated like a Calan Gaeaf acrobat and was inside the Batacgwi's defence before he knew he had been bested, stabbing and clawing like a demented beast.

Cullen dragged his horrified eyes from Kenal's inert body and skirted that fight. He went straight for Serwil's captor, who was now at the water's murky edge. Unlike the rivers he had known, the Vaga was not passive at its weed-clogged fringes, but busy and swirling, and he had a vague image of himself diving into those hungry, merciless depths, drowning as he fought against the current.

The Batacgwi snarled at him. The big man's grin had vanished, but still he had the upper hand, for a human shield, though unwieldy, would be more effective than one of wood and rawhide. The retreating pair's feet squelched now, and Serwil shrieked again as he looked down at the encroaching water. The Batacgwi shook him, a hound with a leveret, and pressed the long dagger to the skinny white throat.

Serwil whimpered, invoking every deity that came to mind, major, minor and everything in between.

The water splashed as it rose higher up the legs of the Batacgwi and his unwilling bounty. Cullen vented a visceral howl of impotent rage. He considered diving at the legs, tripping them both, but they might still end up in the river, with Serwil's throat slit for good measure.

Then Andoc got up. He was still clearly dazed, for he staggered slowly and blinked fast, but he had his sword and his tall frame must have been an imposing sight in the Batacgwi's peripheral vision.

And the Batacgwi looked. Just briefly, his gaze strayed to the side, and Cullen knew it was his only opportunity. Reflexively, he hurled himself, no time for conscious thought. Serwil yelped, perhaps fearing he would be shoved into the rushing black waters, and only then did the startled Batacgwi note the danger, and he seemed to brace, the knife flinching at the Wise One's quivering neck. Cullen stayed high but left his blade low, then he dived, as if pulled by the length of iron, and he opened a gash in the Batacgwi's thigh as he fell, face first, in the stinking mire. The big man might have killed Serwil then and there. Might have drawn back that dagger and all but decapitated the terrified Wise One where he stood. But the arms, both arms, went instinctively to the gaping wound, and for that he had to release his captive, who hurled himself forward, sprawling in a sobbing heap.

Cullen was acutely aware that the second Batacgwi, if he had bested Maeveen, might well rush him from behind, so he rolled away, wrestling the filth that cloyed his limbs. He brought the sword up in a brutal hacking motion that clanged against the helm of the still-doubled

Batacgwi. The man might have been wounded or simply dazed, but it mattered little as he fell back into the shallows, for the Vaga locked its grasping claws about his armoured body and drew him out into the gathering gloom. Silent. Gone.

—

Cassia loitered where a wall of gorse met the river's shallows, and wondered what on earth she was doing. Aoife had sent word, as promised. A messenger had come, and that messenger had made granular what had been the chieftess's broad notion. Cassia had accepted the challenge with bluster she no longer felt. She had not considered the sheer terror that would assail her, or the stomach-twisting reality of waiting to be seen by enemy eyes. It felt like she was drowning, as if the spirits of the Vaga had reached out to claim her for their own. She swallowed hard, cursing herself. Not for cowardice, but because it was all too late. The deed was done, the sluice-gate opened.

Farewells had been said, and the horde had retired to the safety of the far bank, even as the imperial vanguard, unit by gleaming unit, banner by fluttering banner, had trickled off the high ground and down into the valley. She supposed their main camp would be set beyond the rise, a sprawl of canvas flowing back into the east, and tendrils of nausea wormed through her at the thought. That great, temporary city was the heart of the enemy; and the place she now sought to be. At Aoife's behest, but also for her own ends, for if Critheanach yet lived, it would be there, in that nest of enemies, that she would find word of her.

The thought – as she clutched her only possession, a little nettle-fibre bag containing small provisions and a tincture flask – engendered in her a deep, visceral fear that tied her innards in knots. Not least because this new task was taking her ever further from the one person who could temper that fear. Cullen of the Atrebates. Where was he? Did he even live? If she perished behind Roman lines, would he go to his own grave thinking she had betrayed him? Would Aoife bother to seek him out and make good her reputation?

The fear and the doubt and the ache of yearning seemed to unfasten the knots, sending them up her chest and gullet like writhing snakes. She swallowed hard, keeping a wellspring of bile at bay. At least she had the pin. She always had the pin. In the silent time, alone on the riverbank, as she waited and watched, she listened to the Vaga's rushing chatter and stared up at the clouds, and pictured him. The boy, fast becoming a man, who had been so shy when first they met, but whose life, whose very person, had been transformed by loss and fire and blood, and who she loved and longed for in ways beyond her understanding. She tried to imagine him now. Asked the gods, any who would listen, to keep him safe, and she touched the pin to her flesh, letting the pain assuage the ache. And as her mind reeled with the sensations, it wandered, out of this deep valley and into the past, where her father appeared, smiling wide, beckoning her, arms spread. She embraced him – her other self – tight as she could, rejoicing in his warmth, breathing his scent, a little girl, safe and content. And then they melted away, father and daughter, re-emerging on the deck of a ship, surrounded by rolling waves and foaming crests, and swells that stood tall as Rome's greatest buildings, looming, engulfing. Then she was turning, tumbling, and she relived the burn of saltwater in her throat, and she saw again the clawing, desperate fingers of her father as they slipped beneath the thrashing surface. And the sorrow assailed her, whipped her like the winds that had stirred up the Narrow Sea that fateful day, and she dug again with the tiny object, letting the pain pour oil on those torrid waters, the hurt in her forearm smothering the one in her heart. A stinging, raw counterweight, a sensation she loved as much as she hated, and could never live without. She was sobbing, remembering what was lost, her mind staggering, her soft skin striped and torn by her own hand, and then the Romans had begun to descend. They moved carefully, nervous of hidden traps, pits, or sudden ambush. But they came down the slope, fanning out, ever-spreading like ink spilled on parchment, until they filled this side of the valley, occupying the eastern bank of the Vaga as they occupied so many of the world's other places. She put away the pin, asked the gods for their protection, and braced for the moment when, like the adder, she would shed the skin she had worn these ten years and return to her own people. To her true self? She did not even know.

It took them long enough to find her. The terrain at the valley bottom was a treacherous scape of boggy lagoons and tangled scrub. Of mudflats baked and cracked by the sun, half-concealed by the dimming of the day. Gnarled hawthorns, with their rich red berries, harried always by little birds, vied for ascendency with the reed beds and their straggling, strangely amphibian trees, stems sprouting from root balls just above the water's black surface. The tentative scouts, backed up by expendable auxiliaries, picked their way with an abundance of caution, easing through the gorse which had been Cassia's private barricade. She saw them coming, crouched down – a trembling, weeping mess that was not entirely simulated – and let rough hands gather her up. And what had they found? A girl, terrified, dishevelled, with fresh wounds on her forearm, red, puffy eyes, and an expression racked with sorrow. Moreover, a girl who was markedly different from the people of the savage islands they had invaded. All it took was a mumble of hoarse, agitated Latin, and they were sold.

Cassia moaned as the soldiers hoisted her to her feet. She let the pain and the sadness wash through her limbs and torso as they guided her away from the river. Wept as they spoke soothingly, as they put drink to her lips, as they conveyed her back to their lines. She thought again of Cullen, as the distance grew between her and the Vaga. But she felt hope, too. For she was here to find Critheanach and, by all the gods, she intended to see it through. It would be success or death.

–

Adminios swatted a mosquito, its mangled carcass mingling with the thick black hair of his forearm. He smeared it away, as he gazed over the valley from high on the open plateau.

The *cornicines* had brayed their instructions across the marching column, giving the order to pitch camp on this wide expanse. They were effective tools, the cornu. Long, curled instruments, like giant metal snails, perched on the player's shoulder, they could belt out commands over a stupendous range. But they boasted no fearsome figureheads, sculpted from bronze, and their call was not laced with a good undercurrent of bone-chilling dread. No, he thought, give him a decent carnyx any day.

He tugged his fur cloak tighter, for there was a chill in the air now that it was getting dark. Not pitch; far from it. But the sun had melted into the western hills and a hoary half-light had settled over the valley. He mouthed a silent prayer to the gods and goddesses of war and victory as he regarded the scene. General Plautius had chosen this place from which to launch his main assault, for it overlooked a tight bend in the glistening Vaga, before the river straightened in both directions, cutting a deep vale that stretched both north and south. It was the bend that interested Plautius, for it represented the shallowest part of the river for miles, and, so Adminios had himself reported, was the site of the only permanent bridge. He had also warned that his brother, unless the great oaf's brains were addled, would have dismantled said bridge, and that act of swift and total destruction had indeed been executed the moment Roman scouts had emerged at the spot on which Adminios now stood.

He prayed again. For now they needed to find a way across. And over the river, where the marshy land stretched away into more wooded hills, the Britons were waiting. Their encampment was vast, expanding in all directions, as far as the eye could see. Tens of thousands. Spears, shields, horses, chariots. It was too dim and far to make out banners, of course, but Adminios was not too proud to admit that his brothers had achieved something not seen since the days of Julius Caesar and Cassivellaunus. A horde of all the tribes. A sprawling, uncountable massing of warriors from all the corners of this island that was the farthest extent of the world.

'Thank Jupiter they have gathered in one place,' Narcissus, coming to stand beside him, said smoothly, 'for we may now kill them all with one firm strike.' He adjusted a lock of oiled hair, a languid gesture that made Adminios want to headbutt him. 'Togodubnos has performed a service to us, though he does not know it.'

'Do not underestimate him,' Adminios said.

'On the contrary.' Narcissus clicked his pudgy fingers and, as if by some magic, the jewels on his fist began to twinkle and his neat teeth seemed to glow. 'It is he who underestimates us.'

Adminios realised new light had fallen across them, just as he saw the torch-bearer, a frightened mouse of a boy, bring up his flame.

'Feast your eyes,' Narcissus told the boy, wafting a hand in the general direction of the opposite riverbank, 'on the great horde of Britannia. You will see it is a rabble. Nothing more. They gather behind their river and hope that we shall simply march in and drown.' He stifled a yawn, as if the whole explanation was wearisome, his pupils dullards, and regarded the encampment at their backs. 'Take a look around you.'

Even though the imperial advisor was nominally addressing the torch-bearer, Adminios knew that this lecture was for his own ears. The knowledge infuriated him, yet he turned all the same, as if charmed by the silken voice of the man so accustomed to dripping honey into the ear of an emperor. He found himself staring across the tight tent rows, the lines marked by standards adorned with decorative roundels and depictions of various formidable creatures. A troop of cavalry thundered by, yellowish bronze armour gleaming, tinned edging bright like quicksilver in the new-lit campfires, warhorses as well-armoured as riders.

'This is no ordinary army,' Narcissus crooned. 'It is the greatest war-machine ever assembled, furthering the cause of the greatest empire the world has ever known. Now, come. Walk with me.'

Adminios did as he was told, and the trio strode between the exactingly pitched tents. He could still barely believe it. Mere weeks had passed since the coast of Gaul had teemed, the invasion fleet assembling day by day. Troops, horses, supplies, transports, armour, weaponry, wagons, livestock. It had all seemed a dream. Too good to be true. It still seemed like a dream.

After crossing Swamp River, he had advised Plautius to keep his advance to the northern portion of Cantiaci territory, not far from the coast. The general, mindful of the formidable barriers presented by the great rivers, Vaga and Tamesas, had considered swinging south, finding narrower, shallower places when the time came to cross. But Plautius had no notion of the forest that lay to the south and west. It was passable for the Britons, moving piecemeal as they did. Lone spearmen, nines or even bigger warbands. They could filter through, like sunlight through the layered canopy. But even Togodubnos's chariots would not traverse the dense and trepidatious tangle that would eventually ensnare them. Plautius would need to cut a broad swathe through the seemingly endless woodland if he was to get an entire legion through. Adminios did not doubt the Romans could do it. The more he knew them, the more he realised how capable they were. But, he had counselled, it would all take too long. While the Romans slashed and hacked in the summer heat, Togodubnos would send his warbands into those dark and twisted boughs, lurking like underworld denizens, picking legionaries off, one by one.

So it had to be the northern route, and now, as the sun sank and the stars began to prick the endless purple skies, they had come to the place of reckoning. The legions against the hordes.

Adminios and Narcissus followed the torch-bearer along one of the broad corridors demarcating the arrow-straight tent rows. Soldiers took their ease around flickering fires, ate from pots and sang songs of home. Knots of men laughed and jeered around games of dice, and the clack of wooden swords echoed from makeshift practice grounds. The heady aroma of cooking and woodsmoke lay like a blanket over everything.

'Will we attack at dawn?' Adminios asked.

'I think not,' Narcissus answered without looking round, his bejewelled hands clasped at his back as he paced. 'We have scouts abroad. Roving cavalry, wreaking havoc. Plautius would have them return before our advance.'

'Every day that passes allows—'

'Allows what?' Now the imperial advisor paused, smiling as if indulging a child's stupid question. 'Allows your brother to put another few stakes in the water? I assure you, it will not prove decisive.'

Adminios gritted his teeth as they continued, irritation rising like damp through his chest. 'More warriors will come.'

'He vastly outnumbers us already. When you face a hundred thousand, an additional thousand makes little difference.'

They passed a tent that was larger than most. Outside, a burly smith was working at a forge, its mouth glowing like a dragon's fiery maw. A little way behind the smithy, partially drowned out by the metallic clangs, a brawny standard-bearer could be glimpsed wielding a stick, his silhouette poised above the miscreant whose penance he mechanically meted out.

'Brawn,' Narcissus said, catching sight of the punishment detail. 'Oftentimes of great necessity. But not now, not for us. What will win the day will come from the brain, not the blade.'

'How will we cross without a bridge?'

'We have our ways, dear Adminios.'

'It is shallow enough to wade, but not when the skies are dark with spears and arrows.'

'You will see. And you will know that your decision was correct. Boy?' Narcissus called up to the torch-bearer, who stopped. The advisor indicated Adminios. 'This mighty Briton has joined us to regain no less than a throne. You are looking at the chief of the Cantiaci. Is that not a thrill?'

The lad nodded nervously. 'It is, lord.' His eyes, polished pebbles of jet in the flamelight, flickered from one great man to the other. 'I—'

'Go on, boy,' Narcissus encouraged. 'He does not bite.'

The eyes lingered on Adminios. The boy said, 'How do they fight, lord? Your people, I mean.'

'With ferocity,' Adminios said.

'But disorderly to a risible degree,' Narcissus added cheerfully. He chuckled, teeth glowing in the gloom. 'And fractious to a fault. They're as happy fighting each other as they are a common foe. So, worry not, lad.' He flapped that pudgy paw again, and they resumed their walk. Dropping his tone slightly, he said to Adminios, 'And we have invested a great deal of time and money in sowing division amongst the tribes.'

'Divide and conquer.' They were approaching the encampment's largest tent, its gilt-fringed apex rising above all else, the fat spider at the heart of a sprawling web.

'Quite,' Narcissus said, as hostile-faced centurions strode to intercept them. 'Never more crucial than in this vile place.'

A heated retort formed immediately in Adminios's mind, just as he caught sight of his own reflection in a guard's polished cuirass. The words dried in his mouth. Was he not the very case in point?

The sentries moved aside on recognising Narcissus, though a trio of snarling Molossian hounds, tied to stakes in the ground, strained against thick leashes, trying to get to the newcomers. More sentries pushed the tent flap aside, and a blast of warm, spiced air washed over Adminios.

'One of the benefits of your people scurrying to hide behind their river,' Narcissus said, leading the way as the torch-bearer made himself scarce, 'is that we do not fear a surprise attack.' He swept out an arm, indicating the huge tent. 'So come, be merry with your new allies. With the people, no less, who will give you the throne you deserve.'

They stepped inside, the noise of the rambling camp immediately replaced by the clinking of goblets and the melodious strains of music. Adminios blinked as his eyes adjusted, feeling his stomach growl like the Molossians as the aroma of roasted meat teased him.

'Each soldier belongs to a *contubernium*,' a refined voice was crooning in the dim, tremulous light, 'containing eight men. A century holds ten *contubernia*, and a cohort has six centuries.'

Adminios located the speaker, an official in soldierly garb, who was evidently giving a military lesson to a far shorter, portly man, wrapped in a gold-threaded toga, who nodded sagely behind a goblet of engraved glass that was brimming with dark liquid.

'Four hundred and eighty legionaries, all told,' the officer went on. 'The legion at large possesses ten cohorts, plus one hundred and twenty cavalry.'

The portly man, who reminded Adminios instantly of Narcissus, said, 'And how many legions have we brought to achieve this endeavour?'

'Four,' the soldier said, 'plus an array of auxiliary units.'

'Will that be enough?'

A hand on Adminios's elbow, deftly steering him away from the conversation and deeper into the tent, which was drenched in the soft glow of oil lamps, its canvas panels adorned with rich fabrics dyed in regal hues of crimson and gold. Tapestries depicting triumphant Roman victories hung from the uprights, the shifting dance of lamp-light and shadow breathing life into their intricate designs. At the centre of the tent stood a grand banqueting table, overflowing with platters of meat, fruits and exotic delicacies that must have come across the Narrow Sea with the fleet. Carafes of rich wine stood ready to be poured by an army of clucking servants.

Narcissus navigated an oleaginous route through a host of guests – senior army officers in the main, and various dignitaries from the imperial court – who disported themselves on luxurious profusions of cushions, their togas and tunics advertising prestige. A word here, a joke there, a well-placed, whispered anecdote in an influential ear, he orchestrated the conversations, and the flow of drink, like a seasoned impresario.

Adminios found himself marvelling at it all. The assuredness with which Narcissus, a freedman, could operate in such illustrious company, and the impressive way Plautius had managed to bring Rome with him on campaign. These were men who bent the world to their will. He nodded to faces he recognised, and bowed to those whom Narcissus saw fit to introduce. All the while, the room was alive with laughter and animated conversation, ribald jokes and boisterous toasts to the glory of Rome.

He was shown to a sumptuous couch, which he slid awkwardly into, his hand immediately occupied with a full glass that seemed to come from nowhere. He stared, taken aback by the opulence of it all. His own tastes tended to something significantly more austere, it was true, but he had to hand it to the invaders; they knew how to enjoy themselves.

He watched as pots of sauces were passed around, and meats he did not recognise. There was tableware displaying the plumage of birds he had never even imagined could exist, their feathers boasting more colours than he had words for. There was honeyed piglet, and seared fish, stuffed goose and various other fowl. Roasted and boiled vegetables. Venison and beef. Wine flagons and glass dishes, nuts, puddings and cheeses. A man played a wide drum, affixed to a wooden frame, which he knew to be a *tympanum*, accompanying the penetrating drone of an *aulos*.

'Crayfish, sea urchin or oyster?' Narcissus said to his left. The little man was sprawled on a couch of his own, holding out a platter to him. 'Buttered snail?'

'No.'

Narcissus shrugged. 'You're missing a real treat.'

'I confess, I have never laid eyes on such a feast.' He patted his belly. 'I fear I am unaccustomed.'

The imperial advisor grinned white. 'You'd better become accustomed, dear Adminios. This is what awaits.'

'And how many savages range against us?' someone was loudly asking a figure on the far side of the great banquet.

Adminios squinted, trying to find the man he expected to respond. The broad, unflappable face of Aulus Plautius himself resolved from the murky fug. The general, bedecked in a fine robe, his gnarled fists adorned with glimmering jewels, presided over the evening's gathering. He was surrounded by men, standing and sitting, evidently vying for his attention, though he seemed perfectly at ease, the master of all he surveyed. He gnawed at the roasted leg of a large bird. When he dabbed the grease from his mouth, he said, 'It is anyone's guess. Fifty thousand? Eighty? I care not. They are a multitude, like so many ants. We are the boiling water, and we shall wash their nest clean away.'

'Do they organise themselves in similar fashion?' an unctuous, curly-haired lamb of a man asked as he crammed food into his already flabby cheeks. 'Cohorts and such?'

'Why don't we ask them?' Plautius said, and, for the first time, his eyes slid to the tent's newest arrivals. 'I give you, the lord of the Cantiaci.' He lifted a goblet, which was immediately refilled, and tilted it towards a suddenly self-aware Adminios. 'And soon to be lord of so much more. You all know the service he has provided.'

Murmurs of appreciation. A polite ripple of applause. Adminios offered nods that felt unimaginably awkward, but he knew it was the done thing to accept their appreciation with grace. He had told them of the Vaga, after all. Of the places where a crossing would be foolhardy. Its broad and deep expanses that could drown men and horses, leaving an army in tatters. He had warned of its gaping mouth, where fresh water met grey sea, and the capricious tides that gushed and sucked at the land, leaving it cloying and treacherous. Mortal danger for a marching legion. He had told them, too, that the river narrowed to the south, that there was a stretch, just a few miles inland, that was not a spear-throw wide, and shallow enough only to reach a man's chest. He had, in short, been invaluable to the smooth progress of the invasion, and he would receive their slippery praise because it was no less than he deserved. When the mutterings died down, he reflected on the question, returning as many rapt gazes as he could. 'No cohorts,' he said, letting them titter as expected. 'In pitched battle, my people fight as a single, great body. The clans, tribes and nations come together.'

'Spears, shields and swords in the centre,' Narcissus said. 'Chariots and slingers on the flanks. Is that not so, dear Adminios?'

'Do they form *testudo*?' a beanpole in a white toga asked.

'Shield-wall,' Narcissus translated adeptly, 'with shields high as well as low, encasing the formation.' He winked. 'You will see.'

'When on the back foot,' Adminios said, 'they will form a wall of overlapping shields, though the dishonour of defence makes them reticent.'

'Dishonour of defence!' someone scoffed. 'Can you credit the notion?'

'And on the front foot?' the beanpole pressed.

'They tend to rush like rabid wolves,' Plautius said with a certain amount of relish, 'screaming death-curses as shrill carnyxes blast at their backs. But at all other times – tracking, hunting and in the ambush – the warriors of the Isle of the Mighty are grouped into units of nine.'

'Nine, general?' the skinny man retorted with a snort. 'How queer.'

'The number is beloved of the gods,' Adminios said, biting his tongue, lest his temper get the better of him.

'And what after the Vaga?' beanpole asked, making heavy weather of the final word, so alien was it on his tongue.

'There is another large watercourse, the Tamesas,' Plautius replied, 'but we will negotiate it. Then we march on Camulodunon.' He glanced at Adminios. 'Fortress of Camulos, no?'

'The god of war, no less,' Narcissus chirped. 'The *oppidum* is one of two great settlements around which tribal power turns. The other being Verlamion, away to the west. We first must take Camulodunon to break the alliance of Catuvellauni and Trinovantes.'

Plautius nodded, drank deeply, belched fulsomely. 'We understand a great many other tribes have sent contingents to swell the enemy's ranks, but, in the main, we are facing the armies of those two nations. Break them, and this part of Britannia is ours. Camulodunon is key, as lord Narcissus says.'

Narcissus popped a hunk of cheese into the side of his mouth. 'Lord Adminios, here, was chief of the Cantiaci, whose territory we now occupy. He has been key to our planning, and, consequently, will sit upon the throne once more. More than that, he will rule much of the neighbouring lands as well, with the legions as his guarantor.'

'I thank you,' Adminios said, first directly to Narcissus, then, gazing left and right, more broadly. 'All of you. My father, Cunobelin, was a friend to the empire. Trade flourished. The people of this island had never been so wealthy, so comfortable, so prosperous. My brothers have sacrificed that prosperity for ambition. Personal avarice. With your help, we can save the Isle of the Mighty.'

More applause. The musicians struck up a merry tune, which some of the guests began to accompany with slurring voices.

Narcissus leaned across. 'A good speech,' he said in a low voice.

'I hope it convinced them.'

'It does not matter. Your restoration is a noble objective, dear Adminios, but we have other reasons for being in this,' he paused to slap dead an insect that had been harrying his brow, speaking as he inspected the tiny carcass now smudged upon his palm, '*interesting* land. You mentioned your father's trade, and that is certainly on the emperor's mind. He would not suffer the dereliction of those established, and profitable, relationships.' He wafted his wine glass airily, encompassing the whole tent. 'But look around you. Not every face here hails from the Appian Way. Rome is a patchwork. A coming together of peoples and cultures. A melting pot of races from across the world. If Britannia broke all ties, it might very well persuade other nations – subjugated nations – to follow suit, and we cannot allow that, dear Adminios, can we?' He sipped briefly, daintily. 'Besides, we hear Britannia has great wealth, hidden in its desolate places. Iron, silver, pearl, lead, copper, tin. See Fronto over there?' He indicated the beanpole with a waggling little finger. 'He oversees our Spanish mines. Rumour has it that his resources are depleted. What a boon this place will be.'

Across the table, startling Adminios, the big frame of General Plautius rose to loom above the assembly. 'Yes, gentlemen!' he boomed, throwing wide whatever conversation he had engaged in, and raising his goblet, waiting for the others to follow suit. 'The gods are with us, and we shall dye the river red with their blood!'

As the gathering cheered their leader, Narcissus gazed from face to face, mouth curling in a private smile. Adminios watched him and knew that he was studying reactions and gauging loyalties, weighing the worth of every person under the expansive awning. When that measured stare fell upon him in turn, Adminios cheered too. He hated himself for trying to please the little politician, and despised the ease with which he had been seduced, but he was captivated by the sheer spectacle. The opulence, the extravagance, the elaborate display of wealth and power, even in this unlikeliest of places, a midge-bitten hill above a swamp. It was Rome. They had brought the empire to an anonymous riverbank in the furthest corner of the known world, because it suited them. Now that, he could freely admit, was real power. Power he could not wait to wield.

–

Cullen had washed at an animal trough by the light of a glowing brazier, scrubbing away the crusted blood and river muck as best he could. He had walked the perimeter, made sure there were no more incursions, then taken stock with his nine and the villagers, who had so vigorously defended their homes. One man had lost a chunk of his ear in the fight, and Baglan had been winged by a blade, but not seriously. Maeveen had dispatched the man who had killed Kenal, who, in turn, was placed in an abandoned house, there to have the death rites performed by a ghostly pale Serwil. The Batacgwi cut down by Andoc had survived, barely, his guts exposed by a deep gash that would, in time, put an end to him. They dragged his writhing form into one of the huts. Exhausted,

Cullen had given tasks to Clesek and Andoc, and then he had dozed, fitfully, as night's veil drew in.

As the sun rose after what seemed like a fraction of a moment, Cullen went to sit at a low table close to the central shrine. He ate some bread and cheese, and cleaned his sword and shield. When his eyes settled on the image of the magpie, he thought of that bird and how it had once seemed to be his shadow. Iconic of the underworld, for so long he had read its presence as a bad omen. Now its absence put lead in his stomach. Had it deserted him? Had Taranis himself grown tired of the goatherd from Calleva?

'You could have killed me.'

Cullen looked up blearily. 'I saved you.'

Serwil stood a few feet away, blood-spattered and apple-eyed, wan with residual horror. At length, he said, 'Yes.'

'Is that thanks I hear?'

The Wise One offered the tiniest nod. 'It is.'

'Thank the gods too, for they heard your plea.'

Serwil glanced at the shrine, with its offerings and antlers. 'Perhaps you were right. Perhaps they listened.' He stepped closer, swallowed hard, wrung his hands, which were gently trembling. 'I have been unfair.'

'I need you alive.'

'Even so. You are no coward. I will tell Arthmael when this is over.'

'When this is over,' Cullen echoed, though the words felt empty. He tried to imagine this nightmare concluding with anything but their deaths, but nothing would form in his mind's eye. Only a descending shaft of blood red and pitch dark that led to a bottomless pit. 'Kenal,' he said, remembering with a hollow pang. 'Have you prepared him?'

'The gods prefer their people to be interred outside of boundaries.'

Cullen chuckled bitterly. 'They may make an exception this time.'

To his surprise, Serwil returned the smile. 'Cremate him. On the longest day. Show the gods our suffering. The sacrifices we make to preserve the old ways.' The smile vanished. He balled a hand into a pale fist. 'Remind them what they stand to lose if they remain ambivalent to our plight.'

He walked the perimeter again, anxiety putting strength in his legs. Always, he paused to stare out; at the fields and the woods and the river. Nothing seemed to stir. He found Garn and Maeveen playing a game of strategy in one of the empty homes, their oaths punctuated by clattering as frustrated or triumphal palms slapped the board upon which glass beads were arrayed.

'Sleep well?' Garn said, gaze intently fixed upon the board.

Cullen snorted. 'No.'

'He'll try again, the leopard-man.' Maeveen spoke as she took her move, plucking one of Garn's pieces from the board as she did so. 'He's wearing down our resolve.'

'Yes.'

Now she glanced at Cullen. 'Time to ride for the ford? Cut our way through?'

Cullen shook his head. 'He'll kill us all and take the stone.'

'Let him have it,' Garn growled. 'Serwil too.'

'We've come too far for that,' Cullen said. 'Too many deaths on account of that stone and its keeper.'

Maeveen sat back now, biting her lip. 'I could not save him,' she said in a suddenly distant voice.

'I know,' answered Cullen. An image of Kenal, face down in the mud, arms flailing, came to him and he suppressed an icy shudder.

'On to the next,' Garn said.

'On to the next.'

—

'How many to a legion?' Nills asked Cullen. They were at the fence, squinting against the climbing morning sun, trying to pick out movement from the treeline.

'Five thousand, Cassia says.'

'She is your woman?'

'Yes.'

'And she is Roman?' Words laden with astonishment.

Cullen laughed. 'Strange, I know.'

Nills worried at the twisted ends of his whiskers. 'Strange indeed.'

'She was shipwrecked as a child. Washed up on our shores. She was taken in by the Catuvellauni.'

'And she says five thousand men?'

'To a legion.'

Nills frowned with concern as the light of understanding came into his eyes. 'And how many legions have crossed the Narrow Sea?'

'Four.'

Nills whistled softly. 'Twenty thousand.'

Shadows shifted amongst the far-off trees. Cullen sighted one particular shape, followed it as it emerged, became a man and a horse. 'They bring auxiliaries too.' He jutted his chin in the direction he stared. 'Like our friend over there.'

They both turned, because behind them, close to the central shrine, there was a hubbub of some kind. A knot of bodies, raised voices, agitated pointing.

'Why do they do it?' Nills asked. 'Why fight for that greedy emperor?'

'Money, regular meals, safety,' Cullen said, though his attention had been snagged by the imposing form of Andoc, who had pushed out from the agitated group of people and now strode towards him.

'And how many come to our land?'

'The same again.'

'So we face forty thousand in all?'

'Perhaps more.'

Nills tugged at his moustache again. 'Camulos protect us.'

Cullen was moving away, jumping down from the chalk step to greet his friend. At the best of times, Andoc had a sallow complexion, his eyes sunken and shaded, his expression sour, as if every day were the worst he had ever lived. Now, he seemed positively disconsolate. Cullen moved to intercept him, his skin turning to gooseflesh.

'What is it?'

Andoc opened his mouth to speak, but he was interrupted by movement at his feet. They both looked down. A small dog pushed up against his ankles. Ludris's pup, whimpering as if for its mother. The animal threaded its way about Andoc's long legs, and then moved on to Cullen's, keening and pawing, begging to be picked up. Andoc said, 'Yorn has—'

Cullen was already running. He ignored the dog, stepping clean over it, and ignored Andoc, and Nills speaking at his back, and the yapping dog too. He ran towards the fractious folk still mingling at the shrine, and he was shouting Ludris's name, over and again, and as he did so he could feel his heart sinking towards his stomach.

'What did you do?' he cried when he reached the group and found Yorn at its centre, as he knew he would. Ludris was not present. He glared. 'Where is the boy? Yorn, what have you done?'

Yorn, taller by a head, gathered himself up, folding those long, sinewy arms across his body, his expression belligerent. 'I have done what must be done. Saved my kinsmen and our homes.'

'Where is Ludris?' Nills said, panting. 'Yorn?'

Yorn's lips pressed into a firm line, like a child refusing to admit a misdemeanour, but his eyes drifted sideward, to where the village gate stood. Rather, where the village gate was being barred by a pair of sentries. Someone had walked out into the meadow.

Cullen stared after that person, at the closed gate, at the guards who feigned indifference, and he knew precisely who had gone. 'You stupid boy,' he whispered.

CHAPTER TWELVE

Becan and Drest drained their ale pots and exchanged belches. They were sitting, cross-legged, halfway up the slope, staring down at the water, and the armies gathering on the opposing banks.

'Did they cut down the weeping willows?' Drest asked.

'No,' said Becan, scanning the thick stands with their low, dense canopies. 'They've stationed warriors amongst the low fronds.'

'Ready to ambush the reds,' Drest said with a dry chortle, 'should they make it across. Bring them onto our spears, says I.'

Becan observed the gushing, swirling surface, grateful that it was a vicious, capricious barrier for the enemy to negotiate. A rising disquiet followed the thought, and he gave a half-hearted grunt. 'This stretch is narrower than elsewhere, shallower too.'

'They'll have a stiff task to wade it, lad,' Drest said hopefully. 'Given the strength of the current and the hail of stone and iron that awaits them.'

'Gods give us courage,' Becan muttered. The Romans would indeed face a difficult crossing, however they eventually tackled it. But they were more than mere soldiers. They would have artillery, according to Cassia, and those murderous machines could hurl a bolt or stone clear across the Vaga without difficulty. Mercifully, he had seen none of the brutal contraptions brought up thus far, but that did not mean they would not soon be deployed. He looked across at Drest. 'At least the bridge is no more.'

The old man leaned back, planting palms on the trampled grass. 'Togodubnos knows his business.'

Footsteps behind. Becan turned to see Dan come down the slope clutching three more frothing wooden pots. 'Your wound may have quenched your words, but not so your thirst.'

Dan shrugged, handed out the drinks and sat down.

'I prefer,' Drest said, raising the ale to his cracked lips, 'to sup from an old skull.'

'A human skull?' Becan asked wryly, 'or will any creature do?'

'To sup from an ancient skull is a precious act,' Drest went on, undeterred. 'Life begotten from death.'

Becan blew out his cheeks as he gazed across the valley. 'There will soon be a lot of death.' He regarded the preparations on this side of the river. There were sharpened stakes in the water, visible above and hidden below. On both banks there were networks of great rocks and deep trenches, breaking up the terrain and providing a significant hazard for advancing cavalry. Earthworks were under construction too. On the slope at their backs, midway towards the high forest, workmen had created banks and ditches that would become fortifiable positions, while a long trench was being carved from the watery slop beside the river. 'I suppose this is as good a place to defend as any.'

Dan tapped his shoulder, gesticulating at something away to the left.

Becan followed his outstretched arm. Set back from the riverbank were the cavalry and chariots. Scores of horses, tacked and saddled, ready for the off. Scores of wheeled, wicker platforms, painted for battle, arranged in regimented rows. They waited with attendants who scurried amongst them like so many mice, adjusting kit or making repairs. They were stationed on islands of dry ground, held back for the decisive moment when the first legionaries managed to break onto this side of the Vaga.

Becan said, 'You're right, Dan. We must have faith in our secret weapon. Chariots,' he added for Drest's sake.

'Hardly secret,' the old man said. 'Let them see. It makes no difference. They say the Gauls and old Belgae have not used charioteers for generations. The legions will not know how to engage them. If they get across, and the gods are with us,' he thumped a veiny fist into his palm, 'that will be the source of our victory.'

—

He intends to parley with the Batacgwi. Send an envoy. The words echoed around Cullen's head like a scream in a quarry.

There he was, Yorn's envoy. A small figure in a tatty tunic, thin of frame and bare of foot. Ludris walked steadily across the meadow towards a treeline infested with enemies. In his hand, held out for all to see, was a small purse, which he jingled every few paces, making clear his intention. Cullen's shouts for him to return fell on deaf ears. Amongst the trees, light and shadow conjured shapes that began to move. Vipers stirring in a dark nest.

The riders emerged. A dozen on horseback, dipping to avoid the low canopy as they cantered out. At their head, dressed in his starkly golden pelt and brightly crested helm, the leopard of the Batacgwi.

Cullen pushed his way to the gate, all the while shouting for Ludris to turn back. Somehow, deep in the recesses of his mind, he knew it was futile. The boy was too far away, the riders approaching too quickly. Still, he shouted, still he fumbled at the heavy bar and, when his panicked groping yielded no success, he clambered up and threw himself over, landing in an undignified heap on the earthen bridge.

'Too late,' a voice hewn from gravel and thunder came to him from above, and for a moment he thought Taranis himself was speaking from the Dreaming Realm. Then a fist, massive and powerful, took hold of him, like a pup by the scruff, pulling him to his feet in one smooth, irresistible motion. 'It is too late, Wolf Scourge,' Garn repeated his warning. 'To go is to slaughter yourself, as well as the boy.'

Cullen made a show of resisting, of trying to throw off the bear-paw grip, but he knew Garn was right. Even as he shouted again, the Batacgwi had reached Ludris, encircled him. He stopped, presenting the purse like a harvest sacrifice.

The exchange was brief. Some chatter, a ripple of laughter. Cullen glimpsed the boy's face for the first time, white flashes as he turned, seeking a way out. Even from this distance, the alarm was plain, the eyes wide and searching.

Grimoald spurred away from the group, trotting towards the village. Cullen, still on the bridge, felt himself clench involuntarily. He sensed, too, the heads of the villagers poking up from the other side of the palisade. So many frightened stoats, a hungry adder at the woodpile.

'I have enjoyed our time here!' the Batacgwi called. His approach was casual, the reins loose in his lap, though he had wisely brought a shield. The horse took him to within forty paces, where he brought it to a standstill with clicking tongue and expert knee-control. He jerked his bronze-clad head backwards. 'It is picturesque. The woods hold plenty of game, and, with the river, it reminds me of my homeland.

The River Renos, where my people learn to swim before we are free of our mother's milk. Where we practise in the water, imbued with the spirits of fish, until our limbs are as fins. Where we weight ourselves down, first with spear, then sword, then armour.' He spread his arms. 'Until finally, we are as you see. River warriors. River *gods*. Superior to other men. Set apart. Set above. Never to be denied.'

'Release him,' Cullen said.

'There used to be a hamlet, that way,' Grimoald went on as if Cullen had not spoken. 'Sadly it has ceased to exist, but it fed us for some time. You see, we take what we want. We do not negotiate. We do not relent.'

'He is a child, Grimoald. No threat to you.'

A lazy smile spread across the big man's face. 'You are a child, Cullen of the Atrebates. Should I release you too, when this is done?' Grimoald licked his lips slowly. 'I think not. A rat is a rat, whether young or old.'

Cullen rasped free his sword. A vain gesture, he suspected, but he was feeling himself stumble into a dead end, the situation unravelling like a fumbled ball of twine. He waved the blade vaguely at the shield with its black sigil. 'A cat can be skinned, whether small or large.'

The smile spread like spilled water, revealing those big, white teeth. 'Brave words. A surprise for someone who sends a stripling to do his work.' Grimoald paused, his eyes sliding from face to face. 'Ah, I see. You did not send him?' He tutted softly. 'All is not united down at the pretty riverside.'

The grin contracted into a firm, determined expression as Grimoald brought his hard gaze back to Cullen. There was a promise in that look. One that froze the blood in his veins. Up went a hand, a signal to the waiting horsemen. Cullen dragged air into his lungs, intending to scream at Ludris, but the breath just trickled away, for he knew it was all worthless.

A brace of Batacgwi kicked forward, splitting to either side of Ludris. One leaned across his saddle, snatching the purse of coins from the startled boy's hand. At the same time, on the opposite flank, the other man leaned down too, revealing a long, broad sword in a single, fluid, upward arc that ended in Ludris's head falling clean from his shoulders. The boy's body barely registered the blow. The arm was still outstretched, the torso quivering for a heartbeat, then the legs crumpled at the knees, and Ludris, what was left of him, toppled heavily into the grass.

Cullen heard someone scream. Long, lingering, desolate. It was his own voice.

—

A maelstrom.

Pushing and shoving at the palisade, shouts and threats and pleas and curses. Horsemen wheeling away, waving arms and crowing voices and mocking laughter. Noise and horror. Cold skin and hot tears. Crows descending on the fresh corpse, which looked, for all the world, like a sack of meal, dumped in the long grass.

Garn was still holding Cullen, his single hand an immovable vice. Cullen resisted, tried to wrench himself free, but the man with hair and beard the colour of driven snow possessed the strength of two men, and he clung on with ease.

Only one Batacgwi remained in the field. Cullen begged cruel vengeance from Taranis as Grimoald's black stallion cantered a little nearer. He hissed promises to the thunder god, pledging all manner of service and sacrifice if he would just come down from his cloudy lair and strike the leopard of the Batacgwi with a single, devastating bolt.

Nothing. No thunderclap, no lightning. Not so much as a raindrop. Only the thrum of hoofbeats as Grimoald drew up.

'You all bear witness to the wrath of the Batacgwi!' the cavalry leader bellowed, his accent thickening with the added vehemence. 'You all know what I require, and you all understand that no compromise will be entertained!'

Cullen still gripped his sword. He held it out. 'I will kill you!'

Grimoald laughed, mirthless and derisive, not even bothering to reply. Instead, he scanned the faces ranged across the wattle barrier. 'Banish these men who would bring death to your home. We do not want you, or your meagre coin or your putrid fish. We will not burn your buildings or ravish your women, that is my promise, before all the gods.' Only now did he look at Cullen. 'We want this whelp, his druid and the treasure. Give these things unto me, and I will not do any more of this,' he gave a cursory chin-jerk over a shoulder, indicating Ludris's crow-picked body, 'to you.'

A rustle of discussion behind Cullen. Hesitant initially; growing quickly. The villagers weighing their options, no doubt. Cutting through it all, Garn's throaty voice, 'Put on the mask, lad.'

Cullen did not answer, but somehow the words registered in his conscience. Inwardly, silently he concurred. He breathed in, called out, 'I am Cullen of the Atrebates!' Another deep breath, steadying himself. 'Cullen Wolf Scourge; a name I have earned by battle.' He lifted his sword vertically, so that Grimoald could see its full majesty. 'This is Lightning-Strike. Forged at Verlamion, bestowed upon me by Moranna of the Silver.'

'And what do I care for such things?' Grimoald shouted back, though his eyes were drawn inexorably to the weapon, as if the oiled iron beckoned him.

'Slayer of Tellos,' Cullen went on unabated, 'beside the Castrogi Brook, and rinsed in the blood of Rome at Swamp River.' He raised the blade higher, like a banner. 'It will drink of your blood, Leopard of the Batacgwi! Feast of your flesh!'

A pause. The ghost of tension flickered across that brutal face. Then the easy, languorous chuckle again. 'A wolf cannot best a leopard, boy.'

'But this is the Isle of the Mighty! Here, the wolf is the fiercest beast of all!'

Grimoald held his gaze for a heartbeat longer than Cullen had anticipated. He broke off with a shake of his helmeted head, and addressed the wider population once more. 'Deliver this pathetic child to me! This coward, who has brought doom to your home!' He gathered up the reins, wrenched hard so that the stallion whinnied as it wheeled, and bellowed once more as he rode away, 'Heed my words!'

Garn released Cullen, who sheathed his sword, clambered back over the fence, and punched Yorn in the throat.

–

'Your father was a physician at Gesoriacum,' the young patrician in the red tunic said, as he leaned back in a fur-cushioned chair and sipped wine from a fine goblet. Cassia was standing before him, and he let his shrewd brown eyes inspect her, inch by inch, head to toe. 'Until, that is, his untimely drowning.'

He had introduced himself as Gnaeus Hosidius Geta, and, though his complexion revealed a man of limited years – no more than twenty-five, she guessed – he was legate of the Ninth Hispania. A man, in essence, whose name could silence rooms, whose decisions had power over life and death. And now she was in his presence, the heat of fear prickling her skin, heart thundering so loud she was certain he could hear it. 'But you survived,' he added lazily, 'praise Neptune.'

She glanced up, through her eyelashes, blinking deliberately, aware of the performance that was required. Even so, the words echoed like bells in her head. Her lungs refusing to fill all the way. 'I remember the sand, *dominus*.' She looked pointedly at her freshly bandaged arm. They had thought the wound a legacy of captivity, and she had not disavowed them. 'The rocks, where they flayed my skin.' A minute shudder. 'The pain.'

They were out in the open, the legate claiming his grand campaign tent was too muggy for a man to think clearly. Cassia had been conveyed to his presence, for it had been members of the Ninth who had found her. No, she rebuked herself inwardly, not found, but rescued. They had rescued one of their own, a slave to the Britons, now repatriated with her own kind. She repeated the words silently, letting them drum in her skull. For them to believe the charade, she must believe it too.

Geta yawned, stretched a little, sipped a lot. His neck was long and slender, his hair auburn, tightly curled. His tunic, dyed red to honour Mars, the god of war, was very much akin to the standard military issue, but for the golden thread shooting through it in zagging patterns that brilliantly caught the sun. His bearing was straight as a rod, yet somehow casual, as if the young man were utterly at ease in his own skin, the world revolving around him and his every gesture. Which, she supposed, it did. Here, amongst the men of the Hispania, at least. As if to prove her private conclusion, he snapped beringed fingers and a servant scuttled forth to top up the goblet.

'Ten years a slave to these barbarians.' An affected shudder, almost amused. 'Perish the thought. But you are a slave no more, girl, so you may dispense with *dominus*. *Legatus* will suffice.' His eyes, glimmering, narrowed a touch, and he licked his lips slowly. 'Tell me,' he said, voice suddenly thick, 'to what cruel depravities did those savages sink? Were you employed in a very… *beastly* fashion?'

She knew full well what he meant. What he wanted to discover. Knew that his mind would be boggling, conjuring. Very well, she thought. Perhaps the revelation would keep the roving confined merely to his eyes. 'In every possible way, *legatus*.' She forced a heavy, racking judder for good measure. 'It has been a nightmare from which I have not woken, until now, thanks to you.'

He nodded, furnishing her with a smile that missed its evident mark, falling nearer crocodilian than benevolent. 'You understand, we cannot send you home immediately.' An expertly manicured hand, wafted lazily, taking in sentries, campfires, supply wagons, prison chains and everything else. 'Duty calls.'

'I am safe. That is enough.'

He glanced at her bag. 'They tell me you have the healing knowledge. The savages taught you?'

She screwed up her face, hoping the expression looked as bitter as she intended. 'I taught them.'

A bark of laughter. 'Yes, I can imagine their methods put the *rude* in rudimentary.' The brown eyes snagged her, serious and keen. 'You helped them?'

It was a challenge. An accusation, even. She jutted her chin defiantly. 'They forced me,' she said, holding up her bandaged arm. 'It is why I yet live.' She noticed the wide table out the corner of her eye, tilting to and fro as a pair of grunting servants hauled it into the space before Geta's chair-cum-throne.

The commander of the Ninth Legion Hispania leaned forward to peruse the scrolls that the men were flattening and weighting with admirable speed, his guest apparently forgotten. 'We'll need more *scorpio* bolts,' he said to one of the aides. 'I want to flay them as we cross.' His eyes drifted down the page, and he muttered a stream of words she did not catch. It was an inventory, she presumed, and that realisation set her mind to race.

Geta snapped his fingers, jolting the formulating ideas from her head, bringing her eyes up to his. He brandished that reptilian smile again. 'Forgive me, girl. The business of war is never done.' He tilted his head to the side, determining her fate. 'I have it,' he announced brightly. 'You will go to the *medici*. Assist them. Oh, do not worry, you are no servant, but my guest. And yet I feel your knowledge of the local flora might prove invaluable. What say you?'

She opened her mouth to respond.

'Good!' Gnaeus Hosidius Geta snapped while the words were still on her tongue. 'Then we have a resolution, and thank Juno for your liberation.'

—

'That's ten sacks of goat pellets,' Gwidion said, counting off each stinking bundle on his bony fingers.

Becan screwed up his face at the stench. 'That is a lot, uncle.'

'Do not *uncle* me, Becan half-man,' Gwidion retorted, his thorny brow bunching, 'I have not seen so many more winters than you.'

'Ha!' Drest barked as he hovered at the edge of the makeshift healing place. 'I could be the boy's grandsire, and you are older than I!'

Gwidion harrumphed theatrically and went back to the fly-plagued sacks. 'It is a lot of shit, because there will be a lot of killing.'

'The goat turds soak up the blood?' Becan asked, bemused.

'Dry the pellets,' Gwidion said sagely, 'and make of them a powder. Mix that powder with barley and water, boil the lot, and have a wounded man sup of it.'

'That'll put him out of his misery, I suppose,' Becan said.

'Foolish boy,' Gwidion blustered. 'The potion will staunch bleeding. Especially from within. A stomach injury, and the like.' He bit his lip, eyeing the various tools of his trade. 'We will require a lot, when the time comes, and more besides.' He tutted again. 'Gods spare me from slow-witted, smart-mouthed assistants.'

'I did not choose to count goat shit, Gwidion.'

'No indeed. Your esteemed mother chose to foist you on me. The cripple and the blind man. How very generous of her.'

The old healer had trundled up to the bend in the river when word had reached him of the enemy's arrival. He had learned of Cassia's expedition, taken it without much grace, and begun preparing an area that could quickly respond to incoming injuries. All around them, on the slope to the riverbank, up on the high ground and out in the flanking forests, the warriors made ready for what was to come. Chequered cloaks and bracae whirred past as horsemen carried messages from section to section. Faces and torsos were painted. Spells written in woad, charms etched with crow-bone needles. They said their protection pleas to ancestors, and daubed themselves in sacred battle marks, each brushstroke imbued by a Wise One's incantation. Their spears boasted new blades and their shields were freshly decorated. Horses and chariots thundered at the rear, while war hounds, huge and shaggy and slavering, bounded all around, sensing the tension in their masters.

'Your mute friend,' Gwidion said, 'has gone to join a warband?'

'Dan,' Becan said. 'He went to find Aoife.'

'His wounds were grievous.'

'He cannot speak, but he can still draw his bow.'

Drest had turned to face the river, as if he studied the manoeuvres on the far bank. 'Are they ready?'

'Not quite,' replied Becan. 'They are moving two legions down to the water, by the looks of it.'

'When will they attack?' Drest asked.

'Imminently,' Gwidion said, 'lest they wish to run out of food.'

'They'll have brought shiploads with them,' Becan said.

'An army cannot sit idle,' Gwidion replied, 'even if it is one as famously disciplined as our current foe.'

'My mother,' Becan said, 'expects it to be soon. They cannot risk the rains, for the river will flood and the marshlands will become impenetrable. But it's more than that. She says, above all, that the emperor needs a victory.'

—

'Emperor Claudius requires a victory.'

'And you will give him one.'

Aulus Plautius looked down at Narcissus, who was wafting a fat hand at a cloud of hungry gnats. 'Overconfidence will be your undoing.'

Narcissus smiled. 'I am merely assured by your abilities, general.'

Plautius grunted as more of his senior officers, uniforms emblazoned with the insignia of their units, came to join them on the crest. They saluted Plautius as the commanding general, but he kept his eyes and his mind on the gaping valley that stretched before them. It was a patchwork of greens and silvers and browns, littered, now, with humanity. On his side, the massed blocks of the legions, shunting into position, and on the far bank the eclectic, disorganised, teeming horde that was the combined army of the Britons, the different tribes massing around their various ragtag banners.

He regarded this panoply cooly, always calculating. To his right, away in the north and east, the river widened on its way to the sea. To the left, beyond the skeletal remains of a pair of once-quaint settlements, wrecked by the converging armies, the glistening band of the Vaga vanished into the thick forests that clothed both banks. He wondered what barbarous peoples lurked in those misty depths. Suppressing a small shudder, he cast his gaze over the mostly cleared terrain that sloped all the way down to the river. In peacetime, it would be a paradise, to be sure. Tall grass, glassy pools, nesting birds, and basking lizards. Perhaps it would be again, once the land had become a province, subject to the civilising influence of Rome. 'Our plans will come to fruition,' he said bluntly, not willing to elaborate too much, lest the oily little worm take more than his share of credit.

'The water here is deep, but fordable, yes?' Narcissus asked, raising his voice.

Adminios was standing a little way down the slope, a cuckoo in the nest with his full beard, his hairy arms and his skin blemished by faded depictions of old, defeated gods. 'Above the waist,' he answered. 'Shoulder depth in places, and fast. Treacherous, but viable, if certain measures are put into place.'

'Measures?' Narcissus echoed dubiously.

Plautius smiled. It was a fine thing to see the imperial fixer squirm. 'If we wade across, it will take too long, and they will kill us before we reach dry land. Indeed, it is what they expect us to do, and how they expect to defeat us.'

'Then?'

'A diversion.' Plautius pointed to a sharp bend in the river, a mile or so to their left. It formed a 'U' shape, the isolated land occupied by enemy spearmen. 'Vespasian will take his legion upriver and capture that islet. Adminios informs me that the river there is passable. When he establishes a bridgehead on the far bank, Geta and the Ninth will cross,' he swept his arm to the right, at a straight section of the watercourse, 'there.'

Narcissus's nut-brown eyes shone. 'Will that be enough?'

Plautius looked at him levelly. 'No.'

Cullen was in a state of numbness as he witnessed the breaking of the new day. He had not slept, instead keeping vigil over Ludris's body through the muggy night hours. He had taken up position not far from the gate, standing on the drift of compacted chalk that formed the fence's fighting step. Out in the dark, hooves softly thrummed to signify Batacgwi patrols. The boy's headless corpse had had to remain where it was, picked at by a lone owl that came like a ghost from the woods, its white plumage glowing in the moonlight.

Now, as the clouds turned silver, backlit by a fledgling sun that gradually emerged from the hazy purple, the corvids and kites descended to take their fill. Along from Cullen, slingers hurled their stones to disperse the macabre feast, but even they could not keep the hungry scavengers away for long.

Andoc came to stand with him, staring out at the body, and at the riders keeping ominous vigil. 'The dig progresses.'

'How far?'

'More than halfway.' Andoc held up his big, bony hands, the fingernails black with grime. 'It is hard work, but we will do what must be done.' He peered down his long nose at Cullen. 'And so must you. We cannot all escape. When the time comes, *you* must go.'

'We all must—'

'It is imperative,' the tall man cut him abruptly off, 'that Serwil and his rock get to Togodubnos. The king has his plans. The legions will soon be upon them. We must instil our spearmen with valour.'

Cullen breathed out, forlorn and empty. 'Andoc, I—'

'You lead this nine – what's left of it – because you are favoured by Taranis, and because Ulla himself saw greatness where others saw youth. I once doubted you,' he shot a sideways glance, 'goat-fiddler.'

Cullen smiled. 'Despised me.'

Andoc nodded. 'No longer. You are a war-giver, of that there is no doubt. Now, you must do what must be done. We can hold this site for a few more days, at least, but we cannot risk the Wise One any longer.'

'The fisherfolk are simple,' Cullen protested as he turned inwards, eyeing what appeared to be an impromptu gathering around the shrine and communal hearth. Folk were lashing long timbers together into a frame, while four men manhandled a large log between them, bringing it up to the newly rigged structure, and laying it carefully across the top. 'They are not warriors.'

'They are brave and they fight well,' Andoc said. 'Their sling-men are better than most. But Serwil – the Batacgwi almost got him. He'll go the way of the boy if we tarry any longer.'

Cullen looked back to the pile of rags that was once Ludris. 'On to the next.'

'On to the next. It is Heuldro'r Haf, did you know?'

'Midsummer? When?'

Andoc gestured for him to acknowledge the growing congregation at the shrine. 'Now.'

'Time has warped since we've been here.'

'That it has.' He indicated Serwil, whose pale presence was moving amongst the crowd, overseeing the positioning of a straight length of wood directly beneath the large crossbeam. It would run vertically between that beam and the hearth, forming a huge spindle. 'But the longest day has come.'

Cullen looked up at the willowy man. The expression was as spare as ever, but he knew Andoc well enough to detect the subtle changes in his perpetual frown. 'I'll not abandon my brethren, Andoc. We have lost Kenal. No more on account of my decisions.'

He found himself on his tiptoes, lifted by Andoc's long, deceptively strong arms. His friend had him by the shoulder, a fistful of tunic, and shook him gently. 'Listen to me, goat-fiddler. There is more you must do. Get word to Aoife.' He jerked his narrow chin in the direction of the forest. 'These Batacgwi, they are fiends. Born of the water somehow. You saw them swim in full armour. It is unnatural. Impossible, even.' He let Cullen go, gathering himself so that he spoke more levelly now. 'That is how they will cross the Vaga.'

'The reds cannot—'

'How many of these swimming demons do the reds possess? Is it only this handful, or many hundreds more? You blame yourself for the deaths here. For the boy's death. So be it. But what's done is done. You were charged with bringing the stone to the king. Do so. And bring him more than that. Bring him word of what you have witnessed here.' He looked back to Serwil. 'Have that snivelling turd work his magic, and then make your move.'

Cullen followed his gaze. 'He claims it is useless. I ruined the stone when I took it from Smith's Ring.'

'Wrong. We saved the one-eyed bastard from being dragged into the river.' Andoc raised one droll eyebrow. 'He has rediscovered his faith.'

—

Cullen joined the crowd. Every man and woman present – save the watchmen on the walls – observed the sun as it ascended, welcoming the longest day. It was a surreal morning. What should have been the joyous and hopeful feast of Heuldro'r Haf, reduced to a near-empty husk. No revelry here. No joy. No hope.

There should have been handfasting in the dazzling sun. Man and woman, clothed in the most intricate garments the loom-workers could create, joined together in sight of gods and kin. Reverence, music, song. There should have been tapestries hanging from thatched eaves, adorned with symbols of fertility, prosperity and union. The air infused with fragrant herbs and flowers. The central altar festooned with the sacred and mysterious objects of the Wise. Instead, the sunrise was witnessed in muted fashion, though they did their best to observe the traditions.

Serwil, though, played his part to the fullest, as the sun turned the meadow dew to gemstones. Where before he had peered with his milky eye into the Otherworld, now, with the veil between the realms lifted, he could take a step, and he donned the antlers that were housed at the shrine, becoming a half-human pastiche of the great god, Cernunnos. He exulted that god, and more besides. Welcomed the fae folk, who came on the warming rays to frolic in the Waking Realm, and he asked the gods and goddesses of the fields to bless cattle and crops, though the former had long been driven into the interior, and the latter had been left to moulder. He led the villagers in procession to the riverbank, there to present gifts to the spirits of the Vaga, tossing precious items into the rushing waters and chanting mystical words that were imbued with archaic intensity. Then, as the sun reached its zenith, he guided them in worship of Belinos, he who sustained the earth with his warmth. Each participant contributed a small item, placing it at the altar, as Serwil thanked the sun god for his gifts, and for the turning of the seasons and the bounty that sprung from soil, river, tree and animal.

Serwil then instructed the men at the timber framework to wrap a long, stout rope around the middle of the great spindle, while others were directed to build a nest of tinder-fungus and kindling-sticks in the hearth. The rope-men, on opposite sides of the fire churn, pulled in steady rhythm, and smoke fingers quickly began to coil up and away as the friction did its sacred work. When the flames sprang free, the Wise One led the procession around the burgeoning fire, and in his hands he carried bundles of herbs and flowers to invoke the elements and spirits of nature, acknowledging their presence and requesting their blessings.

After that, they shared what meagre food could be found in the dwindling stores, and drank precious mead, for the reserves of barley ale had long gone. A weaver played tunes on his whistle, while a wood carver recited what poetry he could recall. Some folk played hog knuckles to win trinkets and coins, while others challenged their peers to jumping contests, long or high.

They wrestled extensively, as was the custom in this part of the valley. Two men, donning jackets of tough hide that would enhance their ability to grip, would do combat in a ring scratched out of the dirt, each attempting to throw their opponent and cause them to land as flat as possible. Four pins were located on the back of each combatant, two at the shoulders and two just above the rump, the scores derived from the number of pins hitting the floor, monitored and totted at all times by a team of sticklers whose job it was to oversee proceedings.

Cullen enjoyed the contests, despite his black mood. Almost caught himself cheering when a tussle ended in an expert manoeuvre or powerful throw. But all the while he was haunted by the men outside and by the boy they had slaughtered.

'I will perform the ceremony.'

Cullen was seated on a bench, eating whitebeam berries from a wooden pot and sipping a fine mead that was gently fragranced with herbs. He knew the voice like he knew his own, and did not look up at the figure standing before him. 'You will not regret it.'

Serwil of the Wise took a seat uninvited. 'The rites of Gobannos would be better observed at Smith's Ring, of course, but the gods answered our pleas when my abduction was imminent. Perhaps, as you say, Gobannos will reward our tenacity.'

Cullen sipped from the cup as he considered the smith god and what, indeed, would please him. He had not expected to see Heuldro'r Haf, yet here he was, still alive and still in possession of the stone. Perhaps, in spite of everything, Gobannos *was* with them.

'Besides,' Serwil went on, 'these people need courage.' He looked hard at Cullen. 'Is our prisoner alive?'

Cullen pictured the wounded Batacgwi, who had never regained consciousness after Andoc had opened his innards. The man sweated and trembled in the corner of his stinking hut, locked in a terrible sleep, waiting for his summons to the Dreaming Realm. 'Barely.'

'I will need him.'

A raucous cheer made them both observe the raising of a victorious wrestler's arm by one of the sticklers. 'When?' Cullen asked, proffering his cup to the Wise One.

'I will let you know.' Serwil waved the offer away. His face clouded with concern. 'That boy—'

'Ludris.'

'He was brave.'

'He was foolish.'

'Brave and foolish,' Serwil said. 'Like many young warriors. It is not your fault.'

'If not mine then whose?' Cullen said bitterly. He tossed more berries into his mouth, letting the juice ooze down the back of his throat.

'The man you struck.' Serwil paused as a new pair of fighters entered the ring to noisy encouragement. 'Yorn, was it?'

'I should not have done that.'

'You did what you believed the moment required.' The Wise One cleared his throat awkwardly, as if girding himself to admit a tremendous crime. 'It is the behaviour of a leader.'

Cullen held up the mead cup again. This time Serwil took it.

They watched the rest of the bout, parting when it was done and the victor rapturously hailed. Serwil slipped into the crowd, Cullen went to the wall. It was when he was passing the large firewood pile that movement flashed in the corner of his eye. Grey and white and black. He froze, startled, at first thinking it was a badger. But astonishment gave way quickly to amusement as he saw that the creature's legs were too long and the ears – one of them, at least – too pricked, and he caught himself smiling as the pup lolloped out from its hiding place, veering suddenly to pounce on a beetle. Cullen crouched, clicking softly with his tongue as he held out a hand. The dog cocked its head, regarding him with a moment's suspicion, then approached, gingerly, black-striped muzzle twitching as he inspected Cullen's fingers.

'Well met,' Cullen said softly, keeping as still as he could, allowing the animal to inch forward at its own pace. 'You lost your master. I lost mine. Ulla was his name. On to the next, eh?'

The dog came closer, letting Cullen ruffle its coarse grey fur. It keened softly, pushing itself into his thigh, tail swinging.

Shadows above. He looked up. Nills and Garn. The latter said, 'Well done, Wolf Scourge. We shall dine on proper meat this night.'

Cullen smiled, gathering up the dog as he stood. 'Alas, he is all gristle and fur.'

'Perhaps you're right.' Garn swept out his truncated arm. 'Shall we?'

They toured the defences, speaking with sentries and examining weak points. Nills said, 'It gladdens me that we may recognise solstice, even in such challenging times.'

'The wrestling was impressive,' Cullen said.

Garn grunted. 'The feast less so.'

'Any sign of attack?' Cullen asked.

Nills shook his head. 'They wait and watch. If they spot any significant movement, they ride out to intercept.'

'Ludris?'

'They use his body as bait. Too dangerous to retrieve.'

'Have they approached from the water again?'

'No, thanks be to the gods.'

'Let us attest to that.' They walked northwards through the settlement to the open section of the earthwork that should, by rights, have been amply protected by the rushing brown depths of the Vaga. Cullen spotted one of the spearmen, who returned his nod of greeting. The man leaned against an old barrel. He looked drawn, his eyes dark. 'Change the watch soon. Give the men respite.'

'They missed the grappling,' noted Garn with chagrin.

'They may yet get to eat,' Cullen said.

'And sample the mead,' the big man said, smacking his lips.

They moved along the open riverbank to the tune of nightjar and bullfinch, until the run of stakes, ditch and wattle resumed, acknowledging each of the sentries manning the chalk step.

'How does Yorn fare?' Cullen tentatively asked of Nills.

The bushy moustache rumpled as the tall fisherman grimaced. 'It pains him to swallow.'

'I regret striking him.'

Nills's eyes strayed to the dog, happily melted into the crook of Cullen's arm. 'He is alive when Ludris is not.'

They traced the line of the wall for thirty paces or so. Beyond and above it, the old chief's intended tomb reared up. The mound and its great rocks that were as old as the valley itself, embellished by the recent addition of a circle of tall posts, beautifully painted and intricately carved. They clambered up the slope of compacted chalk to look over the monument. Through the screen of timber uprights, they could see the perfectly balanced collection of stones, settled and solidified over centuries, and the huge, grey capstone looming above the gaping maw of the tomb's entrance. There were two spearmen close by, intently scrutinising the far-off treeline, nervously watchful. One of them was Andoc. Cullen hailed him.

'Done,' the tall, wan figure said curtly as he nodded to each man in turn. 'I smashed a few of the old bones, gods forgive me, but it fits.'

Cullen regarded the ancient site, hoping Taranis would overlook the desecration. 'Will it work?'

Andoc shrugged his thin shoulders. 'Probably not.'

Cullen laughed, despite himself. 'Ever the optimist, my friend.'

'I do as I am instructed,' Andoc said drolly. 'I can but hope the stone's power will aid our cause.'

'It will,' Cullen said. 'It must.'

For the remainder of the afternoon, he walked, greeted folk, inspected the defences, the pup always at his side or in his arms. He paid his respects to Kenal, whose body rested in a small hut that lay, cool and quiet, in the shadow of the chief's roundhouse. As he left the space, bowing in acknowledgement to the spirit of his comrade and those that came to take him to the next life, two villagers appeared at the door, bearing a wicker hurdle between them. Behind, head obscured by a cowl, Serwil of the Wise said, 'It is time.'

CHAPTER THIRTEEN

It was hot inside the medical tent, the air thick with the odour of human bodies, ointments and herbs. A middle-aged man in a plain tunic, his arms covered in a mix of blood and grime, was bent over a soldier's leg, trying to bind a wound. He did not look up as Cassia entered, too focused on the task at hand. She went to a chest containing vials of ointments, bundles of cloth, bowls and tools. She took two rolls of linen, moving swiftly to assist the binding.

Now the *medicus* glanced at her as he took the extra bandage. 'How do the barbarians do this? Moss and mushrooms, I shouldn't wonder.'

She moved to hold the patient by his shoulders as he tried to buck against the pain. 'There is a certain amount of moss, I confess.'

The medicus grinned triumphantly, showing a large gap between his two front teeth. 'I knew it.' He nodded in the vague direction of the west. 'They say it's all head-hunting and sacrifice. That their druids make potions and burn virgins.'

'They are animals,' Cassia agreed. 'Barely more sophisticated than wild beasts. It is a great joy to be back amongst my own people.'

Wild beasts. They had taken her in, the Britons. She had been dragged, half-dead, off that wave-washed shore, and brought back to life. She had been enslaved at first. Handed to Critheanach as her servant. But Critheanach, dear Critheanach, had been anything but cruel. For all her cantankerous, eccentric ways, the healer had proven a kindred spirit. One just as lonely, just as isolated, as Cassia herself. Critheanach had been trained by the Wise, but she had failed to reach their lofty standard, and her fate had been to be cut adrift. She was kind, and skilled, but bitter towards life. And then Cassia had arrived, and theirs had been a bond that had saved them both.

Animals. She glanced at the chest, wherein the scalpels waited, calling to her. The guilt needed expunging.

'You have shown yourself adept at this work,' the medicus said, 'despite your privations.'

'My father taught me well enough, prior to my captivity. I merely wish to be of use.'

Of use to the medics, she thought, and also to herself and to Aoife the Dread. She would work, and she would heal, but she kept her ear to the ground always. Overhearing fragments of conversation between officers, as they spoke of movements along the river, of reinforcements arriving. She committed every detail to memory, knowing just one nugget of information might prove crucial. There had been nothing of note so far, but she would persevere, and all the while she could ask, gently, subtly, as to the whereabouts of Critheanach.

'Here,' someone barked. The tent flap flew aside, a pair of orderlies burst through, hauling the limp frame of a legionary into the room.

The leg binding was complete, and both Cassia and the medicus moved immediately to intercept this new patient, ushering the orderlies to the readied bedframe, and gathering the tools of their trade with professional efficiency.

'Ambush, up towards the coast,' one of the men said, as he manhandled the soldier into position. He slumped, moaning incoherently, onto his back. 'Spear took his thigh. It's shattered.'

The urge to hurt herself ebbed as Cassia felt her focus sharpen on the task at hand. The others had stripped the soldier's legs so that they could inspect the large wound, which gaped grotesquely at the outside of the man's right thigh, glistening like a giant ruby. Cassia bent to it, squinting. She took up a thin tool and probed the edges, then, when the swooning patient showed no reaction, went deeper, checking for shards of bone, bits of wood or fragments of cloth.

'It looks clean.' She addressed the others firmly. 'We need to realign it.'

The head medicus watched her closely, his eyes lingering on her every move, clearly impressed. 'Not bad.'

She ventured a small, tight smile, trying to show that she was capable without overstepping. 'I remember my father setting bones at the *valetudenarium*.'

The medicus nodded, indicating for the orderlies to take the injured man by the ankle. 'You heard her.'

Grimoald rocked back on his haunches and drank water they had collected from the river. It tasted like mud, despite having been boiled at the same fire over which they had roasted a small roebuck. He spat, swearing harshly, the flames responding with a crazed hiss.

'Assault the gate again?' Felix, crouching on the far side of the small ember pile, suggested hopefully. 'It is getting dark, and we have the numbers. They cannot keep holding us off.'

'We'd lose men,' Grimoald growled back, staring into the glowing logs. Above them, a pair of squirrels quarrelled in the gloomy canopy. 'I cannot afford any more failures.'

A sheepish look tightened his subordinate's features, incongruous on that broad, belligerent face. 'Perhaps, then—'

Grimoald heaved himself up, impaling Felix with a baleful stare. 'Say it. Perhaps we should leave. Perhaps we ought to cut our losses and ride back to the legions.'

'Lord, I—'

'Lord, I beg your forgiveness,' Grimoald snarled. 'Lord, I humbly retract any and all of the mutton-witted offal that was spewing from my flapping mouth.'

'All of that, lord, aye,' Felix blurted, suddenly fascinated by the flames.

'Let me say this, to which you will be attentive.' Grimoald had shed his extensive pelt, too hot was it in the lap of the fire, but now he retrieved the great cloak, swirling it over his shoulders. 'I am charged with harrying, burning and slaying the Britons. My work is to frighten them. To soften their resolve in the face of the main advance.'

'And you have done that well, lord.'

Grimoald threw him a look that could wither corn. 'But what reward shall I receive when the emperor learns of the great treasure I have captured? What lands will be mine when he discovers I have slain one of their barbaric druids? How many slaves would befit a hero of empire?'

Violent rustling in the gathering dark. They both turned, eyes straining, as a low bough was shoved roughly aside. One of their company strode to the fireside. 'Lord Grimoald, there is movement.'

'Where?'

'Beside the river, lord.'

Grimoald looked instinctively in the direction of the water, though it was too far and too dark to see anything but the nearest trees. 'Boats?'

'No, lord. They have crossed the ditch near the temple-mound. They gather amongst the painted posts.'

'The midsummer ceremony,' Felix said. 'Litha.'

Grimoald spat. 'Fors Fortuna,' he said. 'We are Roman now.'

Felix grimaced an apology. 'Should we attack?'

Grimoald waved a hand in the direction of a nearby tree, and the messenger scurried over to collect the weapons stacked at the base. 'The mound is too close to the earthwork,' he said, taking his sword and scabbard. 'Within range of their sling-men.'

'But it is getting dark,' Felix said. 'Difficult to aim a stone.'

Grimoald buckled the scabbard, kissed the gold ring at his knuckle and shrugged the gorgeous pelt into place. 'Fetch the mounts. Let us see what they're about.'

—

'Gobannos, great spirit, smith god, flame of the world's furnaces, we supplicate ourselves before your purging fire.' Serwil of the Wise, hooded and sombre, held the stone aloft, cradled in a two-handed gesture, like the most precious babe. The size of a man's fist, with rust-coloured stripes and a notch for inserting a staff, it was unremarkable in the main, but at this moment, as the sun made its final dip into the west, melting into the distant, brooding haze, it might have been the most precious gem in all the world, to judge by how many gazes were transfixed upon it.

The Wise One was standing at the edge of the monument that had been erected by the absent chief around a tomb that was as old as the earth itself. The great, pale blocks that formed the core of the sacred mound glowed as the surrounding flames licked higher.

'We bring to your hearth this stone; *your* stone,' Serwil intoned. 'The whetstone of the Dreaming Realm, that, imbued with the power of the setting sun and the heat of the sacred flame, will grant unto its possessor unmatched strength, untold courage.'

It had been risky, preparing the ceremony, for killers lurked in the dark. So they had formed a human chain, passing bundles of dry sticks in a long line, hand-to-hand, from within the village to without. The final pairs of hands placed those kindling sheafs in between the carved uprights, adjusted them so that they fit snugly, and retreated to the fence, lest the enemy come. Then they had gathered, close to the ditch for safety, and witnessed the solemn transportation of Kenal's body on its hurdle, brought up by his comrades, Clesek and Baglan. That body had been placed within the monument, positioned on and under more brushwood.

Then Serwil had made the sacrifice. The wounded Batacgwi – naked and ashen-skinned and stained all over in his own blood – had been dragged up by all-too-willing villagers. Serwil had taken a knife and opened the man's throat, ear to ear, and he had collected the pulsing blood in a wooden bowl and sprinkled it liberally about the monument. The villagers had tossed the fresh corpse onto the brushwood with none of the care afforded to Kenal, and then a torch had been ignited from the communal hearth and touched to the kindling.

Now they watched in reverential silence, as a light breeze whipped the flames into giants, and a stifling heat emanated from the shrine. Embers flew as the painted posts turned black. The corpse and its pyre vanished within a curtain of curling, agitated smoke.

At the edge of the flaming circle, Serwil eased towards the inferno until he could get no closer. 'Subject our enemies to a fury that runs hot as molten iron. Grant us, O Gobannos, your protection through our tumult. Inspire us with your knowledge.' He set down the whetstone, close to what was left of the nearest brushwood bundle, reduced now to a pulsating orange mass, crackling and spitting. 'Sharpen our spears and swords with your great magic. Let your whetstone be our banner as we face the invader.' He raised his empty palms skyward, reaching for the gathering dark. 'Gobannos!'

'Gobannos!' the assembly echoed as the wind whipped and the embers flew. 'Gobannos!'

Serwil bent, retrieving the stone with hands swathed by his sleeves, then dipped his head, walking forward, as if entering the flaming monument. The throng shouted again, but this time the sound was sliced by different, shriller calls, more urgent than their unified chant. Warning calls, further off, at stations along the landward stretch of the defences, and deeper into the gathering dark, where outlying watchmen scrutinised the meadow and the treeline. The chanting diminished, falling away piecemeal, like flaking fish scales, as heads turned and folk understood. Riders were coming.

The smoke was thick and black now, subsuming the outer structure, billowing in a great pall to obscure the riverbank before slewing down towards the water. The central pyre, adjacent to the original tomb, raged bright through the acrid curtain; oranges, reds and yellows rippling, ebbing and lashing, tussling for dominance like the wrestlers from earlier in the day. Garn's booming voice roared above those of the fleeing villagers, who scurried back over the ditch, ascending the timber ladder that had been set against the palisade. He corralled those who would fight, bringing them to the space between the ditch and the inferno, and organised them in a crescent to screen the retreat.

The huge warrior stepped to the fore, raising his iron-studded stump. His teeth, hair and beard were white against the black smoke, and his eyes bulged as battle-joy flooded his veins. 'Shields!'

—

Cullen heard Garn's snarled command, and it touched ice and fire to his skin. It was all he could do not to run outside and join them.

'Now?' Serwil of the Wise asked, his voice timorous as a baby bird.

'Now,' Cullen agreed. He was staring at the Wise One, to reckon by the man's voice, but he could not see a shred of anything beyond his own nose. The chamber, cool despite the inferno outside, was pitchstone dark. Still, his mind's eye rendered an image of a milk-pale face and wide eyes, red-raw and terror-filled. He was gripping a curving length of willow, made smooth by a covering of soft animal skin. He shook it. 'Help me with this.'

'It is heavy.'

'It is wedged,' Cullen said. The object was as wide as the tunnel and solid as any vessel they might have hoped for, but heavy it was not. Together they shook it again, jerking it free of the mud that clung to its outer edge. With a jolt, it came unstuck. 'There,' he grunted, momentum throwing him back. He felt the gluey, newly exposed soil on his back, crumbling in wet nuggets down his neck. He ignored it, shoving himself up onto his knees and grabbing hold of the upholstered willow with renewed vigour. He grimaced as he heaved, fighting to drag the thing along the tight tunnel, half pulling Serwil with him.

Scrabbling, grunting, cursing, they grappled their way in the dark, negotiating tapering walls and snagging stones. The stench of smoke pursued them, along with the cries of a fight out beyond the flames.

And then freedom. They burst from the rear of the mound, the wan capstone looming behind them. They could still see precious little, for the moon and stars were obscured by the roiling bitter blanket that surged off the flaming monument. Indeed, the air outside was more stifling, more choking than that within the passage. But they were out, nevertheless. Before them, stretching in both directions, the great Vaga gushed. It might have been a river of pure gold and gemstones, so glad were they to lay their eyes upon it.

'Will they see?' Serwil rasped through a sleeve pressed tight to his face against the noxious fumes. He was looking back at the ghostly shapes that shifted manically on the far side of the fire. The clash of iron rang out, as if a dozen smithies occupied that space.

'Not while they're trying to kill Garn,' Cullen said, hoping he was right. He felt at his belt for the large hunting knife and its slender cousin, then hefted his side of the coracle. It was smeared with the mud of the tunnel, and he whispered private thanks to Andoc, who had spent so many laborious hours scraping away at the burial chamber, widening it for the bowl-shaped vessel, and punching the passage all the way through to the riverbank.

Serwil lifted with him, perusing the boat of finely interwoven willow dubiously. 'This will bear our weight?'

'Comfortably.' Cullen made a mental note of the scabbard knocking against his leg, reassured by the weapon's presence, then walked backwards, shrinking low as they passed through a gap in the flames. 'These folk know their business. You have the stone?'

'Of course,' Serwil replied archly. 'What the——? By all the gods, he'll give us away.'

The breeze had changed now, and the smoke was slewing low, like fog. They could see little, gauging their distance from the water's edge by ear. The only sights were the tall pillars, rapidly turning to withered sticks of flame and cinder, the pyre on which Kenal had been cremated, still heartily ablaze, and the patchy outline of the tombstones, high on their excavated mound. Yet out of that unreliable smog came a small parcel of grey, scurrying in agitated circles like a large rat. But its ears were pricked and its tongue lolled.

Serwil exclaimed again, thrusting the coracle at Cullen, trying to propel him the last few paces. Cullen held firm. For a moment he had been caught in two minds, but he had been searching for a sign for so long. No magpie had appeared. No lightning. He would take what he could get. He dropped the coracle, stooped to gather up the dog, ignoring Serwil's desperate pleas.

'Come, little one,' he said, the decision made. They hurried down to the waiting Vaga. 'You may need to learn to swim.'

-

The shallows were black as the smoke and more treacherous. It was a marsh, after all, clogged with reeds and tangled by all manner of aquatic hazards. They eased further in, deeper and deeper, pushing away the hissing rushes and carefully high-stepping over great, gnarled roots and the massed twigs of wildfowl nests.

Cullen scanned the gently sloping bank, examining every shape, every flicker of movement for the Batacgwi, but nothing came bursting from the filthy, slewing miasma. He tripped, almost toppled backwards, only his grip on the coracle – and Serwil's reflexive tug o' war – holding him up. He peered into the sludgy mire. A hollowed-out tree stump lurked therein, its crest a glistening ring, just above the water. Flowers and carved figurines had been placed at its core, votives to the capricious sprites of the depths. Cullen breathlessly thanked them now for their restraint.

They set down the little boat and dragged it deeper, wincing at every splash that now seemed unnaturally loud. The water, painfully chill despite the balmy summer air, crept up Cullen's limbs, numbing ankles, shins, knees, stabbing viciously as it met his crotch. When he was happy with the depth, he wordlessly indicated that Serwil should clamber aboard, and the Wise One, encumbered by his waterlogged cloak, hauled himself awkwardly into the craft, Cullen bracing it against his shivering midriff. He tipped the puppy in too, the animal rolling haphazardly over the latticed willow until Serwil put out a steadying hand.

'What did the boy call it?'

'He never said,' Cullen answered, still gripping the coracle to keep it stable.

'The boy was named Ludris?'

'He was.'

'It is a strong name.'

'Yes,' Cullen agreed.

He was intending to say more when he saw the riders. Grey shapes, resolving from the smoke, gaining lines, growing features as they thundered from the side of the burning monument and down towards the water's edge. Cullen threw himself into the vessel, sprawling on his face as the dog had done, twisting back, his mouth hitting something hard – a knee or shin – his lip growing immediately fat. He felt nothing, the fraught nature of the moment salving pain and quickening senses. And he was hanging over the side, slapping madly at the water, his arm a frantic paddle. Serwil followed suit, and they both pounded the gushing, black Vaga, propelling the coracle into deeper water even as they heard their pursuers close in.

It was surreal: a nightmare. An impossibility. The Batacgwi should have drawn up in a welter of flinging mud and skidding hooves. Should have cursed their luck and spat baseless threats as they splashed impotently in the shallows, fetlock deep and utterly frustrated. The horses waded, instead, up to their muscular shoulders, where the current frothed and bubbled at their chests, their apple-eyes white in the gloom. And then their riders slid from the saddles, entered the water, and swam. They wore armour, the Batacgwi. Kept on their boots and helmets. Spared no thought for the scabbards at their waists. They cut through the surface of the river like a brace of dolphins, smooth and efficient.

At a different time, in a different place, Cullen would have marvelled at such a thing. Cheered their courage, applauded their skill. Now he paddled like a man possessed.

—

Garn Grey Boulder stood at the centre of his short defensive line. Hardly a shield-wall, for it consisted of only nine shields, and two of those were held by untested villagers, Cullen and Kenal being absent from the warband. But the wall was stout, for the spears were sharp enough to make the horses shy away, and the slingers on the flanks were as stinging and vengeful as a hornet swarm. The Batacgwi charged in ones and twos, but they veered away at the last moment, lingering only to slash at Garn's line. If they had come to the attack in one body, they might have found success, but he had the sense that their leader, the leopard – whatever creature that was – intended to lose no more men. He wanted Serwil and the whetstone. Wanted Cullen too, if only to punish the lad for his impertinence. But not at the risk of weakening himself before the main Roman advance. That was why they flitted, now, about the seething, broiling remains of the chief's tomb. They were searching for their quarry, sensing whatever ceremony had taken place would have featured the Wise One. Their attacks on the village defenders were merely half-hearted. And that was why Garn had stayed out here so long. Snarled so viciously at the invaders. Berated any warrior or villager who dared take a backward step. They were buying time. Keeping the leopard's cold gaze in the wrong place.

'Fall back to the ladder!' Garn Grey Boulder bellowed, satisfied he had done his duty. They filed back, carefully, watchfully, the slingmen covering the retreat. Cullen had had time to make his escape, and that was all that could be asked of this ragtag group. All that could be chanced, so impulsive were the gods. He slapped the nearest man's back. 'By thunder, you did well!'

–

The two Batacgwi propelled themselves expertly through the water with little fuss and barely a splash. Cullen watched in horrified awe as the metallic river-beasts bore down on them, pale shapes in the black, pitiless, relentless. He scrambled to the coracle's edge, the surface of stretched hide slippery, the craft bucking and lurching at the sudden movement. The pup at his feet, already drenched, keened softly. Serwil, too, was making strained mewling sounds, seeing his own death approach.

Cullen cast his gaze frantically about. He would have liked a spear to throw, but a low branch would do. Something to keep the swimming soldiers at bay. Yet they were out in deep water, isolated and turning idly on the current, far from the low-hanging boughs and the tangled reed beds that might have been of use. He thrust his arm back into the swirling cold, pulling and pulling, dowsed with chilling spray, the coracle tilting violently with each desperate stroke, his movements mirrored by Serwil on the other side.

He stole a glance at the pursuers. The river was broad and deep. It should have been too daunting, yet on they came. Serwil must have been checking for them too, for his worried yelps became increasingly panicked, his strokes more ragged, the coracle seeming to falter. Such vessels were designed for calm waters, but it was all the fisherfolk could fashion with the resources and time available, and it rocked precariously under their weight and their hurried movements.

Cullen ceased paddling, took a deep, steadying breath. He crouched, like a lynx poised to pounce, and drew his sword. An awkward motion, given the dizzying travel and confined dimensions of the coracle, but the iron clattered free, taking a chunk out of the boat's edge as it went. And then the Batacgwi were more than just nebulous shapes. They veered apart, one man aiming for the far side of the vessel, just as his comrade reached them, exploding upwards like a demon from the deep, his arm a tentacle, grasping at the craft's frame. Water streamed from his mail shirt and high-crested helm, and Cullen was again struck by how this man had managed to swim so expertly under all that weight. He was still admiring that undeniable skill when he hit the man clean on the top of the head. The helmet clanged, denting deeply. The clutching fingers wrenched the coracle, tilting it sharply, water sloshing over its rim, then released, setting it to spin wildly, and the Batacgwi's pale face was suddenly red as blood cascaded from under the helmet, immediately expunged by the water as the man sank away.

Serwil squeaked. The second Batacgwi was up at his side, dragging at the swaying vessel, and the Wise One was beating impotently at him with his fists. Cullen tried to shift his weight, forced to negotiate the yapping dog, but Serwil was in his way, and all he achieved was to tip them ever more forcefully. Serwil punched and scratched the Batacgwi, spitting every curse he could think of, and the man in the water clung on, wrenching and snarling, his eyes white in the gloom, his teeth bared. In a flurry of limbs and shouts, the coracle reared and dipped, water flooded in, and then they were over, tumbling pell-mell into the river.

Cullen sucked air into his lungs and then there was blackness. A cold, enveloping embrace. Desperate, struggling noises all around him, muffled and abstract. He thrashed his arms and legs, still grasping the sword, and he could feel himself move, though he had no inkling whether it was towards the surface or the riverbed. Tumbling confusion. Blood rushing in his ears, skull seemingly on the brink of shattering.

Exultation; sudden and shocking. He broke the surface, erupted into the night, mouth agape and lungs afire. His chest heaved, hauling in the smoky decay that was marsh miasma as though it was the sweetest air anyone had ever tasted. He screwed up his eyes to clear them of water, all the while searching, scrutinising every shape for a glimpse of friend or foe. He was perhaps two thirds of the way across the river, the reed beds a black mass on the western shore. The flames still flickered on the opposite side, casting everything in a dull, shadow-thrown glow. The coracle was close, flipped upside down, its hull bobbing uselessly. He strove for it, grabbing hold with one arm as he fumbled to get his sword back in the scabbard without injuring himself, the water rendering it clumsy and unwieldy.

'Here!'

Cullen hauled himself about, seeking the speaker.

'Here, Cullen!' Serwil rasped again, gulping liquid, spewing it back up. He was treading water some dozen yards away, waving a skinny arm frantically. 'Over here!'

Cullen kicked for him, grasping that wan limb and dragging him over to the coracle. 'Do you have the stone?'

The Wise One nodded, then retched again, a stinking concoction of bile and silty water, but he managed to get a grip on the vessel's nodding rim and together they swam in the direction of the west bank.

A yelp in the gloom. High pitched, inhuman. They twisted back. The pup, paddling fast, as competent as the Batacgwi, snout held high. Cullen could have laughed as he snatched up the drenched hound by its coarse scruff and hauled him with them. They kicked again, and the reeds soon emerged, looming tall and thick, a great forest from the night. The gateway to the west bank.

The sounds of splashing and grunting drifted over the river's surface, close but abstract in the murk. The remaining Batacgwi, gaining his bearings after the chaotic capsize. It was unclear whether he had spotted them, but it seemed only a matter of time, and Cullen urged Serwil to redouble his efforts, putting all their remaining strength to the task. The mud clung to their shoes as they reached the shallows, like dozens of grasping hands sprouting from the riverbed. The reeds hissed as they were moved aside. It all seemed so painfully loud to Cullen, but there was nothing for it, and he gritted his teeth and shoved his way into the swaying grasses, mud giving way to a web of roots, the going ever more strenuous. But here was a chance to vanish into the thick, shadowy undergrowth, the natural rustling going some way to masking their movements, and they hauled the coracle deeper until it would be entirely invisible to any onlooker on the water.

And then they stopped. Crouched as they turned back. Serwil gripped Cullen's arm, steadying himself, weakened by their exertions. Cullen, in turn, held the sodden dog, who seemed utterly content, tongue lolling as he panted softly. They stared out through slim gaps in the reeds. The river, calm again amongst its shallows, rippled gently.

A flash of metal. A glint, away to Cullen's right. Unmistakable moonshine on iron. The reeds spoke of violence. No gentle susurration this time, but the hiss of a thousand snakes as the foliage was slashed by a blade. Nesting birds erupted into the gathering gloom. Serwil drew breath to cry out, but Cullen's free hand clamped shut his mouth before either of them had time to think. Their pursuer was close, no more than a score of paces away, wading falteringly towards their position. Slowly, Cullen released Serwil's jaw and drew his sword. The rasp of the scabbard an avalanche to his ears, but, mercifully, the Batacgwi was making plenty of noise of his own. They inched out of the crouch, retreating deeper into the reeds, pigeon-stepping awkwardly, negotiating each other's feet as well as the deceitful tangle concealed by the mud. Cullen used his sword-tip to move each bunch of stems aside, holding them clear like a door-skin, allowing Wise One and hound to step through in turn. The Batacgwi, not bothering to obscure his approach, was gaining, pace by pace, severing clusters of the tall stalks as though he scythed a crop, cursing as he went, promising vengeance on those who had dragged him into this mouldering, treacherous world.

It was no use. Serwil was struggling, limping and whimpering. Cullen shoved the sword home and looped an arm around the Wise One's waist, manhandling Serwil, half-lifting, half-dragging, and they were on the move, Cullen doing most of the work. The sounds of the Batacgwi carried to them, achingly close.

A flicker of movement at the corner of Cullen's eye. He swivelled on his heels, brandishing the weapon. A figure in the reeds, cloaked in shadow, well out of Lightning-Strike's range but tentative all the same. At first he thought it another dog, or even a wolf, but the fronds moved, higher up, revealing a taller shape, distinctly human, but cadaverously thin and bald of pate.

The figure stepped forward. Features grew on the intangible shadow. A hooked nose below bushy brows. Wide-set eyes that drooped slightly at the corners, giving a sombre aspect to the weathered face. A fulsome, grey moustache, worn long to the chin, framing thin, bluish lips. The man's forefinger pressed to those lips as his gaze moved beyond Cullen to scrutinise the dense reeds. After a few heartbeats, that same finger extended, then curled, beckoning them to follow as the man melted backwards into the dark. Cullen and Serwil exchanged a glance, wordlessly agreeing to follow.

–

'Let me speak with the whelp!' Grimoald, Leopard of the Batacgwi, held his stallion in check far more effectively than his rage. They had come to the torched burial complex to finish what had been started. To take heads and dispatch souls and capture whatever treasure had been secreted within the village. But the defence had once again proven intractable. The warriors too good, the slingers too well-practised.

'No whelps here, Batacgwi,' a gruff voice bellowed back. Its owner, a bulky older man with white hair and beard, clambered up whatever step had been set on the inner face of the wall, making him visible from barrel-chest up, bathed in the light of torches set at intervals and the ebbing glow of the charred monument. 'Or you would surely have found a way inside by now.'

Grimoald ignored the barb. 'He of copper hair.' He ran a finger in a long arc from his forehead to his temple, then traced a vertical line down through his right eyebrow. 'Scars, here and here.'

The Briton wove his tree trunk arms through a couple of the spiked stakes, revealing a rivetted stump where his left hand should have been. The metal studs looked wickedly brutal in the flame-gleam. 'We all of us bear scars.'

'Then let me help you.' Grimoald wracked his memory. 'Cullen of the Atrebates was his name.'

'Ah, yes. He perished in the night. Cut down by one of your riders.'

'Show me the body.'

The blockish head moved from side to side. 'He takes his walk into the next life. The eyes of his slayers will not dishonour that journey.'

Grimoald felt his gaze flicker over to the night-veiled river. Men had gone into that water. Somehow they had slipped unseen through the blaze. He could not help but wonder as to their identities. Still, his own warriors had been in close pursuit, and they could traverse a river as well as any eel. He needed patience. It did not come easy. 'A pity,' he said, forcing himself to steady his tone. 'His skull was to grace my saddle. The priest, then. If you lead this rabble, the decision is now yours. Give me the druid and his hoard, and I will let you keep your skin.'

'The Wise One prefers to remain. A fact that riles me no end, for he is a quarrelsome bastard at the best of times. But the gods decree his worthiness, and who am I to contradict the gods?'

—

The clang of hammers, bellow of officers, whinnying of cavalry and bawdy campfire songs had long faded, leaving the Ninth Legion's section of the Roman encampment an eerie sea of canvas, dwindling light and soft murmurs. Near the collection of tents that formed the field hospital, Cassia sat on a smooth stone, checking her nettle bag to ensure the unguents and tinctures had not leaked.

She had been with the Romans for only a couple of days, but it was long enough for the soldiers to cease their sidelong glances and start asking her for salves and water without suspicion. It had been long enough, too, for her to learn names. Marcus and Lucius, the orderlies, were around her age, and friendly enough. Their initial surliness at her surprise arrival in their midst had given way to acceptance, not least because the legionary with the broken thigh bone had begun to show signs of recovery.

Across from her, Gaius, the head medicus, emerged from the awning that housed their cauldron, his tunic stained with the day's work but his hands clean. He carried two wooden bowls, steam curling from their contents. 'Barley stew,' he said, handing one to her as she set down the bag. 'Not the feast of Jupiter Optimus Maximus, but it fills the stomach.'

Cassia took the bowl with a nod of thanks. She liked Gaius, who had a surgeon's steadiness and a centurion's impatience, yet was diligent and highly educated. He had treated her well, impressed with her knowledge, despite his disdain for the people who had taught her most of what she knew. Not that she disavowed him of his prejudices, for it was a useful dichotomy. 'After the day we've had,' she said, 'I'd take lizard boiled in ditch water if it came with a place to sit.'

Gaius chuckled – a short, surprised sound. It was the first time she had heard him laugh. He sat across from her, the warmth of the small fire between them flickering across his face. 'You know,' he said, stirring his stew thoughtfully, 'when they assigned you to us, I thought you were just another of Geta's women.'

Cassia raised an eyebrow but said nothing, letting the silence press him into honesty.

He met her gaze. 'But the way you set that lad's leg – clean, precise, not even a flinch from him.'

She felt herself blush. 'He was in a stupor.'

'Even so. It was good. And your other work. The stitching is exemplary, and the onion poultice,' he waved his spoon like a wand, as if struggling to find the apt superlative, 'simply masterful.'

Cassia smiled. He might be the enemy, but earning his respect brought a surprising note of satisfaction. 'I learned a lot from my father.'

He leaned forward a touch, suddenly a little furtive. 'And I suspect you learned slightly more from the Britons than you let on.'

That was a keen thrust, and it placed ice in her chest, catching the air so that she was momentarily struck dumb. A reminder that one wrong move, one misplaced word, would mean death. Or worse.

Gaius waved the spoon again. 'Do not fret. It is no accusation. You have a quick mind. Of course you absorbed their practices.' He shovelled a spoonful of stew into his mouth, swallowing almost without chewing. 'I mean only to say that I was quick to judge. Both you and the barbarians.'

'But I did learn from my father,' Cassia said. Her worry was beginning to ease, but that did not mean she was comfortable. The façade of the brutalised slave was slipping, if only by a fraction, and she needed to gather it back up. 'At Gesoriacum, before...' She trailed off, letting the woodsmoke bring tears to her eyes.

'I am sorry for what happened to you,' Gaius said, his tone sincere, concerned. 'But Gesoriacum? Gods, I grew up near there. I used to steal olives from the market and run through the alleys before the *vigiles* caught me. My father said I'd end up crucified or conscripted.'

'Looks like he was half right,' Cassia said, offering a half smile as she cuffed away the false tears.

Gaius laughed then. To her surprise, she joined him – genuine, relaxed. The fire cracked between them, and for a moment, the weight of the camp, the wounded, and the impending tribulation seemed far away. She looked down to dunk her spoon, and her eye caught the fresh dressing bound to her forearm. She thought of the new wounds beneath, of the pain they had caused and of the relief that pain had offered. Relief from what trauma, she thought? Her grief over her father? The fear she felt for Critheanach and Cullen? Or perhaps, as she looked at this man who knew Gesoriacum, and who spoke her native tongue, she wondered if the real trauma had been the loss of her former life. A life she had rediscovered, in this crude army camp above a waterlogged valley. The notion was troubling.

Gaius leaned back, gazing up at the darkening sky. 'It's strange. Out here, we stitch bones and patch flesh. But it's the quiet moments, like this, that feel like real healing.'

What had he seen in her expression? Panicked, she smothered her concern, concentrating instead on the steaming bowl. 'I am healed now that I am home.'

He held up his own stew in mock toast. 'I am glad you're with us, Cassia.'

The night deepened, the fire burned low, the scent of barley and herbs lingering in the air, and Cassia's mind tumbled.

–

'Don't often see them built for two,' Wilt said, careful to keep his voice low, as he guided them through the marsh. He glanced at the pup, sprawled like a drowned rat in the crook of Cullen's arm. 'Or three, even. Would not a proper boat have been better?'

'We had neither the time nor resource,' Cullen answered at his back.

'Aye, well, your coracle's a quicker build, I'll say that for it.' Wilt cackled softly. 'Easily upended though.'

Cullen traced the river-dweller's movements, step-for-step, acutely aware that the man knew every inch of the capricious shoreline. At least, he thought with private thanks to all the gods, this was the Britons' side of the Vaga. They had made it across. His legs were ice-blocks in the shin-deep swamp-mire, deadened to the marrow and incessantly seized by the viscous mud. 'How much farther?'

Wilt sniffed, cocked his head, as if smelling the way. 'Almost there. Roman'll be lost by now, should the gods will it.'

'Batacgwi,' Serwil said.

'What's that?'

'Roman,' Serwil corrected himself, realising it was not worth the explanation.

'I'd heard they were coming,' Wilt said. He swatted an insect from his sweating scalp that was marked by a filigree of blue veins.

'They're here,' said Cullen.

The rheumy eyes fixed hard on him. 'And you?'

'I fight with King Togodubnos.'

That gave Wilt pause. The old man half-turned. 'King now, is he? Well,' he chuckled, 'if it's him or the emperor, I know my choice. Come on, then.'

Wilt steered them onward, picking a route between the watery channels despite the dark, pulling paths like a sorcerer from the black abyss between islands, reeds and bushes. There were withies every so often, at sharp turns or particular streams, and Cullen realised that they must have been way-markers of some kind, warning of deep water, bottomless swamp or dead end. The moon hung low, its pale light replacing the glow from the fire. The smoky aroma had gone too, the air on this side of the Vaga ripe with the smell of wet earth and decaying vegetation. The only sounds beyond their own words and breaths were the soft rustle of leaves, the calls of frogs and insects, and the perpetual trickle of water.

'Step careful now,' Wilt advised when Serwil stumbled. 'The mud'll swallow you whole if you stray.'

The Wise One muttered something inaudible as he regathered his feet. His breath was ragged, every pace a chore. There was a distant howl. Wilt raised a hand, waiting, listening. They stared into the night, eyes straining for the Batacgwi, but nothing moved. Wilt clicked his tongue for them to continue.

The marsh seemed endless, a labyrinth in which Cullen lost all sense of direction, his only hope lying in the old man's knowledge of this treacherous land. Wilt moved with a surety that belied his age, avoiding the hidden traps that could spell their doom.

'What was your business out here?' Serwil asked when his nerves had evidently settled.

'Leeches.'

'You're a healer?' Serwil asked sceptically.

Wilt chuckled dryly. 'A purveyor. Your people buy them by the sack load.'

'My people?'

'The Wise.'

'But I have not—'

Wilt brandished a grin mostly devoid of teeth. 'You have a way about you. And that milk-shot eye. What else would you be good for?'

'And you saw the fire?' Cullen asked through blurted laughter as Serwil blustered his outrage.

'A blind man would not have missed it,' Wilt said. 'Just as well I came to have a nose, eh?'

After what felt like hours, the reeds began to thin, and the ground grew firmer beneath their feet. The old man quickened his pace, urging his unexpected charges onward. They emerged from the marsh onto a narrow strip of higher, drier land, set above the Vaga but running parallel. They paused to draw breath, and to search the broad band of the watercourse and its glittering tributaries, ensuring no pursuers were approaching from the reeds. Nothing stirred, and Cullen gave private thanks to all the gods.

The earth thrummed. Gently at first, but growing steadily more insistent, a vibration that climbed up through the soles of his feet and into his ankles. Sounds came too, like very distant thunder, away to the right, but clear of the river, level with their own position.

They saw it all at once. A collective intake of breath, a collective gaping of mouths. Shapes in the dark, gaining definition rapidly. Horses' snorts carried on the breeze. Cullen felt his pulse quicken and sweat prickle at the nape of his neck. Moonlight glinted off something as the shapes moved. Metal.

—

Grimoald gazed at the settlement from high in his saddle. Still night, its features were lost to the murk, but he could draw every detail from his mind, as if the place had been branded upon his conscience. It was nothing, really. Just a pathetic cluster of wooden huts, caked in clay and shit, protected by a ditch, a palisade and a river. Yet what trouble it had given him. He moistened his lips as his line stretched to either side. Horsemen arranging themselves for the final charge, their armour jangling, their mounts restless, snorting and pawing at the ground.

'It is time to put an end to this,' he said to Felix, who had come to his left flank.

'I hate this place,' Felix said. 'The sooner we can go home, the better.'

'Oh, but I'll not go back,' Grimoald replied. He looked down, making final checks of his leather straps, his armour, his shield and spear. Counting his daggers and hefting his javelin, making sure his great broadsword would slide free of its scabbard without hindrance. 'We will be rewarded with realms and titles. I do not hate the land, Felix, but the people. I mean to kill them. Erase them. Every last one. Like the vermin they are.' He levelled his spear, bringing it in line with the curtain of sharpened stakes that was this night's barrier. 'The rats' nest awaits.'

He and Felix urged their horses forward a little, bringing them proud of the line by a few paces. He sensed his men tense behind him. He knew they would be whispering prayers, their hearts beginning to race, their eyes sharp, resolve unforgiving. They had failed up till now, and that would rightly give each man concern, but Grimoald's paramount ambition had been to preserve his force. Take what should have been an easy victory with as little damage as possible. He had, it transpired, collided with an implacable and resourceful enemy. So be it. Now, just as the first cracks of new light opened in the eastern sky, he would send his men at the stubborn village once more. They would absorb their inevitable losses, smash their way across the earthworks and overwhelm the inhabitants, whatever the cost. Because Cullen of the Atrebates was dead, and a druid and his treasure were there for the taking.

Grimoald raised his arm, ready to give the signal. At his left, Felix rolled his shoulders and cracked his neck. Grimoald's black stallion snorted, stamped, eager to unleash its own fury. The air was charged, anticipation palpable.

'For Rome!' Grimoald snarled. 'And for the glory of the Batacgwi! Char—'

But just as his arm began to fall, a horn sounded in the east, cutting through his roar like a sickle swipe. He hesitated, held his breath, his arm frozen mid-motion, as the whining call carried to them again. Some of the cavalrymen had chuntered forward, jumping the order in their impatience, but they were professional, held themselves in check, and now every head turned towards the source of a noise they all recognised.

Out of the gloom emerged a dozen riders, galloping at full speed towards the Batacgwi line. Their crimson cloaks flapped wildly, and the gleaming bronze of their helmets caught the burgeoning morning rays, marking them unmistakably as men of Rome. Grimoald turned his stallion to greet the newcomers. He recognised the standard emblazoned on the riders' chests and lowered his arm completely, signalling his men to abort their promised assault.

CHAPTER FOURTEEN

The firelight flickered across the canvas walls of the tent, casting long shadows that danced like spectres. Cassia knelt beside the cot, her hands steady as she applied a poultice to a soldier's fevered brow. His breath came in shallow gasps, his skin clammy to the touch.

'Keep still,' she murmured, her voice soft but firm. 'This will help.'

The soldier groaned, his eyes fluttering open for a moment. 'Who... are you?'

'A healer,' she replied, her tone neutral. 'You are safe. Let the sleep take you.'

'It hurts,' he managed to say, each word a struggle. 'My stomach.'

'*Dolor ventris*,' she said, mopping sweat from his beading brow. 'The upset will pass. Did you drink from the marsh pools?'

She reached into her bag for juice of the poppy. What she brought out was a different flask, one she had carried since her time with Gwidion. The henbane tincture. Part of her, a deep, dark knot in her soul, considered administering it to the stricken legionary. One less for Cullen to fight, she thought sourly. With a pang of horror, she swapped the vials, chiding herself for such cruel fantasy. Or was it something else? Was her reticence in fact because this young man, this Roman, was one of her own? The horror intensified, twisted into confusion. She sat back. Her scabby wrist began to smart. Began to speak to her.

She swallowed down the tormenting feelings and brought the poppy juice to his lips.

'Not drink,' he said hoarsely. 'Eat. Bitch poisoned me.'

'What bitch?' She touched a single drop to his tongue.

He seemed almost to laugh, despite his pain. 'Briton. Crone. Ugliest thing I ever saw.'

Cassia's heart felt as though it would burst right out of her ribcage. She crammed the stopper back on the flask, shoved it into the bag, and grabbed the man by the shoulders. His eyes were already beginning to glaze, but she shook him, roughly, urgently. 'What was her name, this crone? What was her name, damn you?'

He looked at her, a moment of perplexed clarity. 'Some native bitch. Fought like a demon when we captured her.' Now the eyes rolled, half-lidded and mostly white. 'She's—' he added weakly, and sank back into unconsciousness.

A cleared throat, the ripple of a tent flap. 'Ancilla,' a man said at her back. She turned quickly to observe a plumed officer in polished *lorica segmentate*. 'I come from Legatus Geta. He requests your company.'

'Over generations we have fought. Spilled blood for this land. For dominion over the hills and the woods, the fisheries and the rivers. Now others, foreigners, would take what is ours.'

'*You* would take what is ours. It is a mere brace of summers since the Catuvellauni sacked Calleva. Chased King Berikos into the embrace of Rome. It was in revenge for that very attack that the reds have come. Who are you to speak for all the tribes?'

Togodubnos, eldest son of Great Cunobelin, chief of the Catuvellauni confederacy, and de facto king of the free peoples of the Isle of the Mighty, nodded solemnly, light and dark dancing across his ruddy face in the fire-glow. 'I do not deny it,' he spoke directly to his detractor, a bearish brute representing the Regnenses. 'We are different tribes. Warring nations. But we are of one people. One shared blood.'

Cullen watched and listened, his mouth firmly shut, as murmurs rippled through the crowd. His hound squirmed in his arms, uncomfortable pressed against the sodden fabric of his clothes, and he fed it a scrap of meat, urging it to quieten.

Another man stepped forth. The braided gold torc at his neck glimmered richly, reflecting more than just the flames. 'I speak for the Ordovices of the dragon mountains. The most ancient creed in all of these islands. The Catuvellauni descend from the tribes across the Narrow Sea. As do the Atrebates and the Trinovantes and the Cantiaci. Your roots do not sprout from this soil, but from the soil of the Belgae.'

A growl of dissent from amongst the king's honour guard, cut short by a raising of their lord's hand.

The conference had been convened at a wide glade on the high ground amongst the woods that loomed above the river valley. It was not yet dawn, the distant horizon a swirl of half-lit, bruise-coloured clouds, and the glade was crammed with the combined tribes' most esteemed delegates, all vying to glimpse the man who had claimed supreme overlordship of the gathered horde. The man who promised that he alone could bring victory.

The space was edged by broad, rounded beech, bright hawthorn and dark currant bushes, though the receding night had reduced those verdant sentinels to black outlines. A fire had been lit at its centre, around which a circle had been scratched into the earth, scattered with salt and ashes, and spellbound by the Wise, who pranced and chanted until Togodubnos had indicated it was time to speak. Now those with a voice to be heeded – chiefs and elders, warlords and advisors, princelings, law-makers and first-shields – gathered at the sacred circle's outer edge, there to debate the impending cataclysm.

'The ancient ones and the Belgae share a blood tie,' Togodubnos rejoined, 'as the Wise will tell you. Did you learn nothing from their schooling?' He stepped further into the centre, bathed fully in the warm light, so that all could see his arm rings and torcs, his warpaint and the russet hair and beard that had been woven tightly into battle-braids. There were large feathers in those intricate plaits, and tiny, twinkling charms, the mark of a leader with the gods' favour as his shield. 'We are cousins from long ago, and brothers now. But Rome? They are alien to our people. Their customs, their values. They are an enemy who would subjugate this island in the name of avarice. They may claim the restoration of Berikos as their goal, but any fool knows their true object is greed. We, the peoples of this land, have our differences, it is true. But we have a common foe. A foe that would steal everything we own. Everything we have built. They would burn our homes, take our metals and our timber, our game and our pearls. They would send our warriors to the next life, rape our women and enslave our children.'

'Some say they will be our friends,' a warrior called out. 'Make us wealthy.'

'At what price?' someone retorted from deep in the crowd.

Togodubnos turned a slow circle, nodding as he caught as many gazes as he could. 'At what price, indeed?'

A woman came into the ring. She was tall, her eyes ringed in blood-coloured paint, her hair long and loose, falling beyond her shoulders in a cascade that was as red as the flames. 'The time for decision is past, lord king,' Aoife the Dread spoke, the common tongue inflected with the accent of Innisfail, the Isle of Destiny, the land beyond the sea, far to the west. She was resplendent in her battle garb. A war goddess incarnate. The assembly was silent, hanging on her words. 'The enemy has crossed the Narrow Sea. They will attempt to cross the Vaga. All that matters is how we respond.'

Togodubnos nodded. 'We must make our stand, my friends. United under the gods. Not septs, not tribes, but one nation.' He thumped a big fist into a shovel-like palm. 'The Isle of the Mighty.'

A growl, becoming a cheer, rumbling through the massed bodies.

He waited, turned his slow circle again, inviting comment from the throng, firelight casting flickering shapes on a sea of stern faces. The smell of woodsmoke and damp earth filled the air, mingling with the tang of freshly oiled weapons. The mood was tense, the weight of the impending battle heavy on shoulders and hearts.

The scrape of shoes in the dirt. Cullen peered across the flames to see a big man tread into the speaking space. There was something reminiscent of the king in his face, perhaps around the eyes, but his features were harsher, more angular. He was taller too, and his hair, though styled with similar braid-work, was raven-black, as were his moustaches, which he wore long, around a wide, thin-lipped mouth. 'Stand with us,' Caratacos boomed, his demeanour and tone far more aggressive than that of his older brother. He stalked about the outer edge of the fire, the glow illuminating the symbols and scars etched into his skin. 'Throw the Romans back into the grey waves! Stand with us, and reclaim the stolen soil. My friends, my brothers and sisters. There is only one choice. Fight together or die apart.'

Cullen stared at him. The man who had commanded on the day of his family's slaughter. The man he loathed above all else. The soul Cullen had made a solemn vow to dispatch to the next life. And yet he was enthralled. The man was the greatest of all war-givers. A killer in full war-gear, the image of unyielding power. Fearsome with his blazing stare and belligerent stance. Cullen hated Caratacos, but he wanted to emulate him. Earn the fame Caratacos had earned. He was evidently not the only one, for a swell of cheering rose up at the warlord's words.

'The river is our greatest asset. A natural shield,' Caratacos declared, perhaps seeing a chance to harness this new enthusiasm. 'The Romans will find it hard to cross.'

'We know these lands,' Togodubnos took up the theme, 'and we must use our knowledge. We hold the high ground on this bank. It is for them to come to us. They will be forced to wade into the current at shallow pinch points, whereupon we will turn the river scarlet with their blood.'

Discordant mutters of agreement and disquiet rose up, vying for ascendancy amongst the smoky tendrils. A disembodied voice bellowed out, 'I was at Swamp River, lord king. I have seen the reds fight. They're not like any foe we've faced before. They're disciplined, relentless.'

'I do not deny it,' Togodubnos responded, voice resonant. 'But we have the numbers. We are prepared. They will make great labour of the crossing, and it will be their undoing.'

Caratacos grinned, white-toothed in the gloom. 'Unless they can swim!'

Laughter washed, wavelike, through the crowd. And Cullen stepped into the surf.

He had intended to forewarn the king. Had intended to report all that he had seen. But not here, not like this. Not in reply to the man who now skewered him with ice-pale, dagger-sharp eyes. Still, Cullen moved, his legs carrying him, unbidden, out of the crowd and into the circle. Silence greeted him. His guts twisted. Not for this moment, but because in his mind he was back in Calleva. The callow youth he had once been, orphaned and bloodied, grovelling before this very man. Caratacos the War-Giver. Caratacos the Conqueror. Then, he had expected only death.

A deep, disembodied voice reverberated in his head. Garn's wolf-growl. *Put on the mask.*

So he put it on. Because he was no longer that frightened boy. He met the blue gaze as levelly as he could. 'They can, lord.'

More silence. The crackling fire the only sound as more heads turned to look at him.

Caratacos seemed to smile, amused, perhaps, by the newcomer's raggedy appearance. 'They can *what*?'

Cullen swallowed dryly, trying to ignore his shredded nerves and the rush of blood in his ears. 'Swim, lord. In full armour. I saw it with my own eyes.'

Togodubnos approached him. His massive, muscled frame cutting out the light from the fire. 'Legionaries cannot swim rivers.' He frowned suddenly. 'I know you.'

Aoife came close now. 'Cullen of the Atrebates, lord king,' she said in that sing-song voice, belying the iron in her nature. Her green gaze fell kindly on Cullen. 'You returned in the night?'

'Mere moments ago, lady. A scouting party picked us up to the east. Brought us here directly.'

She seemed to notice his wet clothes and bedraggled appearance for the first time. Her brow furrowed. 'You succeeded?'

'I did.' He cast a look over his shoulder. Serwil emerged from the crowd, the Whetstone of Gobannos in his shivering, pale hands.

'We will speak more of this,' Aoife said. 'Now what is this tale you seem keen to tell?'

Cullen shifted his gaze from the tall warrioress to the most powerful brothers in the land. 'Legionaries cannot swim in full armour, my lords, but the Batacgwi can.'

Togodubnos glanced at Caratacos. 'An auxiliary unit?'

Caratacos nodded wordlessly.

Cullen went on, 'They are impressive, lord king. Deep, fast water, it makes no difference. Armour, weapons, shields.'

'Where did you see this?'

'Upriver. At a place where it runs deeper and faster than here.'

'How is it done?' Caratacos growled.

'They claim to be imbued with power by the waters of their tribe,' Serwil offered.

'But they practise, lord,' Cullen said. 'From the moment they can walk.' He threw out his gaze, taking in so many faces, representing so many peoples. 'As we ride, or throw a spear, or sling a stone. It is done so often, it becomes second nature.' He shrugged. 'The Batacgwi swim.'

He heard a faint murmuring. Sensed the exchange of uneasy glances all around him, the confidence of a moment before starting to waver. One of the king's shield-bearers, a burly man with a red beard, scoffed, though there was a hint of doubt in his eyes. 'We have stakes, rubble-baskets. Sling-men by the hundred.'

'We can fight them,' Cullen readily agreed. 'Even so, we should prepare for the Batacgwi. They can cross where we least expect.' An uncomfortable murmur rippled through the assembly.

'Then?' Togodubnos prompted.

'Set spearmen along the banks, upriver and down. Even where it seems impossible to ford. *Especially* in those places.'

Togodubnos stroked his beard. 'The front is too broad.'

'It is what is necessary, lord,' Cullen said, and, even as the words escaped his mouth, he wondered if he had overreached himself.

When he saw Arthmael, he knew he had.

'The river will protect us,' the wisest of the Wise announced with a finality that brooked no argument. He was just as Cullen remembered. Wizened, ill-favoured and crooked, swathed in the many-hued cloak that spoke of his exalted status. Only kings and queens were permitted to wear more colours. He sidled nearer, leaning heavily on his gnarled blackthorn. An animated cadaver, though his pale eyes were bright as gems. His yellow-nailed feet were bare, and his bald scalp glowed with sweat, the permanently dyed symbols of wavy suns and crescent moons shining in the flamelight. 'The goatherd returns.'

'Lord Arthmael,' Cullen replied, drawing himself up, refusing to be cowed.

Arthmael's lips parted in a malevolent grin. 'He returns altered.' His tongue flickered, showing the split that made it forked like a snake's. 'Has emerged from his chrysalis.' He went to Caratacos's side. The throng shrank back, as if Arthmael's very presence charged the air. As he moved, the cloak flapped, revealing the needled emblems of a long-necked goose and a many-spoked wheel. Cullen felt the skin of his forearm tingle where his own life-wheel had been etched.

'I am a war-giver now.'

'And yet here he stands, sowing fear and division where he may. I did not believe he could insult the gods more than he has already.'

Cullen imagined drawing Lightning-Strike there and then. Sticking it through the Wise One's gullet. Letting his blood stain the turf. But the Wise were the conduits of the Otherworld. To offend one of their order was to offend the gods, and that was a very bad thing indeed. Besides, he did not fancy his chances against Caratacos.

'I am merely giving warning to our lords. Battle will be joined, and we must be ready.'

'Thank you, oh great chief,' Arthmael crooned, eliciting snickers from the crowd as he bowed deeply. He wafted a bony hand in the direction of the brother warlords. 'These humble folk had not thought to prepare.'

'Enough, Arthmael,' Togodubnos commanded.

'Perhaps this boy,' Arthmael went on unabashed, his forked tongue flicking out over the vertical woad lines that ran down his chin, 'can teach us how to ride, or wield a sword.'

'Peace, Arthmael,' Caratacos said.

'He is nothing,' the Wise One spat. 'An insect in this company. Do not listen to—'

'Enough!' the big man snapped. Caratacos waited while Arthmael slunk back into the surrounding bodies, a beetle skulking into a rocky crevice. Then he turned to address Cullen, that familiar glint of intrigue in his expression. 'We thank you for your advice.'

Togodubnos nodded. 'It is heeded.'

Duly dismissed, Cullen moved out of the circle. Even as he walked away, along the ridge crest to find food and shelter, frustration tightened his chest. He knew the sons of Cunobelin were great warriors and clever leaders, but the Batacgwi were unlike any enemy they had faced. The river that had been their salvation for so long, could become their downfall if they underestimated their opponent. He could only hope that, when the time came, the Vaga would indeed prove too great an obstacle, and the Romans would find it as formidable a barrier as Togodubnos hoped. Deep down, a gnawing doubt lingered.

'Wolf Scourge,' a woman called out.

Cullen turned. It was Aoife the Dread, statuesque and terrifying as she strode out of the shadows, the wan half-light distant behind, illuminating her impressive frame and wild hair.

He bowed low, keeping tight hold of the wriggling pup. 'Lady.' He repeated the gesture to the woman who walked beside Aoife. A woman who was half the size, double the age, and just as intimidating.

'Lady Moranna,' he said, 'it is good to see you.'

Moranna of the Silver smiled. 'And you, little red crest.' She was barefooted, as Arthmael had been, and, like him, wore a plaid cloak of many dyes. She was ghost-pale, with long, straight hair framing a round face of snub nose and narrow eyes. Within her silver tresses, tiny figurines of wood and bone had been intricately woven, and about her neck hung a chain of dowels that clacked as she moved. 'Though you are not so little any more. The warrior's path has suited you well.'

'A path I would not have walked without your patronage, lady.'

Moranna's keen eyes settled on his sternum, where his sodden tunic bulged and shifted. 'You appear to have contracted a canker. I can prescribe an unguent.'

Embarrassed, he eased his grip on the dog, allowing it to poke its twitching muzzle into the fresh, predawn air. 'I mean to train him.'

'Very good,' said Moranna. 'Taranis will approve, I think.'

'I have spoken with Serwil,' Aoife said. 'You have done well.'

Guilt stabbed at his insides. Words swirled in his mind as he tried to cobble together a confession. 'It – it was not easy, lady.'

'Nothing worth doing is easy.'

'I was forced to remove the stone from Smith's Ring,' he blurted, 'before—'

Aoife's hand went up to stay him. 'He speaks highly of you, does Serwil of the Wise. Says you saved his life.'

'At great cost.'

'On to the next.'

'On to the next,' he echoed automatically. 'What will be done with the stone?'

'Presented before our horde at dawn,' Aoife said. 'Its very presence inspires courage.'

'It is without power,' Cullen admitted. 'It is merely a—'

'A rock?' Moranna interrupted. 'No, little red crest.'

'I could not wait until the longest day, lady,' he said miserably. 'Serwil could not harness its power.'

'It has more power than that which comes from Belinos,' Moranna replied. 'It is a story. The Whetstone of Gobannos will be presented, of course. It will be paraded before our warriors. But we shall tell of its arrival here. Of its rescue, from the very jaws of the enemy. The stone's magic will come from the telling of its tale. And I have many mouths poised to do the telling.' She winked. 'Some of the best prophecies fulfil themselves, if you let them.'

'Now go,' Aoife said. 'Find rest. Replace the weapons you have lost. Dawn may bring the reds onto our spears.'

'And put on something dry,' Moranna said with a wry smile. Her eyes left him, roaming the treeline somewhere beyond his shoulder.

'Tell that foolish boy to drink his broth. And tell him to remove himself from this valley before the fighting begins.'

—

'Take it away, it tastes like pigswill!'

Becan was sitting on a felled tree, pressing the wooden bowl back into a long-suffering Wise One's hands.

'It is fortifying,' an elderly man was saying as Cullen approached the trio.

The day had begun now, though it was dull and grey. He had been walking the high ground at the forest edge, following Moranna's directions, occasionally glancing down at the valley that teemed on both sides with the metal of armies, when his eye had landed on his friends. He approached unseen, grinning.

The Wise One, fresh-faced and dutiful, presumably one of Moranna's acolytes, tried once more to encourage acquiescence from his unwilling patient, but was roundly rebuffed.

'Strong ale and Gallic wine is fortifying too,' Becan protested. 'Find me some of that!'

'Nettle broth builds strength,' Drest was gently opining.

'I would not be interested in that poisonous brew if it made me sprout legs!'

Cullen laughed. Wretched as he had felt since the war council, a wellspring of joy rose through him as he spoke. 'Your mother says drink it!' he called out. 'And then make yourself scarce!'

'My mother can—' Becan began a retort, then let his jaw loll open. The corners of his mouth turned upwards, morphing into a grin. 'By Nemetona's tits, you lived.'

Drest held out a hand to Becan. 'You owe me a silver minim.'

'Do not listen to this old weasel,' Becan said, swatting the proffered palm away. 'I always believed in you. It is good to see you, goat-fiddler. By Belinos, it is.' He looked Cullen up and down. 'You swam here?'

'Not all the way.' Cullen took a seat beside his friend. 'A riverman rescued us, guided us out of the marsh, then we stumbled into a scouting party.'

Becan frowned. 'Us?'

'Serwil and I. I swear we would have frozen our way to the Otherworld. Fortune favoured us, thank all the gods.'

'All the gods?' Drest placed a withered hand on his shoulder, the skin like dried leaves. 'Taranis pulls your life-threads, lad. When will you start to believe?'

When indeed? The voice inside Cullen's skull whispered. When Andoc and the rest appeared in the shield-wall, hale and hearty? When his decisions did not result in the deaths of those around him?

'What make you of Serwil?' Becan asked impishly. 'A putrid little toad, is he not?'

'He is not fond of your mother.'

'Serwil is a follower of Arthmael the Learned,' Drest said. 'He would be stripped of all rank if he spoke a word in Moranna's support.'

'The Wise jockey for power more readily than any chieftain,' Becan said.

Drest chuckled grimly. 'And when you are ruled by brother-kings, each with his own counsel, it makes for danger.'

'Arthmael the Learned,' Becan spoke the words slowly, as if weighing up each syllable. 'I wonder what they discuss.'

Cullen followed his gaze. Sure enough, the wisest of the Wise, advisor to Caratacos, was walking towards the trees at the head of a cowled cabal. At his flank, stooping so that he could hear whatever Arthmael was saying, strode a warrior so huge, it was as if some magic spell had conjured legs for one of the great oaks. Sego Blood-Swill, Caratacos's first shield. As bald and woad-painted as the Wise One, but there the similarity ended. He was all muscle and long limbs, with a sour face that was a tapestry of interwoven creases and scars. His plaited beard was thick and black, reaching halfway down his barrel chest, and his scalp was adorned with the faded shapes of axes, stars, moons and snakes, the skin expertly etched with needle and charcoal. His movements were at once smooth but powerful; a supreme predator. A born killer.

Sego glanced up, his eyes glittering, and, for an uneasy moment, Cullen had the distinct impression that the great warlord was looking directly at him. He threw his own gaze away, suppressing a shudder. 'Nothing good.'

'Do you suppose he owns a shield, or does his torso serve just as well?' mused Becan. 'Thank the gods that brute is on our side.'

'It is hard to tell just who is on our side,' Cullen replied, watching Sego but thinking of the perfidies negotiated by the late Berikos. 'I saw men of the Regnenses, the Eceni and the Coritani at the council. Was the king not informed of their betrayals?'

'The Dobunni are lost to us,' Becan said. 'They have declared for Rome. We hear nothing from Cartimandua of the Brigantes. But Togodubnos has received pledges from the rest.'

'Of allegiance?'

'Of friendship. They would rather remain neutral.'

'They wait to see how the dice fall,' Cullen said bitterly.

'They have sent spearmen,' Drest elaborated, 'as a gesture of goodwill. And Togodubnos is in no position to reject such an offer.'

'How many?'

Drest spread his palms to show that he did not know. Becan said, 'Token numbers. They claim there is no need to sacrifice their armies until they know Rome's intention.'

'Rome's intention is conquest,' Cullen replied, anger putting heat in his neck and cheeks. 'What of the Eceni?'

'Assurances,' Becan said. 'They have brought spears. Antedios will fight.'

Cullen nodded, outwardly assuaged, but he could not help but recall what Betha had told him. The Eceni princess had warned that her father, the ailing king, was no longer the real power in that nation. Power now resided increasingly with a nobleman named Prasutagus, and he, she claimed, was as trustworthy as an adder, and as ambitious as an emperor. 'Let us hope he is as good as his word.'

Becan clapped his hands. 'Enough of this maudlin chatter. Tell us about this hound you appear to have collected on your travels.'

Cullen grinned, pulling the pup free and holding him up. He presented the squirming creature for Drest to stroke.

'You have a new ally?' the old man said with a laugh, surprised at the revelation his sightless eyes had hitherto concealed.

'Ludris,' Cullen said.

Becan tugged the excitable beast's grey ears as it nipped at him playfully, batting with its oversized paws. 'Well met, little Ludris. A throat-ripper if ever I saw one!' He looked up at Cullen, serious now. 'Where are the others, goat-fiddler? Where are Garn, Rues and the rest?'

'What are the wolves like?'

Adminios looked down at Hosidius Geta, the young commander of the Ninth. A snide little turd if ever he saw one. 'Big, but they keep to the shadows unless it's been a lean winter.'

'The boar are more dangerous,' Narcissus crooned at his other flank. 'Gut you soon as look at you, I hear. Good eating though.'

'How is the ale?' Geta asked.

'The mead is better,' Narcissus said.

'And what about the women?'

Both Romans looked up expectantly at the tall Briton. Adminios held his tongue for a beat, revelling in memory. 'Magnificent.'

They were on the crest of the slope, overlooking the valley from the east. The commanders had gathered for a final briefing, features set firmly in grim resolve. General Plautius himself stalked amongst them, a figure of authority clad in resplendent fur and armour. He strode with hands clasped at his back, gaze firm, as he paused to address certain officers, his tone low and iron-hard.

'The savages do not deserve such women,' Geta said with disgust. He hawked up a wad of spittle, depositing it noisily on the trampled grass. 'I heard they were mostly madmen. Lusting for blood and flesh. I hear they kill their own horses as offerings to the gods, but they fuck them first. Imagine that.'

'We sacrifice to the gods too, Geta,' Narcissus chided.

'But do you fuck your horses?'

Narcissus shrugged. 'Not if there are alternatives available.'

'You say we are brutes,' Adminios growled, working hard to remember his Latin. 'Unthinking animals. I say my people are simply harder than yours. You fear us, so you are forced to invent stories about us. If you did not, your legions would never have boarded those transports at Gesoriacum.'

Narcissus gave a wry chuckle. 'They almost didn't.'

'Ah!' Geta clapped his hands suddenly, startling Adminios, to his eternal annoyance. 'Speaking of women, I am pleased to introduce my new friend, Cassia Severina.'

Cassia thought she might wet herself, such was her terror. She tried to keep her head bowed, gaze trained on the ground, but how could she stop her eyes flicking up to regard such men? Plautius himself. Adminios, son of Cunobelin, brother-foe to Togodubnos and Caratacos. She swallowed hard, her mouth and throat like desert dunes, and bobbed deferentially at the knee.

'Friend, is it, Geta?' a short, plump man said. He had dark, clever, restless eyes, and he raked her with them, weighing her up.

Geta grinned. 'Ever lascivious, Narcissus. Shame on you.' But the legatus immediately belied his words by sliding to her side and taking her hand in his. He rubbed her skin tenderly with his thumb. It was all she could do not to kick him in the balls. 'Cassia spent much time enslaved by the enemy. She escaped, and found her way into my service. Not in the way that you no doubt infamously surmise,' he added quickly, grinning as lewdly as the others, 'but with my medici. She has quite the talent.' He turned to her. 'That is why I summoned you here. The soldier whose leg you so expertly set. That was one of my more valuable aides. I wanted to thank you in person.' He squeezed her hand tighter, drawing her closer until their bodies were touching. His gaze bore into hers. There might have been words inscribed on his eyeballs, so clearly did she read his intent.

'I thank you, *legatus*,' she stammered, trying and failing to move away. She did not know whether to laugh or cry at her own risible hubris. And it had been going so well, the plan working so perfectly. In spite of her misgivings about her people, on both sides of the river, she had inveigled herself seamlessly into the marching camp. In the vast machine of order, iron and discipline, it had not been difficult to avoid attention. And they always wanted healers. No one looked too closely at a helper with blood on her hands and a medicine pouch at her hip. Then the soldier had mentioned the crone, and though no name had been uttered, she had known, deep in her heart, that Critheanach yet lived. And now it was all gone. All that hope, snatched away. 'Thank you,' she repeated, bleakly, hollowly, and he was pressing himself ever closer. She could smell wine on his breath and rosewater on his skin, and something in that sweet and acrid mixture jarred. It repelled her. She wanted to cut herself, to let the stinging rid her of the smell, but into her mind came an image of Cullen. She saw him, and she smelled him. Smoke and sweat – not sharp or rank, but warm, like sunbaked leather and oak ash. It was the smell of home.

She pulled away.

—

Adminios did not bother to fight off his smile as the girl yanked herself free. The arrogant prig seemed to reel from bafflement to anger to genuine hurt, and Adminios would be glad to witness what followed.

'Gentlemen!' Plautius boomed behind them.

The spell was broken. All eyes went to the general. Geta, much to Adminios's dismay, seemed to forget the girl, moving forward like the eager pup he was.

'We are about to engage in a prodigious undertaking,' Plautius went on. 'Are you with me?'

As the other officers cheered, he noticed Narcissus looking searchingly at him, as if he read his thoughts. 'You seem disquieted, dear Adminios. Do you not wish to fight?'

Adminios looked down, examining himself. He was dressed like a legionary, armoured in a flexible cuirass of iron strips, an iron helmet on his head, his cheeks encased in metal flaps. At his belt, the Roman short sword, for stabbing, when the enemy's fetid breath was ripe in his nostrils. The enemy. Who was that, exactly? Positioning himself to displace his brothers was one thing; actually drawing the blood of ordinary Britons was something else entirely. 'I brought you to this place. I saw the legions safe between the forests and the swamps. Was that not enough?'

'Every man must play his part.'

'And what part do you play, *dear* Narcissus?'

A dazzling, well-practised grin. 'Why, I shall be compiling my report. Summarising the day's events. Listing friends, and enemies, of the emperor, for the moment he sets foot on this soil.'

'You think it will be easy? They fight hard.'

'The wildcat fights hard when the pack runs her to ground. She may scratch a muzzle, slice a paw, but she will end the encounter in shreds.'

'Will you shred my people?'

'Hardly your people any longer,' Geta said, not hiding his amusement.

'On the contrary, my dear Geta,' Narcissus corrected. 'When the elder sons of Cunobelin are drowned in the filthy Vaga, their dominions will pass to their surviving sibling.'

Geta smiled nastily. 'So long as you remain well disposed to Emperor Claudius.'

'That,' Narcissus acknowledged smoothly, 'goes without saying.' His eyes shifted to regard Adminios. 'As for shredding the stubborn barbarians, a certain amount of bloodletting must take place. It is unavoidable. You must understand this. We must first break the tribes in order to welcome the future. But that future will be so bright, my friend. We will remake this land. And you will be king of a new and prosperous province, forged in the very image of Rome.'

And Berikos is dead, Adminios thought inwardly. The spoils will no longer be shared.

'As we have agreed,' Narcissus continued, once again appearing to read Adminios's every thought, 'your old kingdom will return to you, with the addition of a stretch in the south, from the Narrow Sea to the chalk downs.'

'Beyond?'

'The seeds you planted with poor Berikos brought abundant fruit. Alliances have been forged. Concessions will be made to those chiefs accepting of our rule.' That oleaginous smirk again. 'Hold firm, dear Adminios. You came to us with vengeance in your heart, and, in the name of Claudius himself, you will have it.'

With a sweep of his fat fingers, he indicated the soldiers below them in the valley, readying to move. No longer marching legions, with their wooden crosses – the *sarcina* – from which they hung their worldly possessions, but warriors, bearing only tools of slaughter. Auxiliaries spread out to the flanks, scattering spiked caltrops to protect against ambush or a surprise counterattack from across the river. The atmosphere crackled, tempered only by the air of disciplined determination that pervaded the ranks of Rome.

Aulus Plautius appeared beside them, a shining bear in his metal and skins. 'I mean to make my play at dusk. But sorcery concerns me more than spear-craft. Black magic will do strange things to men. Intoxicate them. Make wolves of lambs. Lions of cubs. What of your *druidica*, Adminios?'

'The Wise,' Adminios replied sourly. 'Snivelling rodents, for the most part. Overblown with their own importance.'

'I have heard they are as powerful as kings.'

'Not quite. My brothers have allied themselves with the Order of Mona, the seat of the Wise. A viper's nest away beyond the western mountains, beside the Clear Sea.'

'We know what must be done with a serpent.'

'I would rather keep them caged,' Adminios said. 'Poke them with sticks for my own amusement.'

Narcissus placed a hand on his shoulder. 'When you are king.'

Adminios felt a nascent twitch at the corners of his mouth. 'When I am king.'

Orders rang out, spooling up and down the massed ranks. The cohorts shunted forth, moving into position.

'Now we wait for sunset,' Narcissus said.

Out to the flank, an unusual unit was preparing to move. Comprised of foot and horse, they were armed like Romans, but, to the eyes of Adminios, appeared more similar to himself than to the peoples of the Mediterranean: taller, broader and fairer. 'The diversion?'

'Batavians, of the River Rhine,' Narcissus spoke with a hint of distaste. 'Germanic. They call themselves Batacgwi, but they'll answer to our pronunciation.'

'If they know what's good for them,' Plautius said. He turned to his left, gazing upriver, where the silvery water was swallowed by thick forests. 'And once I set them loose, our victory will turn on a flanking manoeuvre. An old-fashioned pincer. Vespasian and the Second.'

'They're out there,' Geta said, almost wistfully, as if he were with them, 'sneaking through the woods.'

Plautius nodded. 'The savages will be busy protecting their precious war-wagons, and Vespasian will take them at the flank.'

'And the other flank?' Adminios asked. 'You described a pincer movement.'

'That is where I come in.' It was Geta, smug and haughty, triumph writ large across his tanned face.

Plautius slapped Adminios hard across the back and stepped away, stretching, limbering up, as if readying himself for a race or duel. 'Can you smell that, my friends?' he bellowed across the crest. 'Death is on the air!'

CHAPTER FIFTEEN

'Then where is she?' Cullen did not ordinarily notice the heartwood figurine, so light was it. Now it seemed hewn from Sarsen, pulling him down, crushing the breath from his chest.

'As I have told you, she was about Aoife's business,' Becan said. He gave a limp shrug. 'Now? Cernunnos knows.'

Cullen slumped back against the tree, nausea rising, guts wrung out. He pushed aside the bowl of bread and cheese, unable even to look at it. They were up in the woods above the valley. He had been revitalised since seeing his friends, the food proving welcome, as well as finding new tunic and braca to replace those now ingrained with the filth of the river. His sword was newly oiled, and a pair of spears had been purloined from one of the many caches that had been positioned at intervals throughout the burgeoning horde's disorganised groups. And a horde it truly was. It had grown exponentially since Cullen's departure, numbering now in the scores of thousands. An army for all the Isle of the Mighty, just as Togodubnos had envisioned. It had given him hope, even as he thought anxiously of the legions on the far side of the valley, apparently waiting for an order to attack. And then he had learned of Cassia.

'Tell me again,' Drest said, his sightless eyes seemingly trained on a distant point beyond Cullen's shoulder. 'These Batacgwi can swim wearing metal?'

'Do not deflect me,' Cullen bit back angrily. 'She has gone to the Romans? Who let this happen?'

'Let?' Becan answered. 'You *have* met Cassia, have you not? She knew what she was about. She spies for Aoife and searches for Critheanach.'

'Gods,' Cullen murmured as he planted palms over his tired eyes. She was gone. Her memory had kept him alive, kept him striving to get home, these past days, and she was not even here. Tumbled into the same abyss that had swallowed Critheanach.

Becan looked up through the canopy at rapidly greying skies. 'Best get some rest. The day wanes, and they'll attack at dawn, like as not.'

'You ought to go north, away from here,' Cullen said, glancing meaningfully at Drest.

'We'll find Gwidion, the Wise One Cassia had been assisting. I'd say we had stepped into her role,' he added with a crooked grin, looking pointedly at one of his sticks, 'but, you know.' With that, he began to heave himself up, groaning exaggeratedly. 'And what of Cullen Wolf Scourge?'

'I'll find Aoife's warband.' Cullen grunted sourly, thinking of the fishing village and all he had left there. Thinking of Cassia. 'A new shield, too.'

'Maybe Andoc will bring it when he gets free,' Drest said hopefully.

'If he yet lives,' said Cullen.

'It was not your fault, goat-fiddler,' Becan said. 'Fate twists and turns, and we must make of it what we can. You kept Serwil alive, and you brought the whetstone to Aoife.'

'I abandoned my nine,' Cullen replied sullenly. 'I was their leader, and I abandoned them.'

'You did what duty demanded,' Drest said gently. 'The gods – and your comrades – will honour you for that.'

Cullen knuckled his tired eyes. He hoped the old man was right, but, deep down, he doubted it.

–

'Elderberry syrup,' Becan said, as he spooned the concoction into the man's open mouth, 'flavoured with herbs and infused with honey.'

The patient had been a spearman until an hour earlier, at which point the unfortunate warrior had dropped a rubble basket on his foot. That foot was now bulbous and purple, and the word spear was unlikely to feature in the man's immediate future.

Becan was seated on a low stool, and he winced in sympathy at the injured fighter's stricken expression. 'We need to get you back behind the lines.'

He and Drest had sought Gwidion as soon as Cullen had left, finding the healer a little way up the slope overlooking the Vaga. They had urged the old man to retire into the great forest, but he had insisted on treating the last few patients.

'They'll be coming,' the soldier opined weakly. 'They gather in earnest. I need to fight.'

Becan shifted his rump to stare out across the broad, brown waters, clouded now with drifting mist and obscured by the gathering dusk. They were a few hundred paces north of the islet carved by the river's tight bend. The offending basket had been intended for that jutting promontory, where warriors clustered thickly, readying themselves to protect the obvious weak point in their defences. The baskets, twinned with rows of wickedly sharp stakes, would hopefully break up any massed assault by the legions against that vulnerable area. Here, though, where the water was wide and deep, he felt relatively safe to tend to Gwidion's charges, and he found himself counting the rows of red shields on the far bank, emerging and vanishing with the movement of the mist.

The Romans had spent the day steadily descending the gently sloping incline. Thousands upon thousands, rigid in their units, so many featureless threats behind *scutum*, *pilum* and helm. They were preparing to cross. They had not hidden the fact. Yet there was no way they could span the river here without suffering huge losses. The tribes' spears and slings would rain down on them, cutting them to ribbons as the water held them in check. And if they somehow made it to the western shore, the most fearsome of Togodubnos's forces would engage them. Chariots, lined wheel-to-wheel, had been drawn up by the score, where the land formed a small plateau that was firm, flat and dry. The horses had been corralled in an adjacent plot to the northeast. The expert drivers, and the warriors they would convey, were camped close by, available for mobilisation at a moment's notice. Not even the legions would relish an entanglement with that fast-moving and agile force. War-chariots had been largely abandoned by the tribes across the Narrow Sea by the time that Rome had swept aside the Gauls and Belgae. But their cousins, isolated on this windswept rock, had kept up the tradition. The legions were unused to such a tactic, and would, therefore, be naturally wary.

Thus, he thought, their only option was a frontal assault, attacking the islet to establish a bridgehead on this bank. Togodubnos, in turn, had concentrated his forces there, ready to throw them back. So what, he wondered, were the Romans waiting for?

'Enough of that, my boy,' Gwidion's dry voice rasped somewhere in the murk. 'Get yourself out of the way and let those who can stand do their work.'

Becan nodded agreement, forgiving the old man his brusque manner. He was as nervous as anyone. He offered another spoonful of the liquid as he said, 'You must recover. We may need you to fight another day.'

The warrior swallowed down the medicine. 'My duty is—'

'Your duty is to live,' Drest croaked. He was seated on a bench, well out of the way.

'Indeed,' Gwidion added as he checked his wagon's traces, readying to follow his own advice. 'Foolish fellow.'

Becan was relieved to discover the Wise One had finally seen sense. They would soon be away from here. Away from the tumult to come. 'Those who cannot fight must retire to the hill crest,' he said, stealing one final glance across the river. The fast-flowing waters looked so serene, the surface and its wispy blanket lit by the last vestiges of a sinking sun and the first glimpse of moonglow. Molten silver, overlaid by glaucous gold. What a beautiful valley this might have been, he thought absently, at a different time, in very different circumstances.

Something was out there, gliding across the shimmering depths, downriver, near the chariot camp. Shadow and movement. The glint of something. A gentle splash. He grabbed his crutches, pushing up, squinting to get a better look at a bevy of swans, or, perhaps, a duck with her raft of newborns.

'All done,' Gwidion said at his back, patting the nag that was to draw the heavily loaded wain. 'We'll stay for the night and make tracks at dawn, yes?'

'No.'

'No?' Gwidion echoed.

'Becan, what is it?' Drest was saying, his tone suddenly tight, nervous. 'What do you see?'

'No,' Becan said again. He was still staring, but now his bowels had turned to water. Whatever was stirring out on the Vaga, it was not wildfowl. 'We leave now. Do you hear me, Gwidion? Drest – get up! Now!'

—

Grimoald, Leopard of the Batacgwi, had a point to prove as he led his black stallion downriver, close to the bank, then, noting the marker – a big rowan with coloured ribbons in its lowest bough – he veered down to the reeds. The engineers had cleared some of the dense beds in preparation, thinning it in places so that men could access the water, but the work had been hard, the boggy terrain unforgiving and the slingstones from the far side insistent. They had been reduced to slipping down to the sludgy edge in ones and twos, making themselves as inconspicuous as possible, cutting back what they could, and retiring before they were spotted. The result was a half-job of narrow passages, barely wide enough to allow a man through, let alone a warhorse in full battle regalia.

Still, Grimoald thought sourly as his horse was forced to wade and wrestle its way through the thick fronds, that was the lot of auxiliaries. They did the dirty work. Took the highest risks. He would, by all the gods of the mighty River Renos, make certain he received the highest rewards when this battle was done. No matter that he had failed to capture the druid or his treasure. No matter that his unit had been recalled just at the moment of his final victory. That was but a flea on the rump of an ox. This – this very moment – was where lasting glory could be grasped. He did not intend to let go.

The stallion was up to his fetlocks now. Grimoald winced at the sound of splashing, though it could not be helped. Fortunately, the mist dulled all noise, a blanket tossed over the wolf-lit dusk. He thought he could hear chatter on the opposite bank. Contented, calm chatter. Good enough.

His boots squelched as he dismounted, signalling wordlessly for the column of riders at his back to follow suit. More men, his brother-Batacgwi from other units, were already out in the river, pushing across. A broad surge of death, unexpected and uncontested. It had begun.

Cold enveloped him as he waded into the water, as if iron bands constricted his ribs, making him gasp. Fear and exhilaration mingled with the numbing embrace. A splash on his lips, bitter and silty, stirred up by his stallion's thrashing hooves. All around him, the saddle-skulls floated, bobbing white. His feet wheeled madly, seeking the surety of the vanished riverbed. He clung to the reins as the horse, eyes bulbous and teeth bared, struck out for the far bank, froth jetting from its roaring muzzle. They were heavy with armour, with weapons, but man and beast were forged in the harsh waters of Germania, and they had spanned wider, faster, deeper and colder rivers than this far-slung stream. What was impossible to other men was as child's play to the noble Batacgwi.

Grimoald kicked by instinct, though his mount propelled them well enough. Water surged around them as they swam, cutting the current, heads high, shield, spear and sword lashed tight to the saddle. Then they were on the far bank, gliding into the reeds. With grim determination, horse and man laboured through the cloying mud, armour dripping. Beyond the rushes, the glow of embers showed them the way. Grimoald mounted as quietly as he could, unfastening the items he would need as the horse took him through the whispering foliage and into open ground. No words were spoken as the rest of his force trundled up in his wake. The sun was diminishing to his left, cloaking the hunters in gloom. Hundreds of Batacgwi. Water lords. Achieving the impossible. Here to prove their worth for all to see. History would testify.

This western bank was quiet and still. The air smelled of woodsmoke, fodder and horseflesh. In the distance, Grimoald could make out the shapes of bodies, like piles of rags. Warriors, settling in for the night beneath their thick animal pelts. They would be kindling fires and preparing items for the pot. There were thousands, all the way up the slope to the freshly dug lines of defence, to the high wooded ridge, and, he did not doubt, far beyond. When roused, they would be a multitude. Vengeful and ferocious. But here, on the lower ground, nearest this difficult crossing place, the guards were fewer, their senses dull, fatally complacent.

Grimoald saw a field full of horses, tied to stakes, their breath steaming, adding to the thinning mist. The first scream rent the grey evening, and he felt his face peel back in a savage grin.

The wagon lurched violently, trundling, far too fast, over a blackberry thicket that had been trampled to an ankle-high wedge by horse, chariot and man. Becan gripped the rail, cursing under his breath. The spearman with the injured foot hissed something significantly more vicious. Gwidion, at the reins, ignored them both, lashing the nag savagely, demanding greater speed.

They were climbing the slope. Running for their lives. Riven with breathless, panicked horror. The riders had come from nowhere. From the very darkness of the river. Emerged in the murky, mist-wreathed dusk like an army of ghouls, conjured from the depths of the Vaga itself. Gwidion had stammered and blustered, calling upon every god he could think of to send these devils back whence they came, but his entreaties had fallen on deaf ears. Still, the riders had come. Still, the slaughter had commenced.

The sound would never leave Becan. Shrieks of disembowelled or hamstrung horses. Cries of sentries and charioteers, run through with ruthless delight by the riders who swept through the encampment with the speed of ravenous wolves, glistening blades dark with fresh blood. All was chaos, all was confusion. Bellows of alarm had risen up, spread like wildfire through the sleeping tribes, joined quickly by horn blasts, but the attack had been so sudden, so unexpected, that the chariot field had been churned to a gore-streaked morass before any meaningful counterattack could be organised. The paddock was now a charnel pit. The war-carts smashed to kindling, the drivers dead, the horses turned to so much twitching offal. Those animals who managed, through their wrenching terror, to break loose of their tethers, were careening up the hill even now, overtaking the rocking wagon, maddened by the killing and likely never to return.

Becan crawled, hand over hand, to the rear of the vehicle, staring back in disbelief at what transpired at the water's edge. Who were these riders and how had they crossed? But he knew, of course. Cullen had told them, warned them.

He was mesmerised. They swirled like avenging demons, cutting and slashing their way to a massacre he could not have imagined only moments before. The horde was awake now. Howling in surprise and anguish, up and down the slope, from water to wood, from east to west. A hundred thousand warriors, maybe more, and they were surging in the opposite direction to the wagon, a great, gushing storm-front of bodies, but it was already too late. The first reached the enemy and were cut down, shambolic and unsuspecting as they were, by javelins and swords, impaled, split, hacked and eviscerated.

One rider in particular stood out, his gold and black cape stark against the rest, his head encased in glittering bronze. He wheeled in tight circles, sword raised, beckoning the others to merge around his black mount. That horse, snorting and rearing as water sprayed from its shivering flanks, had skulls tied to its saddle. They rattled and jerked as it moved, the dance of doom. The rider was shouting orders, braying like a crazed bear, and the enemy went to him, followed his lead, as he decapitated one man and trampled another. Then they were withdrawing, slowly, deliberately. Sinking back towards the reeds, melting into the water, leaving behind fields of mangled corpses, men and beasts entwined in death. The horde was awake now, but their chariots – their greatest weapon – had been utterly destroyed. Their dreams of victory soured to blood-drenched nightmare.

—

Cullen learned of the obliteration of the chariots by way of feverish rumour, long before the messengers howled it out as horrifying fact. He had asked, with all the rest, what was happening. Grabbed men by the shoulders as they ran past. Quizzed them on what they had heard, how many had been lost and what was now to be done. He had deposited the squirming Ludris in the hollow heart of an ancient oak, and gathered his twin spears and buckled his scabbard, and run to join the thousands that surged down the slope towards the river. One small wave in an ocean swell.

He had intended to make for the chariot paddock. To be a part of the fight-back. To punish those who had slipped across the water unseen, who had wrought such chaos, such panic amongst the horde of the Isle of the Mighty. But then horns and drums and carnyxes had wailed and thundered from a different part of the river. It was a din so ferocious to the ears he wondered if the Otherworld itself had disgorged every fallen warrior since time immemorial, a final, cataclysmic judgement upon the Roman invader. But no. The calls were so loud, so vociferous, because they warned of yet another attack. A new attack. A vast, dreadful attack, somewhere upriver.

He veered to the right, going with the throng, uncertain of what transpired but trusting in others who knew where they were needed most. The moon was making inroads now, filtering through mist, turning the valley a hazy grey. Cullen was presented with a broad vista as he sprinted, pell-mell, down the incline. He could see the legions behind their shields and standards, massing opposite the islet that had been carved by the river's bend. Togodubnos had stationed hundreds of warriors on that vulnerable promontory, and thousands more had been set a little way back, in reserve. It should, therefore, have bristled with iron. Far from weak, the islet was intended to provide the perfect bait, taunting the reds into a rash assault, there to be crushed by sheer weight of numbers.

Except that those numbers had stunningly, shockingly thinned. And just like that, he knew what had occurred. The horde, roused by the screams of dying men and horses, had swarmed downstream, towards the paddock, shoaling like myriad fish, heading as one crazed herd to wreak vengeance upon those who had made the audacious incursion to slight the chariots. Which left the islet sparsely protected.

The realisation made his stomach lurch. The mess of bread and cheese crawled up his gullet, bubbling into his mouth, bitter and hot.

Now, as he ran and cursed and begged Taranis for courage, he could see small groups of enemy auxiliaries break away from the main legions and plunge into the river, spears held high above their heads. They were coming in waves, wading by the score, and behind them the legionaries marched in their orderly ranks to the water's edge, shields and swords at the ready, eyes fixed on the crossing.

More carnyx calls sounded, from down in the valley and up on the ridge. A desperate cry from Togodubnos and his battle-chiefs to divert attention away from the lost cause of the chariot field and to the impending crossing of an entire legion. Cullen headed straight for the promontory, where the embattled defenders were already engaging the first of the auxiliaries to make it across. Around him, more and more warriors heeded the cry, surging to meet this new threat, their oaths soaring up with their spear points. They were bearded and cloaked, with beautiful armlets, twisted torcs and intricate necklaces. They wore bracae of many shades, chequered and striped and plain, and their torsos were clad in thick pelts or entirely naked. Their bodies were painted in woad, etched permanently in charcoal, hair long or spiked or braided.

They represented the coalition that Togodubnos had worked so hard to forge. His own Catuvellauni and their vassal-tribe, the Trinovantes. Cullen's Atrebates and the Cantiaci, whose land this rightfully was. Ordovices and Cornovii from the northwest, the Damnonii from the southwest, and the Eceni from the east.

It was a thing of grim poetry. The realisation of Togodubnos's dream. And yet, he thought, perhaps it was all too late. They had been diverted, their attention appropriated by the surprise attack. His guts twisted. For all his warnings, he knew, in the pit of his gut, that the Batacgwi had done precisely what he had feared. What he had cautioned against. They had swum the Vaga and stolen the initiative. And now the legions were coming.

He was fifty paces from the fight now. The spit of land, projecting out into the wide river, was full of warriors, and they were casting sling stones and hurling spears at the advancing ranks. But the Roman auxiliaries had striven all the way across before the full alarm had been raised, and they were through the rows of sharpened stakes, stealing their first steps on solid turf, forming a stoic if ragged shield-wall to secure what they had seized. And, at their backs, the crossing of the main legion was well underway, their scuta lifted above the chest-high water as they waded in a wide front, intending to envelop the promontory and the main shore on both sides.

Cullen reached the water's edge, a little way to the south of the islet, and crashed into the shield of a tall, blond fighter he took to be a Gaul. He brought one of the spears up, found resistance, snarled as he jammed the other home and howled like a wolf as the man fell away. Another Gaul came at him with a wild swing of a club-like weapon, thick and knotted, and he only just managed to fend off the blow with one of the spear hafts, which broke in two. He jabbed the splintered top half into the man's face, the point driving into an eye, letting go of it as the Gaul twisted away in agony. He noticed the first Gaul's shield floating close by, and he stooped to snatch it up, bringing it round just in time to block the flight of a javelin that would surely have skewered his face.

On he waded, deeper by the pace. Shield up, spear sliding at its rim, jabbing relentlessly. The Vaga churned reddish brown. He could hardly tell friend from foe. A mass of bodies, convulsing back and forth in the shallows, the clang of iron only drowned out by the screams of the dying. Sling stones and arrows whirred past his ears. Pila came back, hurled by the advancing legionaries. It was a maelstrom. A hailstorm of murderous projectiles. He wanted to shut his eyes, but he knew that would only hasten death, so he squinted, as if stepping out into a snow flurry, and he crouched into the shield, putting as much of his body behind its curved face as possible, and he stabbed low, stabbed high, stabbed anywhere he could. Out of the corner of his eye, he glimpsed one of those heavy iron javelins slam straight through the neck of the man beside him, snatching him back. Water splashed. Another warrior filled the gap. Cullen paid no heed.

The auxiliary units had dissipated now, pushed back or killed, subsumed by what came behind, and the massed, interlocked red shields of the legion ground their way inexorably forward. These were men in bronze and iron, red-cloaked and snarling, their leaders big and broad-shouldered, with plumed helmets and muscled chest-plates. A standard bobbed high above the seething mass, bearing the image in gold of a beast, its head that of a goat, its tail inspired by a fish. The banner was hefted by a tall man in a strange animal pelt, not so dissimilar to that worn by Grimoald of the Batacgwi, and Cullen wondered what had become of his foe. He wondered what had become of the comrades he had left to face Grimoald's ire. The thought shamed him; enraged him. He bit down so hard that his mouth filled with a bloody tang, and he pushed on, shoving and battering at the advancing shield-wall. But the men on the other side of those barriers were not wild Gauls. They were disciplined Romans, and they held firm, absorbed the crashing tide, pushed back along a broad front, their short stabbing gladii flicking out below shield-rims like giant, gleaming tongues, their touch as deadly as any viper's bite.

Commands punctuated the din, a spew of unintelligible Latin, and the legionaries, faceless in their implacable units, grunted as one, shunted as one, and Cullen felt himself stagger back. He jammed the spear against the nearest shield, bracing, giving himself room to perform a tiptoeing dance to avoid the inevitable gladius thrust. The blade-tip, aimed for the artery at his groin, brushed his thigh, tore the fabric of his braca, though his legs were so wet and numb that he could not discern blood from river water.

More orders shrieked, as indiscernible as all the others amid the pandemonium, though he caught scraps of words, recognised the common tongue. A surge at his back. Warriors of the great horde, fresh to the fight, slamming home to join the tiring men and women in the searing battle-furnace. Wood splintered against metal, the cries of the dying rising all around. It was the legionaries' turn to take rearward steps in the face of a shockwave that rolled all the way along the line. Cullen added his screams to those of his comrades, revitalised by their snarling arrival, and he punched his shield out, knocking a Roman's far enough aside to give room for his spear, and he stabbed hard, meeting resistance. The man before him brayed, sheered away. The spear went with him, the shaft slick with blood, breaking Cullen's grip, sliding free. Cullen let it go, stepped back, opening the range, groping for Lightning-Strike's hilt. He liberated the blade just as the horde surged again, compelling him forward, and he jabbed a low blow at the man opposite. The Roman, obscured by his big scuta, emitted a querulous keening sound as he crumpled, curling about his pain as the cleaved crotch gushed steaming crimson.

Cullen stepped over him. Stabbed him again to make certain of the job. Tried to push, throwing his strength into the combined might of the snarling horde. But the goat-legion held, their line bending but not breaking. They were vastly outnumbered, and most still fought in the river, encumbered by the swirling currents and the cloying sludge, yet they were hard as the iron they wore. Unyielding, disciplined, relentless.

A horn called out from the Roman side. Sharp blasts of different lengths. Instructions issued. The goat-legion moved as one. Cullen took a step back of his own volition, but the second step and the third were entirely engineered by Rome. He fought, shoved, shouldered, cursed. He dug his feet into the morass of squelching silt and trampled reeds, scrabbling for purchase, but still he found himself sliding back, an unwanted retreat. He was forced to look down, putting his energies into avoiding the gladii that still darted at the side edge of the scutum opposite, and all the while the water grew shallower until he found himself on dry land.

Dry? No. It had been liberally decorated in blood and entrails, clumps of flesh and dashed brains. But it was land, nevertheless. The legions were advancing successfully, steadily, momentum firmly with them now. There were hundreds – thousands – of shields presented in perfect formation. An armoured beast, unflappable and unstoppable, spear and stone bouncing impotently off its metallic hide. It had been a bold move. Togodubnos, Caratacos, Aoife and the rest of the tribes' high leaders had undoubtedly anticipated a dawn advance, giving the Romans a full day to take the valley. A dusk attack, with the light fading fast, was as fraught with risk as it was unexpected.

Cullen was exhausted. His arms screamed in pain as he fought to keep them up. The fighting was brutal and close. Swords clanged against shields, spears probed for flesh, the air pungent with the stench of blood and sweat, piss and vomit. He could see the islet out the corner of his eye. The epicentre of the fight. The reds' objective. The warriors there were giving ground too. Buckling under the impossible pressure. Another section of javelin throwers was wading across from the far bank now, and they twisted sideways, still twenty paces short of the bank, and hurled their pila as one; a high, looping arc that sailed over the heads of their own foremost ranks and thumped sickeningly into the massed warbands. Bodies dropped. Gaps opened in the raging horde, to be filled instantly by those coming up behind.

Cullen shut out the scene, funnelling his focus on the man immediately opposite. He rumbled forward, thrust his shield into the scuta, its gold leaf scarred now from a hundred blows. He sprung on his toes, a tired half-jump, bringing his arm up and over, trying to smash Lightning-Strike down on the Roman's head. The man's gladius tracked its sweep, parrying at the last moment, and the world flashed bright as its hilt punched him square in the nose. He reeled, slipped in the bloody grass, collapsed on his back, brightness dissolving to black. He cursed savagely, refusing to let the dark take hold, and suddenly, mercifully, he could see, though it was through a curtain of tiny stars. He had let his sword fall, so he wrenched himself to the side, anticipating the death-blow, and heard the wet thwack of a shield's bottom rim slamming into the earth where his throat had been. He barrelled into a fur-swathed corpse, groped for the spear shaft still grasped in the lifeless fingers, tore it free and stabbed upwards as hard as he could. Blood sprayed, warm and slick. Not his own. He twisted again, still bleary, scrabbling for Lightning-Strike and thanking Taranis when his fingers slid down the slick flat of the blade. Up he got, fighting the wooziness that worked its way through him like poison, knowing the next Roman would step into the expertly controlled line in a matter of moments. He blinked away blood, hauled breath into his lungs, ribs aching, vaguely aware of a force holding him upright, keeping him steady. He glanced to his left. A warrior, taller than most, loomed over him, his big hand gripping Cullen by the scruff of the neck.

'Stay with me, Atrebates,' the voice intoned.

'Kurd,' Cullen managed to utter, still regaining his breath.

Kurd Long Arm grinned like a denizen of the underworld, his face a gore-spattered nightmare. He was bare-chested, as was his way, the woad paint covering his torso smeared with blood, and his carefully curated whiskers – normally twisted to sharp points with lashings of beeswax – were reduced to a wiry mess.

He let go of Cullen, and lunged at the Roman shield-wall with a wild sweep of his huge battle-axe, cleaving a gaping hole just above the scutum's boss, dragging it down to expose the man beyond. Cullen saw the opening, shouldered himself in, stabbed hard at the shocked face with Lightning-Strike. The man's features dissolved in a crunching welter of blood.

Kurd snarled approval, yanked Cullen back as the Roman line slotted into shape again. 'Ulla would be proud!'

Cullen lifted the shield, absorbing a brace of quick blows, replying with a hefty slash of his own. An image of Ulla's hard face came into his mind. The famed war-giver, slain in a fight with the Silures, had been his first battle chief. Cullen had learned his craft under Ulla's stewardship, shoulder-to-shoulder with Kurd Long Arm. It was reassuring to see his old comrade here, in this direst of places.

'Push forward!' a disembodied voice bellowed from further back. 'Forward!'

'You heard him,' Kurd grunted, and went to work with his great axe.

The opposing lines convulsed again as the defenders offered a renewed surge. The Romans took a rearward step, then another, their formation bowing. A great howl of triumph rose up from the native side.

But the enemy would not break. Cullen rapidly understood that the flexing of their formation simply absorbed the new pressure, but it was never close to fracturing. Indeed, even as he hacked and slashed and shouldered and cursed and spat, he found himself sliding back again as the Romans straightened. It was impossible. Unthinkable. For every legionary there were ten native warriors, yet the reds' advance was inexorable, and they responded with an onward pulse of their own.

Step by agonising, bloody step, they shunted forward, driving the tribes back, gaining a foothold on the promontory.

Behind Cullen, far behind, where the slope was broken up by the new earthworks and barricades, horns began to wail. A message transmitted up and down the valley. He gritted his teeth, hissed a bitter oath, refusing to heed, battering again and again at the monstrous, relentless shield-wall. But Kurd was there, grasping his shoulder, hauling him away from the carnage. His heart sank. Because the horns were sounding the retreat.

—

Aulus Plautius raised a goblet. 'Gentlemen, we have our foothold.'

Adminios lifted his cup with the others, toasting their small victory as the general began his summation of the evening's efforts. He sipped the wine, careful not to imbibe too much, knowing that the Vaga was far from theirs. As the rich liquid slid warmly down his throat, he poured himself into his immediate surroundings, trying to shut out the disembodied screams that rent the night air beyond the command tent.

The room itself was dimly lit, ripe with the twined odours of sweat and smoke. Flickering oil lamps cast long shadows across the canvas walls, making a ghoulish mask of Plautius's campaign-weathered face as he consulted his sprawling map. He glanced up, finding an aide in the gloom. 'Toll?'

'Near a thousand, general.'

'A necessary investment.' Plautius jabbed a finger at the map, tracing the winding river's route. 'The Batavians did what they do best, knocking the cursed chariots off the board.' He threw his gaze about the assembly, eyeing the officers who had climbed the slope to convene this special council. He let his gaze linger on each face, as if his sombre expression drilled the importance of the coming hours into their minds. In the silence, they could hear the low murmur of the camp outside, the occasional clang of armour, the distant crackle of the campfires. An army exhausted from battle, preparing to go again with the coming of the sun. Plautius returned himself to the table, his silvered hair catching the light, giving him an almost spectral glow as he inspected the lie of the land. His finger moved, sliding upriver until he reached the bulge on the west bank that Vespasian's legion had assaulted. Where once a wooden counter had been placed to denote an enemy warband, the spot now proudly bore a small wooden figurine in the image of an eagle. 'The Second Legion paid in blood, but they have bought us a crucial platform. We have established a bridgehead on the bend, here.'

Adminios perused the map. The shaded lines on either side, denoting the opposing hillsides. The stick-figure trees that showed where woodland obscured terrain. The incongruous zigzags at the points where the Britons had dug in behind wickerwork barricades. And, of course, the serpentine watercourse at the centre of it all, thinning and bulging as it progressed through the valley bottom. His eyes raked the blank expanse that had hitherto displayed square tokens in lieu of chariots, since knocked, with unabashed gusto, from the table. His skin prickled as he imagined what had occurred there. He blinked the images away, letting his gaze slide down the map – upriver – to linger on the promontory where the main fight had taken place. He had watched the Second's advance as the evening slipped gradually into night. Had stood on the ridge, mouth agape, as Narcissus had crooned and the tribes had dashed themselves upon the most expertly executed shield formation he had ever witnessed. Had surprised himself at the flicker of pride he had felt as those same tribes, roundly outfought and quickly thrown back, had managed to retire in good order, preventing the legions from gaining a complete rout before the day was done. Had thanked the gods that he had not been called to fight. Now it was stalemate as the campfires burned and the wounded moaned in the dark. A battle half-done. He looked up from the map, at Plautius. 'Does it hold?'

The general nodded, indicating the extreme left side of the map, where green lines denoted the fringe of the western woods. 'Your brothers have retired to the forest.'

Someone said, 'Then may we not advance?'

Plautius raised an eyebrow sardonically. 'At night, into a wood we have no knowledge of?'

'They have not retreated further,' Adminios warned. 'They wait only for dawn. Expect them to contest any further crossings.'

'My dear Adminios,' came a voice from near the tent flap. The outline of a plump man, his teeth flashing white as he smiled. 'We are counting on it.'

Adminios could not see Narcissus clearly, but he knew to whom he replied. 'Do not underestimate them,' he began irritably, 'for they—'

'I have not come this far,' Plautius cut him off, 'by misjudging my opponents.' He tapped the table, forcing Adminios to look down at the intricate sketch-work and movable counters by which he made his plans. 'We have taken the promontory, but at great cost. They have removed the bulk of their forces to the higher ground because they expect us to be cautious, to consolidate.' Plautius looked up, an almost menacing determination glittering in his obsidian gaze. 'We shall be anything but.'

Adminios put his own fingertips to the eagle figurine and the markers up amongst the treeline, moving one westward and the others east, so that they butted into one another, the latter quickly outnumbering the former. 'If Vespasian advances from his position, they'll engage him. You cannot bring enough men across that section of water before the Second are overwhelmed.' He stopped, the memory of an irritatingly self-satisfied officer roaming freely into his mind. 'Geta.'

Plautius smiled. An indulgent gesture, as if to a pupil. 'He moves even now.' The smile broadened, evidently noticing Adminios's roving gaze as he searched the tent for the young patrician. 'He takes the Ninth down to the waterside.'

CHAPTER SIXTEEN

The smoke from the watchfires hung low, clinging to the earth like the breath of something ancient and lurking, mingling with the mist to form a thick, ominous miasma. In the desultory light she moved, tugging the hood over her head, biting down the regret at having stolen Gaius's cloak. The tents of the Ninth stood in rows all around – orderly, clean, but empty. The legion would be massing at the riverbank, somewhere downstream, ready to unleash the fires of Tartarus on the unwitting sons of Britannia.

Britannia? No, she thought. This was the Isle of the Mighty. She could feel it through the soles of her shoes. The magic that welled up through this land. Moranna's land, Aoife's land, Cullen's and Becan's.

Cassia's.

She moved like a shade between the rows, body wrapped tight, dark hair bound under a scarf so that it would not betray her sex to the tense, predatory ranks of men. In her hands she clutched a brace of amphorae, and she held them tight to stop her hands from trembling, the ceramic handles clinking.

Down the slope now, skirting any gatherings numbering more than a few, into the midst of the main army. But what pervaded was obliviousness. All eyes faced westward, trained on the horde that awaited them, on the little fires and the glinting iron that sparked like so many stars against the black hillside.

She made it to the river unmolested, where a group of legionaries clustered about the carcass of a desultory fire. These men noticed her, of course. To ignore her was more than their lives were worth. Yet there was no apprehension, nor even urgency, for this was the section that immediately faced the far promontory, captured the previous evening by the Second Legion. With both banks occupied by friendly troops, the mood seemed more relaxed than elsewhere, the threat of counterattack – or even just a potshot from a sling – significantly diminished. This was, she had reasoned, the only possible opportunity.

She quickened, passing the group before they could rouse themselves to accost her, and picked one of the guards at the water's edge, making directly for him. He stood at the entrance to a crude wooden pier that jutted out into the slow, murky flow of the Vaga. A row of flat-bottomed ferries bobbed in place, half-shrouded in mist. From the bow of one, a tow line extended into the water, vanishing halfway into the miasma. The sentry had dispensed with his shield and leaned heavily against his pilum, the butt-end jammed into the soft earth, but he stirred into life as she came close, sidling out to intercept her.

'State your business,' he said in a bored tone, and she was pleased to discover he was not only young, but visibly weary.

'I need to see Quintus Caedicius Crispus,' she said in a low, conspiratorial voice. She let her gaze pass his shoulder, taking in the indistinct shapes of men on the curved neck of land that was the prized Roman foothold. 'He is on the peninsula?'

'He is,' he replied sardonically, 'but it is not a place for maids and cooks.'

She bit her lower lip, sliding her teeth back, letting it pop, wetly, free. 'I am neither.' She winked, coquettishly, pushing the revulsion from her mind. The objective was all that mattered. 'He has won a victory. Legatus Vespasian sends his...' she pushed back the hood and scarf just enough for a tendril of thick, glossy hair to fall across one eye, 'compliments.'

'Compliments?' The whites of the sentry's eyes grew large. 'Oh.' He turned back to look across the river. 'Equestrian stock. By Minerva's tits, they don't know their luck.'

'Vespasian sends his regards to you all,' she said smoothly, holding up one of the amphorae. 'Warmed posca. Said it'll put fire in your veins. The herbs are not fresh, sadly, but I believe it will be to your liking.'

He took the proffered vessel with a grudging sniff, evidently accepting this was the best proposal he would receive tonight. Hoisting it by one of the handles, he quaffed a couple of deep gulps, nodding appreciatively. 'Not bad.'

'That one is for you and your friends,' she said, lifting the second amphora. 'This one is for Tribunus Crispus.'

The boat slid easily across the water, for here, where it hugged the promontory, the Vaga was calmer than elsewhere. The grunts of the men on the far side carried to her, muffled and indistinct, as they pulled the tow line, hand over hand. That line, taut and dripping, a handspan above the surface, was propelling her little boat cleanly through the current.

Cassia counted the pulls. Each time the legionaries grunted, each time the ferry slowed and the line slackened. She had reckoned on twenty beats, but by a dozen she was well over halfway. So she lay the second ceramic jug on the floor and stamped on it, hard as she could, making the boat lurch and the amphora shatter.

She paused, listening intently for cries of alarm. There would be nothing at her back, for the sentries she had left behind would be well lubricated now, and the posca contained both poppy juice and crushed henbane leaves, obscured by the benign mix of mint, herbs and a few drops of resinous myrrh. Not enough to kill, but their wits would be gradually unmooring.

The men on the bridgehead, though, were a different prospect, not least because they were effectively besieged in enemy territory. Their senses could not possibly be keener. So Cassia stooped to rummage in the debris of the amphora, and plucked free the only thing it had contained. A medic's knife, sharp as a whisper in silence. One more beat and she was as close to the promontory as she dared get. The shadows sharpening, gaining features, becoming men, snatches of their soft words slewing over the water, as if attached to the tow line.

She scrambled to the bow and severed the rope. The water hissed as the line twanged loose, coiling along the surface like an impossibly long serpent. Cut suddenly adrift, it felt as though the ferry were in violent reverse, and Cassia almost pitched headlong into the river, but she clung on, by desperate fingernails and hooked legs, the blade plopping harmlessly into the abyss. Now the shouts came. Not in alarm so much as surprise. They had lost their traction, probably fallen in a heap at the river's edge, and presumably now wondered which of their comrades was meandering downriver.

Cassia let the vessel drift. It turned circles, moved entirely by the vagaries of the Vaga itself, and she was rapidly putting distance between herself and the promontory. She was close to the reeds on the western shore, though. To the side where the Britons lurked in their thousands, and then the splashes began as spears were hurled from the dark. The warriors assumed this was a hapless boatload of reds. Of course they did. She squinted into the gloom, trying to anticipate the flight of the shafts, trying to dodge. A low hum emanated from the bank. The whine of twirling slings, and she knew there was no avoiding this new threat.

Cassia screamed. She forced all notion of her father's language from her mind, lest she say the wrong thing and entice the warriors to redouble their efforts. She was a woman of the Isle of the Mighty. She had killed for these people, spied for them. She had betrayed her own kind, because, despite the memory of her father and the comradeship, the comfort, she had felt with Gaius, she was in love with a Briton. She shrieked out curses and pleas in the common tongue of these warlike islands, begging the gods for mercy and fully expecting a death blow to erupt from the dark.

—

A league to the west, amongst the dense woodland above the Vaga valley, a great many fires lit the night. The horde of the Isle of the Mighty rested; bloodied, but far from beaten.

Ludris's tiny paws were a blur as he fought to keep up with Cullen. After an initial moment's worry, he had found the pup close to the oak-hollow, sprawled – sleepy and soil-dusted – in the midst of a half-dozen chewed twigs and several shallow craters. He had suffered the creature's slavering attentions, understanding that the licking of crusted blood from his face was not a matter of negotiation, but, when the dog had finally settled, they had sought food and water, weaving their way through the throng of exhausted, battered warriors, clustered mostly in their nines, warbands or wider tribes.

The night was at its deepest hour now, the moon hanging low, a silver nugget in a sheet of pitchstone. All around, beside every tree, in every glade, the warriors took their ease, their faces hollowed by exhaustion, dirt and grief, their bodies slumped but still strangely tense. Some leaned against rocks or logs, their breaths shallow as they wrapped furs around themselves for warmth. Others tended to the injured with practised hands, using herbs and salves to staunch bleeding or dull the sharp edge of pain.

Cullen glimpsed the moon through the canopy as he picked his way through gulleys trampled in the fern-banks and bramble-patches. There were bilious clouds scudding in the north, loitering bales of grey above the churning sea, and on the breeze, always, the sounds of distant chatter, words uttered by foreign tongues, a whisper of impending threat.

He found the painted sign of which he had been told, hammered into the scrub amongst a run of black poplars. The marker denoted the personal forces of Aoife the Dread, and he crossed between two of the distinctively forked trunks, coaxing Ludris to follow. They found themselves in a large clearing, where men and women clustered in groups, tending wounds, eating, sleeping. The air was damp and thick with the mingled scent of blood and smoke, roasting meat and burning tree sap, broken only by the occasional cry of a wounded warrior or the murmur of quiet conversation. A whistle played somewhere out in the blackness, a mournful tune that spoke to the prevailing apprehension. He walked on, weaving through the groups, nodding to those eyes he caught as he searched the faces for one he might recognise. This night, above all others, was not one to observe alone.

Above him, an owl took flight from a high branch, the silent wings a brilliant splash of white in the canopy. He hoped it was a good omen, and instinctively kissed the life-wheel marked upon his forearm. For good measure, he fished the heartwood carving from its home at his breastbone and pressed his lips to that, too.

As he let the carving drop, dangling by its string, his eyes alighted on a low bough at the clearing's edge. As nondescript as the rest, except for the pale skull that had been nailed to the cleft where it met the trunk. It glowered sightlessly at the warriors gathered about the adjacent fire, snout long, teeth remarkable for the ferocity they implied.

Cullen veered towards the fire. 'The badger on the wych elm,' he said to Ludris. 'Just as Kurd said.'

A dim, flickering glow bathed the assembled figures as he drew close. He could see Kurd already, the tall figure with his incongruously overgrown limbs loping around the fire's edge to kneel beside a far smaller figure, unravelling a roll of linen with which he began to bind a proffered arm.

'The Eceni man the earthworks while we rest,' Kurd was saying. 'The reds wait for night to pass, but they'll come again at dawn. Try to bring the other legions across.'

'We'll stop them,' said the other. A woman's voice. It might have been a carnyx blast to his ears.

Cullen stopped dead in his tracks. 'Maeveen?'

Every huddled body twisted in the gloom, as a score of flame-lit faces, dull with fatigue, tilted up to regard him.

—

'They made fools of us,' Garn Grey Boulder said, his deep voice strangely hollow, the pain of the dusk-shadowed battle bubbling beneath a façade of stoicism. His gaze was distant as he poked the embers with a blackened stick. 'Fools.'

Rues Seeker was standing by the fire, his wiry frame outlined against the soft glow. His arms were folded, his brow furrowed in thought, though his presence was steady, like the ancient trees surrounding them. 'We are not defeated.'

'Even so,' Garn rumbled, 'they destroyed our chariots.' He shook his broad head, the white plait brushing his crossed legs. 'A masterstroke.'

'Do you think the leopard was there?' Maeveen muttered, peering down at her wounded arm, grimacing as Kurd tied off the bandages.

'No doubt,' Cullen said. He looked fondly at each warrior in turn. All of them dear to him, each one a blessing from the gods. Some, like Kurd, had been members of his old nine, the hawks, which had fractured after Ulla's death. The rest were his recent comrades, who he had feared dead. He could hardly believe they were here. They had arrived, they regaled him, in the valley just before the Roman advance, having crossed at the ford beside the fishing village and ridden hard to join the horde. They had found Aoife's battle standard, even as the alarm had been raised and the screams had risen from the chariot paddock. Like Cullen, they had been caught up in the sudden rush for the promontory, and like Cullen, they had been forced to retire, frustrated, to the higher ground.

'If only he had attacked that last time,' Garn said bitterly of Grimoald. 'I'd have torn his arms from their sockets.'

Andoc, sombrely staring into the fire, lifted a water skin to his thin lips. 'Or your skull would now be swinging from his saddle.'

Maeveen cocked her spiked head at Garn, evaluating him as she would a fresh foal. 'Too big. His horse would be lame in a day.'

Cullen leaned forward to cut a strip of meat from the hare sizzling over the flames. 'I am glad you found your way back.'

The clean-shaven face of Clesek beamed from the far side of their little ring, his fair hair glowing gold. 'We brought this.' The young Cantiaci reached into the shadows at his back, grunting as he dragged a large object to the fore, bracing it in his lap as he held it up. 'I fetched it from the baggage when we heard you were here.'

Cullen felt his face crease with pleasure. It was a shield, its façade divided into four, each part painted with a sigil. The magpie, the triple-tailed horse, the life wheel and the twin snakes. *His* shield.

'This too,' Clesek went on, tossing a bundle of material across the space.

Cullen caught it, unfurling his mother's old cloak with an unabashed grin. He slipped it on, spirits lifting. 'And Hog?'

'Roots in the leaf mulch,' Baglan said, stroking his iron-grey moustache as though it were a pet. 'Happy as… well… happy as a pig.' He jerked his head back, indicating an abstract location to the west. 'All the mounts graze in pasture beyond the woods, at the place where the alders give way to the yellow marsh.'

Beyond the woods. As pleased as he was to learn of his horse's whereabouts, Cullen's hopes frayed a little. This was not a battle that would be easy for mounted warriors, and keeping them back was arguably the pragmatic option. But it would also be sensible in the event of a hurried retreat.

'To think,' he said, forcing the disheartening notion from his mind, 'we protected the ford, and they did not need it.'

'The ford remains hidden,' said White Tal brightly. Another of Ulla's old war-party, he was lean and hard, indispensable in a shield-wall, yet somehow set apart. His perfectly white hair and eyebrows made him almost ethereal. Like some kind of snow-prince, exiled from the dreaming realm to walk amongst the living. 'The reds are yet forced to cross the hard way. There is no shame in what transpired.'

Cullen nodded acknowledgement, craned forward to stroke Ludris, a contented furball at his feet. He looked to those he had left at the village. Abandoned to Grimoald's mercy. From Garn to Maeveen, Rues to Clesek, Baglan to Andoc and Erbin. 'I am sorry.'

'You did your duty, Wolf Scourge,' Maeveen said. 'You acted as you were commanded.'

'It is honourable in the eyes of the gods,' White Tal added, glancing up at the canopy as if his perception exceeded that of mortal eyes, 'and your ancestors.'

'In the eyes of your blade-brothers too,' Andoc said, catching his eye pointedly.

'I warned them of the Batacgwi,' Cullen said. 'I told them.'

'It is done,' said Rues. 'Do not dwell.'

'It was a mere distraction,' Garn said. 'While we raced to avenge the chariots, they forced their way across the water. I could not believe my eyes.'

Maeveen spat, the flames hissing. 'Getting a few legionaries onto this side of the Vaga does not constitute victory.'

'They'll bring more in the morning,' Andoc said morosely.

'And in the morning,' Garn growled, 'we shall slaughter them.'

The weight of those words settled over the group like a pall. The morning. Dawn would come soon enough, and with it, the promise of more death, more blood, more shattered shields and spears broken on that remorseless Roman line. The thought of it gnawed at the edges of Cullen's mind. He hunkered in to Ludris, gleaning comfort from the hound's soft pelt. Indeed, he thought perhaps sleep might come, if only for a short while. Which was why it was with a sinking heart that he saw the party of grim warriors and cowled Wise Ones stride across the clearing towards them.

—

Aoife was in a combative mood. The battle had begun, after all the manoeuvring and the waiting, the staring across the river and second-guessing of strategy, the Romans had at last made their move, and that very fact seemed to have charged Aoife the Dread with renewed zeal. This, Cullen thought, as he got wearily to his feet and affected a low bow, was what the famed warrioress lived for.

'Come dawn, they will advance,' Aoife announced. She stood with a wide stance, hands on hips, cloaked in fur and touched with gold and silver. A war-goddess to Cullen's eye. She had come to this land, they said, from across the Clear Sea, where the Isle of Destiny met the boundless ocean. The very end of the world. He wondered if she had come from beyond even there. 'We will meet them and turn the Vaga red with their blood.'

She did not address Cullen alone, but the entire clearing. Indeed, her voice, authoritative and penetrating as it was, seemed to resonate far and wide, drifting into the bracken stands and the tangled brush, through the meshed canopy and into the dark web of animal tracks along which so many knots of warriors had made temporary camp. The place, in turn, was silent as it accepted her words. Thousands of warriors standing to receive her, pausing their much-needed meals and running repairs, their tall stories and their whispered prayers.

'Behold,' Aoife said, 'the Whetstone of Gobannos.' She was thirty paces from Cullen, but he could see her green eyes glimmering like polished emeralds, invigorated with the ardour of her tale. With a movement as smooth and quick as a cat's paw-strike, she freed her great sword. 'Imbued with the light of Belinos and power of the smith-god! Retrieved from its sacred home and brought to this place: the site of our great defiance!'

She waited while the crowd cheered, revelling in it, closing her eyes, as if absorbing its fervour. A slow, triumphal smile spread across her handsome features as the noise ebbed. 'The stone was kept safe by our warriors in the face of divers dangers,' she went on eventually, 'so that we may hone our blades upon its mystic surface.' She brandished the sword high, like a war banner. 'I sharpen Lynx-Bite with its magic.'

One of the hooded figures shuffled into her midst. Cullen had paid no attention to the Wise until now, so reduced were they by her stately radiance, but now he watched with renewed interest as the cloaked acolyte presented the very rock for which he had risked his neck. As he looked on, the cowl slipped a little, revealing half a pale face that was set with a sightless, milky eye. Serwil, playing his part, knowing the stone had long since departed its shrine when the rays of solstice had kissed its dull surface. He felt the pang of failure then, a cool worm writhing in the pit of his being. He wanted to look away in shame. But Aoife was reverently placing her sword against the tendered stone, aligning one cutting edge with the rusty bands that were the mark of its function. She held the hilt in a double grip, drawing the weapon slowly backwards, bringing the pommel into her midriff as the blade hissed. It was all ceremony, of course. The edge already as keen as it could possibly be. But so far as the onlookers could tell, it now possessed whatever power Gobannos had to offer, and that was enough. Indeed, hundreds of swords sung in unison as they were pulled from their scabbards. Hundreds of voices cried out with restored courage. Warriors were moving all around him. Coming out of the shadows, converging on the stone. Despite himself, Cullen could almost feel the air crackle with their collective anticipation.

'Dawn is when the tide turns!' Aoife called, a demi-goddess in fur, leather and metal. One of her confidantes appeared at her side, and she stooped to hear what was relayed. Her expression darkened, tightened. She nodded, turning quickly, with renewed purpose. As she slipped into the throng, she paused only to thump a fist to her chest. 'Life with glory, and death with honour!'

Cullen heard himself repeat the expression, lending his voice to so many others. It was the way of the warrior. A convention that mattered, never to be ignored. And yet his words sounded hollow. He could feel the change in the air, belying his misgivings, the Stone of Gobannos working its magic, bringing courage and unity to this disparate collection of nations. But at what price? What glory had there been in barricading himself within a humble village and turning meek fisherfolk to lambs for a leopard? What honour could be found in the deaths of Ludris and Kenal? What future was there, if it would be without Cassia?

Even as he gathered up his weapons and shield, intent on walking off the black dirge that had descended like a thundercloud on his mind, he was waylaid by another of Aoife's aides. The woman was auburn-haired and bright-eyed, short of stature and sharp of feature, with darkly mottled teeth. She spoke quietly, but firmly. 'Lady Aoife commands you to the chariot paddock.'

'That is the left flank,' Cullen said, his eyes straying back to the fire, where the great woman had hitherto stood. 'Aoife holds the right, does she not?'

The aide seemed unmoved by his reply, simply pulling a fur-trimmed cloak tighter about her narrow shoulders. The copper armlets encircling her forearms chinked softly. 'Come sun-up, you must be where you are most needed.'

He pictured the valley in his head, constructing the skeleton of a map, the way the tribes were arrayed. 'That is the Eceni section.'

'There are many besides the Eceni,' the aide said brusquely. 'We are one army. Aoife has work for you there.' She gave a final nod, concluding matters. 'We do not expect the legions to advance before first light. Make sure you are in place by then.'

'I will,' Cullen said, for what did it matter where he lent what strength remained in his bones? How the horde was deployed did not concern him. Indeed, the Eceni had been named on Berikos's list. Were they traitors in waiting? At least this way he could watch them. He gave a final bow. 'Of course.'

—

'You're certain?'

Cassia peered up through eyes stinging with exhaustion to regard Aoife the Dread. 'I was in the presence of General Plautius himself, lady.'

Aoife blew out her cheeks, astonishment momentarily wrong-footing her. 'By all the goddesses of all the lakes in all the land, you have done well, Cassia.' She gave a thunderclap of rueful laughter. 'I can hardly countenance it. Is it really you, returned to us, or an apparition? Do the spirits taunt me?'

'It is I, lady, truly,' Cassia said, though she barely believed it herself. The frantic babble of pleas she had blurted over the water-edge reeds had silenced the sling-song and the shower of spears and stones had ceased. Warriors had come to her in the gloom, hauled her out of the boat, gathered her up. They had been wary enough, but a single, unarmed woman, wailing in the common tongue, had been enough to stay the instinct to slaughter. And she had swiftly, mercifully, found herself conveyed up the slope.

They had found Aoife in the midst of a solemn progress through the many thousands of warriors at her command. The people ebbed and flowed all around her, jostling to catch a glimpse, hear her words, their faces obscured in shadow and firelight. It had seemed an impossible task to snag the great woman's attention, but when one of Cassia's saviours had managed to get word to her, Aoife had broken off her work, her guards and aides carving a space for her, away from the throng. They had ushered her into a clearing fringed by glossy holly bushes, and rammed a torch into the ground so the warrioress might regard her properly. There had been a sacred object in her keeping, but she had passed the item to the Wise, who seemed happy to continue the work. Now Aoife clicked her fingers. One of her advisors, a stout, moustachioed man with a flat slab of a face, scurried up. The tall war-giver addressed him, fast and imperative. 'They plan to put a legion across, downriver. The enemy on the islet will launch a dawn assault, drawing our attention, and another legion—' She glanced at Cassia.

'The Ninth,' Cassia reiterated.

'The Ninth Legion will simultaneously attack. They'll catch us in a pincer. Go, immediately. Find the high king and Lord Caratacos. Warn them. Lord Sego commands Eceni and Catuvellauni warbands in the vicinity. He will need reinforcements.' The slab-faced man broke at once into an ungainly run, making for a horse that was held by the reins nearby. Aoife watched him go, then turned to Cassia again. 'You are a force to be reckoned with.'

'The Eceni, lady,' Cassia ventured. 'They were identified—'

'As were a number of others,' Aoife cut her off. 'Berikos's list of names was a timely warning to Togodubnos, and he has dealt with it accordingly. To treat with the former king of the Atrebates does not prove betrayal. The Eceni will hold their nerve, because Sego Blood Swill's eyes are upon them.'

'Lady,' was all Cassia said, for she had already overstepped the mark.

'What of your friend?' Aoife asked, brighter now.

'She lives, I think.'

'Then we shall find her,' the great woman said firmly. 'You have my word.' That thunderclap laugh again. 'You've saved us, Cassia! We shall beat them yet!'

—

When he had communicated his new order to the others, Cullen's mind turned to the coming confrontation. It would be a battle for the ages, and he knew that he was not yet ready. Too young still, too inexperienced. A blanket of anxiety fell over him, his skin crawling, as though swarmed by ants. He needed to walk, to stride his troubles into the earth, and he left the campfire, plunging into the night, letting his legs carry him away from comrades new and old. He felt sick as he walked deeper into the woods, the pup he had named for a dead boy skittering contentedly in his wake, oblivious to his melancholy. He passed horses tethered to trees, and knots of warriors; sleeping, drinking, telling tall tales and singing songs of heroes. A faint skein of woodsmoke clung to the air, softening the edges of the world, thickening as the clouds drifted lower. He wandered on, along a track that was like a funnel, flanked by scrub and tree. Shivering at a slight chill, he shrugged deeper into the beloved cloak of beaver skin and aimed, absently, for a tremulous orb of light that seemed to beckon him at the track's end. He emerged, finally, into a clearing lit by a single, lonely torch that had been rammed into the soil. At the edge of the space, the leaves of holly bushes shone in the glow. And there he stopped. Dead in his tracks. He gaped, arrested, words swilling in his mouth, unable to form.

The woman on the clearing's far side returned his stunned stare. The torchlight cast her in gold and shadow, gleaming in the liquid brown eyes and fiercely black brows, along the curls of her cascading hair, her olive skin, her straight nose, her full lips. The most exotic creature he had ever seen. Her jaw seemed to loll, mirroring his own. He tried to say something, failed again, barely able to believe that she was real.

—

The breath caught in Cassia's throat.

He was here. Somehow he had found her. For so long, the image of him had lingered in her mind, the curve of his jaw, the jagged cleft made by an axe in his brow, the wildness in his demeanour, offset by the gentleness in his eyes. All that which she remembered, resolving before her, definition added with each step he took into the light. He was taller, broader than the memory she had so jealously guarded. He was slender still, at hip and midriff. The fluff at his chin and the nascent moustache all added to the air of youth that she knew he was desperate to shake. But the power in his knotted forearms and thick shoulders, the roping sinews of his neck, the scars on knuckles, arms and face. It all spoke of a man. More than that. A warrior, fully-fledged. She felt herself smile. His copper-red hair was still a tangled shock, untamed as the hills of his childhood. His braca and tunic were new, but his mother's old mantle, taken from her house the day it burned, was wrapped loosely about his muscled frame and his gaze was locked on her, sharp and piercing, as though she were the only person left in the world.

She reached for him, touching fingers to his. A surge of emotion roared up through her gut and into her chest, making her breaths shallow and her skin pulse.

For a moment, neither of them moved. The air between them vibrated, dense with longing. Then, in a heartbeat, he reached up, brushing her cheek, his touch coarse but tender, as if she might vanish at any moment, a wraith conjured by fatigue.

'Cassia Severina,' he said thickly.

'Cullen of the Atrebates.'

She stepped into him, desperate for him to know she was real. Her hands pressed against the solid warmth of his chest. He winced – an unseen injury – but did not step back, gathering her up, squeezing as though she might slip away with the smoke. She tilted her head to look up at him, his face close, so familiar, yet new again. She rose onto her toes. Traced the line of his mouth with her own, brushing lightly, pressing harder. His lips were rough, but when they responded, the world collapsed inward, the weeks of separation, the gnawing, chronic worry, dissolving in crushing, lambent heat. She gasped against his mouth, teeth chinking, her fingers tangling in his hair as they kissed deeper, the desperation between them palpable.

When they broke off, Cullen took her arm. She let him guide her into the trees, away from the prying torchlight and deep into darkness.

–

Time seemed to stretch and bend, a haze of hunger and pleasure, made urgent by the knowledge that this night might prove their last. Finally, when the last tremors faded, Cullen collapsed beside her, pulling her into his arms as they lay on the cloak, their breaths mingling in the cool air.

For a long time, neither of them spoke. Cassia rested her head on his chest, listening to the steady beat of his heart. He revelled in her warmth. It grounded him as the world slowly began to reassemble around them. His fingers traced lazy patterns on her skin, and she smiled, eyes closed. After the privations of recent weeks, the deaths and the fear, the guilt and the despair, he realised he was content. It was the first time in what felt like an eternity.

'I thought I'd lost you,' she whispered.

Cullen's hand stilled, and he tilted her chin up to meet his eyes. 'And I you,' he said. 'We'll never part again.' They both knew such a promise was not in his gift, but he could see that she believed every word. Here, in this moment, it was enough.

She pushed up and away, propping her chin on an elbow so that she could regard him properly. 'The names I took from Berikos,' she said, fiercely enough, though her curious sing-song accent was honey to his ears. 'Aoife says the king got to hear them. That is something, I suppose.'

He nodded. 'Much good it did. Most have sent no help. A couple claim to have been misled. They've contributed spears, pledged support.'

'Cogidubnus of the Regnenses, Boduoc and Corio of the Dobunni,' she bit the names off harshly, the handwritten words of the former king of the Atrebates apparently seared onto her brain, 'Volisios of the Coritani, Cartimandua of the Brigantes, Antedios of the Eceni.'

All he could do was shrug. 'I have tried, Cassia.'

'I killed that man with my own hands,' she said of Berikos. Perhaps she was remembering how vomit had rumbled into her mouth as she had pushed her dagger into the old king's belly. Perhaps she saw again the light fade from his eyes as he groped at the wound, shock gradually displaced by realisation. 'I still dream of him. His face. I am a healer, Cullen, and I took a life. Tell me it was not for nothing.'

'I do not know,' he said desolately.

Somewhere, out in the gloom, men screamed, high and pitiful. They shared an uneasy glance. Down near the river, they would be sacrificing Roman prisoners, ostensibly as offerings to the gods, but, more pragmatically, as warnings of what to expect. The mutilated corpses would be draped like macabre puppets along the earthworks, staring sightlessly out over the valley.

'Where will you be, come dawn?' she asked. 'The Romans will come on both flanks.'

He gave a grim huff of laughter. 'The river's edge. With the Eceni.'

'The left?' She frowned. 'Sego is down there, Cullen.'

'Good. Sego is a powerful war-giver. He will watch the Eceni as I once watched my goats. Keep them from trouble.'

'I see him with Arthmael,' she said earnestly, 'often.'

'Time heals. Perhaps the wisest of the Wise has softened towards me.'

She punched him lightly. 'Do not be so foolish. A fox will grow grey, Cullen, but he will never grow good.'

'I am sure Arthmael has bigger game to hunt than I,' he reassured her. 'Battle will come with dawn. Besides, Sego barely knows I exist.'

'You defied the wisest of the Wise,' she retorted. 'Stabbed him! Ruined his ceremony and humiliated him! You think Sego Blood Swill has never heard of you?'

'All will be well,' he persisted gently, 'if we survive the dawn.'

'I heard they were parading the Whetstone of Gobannos earlier,' Cassia said, brightening. She canted her head, regarding him with mild amusement, as she had the first time they had met. 'You have earned the fame you so craved.'

'I did not crave fame, Cassia.'

She punched him again. 'Do not bear false witness before the gods,' she chided. 'What would Moranna say?'

He could not stop the bashful grin from climbing up his face. 'Perhaps a little,' he allowed. A thought struck him then, a black cloud scudding across a bright day. 'We lost Kenal. Others, too.'

'This is the life you wanted, Cullen.' She rolled into him again, the tops of her honey-brown breasts swelling as she pressed against his torso, the heartwood carving clamped between their bodies. She kissed his cheek lightly. 'The path you chose to walk.'

—

Grimoald held his palm flat, whispering soothing affirmations as the stallion greedily snaffled the oats, deftly picking them from the clefts between his rough fingers. It was good quality stuff, he reflected. Brought over with the vast Roman supply fleet. None of the inferior mix of barley, grass and beans the Britons offered their mean nags. No wonder their mounts were smaller than the continental breeds. Hardy enough, granted, but stumpy and weak by comparison with those of the Batacgwi or imperial cavalry. Besides, he found the native muck made his stallion break wind like a wild boar, and that alone was enough for him to stick to Roman oats.

'Good?' he muttered in the snorting beast's pricked ear. It was still fully dark, the night further obscured by a gathering mist, but the animal's black eye glimmered wetly as it regarded him. 'Only the best for you, my friend. Take your ease, boy. There is yet work to be done.'

'I do not trust the ostlers with him,' Felix said. He had stridden out of the funereal gloom, soft-footed for one so big, but was staring back towards the legions' makeshift pens, where the Batacgwi mounts were corralled.

Grimoald followed his gaze, though he could not see the object of the man's disgruntlement. 'Nor do I. But I have had words with them.' He gave an amused grunt. 'They agree that to court my displeasure would be foolish. Our horses are well cared for. When the order to attack comes, they shall be fresh.'

Felix's golden moustache rumpled in a bitter sneer. 'Do they not understand that our mounts swim better than their puny men?'

Grimoald stroked his own horse's neck, a sleek wall of sinew and muscle. 'The general feels they are too conspicuous. The flanking strike relies on stealth.' Unconvinced, Felix spat in the direction of the pens. Grimoald chuckled. 'My sentiment precisely, but then I am not in command.'

'You should be, lord.'

'Now that would be a fine day.'

Felix turned to observe the broad stretch of river, most of which was clothed in reed beds and scrub, white miasma gathering like a second river across the surface. On the far side the lights of ten thousand fires flickered as though the very night sky had fallen into the valley. 'When do we move?'

'Soon,' Grimoald said. He waved a hand to his left, indicating the unseen bend in the river, some thousand paces into the gloom, that had seen the majority of the evening's action. 'Vespasian has a foothold on that spit of land. He will look to forge ahead, bring more men across. If he has any sense, he is doing it already, while the Britons are blind. When they wake to see he has encroached further, they will try to stem the bleed, and the trap,' he clicked his fingers, 'will snap shut.'

'They're watching the entire bank, lord,' Felix said uncertainly.

'Four legions is a lot of bank to watch. While they try to pin down Vespasian and the Second, they will take their eyes off the rest. But which legion will strike?'

Felix breathed deeply, steadying his nerves. 'Will it work?'

'It had better.'

A disembodied scream echoed across the valley, from the west bank to the east and back again. A torch moved on the enemy side, tracing a path a third of the way up the slope. Grimoald watched it, like a firefly against the blackness, and he knew it came to rest around the area of the earthworks that would be the Britons' second line of defence, once the river had been fully breached. The torch was joined by others, and they swirled together, dancing with shadows that flitted in and out of their glowing orbits. Druids, he guessed. Capering and chanting like moon-touched lunatics, as was ever their way. Drums started up too. A dozen or more, playing an incessant rhythm that was like a heart's pulse.

'They're making sacrifices,' Felix said grimly.

'The last desperate plea of a conquered people.'

'Conquered?'

'It is done, Felix,' Grimoald said as one of the Roman ostlers came to take his stallion. He handed over the reins, not taking his eyes from the torch-dance. '*Victorum*. They're beaten, the Britons. They simply do not know it yet.'

—

The last of the legionaries died long after he lost his balls. Indeed, he groped mindlessly at the bloody maw between his thighs, as if they might return with a concerted search. All that happened, of course, was that blood drenched his hands and ran like a fountain from his elbows to dapple the planks of the barricade upon which he was impaled. He writhed and prayed and spewed a mixture of vomit and desperate, slurring Latin, difficult even for Arthmael the Learned to decipher.

Arthmael read the omens in that particular death. Scraped shapes and lines into the vomitus blood-pools with a shard of chicken bone and watched for the shadows that slid across the gore when an underling brought forth his torch. Not much to see. Only death on the horizon.

'What a surprise,' he said to no one in particular, though the acolyte nodded sagely. He unfolded himself from the low crouch as the last of the light left the legionary's eyes, and straightened, back and shoulders clicking wildly. The warriors of the Isle of the Mighty, ranged across the slope, from the earthworks all the way up to the forest, were watching him, silent and expectant. 'The gods favour us!' he shouted. 'Victory will come with dawn!'

The fools cheered. Arthmael knew it was no more than the bleat of a frightened flock. Still, he thought, the very nature of hope gave them a chance. If they believed they would win then perhaps it would come to pass. He turned to gaze across the valley, hoping, too, that the opposite would befall the legions lurking in the dark. If fortune was on the right side, then every scream of the sacrificial prisoners, every single gut-wrenching shriek, would put the fear of the gods into the invaders. And fear might be the tribes' best chance. He looked back to the limp sack of torn flesh that had once been a soldier. To the others, naked, blinded, gutted and gelded, that dangled at intervals along the defensive works. Fear would greet the Romans at sun-up. Raw, pulsating, stomach-twisting terror. They had brought their mighty legions, with their bizarre language and their false gods and their stupid banners. Filled this valley with them. Made great display of their discipline and their weaponry and their reputation, counting on anticipation as their ally. The wait would prove too much for the natives to bear. Well, Arthmael had told Caratacos, let the reverse be true. Let the Romans see what awaits, should they cross the Vaga. Let them imagine their own fate at the hands of the Wise Ones. No – let them hear it first, in the dark, through the mist.

He smiled at the new-made corpse. It had been a pleasure indeed. He had used a ceremonial dagger for the job. Black as the night, beautiful and translucent as Egyptian glass. When knapped, it broke away in flakes, akin to flint, but sharper than honed iron. It was the material of the Otherworld, mysterious and deadly. It was what, so reckoned Arthmael, they must have used in ancient times to slay dragons and giants. And it was what he would use to teach the reds a lesson that would haunt them for as long as they chose to occupy lands not their own.

He put the dagger into his belt, protecting himself from its unfeasibly keen edge with a fine sheath of stitched leather. Then he fetched up his stick, leaned into it, revelling in the easing of weight from his feeble frame, and turned to struggle up the slope. At the top of the rise, near the first trees, men and women of his order were busy constructing a wicker effigy, tall as two men, eyes made of white shells that glowed in the dark. It was as he regarded the monstrous figure that he noticed the auburn-haired woman hurrying towards him. 'What news?'

She bowed as she reached him, bringing up her hood as she straightened, satisfactorily furtive, though she smirked triumphally. 'Lord Arthmael.'

'Speak,' he prompted irritably.

'I have given him the order. Cullen of the Atrebates will do as bidden.'

The corner of Arthmael's mouth twitched. So did his groin. 'You've done well, Myrna. You'll be rewarded. The alewife will suffer, as promised.'

She licked her lips slowly, grinning. 'Then you shall be rewarded too, lord.'

CHAPTER SEVENTEEN

Cullen trudged slowly down the slope, in no hurry to leave Cassia. But he knew it was right. He was duty bound to fulfil his orders. She would, he hoped, go through the forest and out the other side, taking Hog from the alder wood and riding fast, seeking a return to the Wise One, Gwidion, there to await the imminent wave of casualties in relative safety.

Thus, after parting in a welter of kisses and tears, and after convincing her to take care of Ludris, Cullen had rejoined what was left of his nine. Now, as a faint glow clambered like a ghostly rainbow out of the eastern horizon, they were descending into the valley. They wove a route between myriad stuttering fires, around which warriors stole their last moments of sleep, and picked their way through the zigzagging passageways that were the consequence of the staggered earthworks Togodubnos had had constructed along the face of the slope. Men and women chattered all around. A whistle-player added his haunting harmony to the low thrum of a hand-drum. Someone sang sweetly of home, far-off and much missed. The river itself was utterly black, hidden by the night and the roiling, almost liquid fog that had spilled rapidly over its broad surface, smothering the valley bottom.

'It's a fight on foot,' Clesek grumbled as they reached the lower section of the incline, where the paddock had been, and where debris remained as a memento of the previous evening. 'No place for chariots.'

'The Romans are fearful,' Kurd Long Arm said. He and White Tal had joined them, for want of any designated location within the vast horde.

'Didn't think they feared anything,' Clesek said.

'They're unaccustomed to chariots,' Garn answered the younger spearman.

'The Gauls,' Cullen said, recalling what Cassia had told him, 'abandoned war-chariots generations ago.'

Garn grunted mirthlessly, staring down at the unhitched vehicles they glimpsed through the mist, worthless now that no beasts remained to draw them. 'Well, now they're fit for the fire.' He thumped his chest with his studded stump. 'We must do the work.'

Maeveen pointed back at the barricades, decorated with grisly, naked cadavers. 'The Wise have prepared the way.'

'Appease the gods and show the reds what awaits,' White Tal said portentously.

'If it helps,' Andoc said, 'then let them geld who they may.'

A group of cowled priests came out of the paddock and started up the slope, so that Cullen was forced to move to the side, lowering his head deferentially.

'The chief sack-slicer himself,' Andoc said dolefully.

Cullen glanced up. Sure enough, Arthmael the Learned walked at the head of the group, loping gait unmistakable. The wisest of the Wise was staring straight back at them as the two groups closed together. He was grinning, his forked tongue slipping in and out, as if with its own mind. Then they were gone, shuffling up the slope, chanting in low, harmonious voices, calling down the power of the Otherworld with pleas and curses in languages half forgotten.

Cullen watched them go. 'Children make contraptions of feathers and twigs to capture their nightmares. I must look mine in the face.'

White Tal shook his head. 'Taranis stepped in when the Wise tried to offer you to the gods. Arthmael knows he cannot touch you.'

Cullen swallowed. It felt like his throat had sprouted thorns. 'I hope you are right.'

A hooded figure separated itself from the back of the departing party, lingering a moment, as if it wanted to put distance between itself and the larger group. Then it slipped down the hill, silent-footed, a black wraith headed straight for Cullen.

'Serwil of the Wise,' Cullen said with a short bow. 'I see you have been busy.'

The hood was pushed back by pale, spidery fingers, and Serwil acknowledged the bow with a nod of his own and glanced up at the sacrifices. 'We make the enemy welcome. I dare say Togodubnos would prefer we carried spears, but we play our part.'

'And the stone?'

Serwil slipped a hand into his cloak, producing the grey rock Cullen knew all too well. 'The warriors are encouraged.'

'She let you keep it?' Cullen asked in surprise.

'I am the custodian,' Serwil said matter-of-factly, apparently struck by Cullen's stupidity. 'Unless the gods tell me otherwise, it must remain in my possession until such time as it can be returned to the shrine at Smith's Ring.' The lone eye shifted to a place beyond Cullen's shoulder. 'You are for the river?'

Cullen, too, peered down into the sliding fog. 'Aye.'

'Then I wish you well.' Serwil's arms extended suddenly, taking Cullen's hands in his. Before the latter could tell what he was about, he had pressed the cold stone into his palms. 'Gods be with you, Cullen.'

—

In truth, it was a little annoying. Cullen had sword and shield, sling, daggers, spear, helmet and cloak. It was enough to weigh him down, without the compulsion to lug a rock into battle as well. But the Keeper of the Whetstone of Gobannos had offered its protection, and, he reckoned, he had probably pushed the favour of the gods far enough already. One more slight would be imprudent.

So it was that the stone went with him, a giant mass in his leather pebble-pouch, as he led his men – and one woman – the final strides down to the former paddock, plunging into the fog as soon as he spied the banner of back-to-back crescent moons; the mark of Antedios, King of the Eceni. The moons were cast in metal, painted yellow, and mounted on a tall pole that, for now, had been thrust into the dewy turf. Visibility was astoundingly poor down in the lowest part of the valley. They were close to the Vaga now, could hear its rush, but saw not a droplet of water at all. On the far side, the glow of torches penetrated the miasma only as intangible distorted orbs, hovering off the ground like night-ghouls or river sprites, prancing in the darkest hours when no humans were abroad. Except, Cullen knew, there were many thousands of humans on that distant back. Hidden, lurking.

'We have been sent by Aoife the Dread,' he said as they were intercepted by a tall, skinny woman with blue woad-stripes under her eyes. 'Perhaps Lord Sego expects us?'

'Downriver, four hundred paces.' She pointed into the murk, as if that would help. 'Where willows hang over the rushes.'

They picked their way through the loitering army, camped in disorderly fashion all along the valley and up the slope. Most warriors were sleeping. Some murmured entreaties to the gods. Some stared, transfixed, at the fog-blanket that might conceal their very doom. Occasionally parties of cavalry trotted by, snaking across the incline, proud on their high seats. Gangs of youths, not yet ready to walk the warrior's path, showed their eagerness by passing messages, gathering firewood or stuffing pots with grease and rags, ready to be lit and launched when the fighting began. Always, Cullen stole glances up at the black line of the ridge. He could only make out small patches of trees where they were illuminated by braziers, but he pictured Cassia there, looking down, searching for him. He knew – he hoped – she had long since departed, but that did not stop his wistful imaginings.

More moon banners had been planted at intervals along this stretch of the river, coming in and out of the slowly drifting fog. Then another stood out atop a long pole, the sigil nailed upon a crosspiece. It was tall enough to brush the lowest-slung willow fronds, the emblem a red half-circle. A blood moon. A thing of dread repute, for those who listened to the poets' battle-tales. Beneath it, a single torch burned in the hand of a mail-clad teen. Cullen could not prevent his eyes from lingering on the standard as he passed underneath, feeling a flutter of icy fingers at the nape of his neck.

The outlines of a hundred people greeted them as they leapt over a deep, watery trench – running parallel to the Vaga – that men and women were covering with branches. They were in a field immediately downriver of the chariot paddock, a scrap of sludgy marsh, hard by the water's edge, and only visible by dint of the season. In a few weeks, it would be swallowed, given over to fish and fowl. To the right, cloaked now in thickening mist, the willow stands were tangled with the reed beds, making a run of almost impenetrable vegetation that would, it was hoped, offset the relatively shallow section of water beyond.

'Strange that they need us here,' Andoc was saying as they moved deeper into the field, careful where they placed their feet for fear of slipping in the soft mud. 'The Eceni have plenty of spears.'

Cullen nodded uneasily. 'I am told they have tasks for us.'

'The Eceni?' Garn asked, his voice dubious. 'Or Sego?' He touched fingers to his badger-tooth necklace. 'Who gave the order, Cullen?'

They heard the scrape of iron before they saw the blades. A score, at least, quickly drawn, a serpentine rasp, the universal language of danger.

Once more, 'Who gave the order?'

Cullen looked at Garn, at Andoc, at Rues. Faces in the gloom, eyes wide and white, postures immediately tense. Only questions there, not an answer between them. The figures came closer. Shadows gaining gradual form and detail. The weapons grew clearer too, and with them, the intent.

Cullen sensed his own people level their spears in reply. He held up a staying hand. They were vastly outnumbered. A misunderstanding, surely. Nervous people in a foggy night, a matter of a few hundred paces from those who would bring death. Hardly a surprise, given the circumstances.

'The hawks,' a young man's tone. 'Welcome.'

Cullen sought the speaker amongst the advancing group, straining his eyes against the night. 'No longer,' he called out, spear lowered to show peace.

The man that stepped from the pack was barely older than Cullen himself, though a full head taller. He had black hair, worn to his shoulders, with a couple of braids dangling across either ear, and finely wrought bands of gold on each forearm. Cullen had no recollection of the narrow face or predatory stare that glinted behind a mask of affability that would not have fooled a half-wit, but a hint of familiarity lingered somewhere at the back of his mind. The young man inclined his head in acknowledgement. 'Since Ulla crossed to the next, I know. But the core of that group persists, I understand.' He glanced at the others. 'Well met indeed. Your fame precedes you.'

'Is that why we have been requested?'

The unctuous smile was too quick. Too forced. 'In a manner of speaking.'

'King Antedios requires more men to watch this stretch of the water?' Cullen asked.

'Antedios is old and ailing,' the man said. 'Prasutagus commands the Eceni spears, with Lord Sego's counsel.'

The name chimed loudly in Cullen's brain. Betha, the Eceni princess who he had rescued from the Silures the previous spring, had been betrothed to a man named Prasutagus. She had warned that he was a snake, a slave to ambition.

'Who are you?' Cullen demanded. The sense of prior acquaintance was rapidly souring into apprehension. 'We were sent here by—'

'Not sent,' the tall man interrupted, 'so much as summoned.'

And now Cullen knew where he had seen that face before. Or, at least, a face borne of the same bloodline. He took an involuntary step back as the giant resolved from the churning mist. A standing stone, hard and unbreakable, animated by sorcery. The giant's movements, though, were far from stone-like. There was a quiet slickness to his big frame, a fluidity. An emperor stag, strolling at the head of his herd, huge but silent, disdainful of all.

'You have come,' said the one they called Blood Swill. The one whose banner marked this part of the river. His eyes were as black as his long beard, though scorn shone brightly in their depths. That gaze, hard as granite, pinioned Cullen. 'I am glad.'

Cullen wanted to swallow. Knew his skinny neck would quiver. A chicken to be strangled. He fought the urge. 'We understand we are to fight under your command, Lord Sego.'

Sego watched him. A raptor inspecting a shrew. His face, a tapestry of interwoven creases and scars, utterly unreadable. He glanced over his massive shoulder at the tall young man who had greeted them. 'My son, Kadored.'

Cullen had guessed it already. He bowed to both. He sensed his own warriors following suit. And Sego's fighters still came, filling the ground at the warlord's back, forming a wall of leather and bronze and mail. A wall that seemed to quiver with hostility. Their leader, alone amongst them, wore no armour and carried no shield. His torso was bare, save a torc at his throat, and was ridged with muscle and painted with magic emblems. He had only an axe, long-hafted and double-headed, which he held low in one massive hand, the fingers banded by rings big enough to encircle birch branches. With his other, he wiped sweat from his empty pate, the skin stretching taut, moving the faded etchings that covered the surface. But those were not the marks that made Cullen's innards convulse. He remembered Ulla telling him of the pattern of diagonal lines that ran all the way around Sego's waist. A belt, needled permanently into his flesh. Cullen's eyes were drawn inexorably to that bluish girdle now. Ulla had said they extended down both Sego's legs too, because he had run out of space. Kill marks, each one a named man sent to the next life. Each one a herald of his prowess.

When he straightened, Cullen bit the inside of his mouth, forcing moisture in so that he would not be shamed for stumbling over words. His heart was racing. 'You *summoned* us, lord? Have you work?' He threw his eyes towards the river. 'Should we set more stakes or lie in wait for the reds?'

'Kadored returns from fosterage,' Sego said.

Cullen glanced from one to the other, nonplussed. 'And a fine war-giver he looks to have become, lord.'

'Unblooded,' Sego said, indifferent to the flattery. 'Untested.'

Cullen gestured at the fog-wreathed Vaga. 'That will soon change.'

'Soon,' Sego agreed. 'When the reds come.'

'When the reds come,' Cullen echoed. He eyed the massive axe, still dangling there like some farmer's tool. Not poised for action, but hardly stowed safely away. He swallowed this time, unable to resist the desire. Nothing about this was right. They had been commanded to this part of the river, and they had been expected, but were far from welcome. The tension was smothering, suffocating. 'Lord?'

The giant lifted the axe, one-handed, his forearm rippling with the strain, and he levelled it at Cullen's chest. 'Kadored, son of Sego, is not for her.'

Baffled, Cullen said, 'For who, lord?'

'The hag,' Sego said, in a voice so low Cullen could almost feel it vibrate in his feet. He thumbed over a shoulder with his free hand. 'His bloodline is too pure. Too great. She would have his soul. Gift it to the gods.'

'The hag, lord?'

Kadored spat. 'The king's witch.'

Sego ignored his son. He stepped forward a pace, worth two to a normal man. 'You are her minion. Her slave.' The axe was trembling now. Not from fatigue, but rage, raw and hot. Another huge stride, the gap closing. 'Bent on doing her filthy work.'

Cullen drew himself up as best he could. Tried to seem relaxed. Mentally counted the famous names at his back. Grey Boulder, Seeker, Spurn Joy, Daybreak, White Tal, Long Arm, Staunch. Erbin and Clesek were there too, and they would fight to the death, name or no name. But the numbers were too great. They were surrounded.

Overwhelmed. And Sego Blood Swill was enough to strike a man dead through fear alone. So Cullen's comrades, poised at his back, would do nothing. *Could* do nothing. They would simply stare, appalled, as they witnessed what was to come, helpless as babes. Cullen stabbed his spear into the mud, growing desperate. 'Lord Sego, there has been some mistake. I am not—'

'You will not have my son, Cullen Wolf Scourge,' Sego snarled, a sudden, horrifying storm of unfettered fury. Violence flared in those malevolent eyes.

'Cullen conspirator. Cullen murderer!'

The attack was so fast that Cullen had only time to pluck the spear point free and leap aside. Sego rushed him, howling, the thick axe-shaft held vertical, high, in two hands, the blade cleaving wisps of mist as it fell. A thud and squelch as it buried itself in the muck. It stuck, only for a moment, but Cullen scrambled up and away as his assailant jerked it free with a spittle-flecked curse.

Cullen braced. Not for Sego, but the rest. Was he relieved or concerned to learn that no one moved? The big man's warriors were not here to kill him, he realised, but to prevent his comrades intervening. A slight breeze rolled down the valley, pushing a slew of mist off the river, tumbling between them. Out of it came Sego, his harsh face a bitter brew of grimace and grin. Hard voices cheered as he hefted the axe. Cullen turned himself sideways, presenting the smallest target he could manage, stiffened his shield arm, extended the spear. Prayed.

The axe came down, whistling in the dark. He threw himself out of the way, spooling into the mud once more. His arms, face, knees smeared with cold, cloying grime. He twisted onto his back, sensed the world darken under a big silhouette.

Cullen rolled fast, desperate, gritting teeth. He jabbed out with the spear, keeping Sego at a distance. Drew his sword.

Sego swung the axe in a blurring figure-of-eight. He stepped in, challenging Cullen to stab him, and the latter duly obliged. Except the axe was moving so fast that it curtailed the thrust with almost comical ease. The spear splintered, jarring all the way up Cullen's arm and leaving him with a jagged stick, good for Ludris to fetch but little else. Laughter, all around. He tossed the severed shaft at the bigger man and wheeled about, opening the range again, raking the treacherous ground with his eyes, seeking the shield. A woman's voice – Maeveen, may the gods protect her – rose above the others, alerting him to the object that was lying face down a couple of spear-lengths to his right, half in the reeds. Sego's wolfish gaze went there too, silently noting the shield, and he shifted his feet to his left, cutting off Cullen's route, forcing him in the opposite direction.

Cullen pushed it from his mind. Took Lightning-Strike in a two-handed grip. 'I had never met your son, lord!'

Sego spat. 'You were sent to murder him.'

Cullen shook his head frantically. 'Who told you this lie?'

Sego advanced, without particular urgency, as though savouring the inevitable. Cullen darted high, a speculative jab that made Sego bring up his guard, then dropped into a crouch, swinging low, making a scythe of Lightning-Strike, trying to chop at knee height. The big man stepped nimbly back, easily out of range, wheeling to his right, always sneering.

It was enough. Cullen bolted for the reeds, flung himself, sprawled in the sloppy mire and snatched up the shield. He could hear the splash of footsteps behind and he hauled himself onto his knees, leapt onto his feet, and spun, shield up, taking the huge blow on the iron boss. It sent him reeling. Water was at his ankles. Rushes grasping his legs. He slipped, slipped again, almost lost his footing entirely, slewing side to side like a fawn on an icy pond. Away to his right, cloaked by the shifting mist, he absently noticed bodies moving, walking away eastwards, in the direction of the coast.

Sego grinned in pursuit. Strode into the reed bed. Brandished the axe. Cullen gathered himself, feinted, luring the great man into another arcing swing. It hissed as it sliced nothing, and caught in the tangled fronds. Sego swore as he wrenched the handle, fighting to drag the vicious double-edged weapon free. Cullen took his chance. He launched himself forth, putting his body inside the range of the long haft, and rammed the shield into Sego's intricately dyed chest. He might as well have tried to push over an oak tree. But Sego gave a little ground, his feet sliding as Cullen's had done, and let go of the axe with one hand, using the free elbow to slam down on the fleshy space between Cullen's neck and shoulder. Cullen felt his right hand – his sword hand – go instantly numb. His fingers tingled. He risked a glance down and saw that he had let go of Lightning-Strike.

Sego grabbed him by the hair. Shook him, a hound with a fox cub, lifting him onto tiptoes as he bellowed his victory. Cullen released the shield too, as he was dragged out of the reeds and back onto the trampled grass. The stink of Sego's fetid breath filled his nose. The roar made his ears ring.

And that roar only grew louder when Cullen's skinning knife penetrated Sego's flank. It was not a great thrust. He had aimed squarely, but the mauling had jarred his balance and his stab had gone wide of the mark, the delicate blade slicing the flesh at the very side of Sego's abdomen. A poor strike, then, with a weapon not up to the task. But it was enough to force the most famous man in a horde of heroes to drop him like a sack full of adders.

Cullen collapsed in a heap, limbs splayed, feeling himself spread puddle-like over the mud. Sego Blood Swill stood over him. He was grinning again. The last thing Cullen had wanted to see before his death. But the look was different. Amusement now, rather than hate.

Sego dabbed cudgel-like fingers at the flesh wound, inspecting what came away, as if he had not realised he could bleed. 'A good fight.' He turned, addressing his son. 'He would have given you trouble.'

Kadored spat. 'I do not think so, father.'

Sego shrugged. 'He has some skill.'

The world spun. Cullen swallowed down a bubble of vomit. 'This is all a lie,' he panted.

Sego's hard gaze descended on him again. 'You have courage. Perhaps the gods do favour you, as Lord Caratacos likes to tell me. Still, they will not begrudge me slaughtering the man who would slaughter my beloved son.'

'Wait,' Cullen pleaded. 'You have been misled.'

Sego put both hands around the axe shaft, rolling his shoulders. A forester preparing to fell a tree. Just another task.

Cullen stared up at his killer. The breeze blew again. Fog roiled off the river and through the massed onlookers, cloaking everything in an ethereal haze. Out the corner of his eye he noticed a sliver of light in the east. Dawn. He would not see the sun.

A shout from somewhere. Hard to tell. Encouragement? Dismay? No – it was too shrill, too urgent. Alarm? Cullen lolled his head to the side, taking in the crowd. Not expectant now. Not alive with combat and bloodlust. The heads had turned away. They were looking at some other entertainment, out of his sight, upriver. He recalled the nebulous glimpses of men walking away. Leaving their posts.

Hounds now. Giving furious tongue to the coming dawn. Braying in unison, a chaotic, violent din. A warning, he thought absently. He brought his head round again, determined to look his executioner in the eye. But Sego had gone. And through the tall willows and the roiling mist, drifting like the high calls of feeding kites, came the first blasts of war horns.

—

Geta emerged from the water and through the mist, sodden to his chest. The Vaga, wide and treacherous, standing for so long between him and the barbarians, was behind him. It was beaten. Vanquished. The land of the Britons was there for the taking. The glory *his* for the taking.

He had never liked Narcissus, but now, he had to admit, the oleaginous little bastard deserved whatever remuneration he would eventually demand. Somehow the former slave had used that sharp wit and honeyed tongue to make a deal with one of the tribes. The Eceni, was it? It hardly mattered. All that was important was that they had walked away at the vital moment. The way across the water was beautifully, miraculously clear.

He carried no scutum, for the legionary's shield was beneath his dignity, but he drew his gladius, which was engraved along the blade and ornately filigreed with silver wire about the hilt, and he sucked air into his chest, which was clad with a beautiful muscle-cuirass, and he screamed a battle-cry, unintelligible, vicious, and spittle-flecked. His personal guard, surrounding him like a bristling hedge, followed suit.

Behind them, the Ninth Hispania roared. They formed up at his back, a seasoned force, accustomed to the rigours of battle. The enemy had fortified their positions, confident that the river would deter any advance, but they had not expected this. And away to his left, the artillery was beginning to thud.

Geta allowed himself a grim smile as the mist turned pink.

—

The hounds had smelled them long before their presence had been revealed by the shifting mist. The warning had, at least, given the warriors closest to the Vaga the chance to grab their weapons and form some semblance of an integrated defence. Then the Roman catapults had fired, and the new dawn turned red with blood.

Somehow, under cover of fog-wreathed dark, the legionaries had slunk across the river. Not in great numbers. A hundred or so to begin with, but more coming behind, wading out of the willow branches and reed stands in synchronised lines, their big shields braced in front, a great, impenetrable wall. These were not auxiliary troops: Gauls or Batacgwi. These were reds, their banners bearing the charging bull, and their formation sparkling. A broad swathe of iron and bronze, several ranks deep, grim-faced and rose-hued in the fledgling sun. And they had paused, even as the tribes had stirred into thrashing, spitting, gurning life, and waited for death to fly across the Vaga. Paused to watch the carnage.

On the far side were ranged dire contraptions. Murder-machines. Dozens of fantastical, villainous devices, constructed of wood and metal, animal sinew and rope. Gigantic bows, affixed to stout timber frames. Upon those bows, fearsome bolts were nocked, and winches were cranked back, putting huge torsion into the sinews. And when they fired the air screamed and the shields splintered and flesh was shredded.

Cullen, back on his feet, ducked down with everyone else, staring in disbelief as the long bolts smashed home. The barrage was coordinated, scything the dawn, punching through the foremost men, sometimes the man behind as well, and the shield-walls were breached without so much as a forward movement from the legions. They simply watched and waited, still as statues, silent as trees, the only movement the influx of their comrades, still crossing the water in waves, weaving through the stakes with their shields and javelins held high.

The bolts drove into the densely packed bodies. A beat, a holding of breath, then a collective wail rent the valley basin. Fighters were thrown far back from the battle line, chests and necks and bellies impaled. They were pinned to the mud, screaming for their mothers, legs kicking uselessly as innards spilled. The rubble baskets proved their worth, taking many of the hits, but there were not enough. After all, there were simply too many human targets to miss.

Disarray. Horror. A low moan of dismay, rising from the dumbfounded horde. Fear, pure and unfiltered. Cullen could almost smell it. He shook himself free of the shocked stupor. Retrieving his sword with an arm gradually regaining feeling, and collecting the damaged shield, he looked around. Warriors in all directions, leaderless, headless. He saw Andoc and Garn, Maeveen and Kurd. They seemed just as thrown, just as uncertain. Sego and his son had gone. Vanished into the melee no doubt, spewing commands, trying to coordinate a response, regain some initiative.

'Shields!' Cullen screamed, pushing his way to the front. 'Shields!'

Warriors descended on him. Shields, axes, spears, slings, bows, swords. They shoaled, began to form up, snarling their oaths and invoking any curse that came to mind, readying for the charge. They were prepared, the tribes, but ill-prepared. In situ, in their thousands, but not watchful, not alert. Their shield lines were ragged, their orders lost in the panic, drowned out by the screams of the dying. The cavalry were too far up the slope and the archers too spaced out to make a dense storm of their arrows. The battle was beginning, and it was not going to plan. Whispers of concern, rustling like breeze-shaken branches. *The legions have crossed the Vaga. Again. How could it be?*

The carnyx players added to the cacophony. Up on the ridge they sounded the alarm, their lingering drones joining the barking hounds and the Roman horns, the sounds engaged in their own private duel across the water.

Another volley from the Roman machines. Taut catapults, thwacking, one by one. The range twice as far as a standard bowshot, so the horde's archers and slingers could not reply. The bolts whined in the hoary morn, thumped home, plucking men and women back, spitting them like Calan Haf venison, forcing others to step in and face the strange and deadly weapons.

Another lull. The horde seethed with the cries of the wounded and the grief-stricken. Into that uneasy quiet came a series of gruff commands, uttered in Latin, and the legion was on the march. They advanced inland, slow and steady, from the dense stands of willow that had masked their incursion. More – always more – funnelling through the gaps they had stealthily cut and into line, thickening the formation with every step.

'They waded across,' Andoc murmured, disbelieving, at Cullen's side. 'Through the stakes and the currents. Where are the Eceni?'

'Gone,' Cullen said, for, in spite of his befuddled brain, the list of possible traitors flashed across his mind's eye. Togodubnos had wanted to believe that, come the fight, the peoples of the Isle of the Mighty would unite against a common foe. He had been taken for a fool. And upriver, on the islet, a different legion would be coming. He imagined them pushing inland at this very moment, mirroring the assault he now prepared to face. Pincers. Had they not heeded Cassia's warning? He felt suddenly sick.

Around them, the defenders were bracing again, forming a loose arc, twenty or thirty bodies deep, to engage the Romans. More streamed down from the ridge, and from up in the forest, and their massive numerical advantage began to show. Cullen rapped Lightning-Strike against the splintered face of his shield, beckoning the enemies, challenging them.

Andoc followed suit with his spear haft. 'How were they not spotted? How were they not stopped? Cassia told them—'

But Cullen knew. It hurt his heart to articulate the truth as he looked up into Andoc's mournful eyes. 'Treachery.'

Andoc's deep-set eyes swivelled, as if he sought the people he now understood had long since departed.

'The Eceni have gone,' Cullen said. 'I saw them abandon their posts.' Just as I had warned, Cullen thought. And the Ninth had come, just as Cassia had said.

'The fog was too thick to see,' Andoc opined. 'And Sego's men were watching—'

'Me,' Cullen cut him off, unwilling to let his friend utter the damning words. They were his to bear. As was the shame. 'They were watching me.'

The legion probably had upwards of a thousand men across the river now. He remembered what he had been told, by Cassia, by the Wise, by Ulla and Garn. This strange, impossibly orderly enemy attacked in their cohorts, each one not far shy of five hundred men. That meant there were two cohorts in place, but more would be streaming – flowing – through the bullrushes and willow fronds, and they were forming up with expert precision, moment by moment, bolstering the legion as it shunted inland.

He eyed the vanguard as it progressed, desperately seeking weaknesses, his heart aching as he found precious little to work with. As they marched, the first row held their shields straight, covering themselves from shins to eyes. The ranks further back lifted their own shields horizontal, balancing them on their helmets as each overlapped with the next, forming a makeshift roof for the broad formation. Legionaries on the sides twisted their torsos, walking awkwardly so that their shields presented a solid obstruction on the flanks. It was impressive in the extreme. It slowed the advance, but the effect was a consistent barrier, all the way around.

'Testudo,' he muttered to no one in particular.

'What?' Andoc said.

'Something Cassia told me.'

The distance between the two armies was no more than fifty paces, but still the order to charge did not come. Still, they held their ground, snarled their challenges. The catapults appeared to have fallen silent now that the legion was moving across the face of the riverbank, putting themselves in the way of the bolts. At least the defenders were spared that horror, Cullen thought with a surge of encouragement. More hope sparked as the shrill whine of rotating slingshots came from somewhere behind, and he imagined dozens of the deadly slingers readying themselves at the foot of the ridge.

The whining rose to a crescendo, like swarms of angry hornets, ceasing all at once as the thongs were released. The air whistled briefly. A shower of stones flew over the massed heads of the horde and smacked into the legion. The big shields took the brunt, low and high, clattering manically as stones mangled the fine red and gold leaf, the strange symbols and the painted lightning bolts. A handful made it through, meeting sickeningly with limbs and faces. But the testudo brushed the torrent aside, the legion barely seeming to register it at all. The advance did not even falter. The horde brayed in triumph, exhilarated by the riposte, but a vein of disquiet ran through their voices, betraying new doubt.

Cullen twisted back, seeking leaders. He could hardly see a thing, beyond the immediate bodies, so tightly packed were they. At the rear, on the rising ground before the earthworks, he glimpsed the Wise Ones cavorting in twos and threes. They wore feathered headdresses and animal skulls. Held up the severed heads of the corpses that were dangling on the barricades. Pulled back their robes, exposing themselves, and pissed towards the Romans. They cast spells – grimacing, cackling – tongues lolling like underworld denizens.

The Romans slowed, the shell of the testudo breaking apart. For a moment Cullen imagined them retreating, the fear of black magic proving too much for even the men of this most successful empire to endure. That was when he saw the enemy front ranks open up as the legionaries drew back their throwing arms, the black points of javelins poised at their right shoulders.

—

'See how they melt away?' Narcissus said, smug smile broad and imposingly white. 'Nation after nation, army after army, battle after battle, it is always thus.'

Adminios sucked his whiskers, unable to smother the uneasy feeling that had settled across him like a sodden cloak during the hour since dawn. 'So many fall.'

'It is grim work,' Narcissus acknowledged, 'but progress tarries for no man. If he resists, it comes regardless. Best to embrace the inevitable.'

'This carnage is progress?'

Narcissus shrugged his finely plucked brows. 'Clears the way for progress, naturally. You're losing your nerve. Not a surprise. They are *your* people, after all.' He let his eyes run down Adminios's body, as if sizing up a prize bullock. 'You look just perfect, though. Ready to take your place at the head of the new province.'

Adminios looked down at himself. He felt utterly ridiculous in his legionary's garb, safely ensconced this side of the river, far from the fight. 'If you say so.'

'Your hard work bears fruit.'

Adminios followed the smaller man's gaze, which had returned to examine the fluctuating, metallic tides of the battle. He could see the blocks of the Ninth Legion on the right flank of the fight. Whatever the prearranged signal had been, it had been communicated successfully. The Eceni had left their section of the river unguarded, abandoned the sons of Cunobelin, and Geta had snuck across under cover of the fog. It had been a seamlessly executed manoeuvre, and, though he considered Geta to be a slippery, arrogant specimen, he had to give the man his due. He watched with a mix of admiration and horror as the Roman machine rumbled on, efficiently murderous. 'And that of Berikos.'

'Berikos is no longer with us,' Narcissus said. 'On to the next, isn't that what you say?'

Adminios nodded. 'He made the alliances.'

A beringed hand waved him away. 'The emperor will not care who did the talking.' He leaned in, breath sweet and warm, as he whispered, 'Overlord of Britannia.' Straightening now, and inspecting imagined creases in his robe, he said, 'He'll care who deserves the praise, and that, dear Adminios, is you. The Eceni have been bought. Even now they walk back to their own territory, heads brimming with the promise of civilisation. Good for them. The way is clear for Geta to lead the Ninth to glory.'

—

'Shields! Shields! Shields!'

The pila flew in a high arc, dark streaks in the sky, seeming to hang above them for a moment, then slamming down into the front few native ranks. Cullen shrank low behind his shield. A pilum – two sleek strides of wood and iron – punched straight through the shield of the man next to him, the slender shank snapping, the wicked tip exploding into the astonished face, a fine red spray misting Cullen's peripheral vision.

Cullen swore. Another man stepped into the new-made void just as a second volley was unleashed. More pila rose and plummeted like demonic hail. One long javelin fell at his feet, skidding in the mud, sliding straight between his legs. He whispered thanks to Taranis, snarled threats the Romans could neither hear nor understand, banged Lightning-Strike against the shield rim and tried to think what Ulla would do.

The whir of slings started up again. Seamlessly, the testudo resumed its impenetrable shape. The slingers loosed. The rattle of stones on shields and armour echoed up and down the valley. Another cheer from the horde, though they had precious little to celebrate.

They came on, the Romans, gathering speed as they advanced, an intractable wave of weaponry, only the feet and helmets exposed beyond the curving shields, and Cullen felt his insides spiral like the precious strands of a chieftain's torc. He vomited, a thin stream of yellow bile, and so did the man next to him, and they grinned at each other, bloody-minded and grim, acknowledging the fear, embracing the anticipation. They would kill, and they would likely be killed. The warrior's path.

And then the Romans reached the trench.

CHAPTER EIGHTEEN

It was the gulley that Cullen and his party had been forced to cross in the dark. Dug by teams of toiling youngsters in the previous days, it formed the first of Togodubnos's earthworks. Not a deep trench, barely enough to sink a man to his knee, but it had filled with marsh water, and the foremost legionaries, entirely oblivious to its presence, trod, almost in unison, into that narrow trap, and the disciplined line convulsed as men fell forward, shunted by those behind. That front rank fell, tumbling like rats from the side of a sinking ship. The men following, so disciplined and alert, halted in good order, averting the chaos that had been intended, but the advance stalled. There they floundered, like so many oxen stuck in a mire, their centurions braying for them to clamber up and out. It would not buy much time for the horde. But it might, Cullen thought as he bellowed himself hoarse, be just enough.

He ran. Somewhere leaders would be shouting the order to charge, but it was as unnecessary as the order to raise a shield in the face of a flying pilum. Cullen ran because everyone else ran. They screamed; a shrill, blood-freezing, teeth-shattering howl of collective battle-rage. And they fell upon the stalled Roman line.

It was as if the shee had sailed in on the breeze and carried him to the fight, for, in what seemed like half a heartbeat, Cullen was at the trench, hacking down with Lightning-Strike as the Romans floundered. He focused on an enemy who had been wallowing in the hitherto concealed gulley, and was still unsteadily regaining his footing. He dipped his shoulder at the last, slammed in with his shield to move his opponent's aside, and he drove Lightning-Strike into the opened space with every fibre of his being. The Roman defended the blows with shield and gladius, but the sword of the legions was short, for stabbing, and the parry was awkward, and Cullen's blade slid all the way down the cutting edge, jumped off the guard and took a chunk from the crook of the man's elbow. To his credit, the Roman barely seemed to register the wound, but his arm failed him as he tried to counter, the damage more extensive than was apparent. Cullen brought his own sword up and round, smashing the Roman in the face with the hilt, kicking him in the chest as he wilted. Immediately the next Roman stepped up, putting his shield in Cullen's way, stabbing to the side of the rim, aiming for the artery in his groin. Cullen was forced to shy away from that wicked tip, flicking out like the tongue of the most deadly serpent, but he could not move far, for the press of warriors at his back kept him firmly in the jaws of the fight. He swayed, like some bizarre dance, and let the weapon slide to the side of his hip, then pushed back with the shield, and clubbed at it with his sword, forcing the Roman to stand on his fallen comrade so as to avoid the trench.

They braced against one another, pushing with shields and probing with blades. Cullen's skin prickled, arms pulsating pain. His ears were assailed by rushing blood and brain-curdling screams, his nostrils filled with the stench of sweat and oil, leather and mud, shit and vomit and piss. He could barely see a thing beyond the inner face of his shield and the outer face of the one against which he shoved. He knew not where Andoc was, or whether Garn lived, or if Maeveen had been cut down. Maybe Aoife was there, in the thick of it, screaming a furious battle-cry in her musically lilting language. Maybe Togodubnos and Caratacos, brother-kings and battle-givers for the ages, were galloping behind the line, high on their war-steeds, bellowing oaths and encouraging the horde to show valour and deliver death. Maybe. For now, it did not matter. All that mattered was staying alive, and he chopped and slashed and stabbed at the Roman formation with mindless rage, making of himself a killer, the like of which Ulla Jagged Cliff would have been proud. Or so he hoped.

Despite it all, he felt himself moving back. It was no retreat. Barely even perceptible. But instead of forcing the Romans towards the river, the line of red and gold was shunting inexorably forward, inch by blood-drenched inch, and the warriors of the Isle of the Mighty were sliding away, their shoes greased by cold marsh-slop and steaming-fresh blood. Cullen heaved, felt himself gurn like a toadstool-nibbling Wise One, spittle flecking his chin as he hissed and snarled. They had the numbers, the tribes. Togodubnos had assembled an army of more than a hundred thousand, so folk said. But they were spread all across the

Vaga valley, bound to watch every part of the river, especially since the Batacgwi had proven nowhere was unfordable and a small number of the enemy Second Legion had forced their way across. The Romans, by contrast, had concentrated this legion at one specific point, and now their numbers were building, coming in a swarm to add their weight to the push. In the great, heaving mass, a gilt eagle bobbed atop a long pole. Nearby, a young Roman in a breastplate sculpted into the shape of a muscled chest slashed and stabbed with a short sword that was more work of art than killing tool. He bore no shield, but seemed protected by men larger than most of their comrades. The commander, perhaps? Cullen resolved to get close, to slay the Roman noble, wrest that fancy sword from his dead hand and capture the eagle with it. To earn fame and end the battle in one fell swoop. He imagined the poets retelling his tale in feasting halls up and down the land, and he crouched behind the splintering shield and pushed.

Then the ground began to thrum, a vibration climbing Cullen's legs. Eyes slid to the right, his too, just as horses came from the side, down from the forest in a great galloping arc. Two hundred, he reckoned, though his view was poor, the column's speed a blur, and they smashed into the Roman flank, battering and cleaving as the well-drilled formation adjusted to receive them. They were not enough, could not hope to break the reds' overlapping shape, and no horse could break so dense a thicket of armour and blade, but they might stall the advance, put fear into Roman hearts by savagery alone, give impetus to the horde.

War horns blew, heralding something. Cullen scanned the slashing cavalry column, searching for the cause.

There it was. A chariot swept down from the incline, drawn by a huge, snorting grey and driven by a crouching man, reins looped over his knuckles, his head circled by the gold band that announced his elevated status as a renowned charioteer. The vehicle was gaudy, painted in greens and reds, with the writhing twin serpents of the Catuvellauni emblazoned on its sides, and the spokes of its wheels were chased with silver and gold. It was a chariot Cullen recognised well. His gaze moved inevitably to the warrior standing on the wicker platform, a shield in one hand, spear in the other, a war-god incarnate.

'Caratacos,' someone breathed nearby, 'gods preserve him.'

The great man shone in mail, his shield bore the double serpents, and his helm had huge, yellow wings. He bent his knees a little, bracing, riding the chariot's rolling movements as it thundered across the undulating terrain. Caratacos, second son of Cunobelin, younger brother to Over-King Togodubnos, chief war-giver of the Isle of the Mighty, threw back his head and howled. And the horde howled with him, Cullen howled with him, the man's mere presence a boon to the beleaguered defenders. Spearmen shifted, disengaged, providing room for the newcomers, and the chariot careened into the corner of the front cohort, the horse, whose tail was plaited with golden wire, whinnying madly as it ran the gauntlet of shields and gladii. But Caratacos appeared to grin as he engaged the reds. His spear clanged as it ran along the line, prodding and probing for an opening, daring the enemy to break their close-knit structure.

The Roman formation held firm, let the prince of the Catuvellauni rumble out of range, but the horde was reinvigorated. Cullen could feel it, sense it in their yells. New shoots of hope, springing forth. It was magnificent. *He* was magnificent. Cullen felt nausea rise as he eyed the chariot and its braying cargo. The son of Cunobelin had brought about the slaughter of his village, his family. He despised the man. No – despised himself, because, despite it all, he admired Caratacos. In this moment, yearned to be him. He screamed. At the enemy? At his own treachery? It did not matter. He pushed forward, and as he did so, he remembered the extra weight in his pebble pouch. Now was the time. He pinned his sword under an arm and groped within the bag, pulling free the banal-looking grindstone. He held it aloft. 'The Stone of Gobannos!' he shrieked, his voice crackling like firewood, so parched was he. 'Gobannos!'

Magic. Power. He could feel it surge all around him, rippling through the warriors as they realised what he possessed, echoing his call, by the dozen, by the score, by the hundred. It was glorious, exhilarating. 'Gobannos with us! Gobannos with us!'

The tide of spearmen, shield-men, axemen, daggermen gushed like sluice-water into the Roman cohorts, the Whetstone of Gobannos giving strength to every arm and courage to every heart. Cullen returned it to the pouch, brandished his bloodied sword, and searched the opposing lines for the man in the muscle cuirass.

–

Gnaeus Hosidius Geta bellowed orders to everyone and no one at once. The world shook and his skull ached and his ears rushed like the Vaga in flood. The attack had stalled. Things were turning against him. The element of surprise had gone. Indeed, it had been stolen. The enemy had had reserves, and those screaming horsemen, coupled with the hidden trench, had caused his forward momentum to leak away. Now was the time to dig in. To fight or die. The choice was not difficult.

He saw the red-headed marauder with only a fraction of a moment to spare. He wrenched himself about and brought his gladius up to parry the young Briton's lunge, turning it expertly away while he ducked another man's punching spear point. The latter assailant was cut down in a rapid succession of blows from a brace of Geta's personal guards, which allowed him to deal with the red-head, whose eye had been given a permanent droop by an old scar and whose arms were inked in the barbaric symbols of this doomed culture. He grinned, bloodily and wolfishly, as he beckoned the savage to come onto his blade. They had courage, these Britons, he had to concede. They fought like rabid dogs, and they seemed to know no fear. But, by Mars Ultor's avenging spear, they were as mindless as Narcissus had foretold. This one was no different. Cleaving a path through flesh with his teeth bared and his tongue lolling and his words an inarticulate, animalistic howl.

His guards were closing around him at this new threat, but Geta barked a command and they parted, just a little, letting him engage the flailing lad without compromising flank or rear. He laughed, the exultant, warrior's laugh, and he hit the frayed-looking shield with his ornate gladius, pulverising the crude painting of a bird, and putting his shoulder to it, giving the lie to another shove. But then he pivoted away, relieving the pressure so that the Briton overbalanced, and Geta brought his blade smartly about, going low, as they so often practised, attempting to snag the artery that would finish the job in seconds. He snagged something, for the barbarian yelped, seemed to judder back, and Geta was grinning ever more broadly, but the Briton shifted his weight, as Geta had done, and pounced forward, catlike. As Geta brought up his sword in a desperate block he understood that the retreat had been a feint. Well now, he thought, this feral creature *can* fight. He bellowed a challenge – they would see who knew his work the better – but even as he parried again he could feel the strength of his opponent travelling through both blades, reverberating up his arm, jarring at his shoulder, zinging through his teeth. He stumbled back, deflected again and again, and he tasted a sudden metallic warmth as he bit his own tongue. His guards were shouting in alarm, screaming for him to fall back, but they were assailed too, swamped by sheer numbers of the enemy, and for a terrible moment, Geta could see that they would be enveloped by this crazed tide. Swallowed whole by it.

—

Adminios gritted his teeth and balled up his fists. Not out of triumph, nor sadness, but something else. He was mesmerised as he witnessed this almighty bloodletting, and he could barely contain his emotions. It was a swirl that wrung out his stomach and put needles to his skin and sent his heart racing. A heady mix, for which he possessed no antidote. He simply did not know how to feel. The Romans were winning. Grinding forward, implacable and inexorable. And yet his brothers had done something glorious. They had come from the trees with their thundering chariots and smashed Geta's legion, and now the horde were swarming like ants at a wounded beetle, threatening to overwhelm the Ninth and wrench momentum from General Plautius's grip.

Adminios watched in awestruck silence. He could not see Geta himself, but the legate's personal standard, not to mention his legion's sacred eagle, was coming precariously close to the enemy positions. The patrician risked becoming surrounded. Was Adminios proud? No. But nor was he disappointed. Indeed, he glanced down at Narcissus, at the pudgy face that was drooping in shock, and at the ever-crinkled eyes that now seemed pinned back in disbelief. What a wonderful sight it was. He cleared his throat. 'Geta has overreached.'

Narcissus swallowed thickly, jowls quivering. 'They knew.' He glanced up, almost accusingly, at Adminios. 'They were expecting the Ninth's advance.'

'Geta is not the warrior he thinks he is,' Adminios said. He kept his tone level, though he wanted to laugh. 'And my people are better than you expected.'

Narcissus's eyes were swivelling now, as he searched desperately for one of Plautius's aides. 'Where are the Second? Vespasian was to push out from his position with all haste!'

'I think,' Adminios said, scanning along the river until he found the promontory, 'Vespasian marches, as expected. Do not fret, *dear* Narcissus. But let this provide a lesson.' Now it was his turn to give a smug smile, and it was the best he had felt since throwing in his lot with his brothers' enemies. 'The warriors of Britannia must never be underestimated.'

—

Cullen would kill the Roman cockerel. He would take his silvered sword and grab the proud eagle and win the day. He cried out for Belinos and Taranis to give him strength. Thanked Gobannos for his power. Begged his mother's protection. He fought for the memory of Ludris and Kenal and for the chance to see Cassia again. He was so close. The Roman was frightened, he could see the terror light up the man's eyes. It was a thing of grim beauty.

But even as he allowed himself to dream, so the dream soured. Because the carnyx players had started up again, and the horns were furiously blasting, and a groundswell of new alarm seemed to gush through the assembled warriors. Something was happening. Something bad. They had been a wave crashing in, but now that wave was ebbing, rolling out to sea, taking Cullen with it. He was forced to disengage, leaving the floundering cockerel to stare wildly, panting furiously. Cullen stared too, but he was looking down the line, desperate to see what others must see, but all he saw was bodies. Furs and mail, braids and beards, wild eyes and bloodied faces.

'By the gods,' a voice exclaimed.

'Andraste protect us,' yelled another.

More and more, folk were crying out, turning to the southwest, upriver, where the previous evening's fighting had taken place. The Roman line stamped forward again, shoring up their hitherto fraying formation, stealing a pace.

'Fall back!' came a cry. Nameless, faceless, it did not matter. The order had been expected, and the tribes broke off. 'To the barricades!'

Cullen extricated himself from the shield press, running with the rest. He winced as he went, kept his head down, anticipating a Roman charge or a pila volley, but nothing came. He reached the gentle incline and scrambled up the grass to the first run of earthworks, where staggered ditches scarred the slope, backed by banks formed of the spoil. He took up position at one of the timber barriers, where the corpses of sacrificed legionaries still hung, disembowelled and castrated.

The enemy advanced in their wake. They had come so close – so achingly close – to overwhelming the invader, but that was all gone, the chance squandered. Below, there was a slight shift in the Ninth's ranks as men with pila came to the fore, then they were back in good order, marching perfectly in time, shields interlocked. More files emerging from the misty riverbank all the time.

But no one was really watching them. All eyes had turned upriver. From here they could just about see the outcrop of dry land that jutted into the Vaga, where the enemy Second Legion had gained their foothold during the dusky skirmish. Now the sun was making real inroads, burning away the mist as well as the dark, and Cullen could properly perceive the valley in the fresh dawn. What he saw chilled him to the marrow.

The Romans had pushed in from the promontory. Just as the legion had advanced here, so their brother-cohorts had advanced, probably at the very same time, and they were fighting their own battle against the warriors stationed at that end of the valley. Now the horde of the Isle of the Mighty, so vast and formidable, was fighting on two fronts, their strength cut in half, and, if they could not overcome the twin attacks, they would find themselves trapped between the claws of two entire legions, with more ready to cross the river at a moment's notice.

He muttered a prayer to Taranis, looked back to the nearest line of legionaries. The pouch at Cullen's hip, though heavier than usual, given the presence of the sacred whetstone, still contained his trusty cache of pebble-shot. He sheathed his sword and plunged his hand inside, rummaging for a smooth stone that he must have selected on some long-past day for its weight and shape. He plucked a suitable example free, rolling it appreciatively between thumb and forefinger, and a smile formed on his mouth. He was a warrior, a named man, a shield-bearer, a spear-fighter, but was there anything so satisfying as a perfectly sized sling stone?

'Ever the goatherd,' Andoc's droll tones came from a little way along the barricade.

Cullen grinned, glad to see him. He kissed the stone and took the leather sling from his belt, nodding to the other faces he was delighted to recognise. Kurd, Maeveen, Garn, Rues and the rest. They were all here, all preparing to face the assault, all bloodied, sweat-drenched and bruised, panting and grimacing. Cullen read determination in their faces. Fear, rage, excitement. The battle-frenzy, bright in their eyes, livening their souls, quickening their senses. The Romans were coming, and the battle had taken a dire turn, but these were true warriors. Men and women of renown. Unlike the reds, who fought as they were told to fight and marched where they were ordered to march, the warriors of the Isle of the Mighty were in pursuit of reputation. Of fame that would never fade. They would fight to save their tribes – their nations – and they would have songs sung of their valour until the end of time. The invaders would soon learn.

Cullen leaned into the barricade, a trellis of hazel branches woven between timber uprights, which came up to his chin. Not enough to keep a child out on its own, but with its ditch and bank frontage it would slow the advance and let the warriors do the rest. To his left and right, between the gaps in the fortifications, he was vaguely aware of archers nocking bows, and with them, pockets of youngsters, bringing up pails, roped at the handles. Those buckets would be filled with pitch and pig grease, rags and grass, resin, wool, dry leaves and amadou. Where the pail-bearers gathered, men knelt before prepared braziers, striking fool's gold to flint, bringing forth a blaze.

The legion swept steadily up the hill, a tidal wave that would smash against their line. Forty paces shy now, and Cullen put the pebble in his sling.

'Moranna's slave,' said a man to his left.

Cullen looked past two men he did not recognise. The third wore no helm, leaving his black, shoulder-length hair long, which was braided around a narrow face that was clean-shaven and sour as old milk. 'I mean you no ill, Kadored. Upon my life. My honour.'

'Honour?' the son of Sego spat the word as if it were rancid. 'You have none. You are but Moranna's thing. Her minion.'

'Moranna?' Cullen echoed, nonplussed, even as understanding began to dawn, like the sunlight coming from the east. 'Arthmael. Arthmael has whispered poison in your father's ear.'

'You call him witless? Easily gulled?'

'I call him respectful of the Wise,' Cullen said. 'He believes the lies he is told because he knows no better.'

Kadored was holding a huge sword in one hand and a heavy-headed club in the other. Both twitched as his grip tightened, the armlets glittering as his forearms rippled. 'If the reds do not kill you, Wolf Scourge, then I will.'

The arrows flew, darkening the sky for a heartbeat, before tumbling down upon the first of the cohorts. This time the testudo, constructed under duress and without breaking stride, was less complete, and a smattering of Romans fell. The slingers twirled their arms too. Cullen broke Kadored's baleful gaze and did the same, bringing his throwing arm to a powerful speed before letting fly the stone with a throat-scouring curse.

The reds were thirty paces short now, their ranks bristling with arrows, the formation sliding over the land like some gigantic, spined beast. They paused, the line visibly rippling as they braced, and their pila were flung, arcing over their heads and down onto earthwork, the barricade, the shields and bodies of the tribesmen arrayed along its length. One of the javelins smashed through the wickerwork beside Cullen's knee. Another clipped Kadored's temple, grazing him, before thudding dully into a man further back. Kadored swore, dabbed his leaking head with something like disbelief, and growled for the enemy to come to his blade.

A third pilum slammed down, thumping into Cullen, knocking him back, the slender iron tip bursting through the skin and willow of his shield's painted face, the wicked point poised before his right eye. For a moment it dangled there, the long wooden shaft protruding, bouncing against the top of the barricade. It was pulling the shield down with its lolling weight, exposing him to the next volley, and he swept Lightning-Strike down, severing it from the slender shank so that it fell uselessly away. The point was still lodged, so he battered it with the sword pommel, bending it downwards and away from his face, but leaving it there, a black blight, a reminder of how, in this searing moment, he straddled the doorway between this life and the next.

The legionaries advanced, faster now, almost at a trot, but careful to keep their tight formation. The javelin volley had caused carnage and confusion amongst the defenders, and the reds were determined to reap their reward in the aftermath. All along the earthwork, named men – respected men – bellowed for calm. The warriors closed ranks, dragged bodies clear so that they would not obstruct the spear-line that was taking shape. They snarled to themselves, to the gods, to the enemy, calling down the wrath of Belinos, of Andraste, of Taranis and Cernunnos and Epona.

Cullen readied himself. Sought those of his nine he had not lost in the dash back to the ditch. He found most of them. Garn's broad face, pulpy and scarred. Maeveen's sharp features and malevolent stare. Rues's spiked hair and weather-beaten complexion. Andoc with his dour, sunken-eyed countenance. Comrades, all. Was this the last time he would look upon them?

Fire; bright in the grey dawn. It dazzled him for a moment, so that, as the world blazed orange and red and white, he wondered if he had taken a javelin to the face. He did not fall, and there was no pain. He looked up. Flaming arrows and spears, bound at the tip with oily rags, filled the sky, roaring as they careened down the slope to pelt the enemy, black smoke wisps streaking the air. The young pail-bearers dashed forth too, and their vessels danced with heat, and they slung them down the slope, the rope handles giving extra range. The pails smashed against the front couple of Roman lines, exploding in a welter of flame. Men screamed as they were scorched, shied away from the heat, pushing into the ranks behind.

And yet still they came, their formation an enormous, voracious animal, swallowing all in its path. In the gaps between the cohorts, artillery teams brought up box-like contraptions, made of wood and bound with iron straps. They stood on tall tripods, unaffected by the gradient, and from those boxes spat bolts, smaller than the ones fired by the great machines but equally deadly, and they sprayed the barricade with murderous volleys.

Cullen shrank away from the bolts as the wicker splintered into flying shards. A man collapsed next to him, the short quarrel lodged in his throat, mouth gargling, lips frothing pink. Cullen glanced up, gauging the intensity of the barrage, waiting for it to fade. He noticed the sky was blue now. Daylight had crept up on them, the dawn fog burned clean away. A red kite glided against white, bilious clouds. Gulls and crows swirled, higher up, anticipating the feast that would soon be theirs. He stood, just as the legion reached the earthwork.

The Romans charged those final few paces. They leapt the ditch, smashed the fencing with shields and hobnailed boots, and, though they were challenged by spears and swords all across its length, the barrier began to fray and then collapse.

The men and women of the tribes screamed as the two sides clashed.

Cullen had discarded the slingshot, retaken Lightning-Strike, and used its superior reach to jam the point into a legionary's eye. He jerked it free, the scrape of bone reverberating through his hand, and already the next opponent came struggling up the short bank, using the bottom edge of his scutum to tear at the top of the barricade. Cullen battered the shield once, twice, then used his own to knock it aside, long enough to lunge with his sword into the gap. He did not even see where the blow landed, but the man yelped, tried to twist away, and then Garn's truncated arm lashed past his right ear. The stump, bound and studded in bull-hide and spikes, crunched home, turning the wide-eyed face to jelly. On the other side of Garn was Andoc, taller than the rest, keeping his shield high because he was a plum target. Beyond him stood Clesek, Baglan and Rues. To Cullen's left, Maeveen screeched like a barn owl as she fought. White Tal was next to her, cleaving with a long-hafted axe, and next to him was Kadored, swinging the brutal club, battering anything that came within reach.

The hillside became a writhing, shrieking mess. Each ditch and barricade was somewhere in the region of a hundred paces long, with roughly equal-sized gaps between, and, though they were focal points for the defence, the sheer number of warriors meant that the battle spread like spilled milk, in front, behind and between, shield-walls hastily formed wherever the legions attempted to break through.

Cullen hacked and blocked and hacked again. He spat into the faces of the Romans, beat at them with Lightning-Strike, called on Taranis to send down his power, begged his ancestors to renew his strength. Warriors pressed in from behind, legionaries swarmed up in response, so that he felt sure he would be crushed between the two great hosts. The barricade at which his nine made their stand was crumbling. Romans leaned on it for purchase, craned over the creaking top, thrust their short swords down. One man, a heavy-set centurion with a plumed helmet, tried to clamber over, leading by example, but only had one leg across when he took a dagger to the side of the knee. When he looked down at the wound, someone buffeted that ostentatious plume with a knotted cudgel, knocking him senseless, and he seemed to hang there, suspended, straddling the fence as though he had been caught scrumping for apples. The horde swallowed him up, dragging him onto their side, cutting him to ribbons.

Cullen heaved himself up to the shattered wickerwork, girded his left foot against the base of the screen, twisted sideways, shoving forth with his shield. Pushing back was a fresh-faced legionary, younger, perhaps, even than he. The fear was alight in his eyes as he attempted a battle-cry that seemed more like a whimper. Still, he could fight, for his torso and shoulders, like all the others, were completely encased in segments of plate armour, the lorica segmentata. The stuff could not have been as flexible as the chainmail worn by many tribesmen, but the plates clanged as they deflected Cullen's blows, and his own shoulders burned as he worked to find an opening. They locked together in a great heave. The gladius, as always, came up from below the scutum. Cullen was ready for it, went low with Lightning-Strike, knocking it aside, and then he jumped back as far as the men behind would allow, and the Roman toppled forward with all his weight, crashing through the stockade to collapse on his face. He floundered there, weighed down by his armour, and took a blade in the back of the neck for his trouble. Blood sprayed, blinding Cullen for a moment, running down his collar so that he felt it, sticky and warm, within his tunic.

The Romans streamed through the gap he had made. Kurd smashed one down, Andoc opened the groin of another, Kadored bludgeoned a third. Cullen met the next, shield-to-shield, blocked the gladius with his sword, darted in with a thrust of his own that dented the man's cheek piece. The sword slid on, down the side of the helmet, bouncing harmlessly off the ridge at the back. The legionary's blade was facing the ground, so he brought up the pommel. It crunched into Cullen's mouth. He stumbled back, tasted blood, his own this time. Spat out a tooth fragment. Shook his head to clear the stars spangling his vision. He saw that the entire body of warriors, all along the slope, was gradually giving ground, backing away towards the forest, inch by grisly inch.

He went for the Roman again, lips and gums throbbing, tongue probing the broken front tooth. He caught the next blow on his shield, dipped to a crouch and brought Lightning-Strike up and under the lorica segmentate, into the soft flesh of the man's abdomen.

A big spearman, stinking of ale, garlic and onions, pushed past him into the front line, and Cullen took the moment to catch his breath. He gazed out over the valley. It was full to bursting. Warriors – plaited and moustached and painted – stretched in both directions, as far as he could see. A swathe of war-givers, representing dozens of septs and nations, creeds and clans. A horde for all the Isle of the Mighty. They faced smaller, tighter, more heavily armoured blocks of reds, who marched relentlessly, fought ruthlessly, and advanced like a moving cliff-face, the waves simply dashing against them, fury dissipating as quickly as it gathered. Knots of legionaries had punctured the barricades now, and they swarmed between the gaps in the trench system, leaving those earthworks in their wake. More territory gained. More land stolen.

The warbands fell back, abandoning the first line of fortifications and taking up position at the next. But this second level, another fifty paces up the slope, had fewer barricades and shallower ditches, and Cullen found himself drawing up between two fences, protected only by his shield and those either side. He hauled breath into his lungs, blinked away the blood that lingered around his eyes, and looked out at the scene. This higher vantage opened the entire valley to him. What he saw put a block of lead in his stomach.

In front and to the left, the cohorts trudged up the slope, battered and arrow-pocked, but maintaining their rhythmic pace. Their flags, hanging from tall poles, bobbed proudly, golden writing, a mystery to him, inscribed on each crossbar, along with the strange creatures that were their symbols. Further back, surveying the entire formation, appeared to be a bird. An eagle or hawk with expanded wings, cast in silver or bronze, and perched on its own high staff. The sight was gut-wrenching in itself, for, though they had taken many casualties, their ranks were unbowed and unbroken. But that was not what struck fear into Cullen. Away to the right, lower down the slope, closer to the water, another legion, with its own standards and its own precious, glittering bird of prey, surged up from the direction of the promontory. Before it, juddering raggedly rearwards, was the horde's flank under Aoife the Dread. He had a sudden, vivid picture of her in his mind's eye. Tall and intimidating; a flame-haired, green-eyed war-goddess. She could not retreat. Did not know how. Yet up the blood-slick slant they came. Squeezed, crushed, butchered.

All across the Vaga valley, Roman horns blew, their sounds triumphal to his ears. And in response to those high, lingering notes, came the cries for retreat, uttered in the common tongue of the Isle of the Mighty.

'Never in doubt,' Narcissus said, smile returned, wider and more brilliant than ever.

Adminios dragged his gaze to the west, along the valley, to take in the curving headland that had been captured the night before. 'Vespasian knows his work. Togodubnos is trapped between two talons.'

Narcissus laughed. 'The talons of Rome! I like it, dear Adminios, I do.'

The battlefield's left flank had erupted into violence, just as Geta's legion had teetered on the brink of defeat. The Second Legion, forging out from the bridgehead already established, had faced fierce opposition, for that was where enemy eyes had been trained. But, as the sun poured molten gold in the east, and the defenders realised there had been a surprise incursion downriver, so had their forces been redirected and their resolution waned. Now, Togodubnos fought a battle entirely on his side of the river, on the back foot, and on two fronts.

The outcome, as Narcissus had so often predicted, was looking more assured by the moment. He felt a pang of disappointment at that. It surprised him. He smothered it brutally. There was too much to gain for sentiment, and at least Geta had suffered a bloody nose and Narcissus's smug mask had, for just a short time, slipped. 'Will Plautius send the reserve?'

'To crush your brothers?' Narcissus shook his head. 'Unnecessary. We'll take the valley, chase them into the woods and establish a permanent crossing. Supply trains, dear Adminios.' He tapped his temple. 'Something you'll need to learn, if you're to marshal your own army in the fullness of time.'

Adminios felt his fingers twitch as he imagined wrapping them about the condescending little man's jowly neck. He balled his fists at his sides, wrestling them into submission. 'The bridge was dismantled.'

'The Ninth and Twentieth can commence the construction of pontoon bridges, and we'll have the whole army across by this time tomorrow. You say there are more swamps beyond the forest?'

'The yellow marshes.'

'Treacherous?'

'Aye.'

Narcissus tapped a finger to the side of his nose. 'There you have it. Consolidation first and foremost. Only dead men rush in.'

'My brothers will not surrender,' Adminios warned.

Narcissus gave a grunt of amusement. 'I would never presume otherwise. But we'll have the valley by nightfall, and their army, large as it is, has been splendidly mauled. We hold our nerve, keep talking with the barbarian chieftains. The Eceni have turned their backs on ignorance and look forward, into the light. Who next? There were plenty you and Berikos spoke with. Plenty who see the benefit of empire. It'll be easier to convince them after today, especially when they bask in Claudius's radiance.'

'Claudius?' Adminios echoed stupidly, wrongfooted. 'The emperor?'

'We shall send for him. He will lead the final march to Camulodunon. It will be spectacular. The final conquest.' He chuckled. 'In the end, the tribes will see their way to civilisation, mark my words.'

'My brothers will not.'

'Then it will be only the Catuvellauni, and we shall brush them aside,' Narcissus knuckled his silkily upholstered shoulder, 'like dust from a robe.'

-

Cullen saw Togodubnos. The king – escorted by a score of riders with the twin red snakes painted on the rumps of their mounts – was conspicuous on his huge dappled grey as he raced along the back of the vast army, up near the first of the trees, where the gigantic wicker figurine had been erected. He was more ruddy-faced than usual, presumably shouting encouragement, though Cullen could catch not a word over all the other screams and the clashing of arms and the wails of the dying.

The horde had coalesced now, shifting as it retreated, from three distinct subdivisions, under Aoife and the brother-kings, to one seething mass, edging towards the treeline at the ridge's summit. They still bellowed defiance. They still outnumbered the enemy, of course, and they had the higher ground, and yet a vein of trepidation seemed to run through their snarled challenges as the reds rumbled up through the last of the fortifications. Two entire legions pressed in, weathering storms of spears, arrows and stones. Enduring waves of charging counterattacks. Always pressing, strangling. The horde, jagged and desperate, seemed to groan under the strain.

The native cavalry swept down and into the extreme flanks of the invading force, scything at their shields, their clattering engagements echoing across the water and up into the stands of ash and oak, but they made little impact on the tight, pitiless ranks.

Cullen was the third man from the front. Ominously, he had lost sight of Kadored's party, and he wondered if he would take a knife between the shoulders while he tried to avoid one in the belly. The legionaries smashed home. More of the same. The warriors hacked and spat and cursed, and the Romans presented their big shields in a perfect, overlapping front. It was commendable, in its way. Controlled in its bloodlust. Slow but unstoppable.

Warriors fell. One lost a hand and then had his loins torn open, blood spouting down his braca in a steaming fountain. The next was a woman, strawberry-blonde and bulkily built, her bare breasts embellished with the double white snakes of Caratacos. She feinted one way, shimmied the other, and inveigled herself beyond the shield, blocked a gladius thrust with deft hands, bringing her much longer sword up and round in a wheeling strike that clattered the Roman's temple, denting his helmet deeply. He staggered, eyes rolling, and she tilted back her head in a triumphal shriek that her grandparents would surely hear in the next life. That shriek turned blood-chilling as it was immediately cut short by the adjacent Roman's gladius, her throat chopped open to the bone.

Cullen stepped up, trampling the dead woman, unable to give her the dignity her courage deserved. He pounded his shield into the one opposite, boss to boss, arm zinging with the impact, and brought Lightning-Strike to bear when the smallest of openings was made. It was a thankless, fruitless business. The body armour they wore provided incredible protection, so that he found himself battering thanklessly, his sword bouncing impotently off the iron strips. Throat or groin, he told himself repeatedly, but it was easier imagined than done.

He remembered the blonde woman, and trod back, using her prone corpse as a step. The new height let him hook the bottom of his shield over the top of the Roman's and he managed to drag the scutum down just enough to slide the sword over its rim, crunching straight through the surprised-looking face. He pulled it free, the man collapsing where he stood, and another cleaved at Cullen from the side. Cullen parried high, punched with the pommel so that his opponent had to sway back. The Roman snarled something unintelligible. He was older than most, with craggy eyes, a hint of silver in his stubble and a puckered scar from earlobe to chin. He grinned nastily, spat in Cullen's face as he jumped back in, and jabbed the gladius low. Cullen turned his shoulders to bring the shield round, caught the point, forced it wide, and brought up his own blade. The man's long-healed wound had evidently once nearly cut off his jaw. Cullen aimed for it now, missed, tried again with the reverse and then caught the man on the third pass. Blood sprayed. The dying soldier grabbed for Cullen's shield, clung to the top like a drowning man on a floating spar, and Cullen supported his weight for a heartbeat, then pushed up and away, throwing the soon-to-be corpse into the file behind, buying himself a moment to recover his strength.

The moment did not last long. A short sword feinted low, struck high, hitting his shield so hard that it punctured all the way through the protective hide and the boards beyond, a handspan of bloodstained iron bursting out to narrowly miss Cullen's wrist. The sword's wielder tried to yank it free but it was well stuck, and Cullen let go, the weight of the shield pulling the gladius out of the Roman's grip so that Lightning-Strike could do its work. The Roman crumpled over his opened upper thigh, mouth flapping wordlessly as his fingers tried to stem his lifeblood. Cullen shifted back, exposed without a shield, but the press of men behind curtailed any thought of escape, so he fought on, unthinking and desperate, hacking at the oncoming men, using Lightning-Strike's extra reach to keep away from the snapping gladii.

The horde was in utter chaos. They were fighters, to a man and woman. Born to the spear and trained behind the shield. But their style of war was fought on the front foot. Bravado, challenge, aggression, charge. They grew up with a battle name as their goal, and raw, naked courage as their means to attain it. This was different. Alien. It was like fighting a monster, sent from the underworld. Untouchable and obdurate, devoid of fear or feeling. And they gave ground, the horde of the mighty. There was no choice. They killed the enemy, but lost so many more in return. And those bodies now lay all across the sloping fields and down to the riverbank. They got in the way, their mangled limbs and shattered weapons becoming entwined with the feet of the living, making an orderly retreat impossible. So more died. More souls soared to the next life.

One of those had belonged to White Tal. Conspicuous with his snowy locks, perhaps he had been too visible for the enemy to ignore, for the Roman front rank seemed to bow around him, two or three legionaries chopping at him at once. He blocked and riposted, he bellowed entreaties to the gods whom he knew so well, and then one of the gladii had slid along the side of a scutum when Tal had been dodging another and parrying a third. The blade had chewed up his braca as though it were made of rotten leaves, and the great, pulsing vessel in his thigh had been gouged open. Tal gave a final howl, fell to his knees, tears tumbling down his pale cheeks. The Romans took his head, gripped it, dripping, by the icy hair, and held it aloft.

As if in reply, the sorrowful chorus of a dozen carnyxes floated over the battlefield, their song jolting right through Cullen's body. He did not look round. Did not need to hear a command or see a banner. It was the call for retreat. Behind, up near the trees, men plunged into the woods. He could sense them, could feel the defensive line thinning as more and more peeled away. Roman horns blew, the clarity of their tones competing with the harsher carnyx cries, and the legions seemed to halt, apparently content to let their vanquished foe escape.

Cullen risked a look behind. Searched for Togodubnos, for Caratacos or Aoife. Saw only madness, panic. The horde was breaking rapidly apart, splintering into smaller warbands and nines, fighters finding those they knew, those they trusted, folk beside whom they would make a final stand or flee into the deep dark of the forest. He still had most of his group in close proximity.

'To me! To me!' he screamed, though he knew not if anyone heard. 'Shield-wall! Push them back!'

It was pointless, in truth. The words hollow. A last venting in the face of crushing defeat. Some of them came, and he whispered thanks to the gods for them. Garn and Andoc, Maeveen, Rues and Baglan.

'Where is Clesek?' Cullen panted as they gathered just in front of the wooded crest, turning back to present yet another front for the enemy to negotiate, buying others time to escape.

'Dead,' Andoc said. His dourness, this once, entirely apt.

The Romans were coming again. They had merely used the lull to reform, straighten up, get their shields to overlay precisely. In their wake, all across the slope and down to the reedy bank, corpses were strewn, twisted and grisly. Warriors in their thousands, but legionaries too. Hacked and beaten, arrow-punctured and stone-shot, smashed by club, cleaved by axe and scorched by fire. To look at the refreshed Roman formation, one could not tell. Their dead littered the valley, but it made no difference at all.

All around him, the warriors dragged air into their bruised bodies, shoulders rising and falling in laboured heaves. They were battered and broken, dog-tired and desolate-faced. But they were here, and they would go again, and they turned their shoulders to the side, and clamped the front foot down, chocking against an unstoppable vehicle that bowled uphill instead of down. A swell of pride bloomed in Cullen, and he felt the sting of hot tears. He cuffed them away, tried to stand tall. Without his shield, he drew his dagger, a longer, wider brute than his delicate skinning knife, its heft reassuring in his grip. He looked left and right, saw gazes returned, felt they were seeking some kind of direction. The familiar uncertainty crept up on him, catching him off guard. Many were older than he, more experienced. But still, they seemed to look to him. To the one who had defied Arthmael the Learned and won the favour of Taranis himself. And besides, he told himself, they were all likely to die anyway. What did it matter if his hunch was wrong?

He stepped out of the line, spat a globule of blood between his broken front teeth, and raised Lightning-Strike. 'Our last stand, my brothers and sisters!' he shouted, twirling the blade high. 'Let our lifeblood water this soil, and let our descendants sing of our fame!'

They cheered, half-hearted at first, but then the sound grew as it spread, rippling all the way along the line. They were only a couple of ranks deep now, for most had fled the field. *Not us*, Cullen thought. *Not now.* To his friends, his brothers of the blade, he said, 'Life with glory.' They exchanged grim smiles as they intoned the traditional reply. Then he said, 'Kill as many as you can before they kill you.'

Garn, his white hair and beard turned pink by the day's work, caught his eye and smiled. 'You wear the mask well, Wolf Scourge.'

Cullen looked hurriedly away, suddenly overwhelmed. His eyes went further afield, gauging the throes of the fight now that the earthworks had been lost. Enemy cavalry swirled beside the woods, perhaps four hundred paces from his position. They appeared to be harrying men on foot, their dark shapes and bright markings ebbing and flowing at the treeline, melding with the shadows as individual skirmishes were swallowed by the gnarled trunks and heavy, low canopy, only to be regurgitated in a welter of thrashing hooves and glittering iron.

Cullen watched the fight only briefly, the time it took to draw four or five breaths, for the combined legions were closing on his position. But something jarred in his mind. Something in that eddying clash of horse and spear. A familiarity, that gave him pause.

The Romans broke ranks. It was almost a relief to see their cohorts dissolve, for it made them somehow more human. But he knew it was a small comfort. The Romans could not hope to penetrate the forest – let alone the yellow marshes beyond – in their rigid formation, and so they had decided to overwhelm and mop up the last of the resistance before the warriors were lost to the dense and dangerous boughs.

Cullen launched himself forward, barrelling into a taller, thinner man, whose armour jangled wildly as they collapsed together in a heap. Cullen's dagger slipped under the man's chin, even as he writhed to free himself. He pawed haplessly at his killer, the last breath wheezing out through a mouth full of blood, his eyes washing emptily over Cullen.

Huge strength at the scruff of his neck, hauling him bodily up. Cullen wrenched about, fearing impending death, only to see Garn's blood-flecked face grinning back. The big man released him, moved swiftly on, smashing a Roman with his metallic fist and then cleaving through helmet and skull with his enormous axe. The unfortunate legionary's face was drowned in a flood of his own brain-flecked gore as he crumpled, Garn kicking him savagely away.

The stand was exhilarating and savage. A moment of true carnage unleashed upon the invader, in a style of battle suited to named men and warbands of repute. But those warbands were fading now, their numbers depleted, and the Romans kept coming, kept pressing. They needed to retreat, properly, fully, this time. The day was done. Cries went up to that effect, and the momentum began to shift back to the reds, who, out of their disciplined lines seemed free to crow in triumph to their own gods. A sound that would have sickened Cullen, had he been paying attention. Instead he was looking along the treeline, at the private fight between two bands of horsemen. Because he had finally realised what it was about them that had resonated in his mind.

Maeveen Spurn Joy was nearest Cullen now. A Roman was making for him, but she stepped into his path with a shriek like an injured kestrel, twirled like an acrobat, dropped suddenly, rolled, hacked the legionary's feet out from under him and jammed a blade into his mouth.

Cullen, still staring at the cavalrymen, crouched over the last man he had killed. He dipped his fingers into the freshly spilled blood and smeared his own face with the crimson paint, the raw tang filling his nostrils anew. Then he sprinted for the horsemen.

CHAPTER NINETEEN

The wicker man blazed in front of the trees. A grotesque double-faced ghoul, human at the back, staring sightlessly into the woods, and horned ram at the front, surveying the valley, it had presumably been lit by the Wise to stall the Roman pursuit. The great forest and treacherous marshes they would next need to negotiate were teeming with Otherworld dwellers. Let them know. Let them fear. Let them hesitate.

Streams of humanity ran freely to either side of the rapidly blackening sculpture. Warriors fleeing the fight, leaving the valley to the enemy, their shield-walls collapsed, resistance crumbled. They would surge north and west, through the trees and the swamps, following the tracks and holloways unknown to the Romans, and there gather at an even more formidable river than the Vaga.

Not Cullen. He sprinted below the crackling mass of embroidered hazel, black and grey smoke curling in acrid gouts to mingle with the dense leaves. Behind him he could hear the pounding footsteps and laboured breaths of the motley assortment of warriors who had followed. Some were of his nine, and others, like Kurd, were as good as kin. There were probably a score more, archers and slingers and spearmen, attaching themselves to him for want of any other command. He might have felt pride in that, had his thoughts not bent entirely towards the foe at whom he now screamed his challenge.

—

Grimoald, Leopard of the Batacgwi, was enjoying himself.

'Bring them in and finish them off!' he bellowed to Felix, who was leading the men in an arcing manoeuvre, surrounding the final efforts of fifty or so exhausted barbarians.

Once the battle had commenced, and the legions had insinuated themselves on this side of the river, it was a simple enough thing to lead his auxiliary unit across. They had already done it once, after all, and that had been when a hundred thousand Britons had been guarding the water. This time, it had been something of a leisurely swim for both horse and man.

Now, though, the killing had started. The eight hundred Batacgwi that Aulus Plautius had at his disposal had been instructed to occupy this bank in order to wipe up the mess left in the wake of the reds. It was a slick of gore. A chilling, stinking, twisted blight on the hillside, and strewn amongst the myriad dead were the moaning, weeping dying. The Batacgwi, not as highly regarded as the legions, had been assigned to the dispatching of those dying. At least, the Britons amongst that wretched group.

But Grimoald had a problem. He was lord of his followers. Chief fame-earner and silver-giver, no matter what the Romans thought. To that end, he had promised his men treasure beyond their wildest dreams. Had led Felix and the rest into the enemy's heartland, and found a prize worthy of their efforts, only to encounter a stubborn group of spearmen, commanded by a whelp barely old enough to grow a beard. They had returned to the army empty handed and humiliated, and that could not stand. If they had no bounty, they would soon find another lord. It was unconscionable.

Which was why Grimoald had crossed the Vaga, as he had been bidden, but then he had ignored the remainder of his orders, and had galloped headlong up the slope to the treeline, where he knew he would find some fugitives to kill and loot. They would, at least, collect some fine prizes by day's end. The Britons were well known for their trinkets in bronze, copper and gold. Some wore jewellery of intricate golden wire, shot through with beads of glass and gemstones. Others, it was said, even carried pearls.

This group of walking corpses were, he had to admit, irksomely tenacious. They were mostly big bastards, several rejecting armour so that their uniformly muscular and intricately painted torsos could intimidate the physically inferior Romans. Bad luck for them, he thought with grim pleasure, that they had come across the butchers of the River Renos. Every inch their match.

Grimoald watched contentedly as Felix steered the arc of horsemen. The stubborn knot of Britons were hard up against the trees, refusing to flee. 'One last charge should do it!' he called. 'For the glory of Rome and for the grandeur of the *Batavorum equitata quingenaria*!'

The savages responded with a stream of vicious drivel in their own tongue, most of which he understood, all of which he disdained. They would fight to the death. Hardly a threat when there were trophies to be taken. The leader, a hulking, bald-headed brute with a scalp decorated in various emblems, wore a bronze torc at his neck and fistfuls of fine-looking rings. He was already on his rump, slumped against a blood-spattered tree, his leg a ragged mass of open flesh, the thigh bone gleaming white. He still barked commands at his men, compelled them into some semblance of order, but they were finished, and they knew it.

The horsemen kicked on, gathering pace, swords poised. They fell upon their prey in a crescendo of iron and screams and whinnies. The shield formation disintegrated. The big, arrogant Britons were carved up, trampled, slaughtered. The vast man with the injured leg howled like a wolf in a pit. Grimoald let his excited mount skitter a tight circle, the animal unable to contain itself with the scent of death ripe in its muzzle. As he turned about, he was forced to stick a boot in the face of a tall barbarian who had broken away from the melee. He was black-haired and narrow-faced and wore armlets of a good quality, marking him in Grimoald's mind as someone worth killing. A petty chieftain, perhaps, or a noble's son. Whatever his status, the fellow collapsed, nose broken, dropping the club he had been waving. Grimoald sheathed his sword, swung a leg over his saddle, dropping to earth, and went to collect his reward. He took the curved knife from his belt of bronze and jet, and bent to grab a fistful of the warrior's long hair. 'Your skull will look good hanging from my saddle,' he whispered in the vulgar language of the Britons. It gratified him to feel the man buck helplessly in his grip. The wind blew, slewing thick smoke from the burning wicker effigy across the slope's crest, drawing a screen across his personal slaughter. He put the knife to the convulsing windpipe. Which was when he looked up, startled. Because someone was calling his name through the smoke.

'Leopard!' Cullen shouted as he ran, hoping he had not mangled the unusual word. 'Leopard!'

It was the copper feline, frozen in a leaping pose on the man's helmet, that he had noticed. Then the skulls, dangling beneath the saddle, though they were too far away to be recognised as anything but swinging shadows, like ripe fruit on a low, distant bough. Through the carnage of battle and the fright of capitulation, overwrought by thudding, leg-deadening exhaustion, his mind had not turned quickly enough at first. Not put those fragmentary notions into a coherent pattern. Gradually, they had shifted in his mind, melded together, and, with jarring clarity, he had seen the cavalrymen for what – for *who* – they truly were.

'Leopard!' he called again, bursting through the smoke screen, and this time the man he knew to be Grimoald of the Batacgwi stood up. The man was as impressive as he remembered. Wide at mail-clad shoulders, eyes of icy blue, with one pupil that had a trailing smear of black, like the tail of a newt. His face had once been cleaved by a blade, leaving a vertical scar from his forehead to his yellow-bearded chin, and he wore his helmet with its pouncing leopard. The long cloak trailed behind him, distinct with its strange pattern, crafted from the pelt of the giant cat that was his emblem.

Grimoald had been about to draw his dagger across the throat of a warrior, but he kicked that hapless captive away so that he sprawled in the mud. He spread his arms as if he might embrace Cullen. 'Can it be, the deluded boy who styles himself after the wolf? Do my eyes deceive me?' He spoke in the common tongue, warmly, as if greeting an old friend. 'You made good your escape. I have thought often of your fate.' He looked around, hailed his men who fought in duels with pockets of spearmen. 'Felix. Come. Look at what the gods have brought me!'

'Perhaps they have brought you to me.' Cullen had his dagger and his sword, and he levelled both at Grimoald.

The water-lord grinned broadly. He pulled his own broadsword – more similar to those of the tribes than the short gladii of the legions – from its scabbard, though it was the dagger that he wagged slowly at Cullen. 'Shall we discover the truth of it?'

'For Kenal and for Ludris.'

'Who?'

'It does not matter,' Cullen said. But it did. It mattered more than anything.

He walked forward and to the side, so that his enemy was forced to do the same, steadily circling one another. They crouched a little, ready to give or receive the first lunge. Behind them along the crest, and all the way down the slope, the battle still seethed, though it was in its final moments, the horde reduced to pockets of forlorn resistance. Many of Grimoald's cavalrymen thundered in and out of the treeline, looking for fugitives in the murk. Here, though, where the day had come to a blood-drenched crescendo, cut off from the world by the pall of roiling smoke, the killing had paused. Warriors stopped and stared, Batacgwi and Briton alike, captivated by this private reckoning.

'Kill him,' a voice rumbled at his back. Garn Grey Boulder, beaten but unbowed.

'Vengeance,' Andoc said.

'Kill him,' Baglan Day Break snarled.

Grimoald attacked. It was so sudden that his sword's tip almost made it through Cullen's guard, but Cullen – younger, weaker, faster – was able to twist away as he knocked the stabbing thrust aside. They both spun on their heels, resumed their guard – dagger low, sword high – and got up on the balls of their feet, bouncing a little, gauging always, alive to every flinch and inflection. Grimoald jumped in again, battering down with his heavy strength, cleaving at Lightning-Strike, chopping with huge strokes as if his intent was to snap it in two. Cullen found himself bending awkwardly over his rear foot, the strain going through his left hip and knee as he arched unnaturally over them, sword held level across his face as it took the pounding punishment. It was all he could do to keep hold of the hilt, and he felt his hand losing grip, growing numb. He dropped to a knee, stuck out his left hand to punch the dagger into Grimoald's gut. The Batacgwi shifted his feet with impressive agility, midriff swaying clear, and danced to the side, resetting himself, tutting softly as if to a callow apprentice.

Cullen knew he could not win. He was good. Had been given his grounding by Farrad, the renowned sword master of Verlamion, and then taught in the school of life by Ulla, one of the true heroes of the Catuvellauni. Every day, every fight, he had improved, grown stronger, wilier. Yet this man, this murderer of children, who could fight in the saddle and on foot, and swim a raging torrent with his horse and in full kit, was no ordinary opponent. Both knew it. Cullen gritted his teeth. Grimoald grinned as he feinted with a low flick and dragged the blade hard up, almost snagging Cullen's ear. The latter overbalanced, Grimoald stepped quickly in, and his blow was blocked by Lightning-Strike. They held each other there, wrestling over the cross of iron, but there was only one winner, and Grimoald shoved Cullen away with a look of pure scorn.

Cullen stumbled on the prone man whose life he had prolonged by his interruption, performing a haphazard backwards dance as he fought to keep upright. That man, curled like a foetus, whimpered at the contact, and Cullen saw that his face was smeared by an explosion of blood around a severely canted nose. Despite the injury, the face resounded at the back of his mind. It made him look around, searching for something nebulous, like trying to recall a dream. He took in the warriors, scattered and beaten. His own blade-brothers, willing him on, and the others who had come purely because they needed someone to lead them. Several more, gathered for safety with his own group, bore the mark of a bloody half-moon on their shields and chests. A sigil he knew all too well. He raked the scene with his eyes, scrutinising the twisted bodies, the debris-strewn slope and the shadowy treeline. His gaze settled on the base of an oak, where ferns grew thick, and a giant clutched his tattered thigh with bear-paw hands. Sego Blood Swill returned his gaze. Not with the usual malevolence, nor with the pain that must surely be washing over him like an incoming tide, but with a curiously taut desperation, as if he wanted to convey something but the words were restrained, shackled by some unfathomable fear.

'You are brave,' Grimoald said. 'Skilled, even.' He shrugged. 'But you understand I cannot allow you to retire. Not this time.'

'I will fight,' Cullen said, but now he was looking down at the man with the broken nose. Kadored, Sego's beloved son.

Grimoald chuckled. 'This I know.' He swiped the big sword so that it sung in the smoky air. 'Die well.'

Cullen set his feet again, excoriating himself privately for the hitherto lacklustre display. He checked his breathing, not wanting to let Grimoald know that his body was beginning to wilt. His hip still ached. He must, he absently reflected, have jarred it badly. Then he remembered the extra weight that hung there. He put away the dagger and unhooked the stone pouch. Grimoald frowned.

'The treasure you sought,' Cullen said, upending the pouch. Pebbles scattered the ground. A much larger stone followed, thudding into the mud between his feet. He crouched, slowly, retrieving it, never taking his eyes from the man opposite. 'For which you murdered a child.'

One of Grimoald's yellow brows arched. 'War is war.' He cracked his neck, the monstrous fang at the end of his plaited beard danced a little jig, rattling against his mail shirt. 'The *child*, as you call him, had seen no fewer winters than you.'

Cullen stifled the urge to leap at the Batacgwi. He held out his palm instead, presenting the stone. 'The Whetstone of the smith-god, Gobannos.'

The mounted men laughed. Grimoald sneered. 'That is my treasure?' He coughed mucus into his mouth and spat towards Cullen. 'You would buy your life with a dirty rock? I'll kill you slowly for your impudence.'

'You have heard of Ankou?' Cullen asked, fighting to keep his voice steady and his hand from shaking.

Grimoald gave a head-jerk to show that he had. 'The servant of death.'

'At the world's birth, when the mountains grew out of the sea, and the first men battled the gods of anarchy, Ankou stalked this land, served by his shadowmancers, slaying by mere whim alone.'

'Take his head, lord!' one of the horsemen yelled, but Grimoald raised his sword arm for silence.

'But some of the gods looked favourably upon the world of flesh,' Cullen went on, sensing he had Grimoald's attention, if only fleetingly, 'admiring the courage of those first men. One of the gods was the smith, Gobannos, who sharpened the weapons of the Otherworld.' He raised the object higher, offering it towards the sun, and now he let the fearful trembling overtake him, so that his arm quivered almost uncontrollably. 'And he took his whetstone and bathed it in the light of Belinos on the longest day, and ran the blades of men across its surface, imbuing them with power and sharpness beyond comprehension. And with those blades the first men slew the shadowmancers, and chased Ankou into the dark, there to lurk for all eternity, emerging only to take life when the time was fitting.'

Grimoald spat, rolled his shoulders, stepped forward. 'Enough of this.'

Cullen jumped back a couple of paces, extending the space between them. 'This is the treasure you sought to steal from me,' he said hurriedly. 'The Whetstone of Gobannos.'

'Stripling,' Grimoald growled. 'Sow's turd. Craven liar.'

Half wincing, for fear of sudden assault, Cullen did as Aoife had done in the forest. He lowered the stone, laid his sword flat upon it, aligning its cutting edge with one of the iron stains and scraping it back, as slowly as he dared risk. 'I sharpen my blade on it now.'

He might have felt foolish. The stone, after all, was worthless. A magical vessel, utterly empty. It had been stolen from its sacred seat in the Cantiaci hills. Had not been in place during solstice, nor had the correct manner of rites been performed in its honour. It was, in essence, just a rock.

Might have felt foolish, had Cullen not been entirely exhausted. Had he not seen his blade-brothers fall, had not the tang of his own blood cloyed at the back of his throat. Embarrassment was the last of his worries. So he gurned like a madman, and glared reverently at the stone, channelling the authority he alone had denied it. Did he honour the gods with his charade, or was this the final insult on his way to meet them? But then he recalled the forest before dawn. Aoife's presentation of the stone, and how, despite Cullen's failures, its magic had flowed, the horde invigorated by its ancient wonder. 'It is charged with the power of Gobannos and Belinos, and I feel their power flow through my blade.'

Grimoald watched the performance with something like sceptical veneration. He was frustrated, suspicious, but he could not bring himself to risk defying the gods. He seemed to have frozen. He checked whatever move had been planned, narrowed his eyes, scrutinising the act for authenticity. His twisted mouth spoke of complete derision, yet his blue eyes were transfixed and still he did not move. Cullen ventured a quick eye roll, as though he were in the thrall of something unearthly. The other Batacgwi, watching on from their saddles, murmured concern. Their chief looked round at one of his subordinates with a questioning glance, clearly uncertain.

Cullen leapt at him.

He tried to close the gap before Grimoald could react, and he almost managed it. The Batacgwi leader had been spellbound for just a moment. Serwil had told him the men of the River Renos were as reverent of the Dreaming Realm as any tribe of these beleaguered isles, and despite Grimoald's allegiance to Rome, the Wise One had been right. He blinked as if dazzled by sudden sunlight as he rocked back, hastily throwing up the long sword and the curved dagger as he fended off the younger man.

Cullen pressed, howled, unrelenting and ferocious, knowing this might be his only chance to seize the momentum. His senses were keen now, smells richer, sounds sharper, colours brighter, his soul pushing on the golden gate between this life and the next, and he hacked sideways, one blow after another, trying to smash through the hurried defence. Tried a high angle, then low for the groin. It was a blur of speed and savagery, of sweat and blood and spittle. He withdrew smartly, regathering his strength, and darted in once more, two quick strikes direct at the face, then diverting low with another brace, sending Grimoald desperately reeling, parrying for his life. He was gratified to see the Batacgwi panting now, a wild look in that ice-nugget stare.

The trip, when it came, was as hapless as it was unexpected. Cullen had worn the auxiliary commander down, taken the initiative, only to snag his foot on a dead man's hand as it clawed for the sky. He stumbled forward, his pursuit of Grimoald becoming an exaggerated run that took him into range, and the leopard cape billowed as the big man brought the handle of his sword down vertically, clanging hard against the crown of Cullen's helmet.

The world went white, then black. He opened his eyes, expecting the golden gate to have swung fully open for him. But instead he saw long grass, soaked crimson, and blue sky, smudged a smoky grey, and then he saw Grimoald looking down at him.

'You have given me a great deal of trouble, boy,' Grimoald said.

Cullen flinched as the Batacgwi bent close, tearing the dented helm roughly from his head and tossing it away. He pushed himself up, weakly, groping for Lightning-Strike. Long gone. He went for the dagger in his belt. Fingers brushed the hilt, but no purchase, no grip.

Movement in the trees away to his right. Abstract shapes, nothing more. Legionaries, he guessed, encircling them. It was done.

Grimoald, Leopard of the Batacgwi, sheathed his sword and swapped the curved dagger to his right hand as he stepped over Cullen. He made a dextrous swirl of the blade, cutting so fast it almost left the remnant of the shape in the air. And he leaned down to take a fistful of Cullen's hair.

'I told you I would have your head, Cullen Wolf Scourge. I told you.'

The Whetstone of Gobannos broke his eye socket. That was Cullen's best guess, of course. He would have needed Cassia to make a proper diagnosis. But the broad, confident face crumpled as Cullen smashed the heavy rock home, just below the rim of the ostentatious helmet. The left eye imploded, vanished like the entrance to a collapsing cave, and Grimoald brayed as he plunged backwards. Cullen scrambled up, one arm still near useless, but the other still clutched the stone and he sprawled across Grimoald's prone form as the watching Batacgwi lost their nonchalance and screamed for his slaughter. The shapes in the trees to his right materialised then, and they were not Romans but his own people, and many had bows, ready nocked, which they loosed in a stinging volley to unseat the leopard's men.

The battle sparked suddenly into life all around him, but he only had eyes for Grimoald, who he battered once more. When he saw the blood, it was not Grimoald's but that of Ludris. His blurred vision, swimming with pain and exhaustion, put images that were unreal in front of him, replacing Grimoald's damaged face, and one was the boy's headless corpse, buckling at the knees, slumping into the trampled grass. He felt new tears. Kept smashing, harder and harder. He lost his mind, then. Driven by pure hate, wanting to demolish the leopard of the Batacgwi, reduce him to carrion, as the leopard had reduced Ludris.

When it was done, he rolled away, staring blankly at the sky, hauling in breaths, hearing only his own pulse. He was ready to die. Hands took hold. Firm but not threatening. They grasped at his arms and torso, and the accompanying voices urged him to stand, to head for the trees. And so he went, almost mindlessly, plunging into the gloom. The battle was lost, so too the Vaga. But he was alive, and Grimoald was not. He whispered thanks to Taranis. To Serwil, too. Felt a curious, ragged smile form in the corner of his mauled mouth at the last thought. He stumbled, legs failing in the thickening brush along which he was being dragged. He felt himself begin to swoon. Strong arms held him up, lifted him, turning. He seemed to be on his back, one eye peeling open, regarding the densely entwined canopy.

Screeching chatter above. A bird, nimbly balancing. Black and white plumage, with a streak of blue on its flanks, and dark, shimmering green along its tailfeathers. He let the smile widen, and fell asleep.

EPILOGUE

The yellow marsh stretched into the northwest, a tapestry of reeds and mist, bottomless pools and quarrelsome wildfowl. Cassia rocked silently, letting her body move with the roll of Hog's loping gait. The horse's stoic steadiness reassured her. He was a proud beast, with his golden coat and cream-coloured mane, spattered now from fetlock to tail by the stinking mire. But he was gentle enough, and calm, and he seemed content to trudge with all the rest, resigned to his place in the endless column of bedraggled fugitives that streamed away from the slaughterhouse that was the Vaga.

Behind Cassia, the echoes of battle still lingered. A scream, rending the air. The blast of a horn, the beat of a drum. No carnyxes now. Those shrill cries conspicuous by their silence. She thought of the carnage back in the valley. Of a hillside and a wood littered with corpses, and a river running red. What would her father have made of that? She could hardly imagine. It was as if the last days — the fear, the exhilaration, the death — had filled her mind so that there was no longer space for anything else. The older memories felt like fragments from another life, distant and blurred and, mercifully, their edges duller than before.

Hog drifted to the side of the path, teetering at the edge of a black rill, seeking to tear up a clump of grass. She did not demur, for the pickings were slim in the yellow marsh. Ludris squirmed in her lap. She stroked the pup, cooing into one of those oversized ears until he settled. She caught the glimpse of her own reflection in the water. The face that stared back was one she barely recognised. Neither Roman nor Briton, but something forged in the crucible of conflict and loss. The scars on her arms, once fresh and angry, had faded; the newer scabs itched, but they no longer called to her. She considered that, surprised by the realisation. She looked back to the reflection. There was something hard in that face she had not seen before. A resilience, etched into the skin at the corners of her mouth and eyes.

Around her, the Britons moved with quiet determination, their spirits unbroken despite the retreat. Children clung to their mothers, warriors tended to the wounded, and elders offered words of solace. They chattered, always, in low tones, encouraging one another to keep up the pace, always glancing back, fearful of an enemy on the horizon. Cassia felt a profound connection to them, a shared understanding that transcended bloodlines and birthrights. A sense of peace enveloped her. She had chosen her path, and she knew now that it was the right one. The burden of guilt and grief and confusion, hitherto so heavy, had somehow lifted.

She clicked her tongue softly and Hog plodded on. Amid the whispers of reeds and the soft lullaby of distant waters, Cassia smiled – a gesture not of joy, but of acceptance. Of her choices, of herself. She was no longer a woman torn between two worlds, but one who had found her place amid these beleaguered people. She would find Cullen, if he lived, and then she would find Critheanach. For this was her home, the Isle of the Mighty, and they were her family. She held Ludris close, and spoke gentle words to Hog, and begged the gods to spare the life of the man she loved.

—

'The gods weep.' A woman's voice, vague, illusory. 'The land aches.'

'Why?' A man now, the growled word like an earthquake in Cullen's head. 'Why stand aside and watch, only to weep for what is lost? Could they not have fought? Are the gods so indolent that they allow this slaughter?'

Cullen peeled open an eye. It hurt to prise the lids apart, so glued were they. He put a hand to the place, probing, expecting it to sting where the skin was tacky on his fingertips. Nothing hurt, so he followed the stain of what he guessed was congealed blood. It led him to matted hair and an egg-sized lump on the very top of his skull. He hissed as the pain lanced all the way through his head. He saw sky, still blue, but darkening now, awash with vast swirls of ochre and honey. The world rocked gently.

'The gods will fight,' the woman was saying. Now he placed her. Maeveen, somewhere to his right. 'It is only a matter of time.'

'Time and death,' Andoc said, the bleak tone unmistakable.

'How many more,' Garn Grey Boulder rumbled a reply, 'before the Dreaming Realm wakes to our plight?'

Cullen understood that he was on his back. The blow had knocked him senseless. His head pulsed incessantly. He put a hand to it. The hair was matted, caked in dried blood, so that every flinch pulled, making him wince. He pushed himself sluggishly up to see that he had been placed in a large wain drawn by two shaggy bay ponies. He stared, blearily, replaying the last moments of consciousness in his head. The collapse of the horde, the duel with Grimoald, the screaming hail of arrows.

'Gobannos knows,' Maeveen said. 'He saw. How else do you explain Cullen's survival?'

'I cannot,' Cullen managed to utter, his throat parched and hoarse.

They grinned. He saw that they were walking at the side of the swaying vehicle. The others were there too, in varying states of dishevelment, caked to the knees in mud, their armour dented, weapons crusted with blood. Baglan, Andoc, Rues, Kurd, Erbin. He smiled as they took turns to hurl good-natured abuse at him.

'The explanation,' Garn said, 'is that this goat-fancying youth is favoured by the smith god, as well as Taranis.' He thumped the side of the wain with his studded stump. 'By Epona's mystical teats, he's a lucky bastard.'

'Tal put his faith in the Otherworld,' Kurd said as he loped up ahead, 'and he has gone.'

'On to the next,' Rues intoned.

Many voices echoed the sentiment. Kurd continued, 'I'd rather put my life in the hands of a lucky fighter than a pious one.'

'Where am I?' Cullen asked.

Kurd looked round now. 'One of the almost-walking wounded.'

'Where are we?'

'The road north,' Garn said.

Cullen's vision was clearing now, blocks of abstract shape and colour coming together in a discernible vista. Into the golden evening trundled a great train of vehicles, horses, chariots and men. There were large supply wagons, carts laden with weaponry and smaller hurdles bearing yet more wounded fighters.

A throb of memory, coated in fear. 'The reds?'

'Stopped in the valley.' It was Andoc talking, his long stride affected by a noticeable limp.

'Why did they—'

'Let us leave? Hunger, sleep, reinforcements. They're a long way from their anchorage. We're to gather at the Tamesas.'

'Another river,' Cullen said, sullen at the thought.

Andoc shrugged. 'The next defensible place. There are healers at the riverbank. You'll be taken there. Moranna and her people. Gwidion,' he gave a rare, sardonic smile, 'with his new helpers, gods preserve you.'

'Oh?'

'One for want of eyes, the other for legs.'

'Becan and Drest.'

Andoc nodded. 'Gwidion will put you right. You took a nasty knock. Not much they can do for your smile, though.'

Cullen probed his damaged front teeth with his tongue. One was bent inwards, the other snapped halfway up. He tried to laugh, though it sputtered to a dry cough, which seared his head. To his surprise, he noticed the stone at his feet, tilting gently with the sway of the wain. Its stripes had expanded to envelop the rest, so that it had a uniform rusty hue. A leopard's blood, he realised with a stab of recollection that made his stomach turn. Moranna's words filled his head. *Some of the best prophecies fulfil themselves.* He closed his eyes, steadying himself. When he opened them again, he noticed the other wounded men and women. They were crammed close, shoulder to shoulder, bandaged, bruised and bleeding.

A hand touched his arm. 'I am alive because of you.'

He was startled to see Kadored staring back at him. The young man had had his nose put back into some semblance of its correct position, but it was still swollen and crooked. Cullen asked, 'Who told you I was your enemy?'

'Arthmael.'

'It was a lie.'

'I know that now.' Kadored turned his head gingerly, the pain still raw, and looked pointedly towards the far corner of the vehicle, where a huge, bald man was slumped, his thigh swaddled in tight strips of brown-stained linen. '*We* know that.'

Cullen followed Kadored's gaze. Sego, first shield of Caratacos, nodded at him. Cullen nodded back. Neither yet ready to speak.

Instead, he looked for Andoc again. 'We lost the battle,' he said softly, bleakly.

'Not if the poets have anything to do with it,' Andoc replied, cynical as ever. 'They'll weave their elegant words into a tapestry of victory.'

Maeveen turned. 'Many got away, thank the gods. We'll fight again.'

'And you avenged young Ludris,' Andoc said. 'When you meet him in the next life, he will honour your courage.'

'The bowmen,' Cullen said suddenly. 'They came from nowhere. Saved us all.'

Andoc gave a rare smile, jerked his chin at a group of archers who were walking up ahead of the wagons. 'They were on the flank, fleeing like all the rest. But he saw his blade-brother through the smoke, and he came back to help.'

Cullen stared, until Andoc's high-pitched whistle made a few heads turn. One was the scarred visage of a man he had not seen since returning from the fight with the Silures. His heart swelled.

'Dan Tongue-Torn, they call him now,' Andoc said. 'Doesn't matter whether he likes the name. He can't say either way.'

Cullen grinned, despite the pain, and the mangled jaw of his old friend twisted upwards in return. He rubbed blood-encrusted hands over his face, trying to purge the weariness. Replayed the day, the fight, the deaths and the conversations since waking. A name came to him through the haze of notions. He put his hand to his chest, groping for the heartwood horse that dangled from its string. 'Andoc, wait. You said Becan and Drest were at the Tamesas.'

Andoc glanced down at him. 'So I did.'

'Well? Is she with them?'

'I cannot say, goat-fiddler. But when we retrieved the horses from the alder wood, Hog was absent.'

'Only him?'

Andoc nodded. 'The watch-boys said a dark-haired lass took him. Quoted the phrase.'

'The raven flies at dusk,' Cullen whispered.

Andoc offered a wry smile. 'Now who might have told her that?' He did not wait for an answer. Instead, he leaned across, slapping Cullen on the back. 'You'll see her soon enough, goat-fiddler! Now, sit back. We've a long road ahead.'

HISTORICAL NOTE

The Romans, under Aulus Plautius, invaded Britain in AD 43 with four legions and about twenty thousand auxiliaries. The first book in this series, *The Savage Isle*, described what those early weeks must have been like, as the tribes scrambled to organise some kind of resistance. *The River Warriors* is my attempt at retelling the story of the first major battle, as the legions sweep inland.

Though the Celts left no written account, what we can glean from Roman historians – namely Cassius Dio, Tacitus and Suetonius – is that British resistance emerged predominantly around the Catuvellauni, under the brothers Togodubnos and Caratacos. We know that several tribes were already negotiating surrender by this point, but it seems likely to me that many others would have joined the Catuvellauni alliance.

The Britons set up a strong defensive line on the west bank of the Medway – which I have called the Vaga – believing the Romans would have a very tricky time crossing without a bridge. A reasonable assumption, except that General Plautius had Batavian auxiliaries within his ranks, who were experts at crossing rivers in full kit. Hailing from the Rhine–Waal delta, the Batavians were renowned for their aquatic prowess. Tacitus notes they and their horses 'could cross the Rhine without losing formation,' and Cassius Dio, talking explicitly about the Medway assault, wrote that they managed it 'easily in full armour across the most turbulent streams.'

However it was done, the Batavians were able to reach Togodubnos's lines and wreak total havoc. They disabled the chariot horses, one of the Britons' main advantages, which must have disrupted their overall morale.

Vespasian (yes, *that* Vespasian, who later became emperor) led his Second Legion across, presumably amid the chaos ensuing from the

Batavian attack, and snatched a foothold on the west bank. The following day, the other legions forced their way across too. Hosidius Geta really did lead one crucial advance, and nearly got himself captured, but he fought his way clear and turned the tide of battle, earning high military honours in the process.

The senior Roman characters mentioned in the book – Plautius, Geta, Narcissus, Vespasian – are a matter of historical record. Sadly, most of the Britons are figments of my imagination, with the exception of Togodubnos and Caratacos, and some of the tribal kings.

The Stone of Gobannos is an invention, but I have tried to keep that, and the stories told by my characters, as authentic as possible, drawing from Cornish, Irish, Scots and Welsh myths. The same can be said of the native culture in general, their belief systems and the entire druidic caste. All mistakes are, of course, my own.

ACKNOWLEDGEMENTS

Once again, I am hugely grateful to the whole team at Canelo. I hope this story does their hard work justice. Thanks in particular to my editor, Craig Lye, for his expert and insightful feedback, bringing the initial draft up to something worth publishing.

Thanks to my agent, James Wills, and everyone at Watson, Little, without whom this series would never have been read by anyone but my parents. Speaking of which, my poor mum and dad have been supporting this journey from the very start. Much love and gratitude to them.

Last, but certainly not least, my love to the gang at home. My wife, Becca, and the kids, Josh, Maisie, George and Martha. Thanks for everything.